DIVE-BOMBER

The elf free-fell in the classic skydiver's position, arms outstretched, legs bent at the knees, and head down so he could see exactly where he was going. The roof of the Plantech building rushed at him with what would have been frightening speed, but Khase wasn't worried. Instead he exulted in the feel of the chill droplets and rush of air as he hurtled toward the greenhouse at terminal velocity.

Two . . . one . . . now, Sindje! he thought.

As if a giant hand had suddenly reached out and grabbed him, courtesy of his sister's levitation spell, Khase felt his body slow as he neared the roof. Reaching out with the reinforced glove, he grabbed the gleaming line, using it to guide himself to the four-inch-wide ledge. The elf landed on his toes without a sound, right next to the shaft of the arrow, which was sunk halfway into the plascrete. *Got to hand it to Hood, a three-hundred-meter shot in the dark— through the rain, no less. Damned impressive.* Khase reached around to the pack at the small of his back while he thought to his sister: *I'm on-site. Tell Max we're green.*

SHADOWRUN™

AFTERSHOCK

A Shadowrun™ Novel

JEAN RABE AND JOHN HELFERS

A ROC BOOK

ROC
Published by New American Library, a division of
Penguin Group (USA) Inc., 375 Hudson Street,
New York, New York 10014, USA
Penguin Group (Canada), 90 Eglinton Avenue East, Suite 700, Toronto,
Ontario M4P 2Y3, Canada (a division of Pearson Penguin Canada Inc.)
Penguin Books Ltd., 80 Strand, London WC2R 0RL, England
Penguin Ireland, 25 St. Stephen's Green, Dublin 2,
Ireland (a division of Penguin Books Ltd.)
Penguin Group (Australia), 250 Camberwell Road, Camberwell, Victoria 3124,
Australia (a division of Pearson Australia Group Pty. Ltd.)
Penguin Books India Pvt. Ltd., 11 Community Centre, Panchsheel Park,
New Delhi - 110 017, India
Penguin Group (NZ), cnr Airborne and Rosedale Roads, Albany,
Auckland 1310, New Zealand (a division of Pearson New Zealand Ltd.)
Penguin Books (South Africa) (Pty.) Ltd., 24 Sturdee Avenue,
Rosebank, Johannesburg 2196, South Africa

Penguin Books Ltd., Registered Offices:
80 Strand, London WC2R 0RL, England

First published by Roc, an imprint of New American Library,
a division of Penguin Group (USA) Inc.

First Printing, July 2006
10 9 8 7 6 5 4 3 2 1

Copyright © WizKids, Inc., 2006
All rights reserved

ROC REGISTERED TRADEMARK—MARCA REGISTRADA

Printed in the United States of America

PUBLISHER'S NOTE
This is a work of fiction. Names, characters, places, and incidents either are the product of the authors' imaginations or are used fictitiously, and any resemblance to actual persons, living or dead, business establishments, events, or locales is entirely coincidental.

The publisher does not have any control over and does not assume any responsibility for author or third-party Web sites or their content.

This book is dedicated to my wife, Kerrie Hughes, who spent many a late night listening to me mumble about elves, trolls, orks, dwarfs, spell casting, Seattle, and many, many firearms, with endless patience and good humor.—John Helfers

And to my good friend and fellow runner Kevin Connelly: Hey, chummer—Hood and Einstein miss their old pal Scrod.—Jean Rabe

ACKNOWLEDGMENT

Special thanks to our wiz editor Sharon Turner Mulvihill for giving us an opportunity to play in the shadows, and for providing numerous reference materials to make our run smoother.

NORTH AMERICA
AS OF 2060

Copyright 2005, WizKids, Inc.

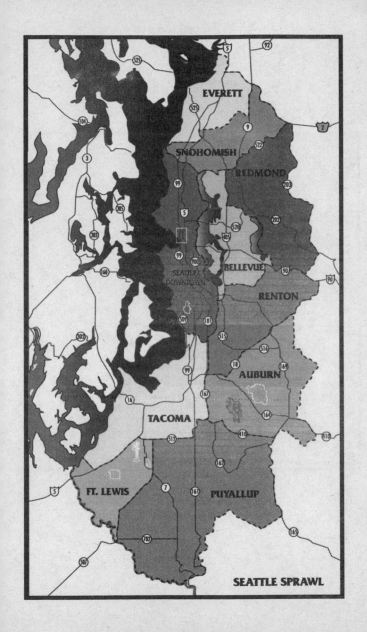

SEATTLE SPRAWL

Prologue

From the air, he thought the terminal looked like a giant arachnid. The concourses were its legs, sprawled across a massive rain-slick slab that stretched toward the edge of the city proper, where myriad lights resembled a starry sky. More than three dozen airlines and airfreight companies used this place, but the LC Platinum II jet he was comfortably settled in belonged to none of them.

Black as the private runway it lined up with, the sleek aircraft lowered its landing gear with a barely audible hum.

"We will be on the ground momentarily, sir."

From his plush window seat, he studied the contours of the hangars below, their boxy forms appearing to waver ghostlike in the evening storm, the lights coming from a few windows looking like dim, curious phantoms. A few maintenance men in coveralls gave the Lockheed an appreciative glance before they hurried into a service door at the base of a concourse.

The jet touched down so gently he barely felt it.

"Sir, we have arrived at Sea-Tac International Airport. We'll be taxiing near the south satellite. The temperature is. . . ."

He ignored the rest of the pilot's words, straightened the tapered lapels of his perfectly tailored Wellington Brothers suit and shrugged into a butter-soft black Europa leather duster. Moments later he was on the tarmac in front of his private hangar, listening to the staccato *tat-a-tat* of the rain against his duster and the ground, sufficiently loud enough to diminish the harsh sounds of other planes coming and going. He stared into puddles tinted neon by the reflected lights of the terminal and taxiway—seeing something far beyond the airport and Seattle. Rivulets of green, pink and electric yellow streamed down a sloping sidewalk that led to a gleaming Rolls Royce Phaeton Deluxe. The liveried driver waited for him at the open rear door of the limo.

"Good evening, sir."

He waited a few moments more, tipping his face up into pattering rain, breathing in the sweet air that was oddly cold for this early in the fall. Behind him, the pilot opened an umbrella and held it over his head, politely ruining the moment.

"Everything is ready, including the team you requested." This came from the limo driver, who appeared nonplussed by the deluge. "They are gathered at Ohgi Ya's on Fourth downtown. I took the liberty of ordering the pressed duck for you. It should be ready when we arrive. Your luggage is. . . ."

"Fine." He stepped toward the limo, the pilot keeping pace and holding the umbrella high. A second limo had pulled up, and attendants loaded several large suitcases into it. A last look at the neon snakes at his feet and the rain drumming all around, then he eased into the limo. The driver bowed respectfully and closed the door.

Sea-Tac International's main terminal boasted magnetic and X-ray scanners, chemsniffers, security patrols and a state-of-the-art host system. Passengers were subjected to a variety of scans, including those from paranormal sources. But he bypassed all of this.

The limo breezed through the UCAS checkpoint on the edge of the airfield and disappeared into the misty night.

1

Khase stood in the doorway of the modified Hughes WK-2 Stallion helicopter, enjoying the spray of raindrops from the rotor's downdraft on his face. He glanced back at the other three members of the team in the cargo area, all concentrating on their own preparations.

His elven sister, Sindje, sat cross-legged on the floor. As always, she was flawlessly organized, from her polished combat boots to her close-fitting silk skinsuit, balaclava and gloves—that all contained the panels of silk/Kevlar combo ballistic armor he'd had custom-woven last year for her birthday. She flashed him a show of teeth that was equal parts grimace and grin. She had never liked heights, and riding in a helicopter through a rainstorm with an open cargo door was definitely not her idea of a good time.

Next to her sat their hacker, Max, her thick fingers dancing in the air as she ran programs from her own customized bodysuit, which had the capacity of a juiced-up Fairlight Caliban commlink built into its various pockets. Tactile pads in the fingertips of her AR gloves enabled her to execute entire suites of programs with a single finger twitch. The wild dreadlocks that normally radiated from her head in all directions had been corralled by a twist of multicolored electrical cable and hung down her back. Although it looked like she was staring off into space, Khase knew her cybereyes were supplying her with everything they needed to know about the current status of their target.

As if she felt his stare, she looked over. "ETA one minute," she said, her tusks gleaming pink in the red security lights of the cargo hold.

Khase nodded, and Max returned to her prep. He couldn't help smiling as he turned to look at the final member of the team kneeling on the patterned metal floor of the Hughes. The huge troll known on the street as Hood braced himself with one massive, muscled arm against the helicopter's roof, his other hand curled around a sleek compound bow almost as tall as Khase. The troll was dressed like the rest of them, in a standard black skinsuit, only his was sleeveless, his broad chest covered with an armored vest that Khase would have been swimming in if he tried it on. The end of what looked like a long, rectangular box jutted up over a huge warty shoulder. The troll's gaze was steady as he looked back at the well-muscled elf.

"You're enjoying this, aren't you, Khase?" The words were a sustained growl.

"Just a little moonlight ride, Hood. Though you know what they say: you should never dive on a full stomach." The corner of Khase's mouth quirked up. He wasn't holding on to anything, yet he easily adjusted to every movement the copter made as it approached their destination. He pulled his own silk balaclava down over his shaved head, adjusting it so that only his almond-shaped mocha eyes were visible.

"Thirty seconds." Max's voice didn't change in tone or volume, her fingers just moved a little faster as she readied her programs.

"Time for a little sneak and peek, *chwaer*." Khase stepped to Sindje's side and crouched beside her, putting his arm around her shoulders. *Chwaer* was the Welsh word for sister. He liked using pieces of their musical language.

She shook her head in mostly feigned annoyance. "Don't let me fall over. I hate coming back in to find myself face down on the floor."

"I won't. Promise."

"See you in twenty." The slender elf closed her eyes and slumped over, supported by her brother. As the Stallion sideslipped in a banking turn, Khase looked up to see Hood point out the door with the tip of his bow. Still holding his sister, he turned just enough to peer over the edge of the

Stallion's floor and get the first glimpse of their objective three hundred meters below.

The rich green hills and fields of Snohomish stretched for dozens of acres to the north, the bright lights and tall skyscrapers of downtown Seattle glittered in the rain-misted air to the south. On the border between the city and the farmland was a thirty-story building of plascrete, steel and glass, its copper-tinted windows reflecting the neon and halogen of the city two kilometers away. Khase's eyes gathered the ambient light as easily as he breathed, enabling him to see through the night and rain to scan the structure.

A glass greenhouse, dark and still at this hour, had been built as one half of the skyscraper's top floor. It overlooked the corp grounds, including the lit sign on the lawn in front of the building: PLANTECH.

"I still think this is too much nuyen for such an easy run," he remarked to no one in particular. "Not that I'm complaining, mind you."

The troll shifted his weight, the bow never leaving his side. "Maybe, but we're all getting paid to make sure it goes down smooth. So let's make sure that's exactly what happens."

"No prob, chummer—" Khase was interrupted by Max, who tapped Hood on the shoulder.

"Airjock wants a word."

Khase, still supporting his comatose sister, glanced at a small vidscreen to see it flicker into life, revealing the face of a human wearing wraparound sunglasses, two day's growth of scraggly beard, and an ancient leather aviator's hat.

"Hoi! I'm right over the place. Why you want to risk your hoops here is beyond me, but that's your business, I'm just the ride. Are you sure you don't want me to hang around in case you need air evac? With what you paid, I'd almost consider it part of the bargain."

Hood smiled and shook his head. "Jock, you've done more than enough getting us here. We've got our exit planned street-side. Thanks for the offer, though."

"No, thank you. And hey, anytime you get another one of these milk runs, you look me up, ya hear? I'll always answer my comm for you guys. Sayonara, and good luck." The screen winked out, and at the same time Sindje straightened and sucked in a huge breath of air, her eyes fluttering as she regained control of her body.

"*Cachu,* they weren't kidding! Even when I knew where my body was in the fraggin' chopper, it was still a trip to get back." Still breathing hard, she shrugged off Khase's arm. "I'm all right, *brawd*. The place is shut down, guards just finished their latest sweep, bored out of their gourds. A third-rate corp like this, we should be in and out in twenty, no more."

"Khase, you're up." Hood opened the box quiver on his back and extracted a long, thick arrow with an unusual, multibarbed head, pulling one end of a small reel of microwire out and attaching it to the arrow shaft. The Stallion hovered motionless as he walked to the edge of the cargo bay and hooked his nylon combat harness to a strap near his head, hanging on it to make sure he was secure. Setting the arrow, he leaned forward out of the rotorcraft, his boots balanced on the edge of the bay door. The troll extended the bow downward, oblivious to the churning whir of the blades slicing the air two meters above his head. He drew the bowstring to his eye, breathed once and then released it, the arrow streaking into the early-morning darkness, taking the microwire along for the ride.

The troll reached up, unhooked his harness, and attached the other end of the microwire to the strap. Then he pulled himself farther back into the cargo bay, slapping Khase on the shoulder as he passed. "Good luck, as Jock said."

"Luck is never a factor." The elf winked as he leaned down to Sindje and pulled a padded glove onto his left hand. "Shall we?"

She managed to look up at him and down her hooked nose at the same time. "Don't get killed." It was the same thing she told him every time they were about to separate.

Khase kissed her on the forehead. "See you there." Straightening up again, he stepped back to the door of the rotorcraft. His gaze followed the slim microwire line until it disappeared in the darkness. One last, deep breath to find his center, and he dove face-first out of the Stallion.

The elf free-fell in the classic sky diver's position, arms outstretched, legs bent at the knees, and head down so he could see exactly where he was going. The roof of the Plantech building rushed at him with what would have been frightening speed, but Khase wasn't worried. Instead he exulted in the feel of the chill droplets and rush of air as he hurtled toward the greenhouse at terminal velocity.

Two . . . one . . . now, Sindje! he thought.

As if a giant hand had suddenly reached out and grabbed him, courtesy of his sister's levitation spell, Khase felt his body slow as he neared the roof. Reaching out with the reinforced glove, he grabbed the gleaming line, using it to guide himself to the four-inch wide ledge. The elf landed on his toes without a sound, right next to the shaft of the arrow, which was sunk halfway into the plascrete. *Got to hand it to Hood, a three-hundred-meter shot in the dark— through the rain, no less. Damned impressive.* Khase reached around to the pack at the small of his back while he thought to his sister: *I'm on-site. Tell Max we're green.*

His sister's cool voice replied inside his mind. *Affirmative. Infiltration commencing.*

Khase brought out a glass cutter and handled suction cup from his tool kit, glancing around out of long habit. *Sure hope those codes worked,* Khase thought as he pressed the rubber cup to the glass and pushed it down, then carved a hole big enough for entry. A blast of warm, humid air *whooshed* out, and he stepped inside just as Max appeared through the rain and night above him, using a mechanical rappeler to control her descent. Braking to a stop, she landed on the ledge, not nearly as gracefully as the elf had, and scrambled through the open window.

"They're right behind me," she whispered, stabbing invisible switches in front of her face. "We're still green, sec has not been compromised."

Khase looked up as a large form swooped down and hit the ledge. Swaying a bit, Hood used the line to steady himself until he got his balance. Sindje clung to his back, her arms wrapped around his neck and her eyes squeezed shut. Hood pointed at his throat, one slim, silken arm encircling it, and stuck his tongue out, making a choking face. Frowning, Khase motioned for Hood to turn around, then reached through the window and plucked his sister off the troll.

"Sindje? It's all right, you're down. I've got you." He

pulled her into the greenhouse while Hood bent to cut the
microwire and removed the arrow from the ledge, putting
it back into his quiver.

"I can't believe I let you talk me into this." The mage
squirmed free, her open eyes flashing with anger. "At least
the nuyen's worth it."

"Yeah, and besides, you wouldn't let me get into any
trouble all by myself, would you? Watch yourself, Hood."
Khase took the large bow and quiver, then helped the troll
squeeze through the hole. The elf picked up the window-
pane and set it back in place, then squirted fast-dry epoxy
from a small tube around the edges and set a large plant
in front of the window. Finished, he turned around to have
a look at the jungle surrounding them.

As befitting its purpose, vegetation filled every square
foot of the glass house. Rows of racks brimmed with trays
of both flowering and leafy plants, potted trees, shrubs and
crop varietals of every shape and size. Sweet fragrances
from rainbow-hued tropical flowers warred with the sharper
scents of spice plants and even what looked like a twelve-
foot Douglas fir in one corner. At least Khase was pretty
sure that's what it was; he wasn't huge on botany. The
nuyen that particular specimens of foliage would bring for
extracting them from here, however, was another matter
entirely—he was huge on that.

"Good job, temperature hardly dropped here," Max said,
her fingers dancing on air as she scanned the room, using
augmented reality programs to keep track of what was hap-
pening both inside and out. "Security is still tight, but it
looks like those codes our Johnson gave us are on the level.
All's quiet on the leafy front."

The troll stood like a statue for a moment, mesmerized.
"Beautiful, aren't they?" He shook his head to clear his
senses. "All right, people, we've still got a job to do." Hood
punched keys on a small datapad. "Sindje, Khase, you each
have your lists, so spread out and start collecting. Max,
please make sure that door to the hall elevator is green,
and I expect that the carts we need will be there?"

"If you're referring to the work order I moved up twelve
hours, you're right." The ork flashed a toothy smile as she
trotted down a narrow aisle toward the main entrance
doors.

"Easy for you to say, I can barely read some of these names." Khase screwed up his handsome features in concentration as he pulled a different glove onto his right hand. "Pachystacky—"

"Not while we're on the clock," Sindje cut him off. "Besides, you know your Latin. *Pachystachys Lutea,* Golden Candle. *Canaga Odorata,* Ylang-ylang. *Plumeria Rubra L,* Frangipani. *Auris Folium*—'Ear leaf'?—never heard of that one. *Manihot Esculenta Crantz* crossbred with *Zea Mays,* some kind of manioc-sweet corn hybrid, probably for third world countries—"

The troll cleared his throat with a low rumble. "As fascinating as the botany lesson is, Sindje, let's concentrate on getting the green loaded and out of here, what do you say?" Hood made his way to the greenhouse's main doors, cradling a pot containing a diminutive rough-barked tree with narrow fronds.

"Aye, aye, Captain." The lean elf sketched a sarcastic salute with one finger as she scanned the greenhouse. "Crop hybrids—there they are. Khase, grab the *folium,* it should be two rows over. I'll snatch the cornroot and—"

"Shh!" At the main doors, Max held up her clenched right fist. "Intrusion alert just went off at the station on level one."

"Did you trip something on the door security?" Hood was right at the ork's side.

"Hey, it wasn't me," the hacker replied. "Drek, it's after three. The codes must have reset for the new day—we're hosed."

Sindje and Khase exchanged pained expressions. "I guess our Mr. Johnson didn't give us all the information he *thought* we needed," he muttered.

A slow, feral smile spread across Sindje's face. "Look's like company's coming."

2

"Patrol squad entering the elevator—hitting that corridor in one minute." Max's fingers flew as she tried to circumvent the door security. "*Vut, Vut, Vut!* I've lost the wireless feed! Main door's maglock has gone to lockdown—I can't open it!"

"You've got sixty seconds to apologize for that lie." Hood set the tree down and whirled his index finger in the air, signaling a team pullout. "Sindje, Khase, finish your sweep and get the rest of our cargo over here. And everybody watch for flash." A standard technique for security forces was to suddenly turn on all the lights in a room, hoping to catch elves, orks and cybered runners using low light vision by surprise and blind them.

"Hey Hood, we're not newchums on an init, you know." Khase pushed a wheeled rack of plants next to the troll. "In fact, I've got all of mine."

"Yeah, turn a couple of cartwheels in the aisle, why don't you?" Sindje staggered up, bent double under the weight of a four-pack of large potted plants. Hood and Khase each leapt forward and grabbed a pot.

"This isn't a race, woman." Hood carefully set his orange and yellow-hued flower down and picked up his bow from where it had been leaning against the wall.

Sindje set the other two pots down and wiped her brow.

"Really? Tell that to the goon squad looking to smear us into wet red paste if they get a chance."

"I've got the door!" Max let out a long sigh of relief, just as the elevator chimed at the end of the hall.

"Max, open it and duck." Hood aimed at the elevator doors at the far end of the hall as the main greenhouse exit began to open. A red light glowed about twenty meters away in the darkness. As soon as he saw the light flash, the troll released his arrow, the tip piercing the metal elevator frame with a *thunk*. All four of them heard a muffled curse from inside. The door opened a few inches, hit the arrow shaft, and began to close again.

"Wiz, very wiz." Khase whistled in admiration.

"It won't hold them long. Max, get those carts in here and start loading. Khase, Sindje, take care of the squad, and remember—no geeking."

"Yes, *tad*." Sindje's eyes glowed with mystical power. "Y'all might want to stay away from the doors for a bit— some overzealous sec goon might put a bullet or two in here while they 'arrest' us." She glanced at her brother. "What's the plan—go out, or let them come in?"

"One who takes position first at the battleground and awaits the enemy is at ease," the elven adept replied.

"You know, you could have just said 'let them come to us.' " The mage touched her brother on the shoulder and he faded from sight. "Take them in the hallway."

"Aw, sis, that's not even fair." The sound of his monowhip sliding free rasped from where Khase stood unseen.

Sindje's reply was clipped. "Maybe not, but they have guns, and you ain't bulletproof yet, *brawd*."

With a screech of rending metal, the elevator doors finally opened, and a squad of helmeted and body-armored sec men spilled into the hallway, each one covering the next as they leapfrogged up the corridor, firearms at the ready.

"Hmm, not your standard wage slaves. These boys have a modicum of talent." Khase's voice came out of thin air. "Ready when you are, Sindje."

The elven mage ducked under a table, her voice distant due to her concentration on the men in the corridor. "Just—one second." From her vantage point in front of the glass-paned double doors, Sindje had an unobstructed view of the five guards taking the hallway. "Eeek, they've got a troll on payroll. Khase, watch out for him. He'll spot you first." Scanning them quickly, she found what she needed. "Ahh, there you are."

"INTRUDERS IN THE GREENHOUSE! THIS IS PLANTECH SECURITY! YOU ARE SURROUNDED!" blared a voice from a speaker mounted somewhere above.

"All that noise can't be good for the plants," Hood said, frowning. He squinted and searched the glass ceiling.

"Or good for my focus." Sindje held out her hands and cast, her fingers curling as if she were holding something. In the hallway, a guard's sidearm extracted itself from his unsecured thigh holster and floated in front of the elevator. Frowning, Sindje concentrated on the mana, pantomiming with her hands. In response, the handgun's slide pulled back, chambering a round, then slid forward. Mana, the very essence of magic, flowed from the metaplanes to this world, surrounding everything with an invisible field of energy. Those who could tap into that energy, like Sindje, could intuitively manipulate it into all kinds of useful spells.

"PUT DOWN YOUR WEAPONS AND EXIT THE ROOM ONE AT A TIME, HANDS ABOVE YOUR HEAD, LYING DOWN IN THE HALL!—"

There was a whir, and as if by magic an arrow shaft protruded from a speaker grill. A brief spray of sparks popped from the housing, and the commanding voice was cut off midword.

"Much better." Hood ducked down, looking for Sindje. "Ready?"

A pair of lambent green eyes blazed in the darkness under the table. Sindje's eerie voice wafted forth as she held her imaginary pistol and squeezed the air trigger. *"Showtime . . ."*

A flurry of gunshots sounded in the hallway behind the security squad. The unexpected attack threw the five guards into confusion:

"—Who's firing? Cease fire! Cease fire, frag it!—"

"—Unknown hostiles behind us—"

"—Get down! Cover, take cover!—"

"—Is anyone hit?—"

Nothing happened for a second, then the members of the squad began to behave very oddly indeed. The lead member, who was lying on the floor still trying to draw a bead on anyone in the greenhouse, found his HK 227X submachine gun wrenched up toward the ceiling. The stock and barrel of his gun split in half, accompanied by a high-pitched screech of monofilament on metal and plastic.

"Hostile is here—" was all he said before his face ricocheted off the floor tile as he was punched into it, rendering him unconscious.

The second man, who had been kneeling behind his partner, did a decent job of trying to cover the unseen enemy with his weapon, but also to no avail. His helmet popped off, and before he could react, his head slammed into the wall. Without a sound, he slumped down to the floor, also out cold.

"Target is invisible," the troll grunted.

"Go to ultrasound!" the lone guard nearest the elevator ordered. Two of the remaining three guards flipped lenses down on their visors, and the troll started to bring his modified Mossberg CM-AMDT short-barreled auto shotgun back around from where he had been covering the elevator.

But Khase was already moving.

"I've got him!" one of the second pair of guards said, tracking the elf's movement with his subgun. "He's on the wall!" In his excitement he triggered his weapon, sending three rounds into the ceiling.

Sindje's heart leapt into her throat fearing for her brother, but her concern was unwarranted. The guard reeled from an unseen blow, the visor on his helmet shattering as he sailed down the hall, impacting the elevator with a crash and dropping to the floor. The guard's weapon hovered in midair for a second while the troll guard stepped forward, blocking half of the hallway as he leveled his shotgun.

"Drop it!" The troll's guttural voice echoed in the passageway. "Now!"

The submachine gun flew through the air at the troll's head, but he instinctively ducked out of the way. His shotgun swiveled right, for all appearances tracking nothing, but then his eyes bulged and he collapsed to his knees, one massive hand clutching his privates. The shotgun clattered to the floor, forgotten. Globs of vomit spewed as he hunched over in agony.

Still, the troll had delayed Khase just long enough to let the fifth member of the sec team get the drop on him. Sindje saw the human cover seemingly empty air with his subgun. "Freeze! Twitch, and I'll paint the wall with your brains. K-Tog, you all right?"

"I'll be—fine—just get the cuffs on this—drekhead," the troll wheezed, looking for his shotgun while gingerly trying to get to his feet.

"Hood!" Sindje was already casting, curling her fingers into a fist and cocking her arm.

"I'm on it." Hood loosed an arrow that hit the guard's weapon, distracting him and knocking it off target. Sindje followed that up with what she called her "mage-slap," a kinetic spell that knocked the human backward. He fell to the floor and didn't move. Meanwhile, the troll guard had just gotten his hands on his Mossberg and was about to get up when his head was rocked back and forth by a rapid series of hard blows. He swayed, blood dripping from his bulbous mouth.

"This is gonna hurt," Sindje said, dropping the invisibility spell in time to see Khase execute a flying front kick to the troll's face, snapping the monstrous head back and sending the huge guard crashing to the floor. The impact made the entire hallway quiver. The elven adept scanned the rest of the motionless sec team, making sure no one else was a threat. Grinning back at the others, he flashed a thumbs-up.

"Time to go!" Khase was already dragging the bodies of two sec men over to the door. Hood, you grab your own, bad enough I almost broke my foot on his face. Max, you got those elevator cameras derezzed?"

"Done, but I don't know how long my prog will hold, so let's get our hoops gone." She bent over the squad leader, holding his face close to her own while she thumbed an eyelid back. "Say cheese, sweetmeat. Got it. Now, how you gettin' us out of here?"

Hood began stripping the troll of his uniform. "I figured we'll stroll right past the guards in the lobby and drive out of the garage, if that's okay with you."

Two minutes later the four-man squad pushed a pair of tall racks and a cart full of plants into the elevator, the troll carrying one of the unconscious sec guards over his shoulder. With the plants all inside, it was a tight fit. Only the troll went visorless; his horns made it impossible to fit any kind of helmet over his head.

"Going down." Khase hit the lobby floor button, while Hood tossed the broken shaft of an arrow out into the hallway before the doors closed.

"Squad Four to lobby, we are evacing with injured, please have Crashcart standing by for removal," Hood said into his exterior mike.

There was a hiss of static, then a reply: "We copy, Squad Four, personnel standing by."

The ride took less than thirty seconds to the lobby floor. The door opened to blinding halogen spotlights, and the squad filed out, towing the racks behind them.

"K-Tog, Squad Four," the troll said, shielding his eyes. "Our lead took a powerbolt to the chest, might have fractures. Fragging mages." The troll handed over the unconscious man, then looked back to the lobby leader.

"Report, officer," the human guard in charge said.

"Estimate at least five hostiles trapped in the greenhouse. We managed to retrieve the more valuable plants it looked like they were trying to steal, but then Morgan took that shot and we evaced out just as Squad Two came up—"

Shouts and the sounds of a heavy firefight suddenly erupted on every commlink among the sec forces. "Main level, main level, this is Squad Two requesting immediate backup! Have engaged hostiles and are taking heavy fire, repeat heavy fire—" the low roar of what sounded like a burst of flame was heard over the channel, and the transmission cut off.

The lobby leader snapped his fingers and grabbed his subgun, pinning the troll with his eyes. "You four, come back up with us—"

"SOP states that we must secure any at-risk flora outside the greenhouse before it is contaminated by contact with an unfiltered environment." The troll glanced at the two racks and cart of plants. "We'll get these stowed and join you back on thirty ASAP."

The lobby leader gave a resigned huff. "Affirmative. Squad Three, you're with me. Squad One, secure the perimeter. No one leaves." The leader took off for the elevator, and the troll and his three companions headed for the shaft that led to the underground levels and the garage, pushing the racks and cart ahead of them.

Inside the elevator, Max handed off her rack to Hood and her fingers began dancing again. "How much time we got?"

"Figure less than a minute for them to get up there and notice that there isn't any fight going on, and another thirty seconds to clear the greenhouse and realize they've been had. We'll have some seriously fragged sec hot on our tail in about two minutes tops." Hood slid his bow and quiver out from in between two rows of bushy plants on the cart. He kept them in front of him as he moved to block the camera mounted in the back of the elevator, hiding the fact that they were going to the garage.

"No problem." Max keyed in one last command. "I love maintenance progs. Love 'em, love 'em, love 'em. Okay, it's ready."

"We're here. Keep your helmets on until we're clear, and get that eyeball ready." Hood led the three other "guards" to a nondescript, battered, gunmetal-gray Ares Roadmaster.

"Mmm, plascrete and gasoline, my favorite smells," Sindje said, wrinkling her nose as she and Khase opened the back doors and unloaded plants into the cargo area. Max jumped into the driver's seat. Hood handed off the last of the plants and stepped inside, his bulk causing the van to tilt back a few inches before settling down.

"Frag, Hood, you're so big I oughta make you jog back." Max stabbed a finger at the elevator doors, causing every light on the level to wink out. The sound of activating mag-locks echoed across the garage. "Good thing I had these seats reinforced. Still can't believe you talked me into using my own ride."

"I promised we wouldn't put a scratch on it. Now go!" Hood made his way through the miniature jungle in the back of the van to the passenger seat and rolled down the window, listening and watching for any sign of pursuit. Max backed up the Ares and headed for the steel exit gate.

"This eyespy program that drek hacker sold me better work—" She let the rest of her sentence trail off as she readied her AR gloves.

"It will." Hood leaned back in his seat, making it creak in protest under his weight.

The van rolled up to the security checkpoint, and three

pairs of eyes riveted on the ork. Max's index finger twitched. "Downloading the retina image now . . . hacking into the scanner program to overlay it . . . eventually."

A light blue beam of light shot out from a scanner, playing over Max's eyes. She sat stone still, letting the beam read her retina. Seconds ticked away, yet nothing happened.

"Should it take—" The troll's question was answered by the security gate rolling up, and a pleasant automated voice saying, "Good night, Mr. Touchstone. Security level three has been engaged. There is a matter on floor thirty that requires your attention. Shall I open a channel to the guards on scene?"

Max stabbed the air with her gloves and spluttered in a voice that sounded exactly like the head of the squad that had been taken out, "No!—uh, no. That's unnecessary, I'll contact them myself. Uh—thank you."

"Very well. Have a good evening, Mr. Touchstone." Although the Roadmaster was built for power rather than speed, Max nearly laid rubber as she squealed out of the garage.

"Hey, careful! Our Johnson said nothing about payment for dead plants." Hood checked their cargo, seeing Khase and Sindje contorted in strange postures as they each held two pots upright. "Good work, everyone, I think we just scored a clean run."

"Clean?" Max snorted in derision. "Clean? Who's your maid, Hood?"

Bright halogen headlights speared through the dark streets and lit up the Roadmaster's mirrors, causing Max and Hood to shield their eyes from the glare. Two pairs of Nissan Stealth motorcycles flanked the Roadmaster, engines screaming as they accelerated. All four riders drew compact machine pistols and aimed at the van's sides.

"Frag it, Hood, this run's been anything but clean." Sindje glared at him from her position on the floor. "And it ain't getting better, either!"

Max gunned the engine and cut across a deserted intersection, tires squawking on the pavement as she caught the cycles by surprise. "Whatever you're gonna do, make it fast. They'll be back on our hoops in a sec!"

3

"**J**ust drive straight!" Hood growled. "The Johnson'll shove an empty credstick . . ."

"Yeah, I know," Max shot back. "If these plants don't arrive in perfect shape, no nuyen. That is the least of my worries at the moment."

She rolled up the window as a squeal cut through the air. Two of the pursuing cycles took the lead, while the other two held position a short way back. One of the closer pair of Stealths gained on her Roadmaster, its front wheel popping up and sparks flying as the rear fender scraped against the street. She floored the accelerator, tapped her left turn signal and then cranked the wheel hard right, leaving the highway. Her simple ploy didn't work this time, the cycles stuck hard on her tail. Max wove from one side of the road to the other, trying to keep them from pulling alongside. The cycles' halogen headlights flashed white in her rearview mirror as they wove in and out behind her.

"Many of these will bruise easily, Max. Please try to take care." Hood had squeezed into the cargo area and managed to position himself so his back was to the driver's seat. His legs were curled, heels meeting, so his legs formed a large "O" that he'd nested some of the more valuable plants in. His right hand gripped a panel of the van, and his left arm was stretched to support some delicate-looking vegetation in a tray. Khase braced his back against another tray to keep the plants in it from tipping over.

The ork snorted and glanced at her side mirror. "Bruise, Hood? If those sec goons catch us we'll be more than bruised. We'll be mulch." She swore under her breath, a string of rasping words in a language she was certain the troll and the elves didn't know. Both hands tight on the wheel, she bit her lip, her fangs sinking into the skin as the Roadmaster's engine wheezed with the sudden strain. She saw the second cycle catch up to the first, and she stomped the accelerator a little harder, clicking her teeth together. The engine made a popping sound and she raised her voice. "This van's as close to new as I'll ever own, Hood. You promised—"

"If you just drive straight you'll keep your van—and the plants—from getting hurt!" The troll snarled when they hit a pothole, sending everyone into the air for a moment. His horns thumped against the roof of the van, denting it. A plant in an oval-shaped pot tipped over, spilling dirt on Khase.

"Dammit, Hood! If you've—Incoming!" Max whipped the wheel to the right again, just as bullets ripped into the van's left side, punching through the stamped metal door and the driver's window, spraying safety glass across the front seats. Max howled and kept going right, brushing the Roadmaster against the cycle coming up on her right side and sending it up on the sidewalk.

"Watch it!" This came from Sindje. The elf was crouched at the rear of the van, her head raised just enough so she could peek out the back window. "Can't kill anyone, Max. Can't afford that heat."

"Frag that! Those *zakhans* shot my ride!"

She turned onto a fairly wide street that angled north, heading toward an old bus station, the outline of which Max could see a few blocks ahead. Beyond that, it led toward the heart of Everett, an effective dead end at an old warehouse. Max wanted to lose the cycles well before that. This early in the morning—in this part of the city— few cars were out, and those that were gave the Roadmaster and the cycles a wide berth, turning off on side streets and pulling over as if the ork's van was a DocWagon speeding to a hospital.

"Bullets, Hood! They've put bullet holes in my van. Busted out the windows. You've dented the roof with those longhorns of yours. Who's gonna pay for this, huh? Who in all of—"

"Faster, Max!" Khase cut in. "And they didn't get all of your windows." The elf brushed bits of glass off him and righted a few of the plants that had tipped over.

"Faster, Max," the ork parroted in a nasally tone. "Easy for you to say. I didn't buy the van for speed."

"No drek, I think everyone knows that now. Look!" Sindje was still watching the cycles through the back window. They stayed several meters back, side by side, the riders appearing to converse among themselves. In the background, the other two riders held their tail positions. The front cycles stayed even for a moment, until the Roadmaster passed the old bus station and appeared to pull ahead just a little. Then the rider who'd pointed to his helmet steadied his bike with his left hand, holstered his gun, and extended his right arm, a trio of snap-blades springing from a forearm sheath. He twisted the accelerator and shot forward, coming up on the van's left side and leaning over.

"Tires!" Sindje shouted. "He's going for the tires!"

"What—where?" Max looked over to see the glint of steel as the cyclist raised his arm to rip into the Roadmaster's engine compartment. "Oh, *VUT!*"

At the same time, the second rider veered to the van's right side, leaned forward until he could barely see above the handlebars as he aimed his machine pistol at the tires on his side.

Sindje whirled to face her brother. "They're going to—" Her words ended in a thump as she pitched forward, sliding into a cluster of foliage. Although not caught by surprise, Khase did have to steady himself against the wall as everything in the cargo area pitched forward.

Max rammed her foot on the brakes, the Roadmaster shuddering as the antilock system clamped down. The sec guards blurred by, one rider slashing at the air with his snap-blades, the other shooting and hitting only pavement. The two cyclists decelerated as well, popping front wheelies as they spun their bikes around for another pass.

Max spun the Roadmaster in a U-turn, tires screaming in protest against the rain-slick pavement, the powerplant seizing and threatening to quit. "Hood, we can't take much more of this." The ork growled deep in her throat, then swallowed hard when she heard metal grating on metal. "C'mon, baby," she coaxed. "C'mon, c'mon." Tromping the gas again, the van shot forward in the opposite direction before the cycles were able to catch up. The second pair of cycles split up to avoid the hurtling Roadmaster as it barreled straight for them. Max jerked the wheel and cut down a side street heading past the old bus station, side-swiping a dented Ford Americar double-parked in front of a dilapidated hotel.

"Totaled, totaled, totaled!" Max hollered to no one in particular about her van, not the newly crumpled sedan. Smoke puffed from a crack in the hood, accompanied by a mechanical belching sound. "Hood, my van's totaled!"

The troll had no reply for that; he just continued to worry about the plants, hunched forward as much as possible, but not able to get his head below the level of the side windows. "Khase, Sinjde, do whatever you can to get these guys off us!"

"Max!" Sindje was looking out the rear windows again. "Two still on us!"

"I see 'em." The ork glanced in her side mirror, a diffi-cult feat now because it had been mangled from the impact with the Americar, and was dangling from one screw. The sec guards were a block back, one rearing up on the back wheel once more. "The milk run ended with the first bullet hole in my baby. Ain't enough nuyen in the world for this job, Hood. Awwww, frag, frag, frag!"

Engines roaring, the Stealths sandwiched the van be-tween them, the rider with the blades slashing into the truck's cowling to get at the engine, the one on the right drawing a bead on the rear tire again.

Max pushed her foot against the floorboard and the Ares' tires howled. More smoke belched from a crack in the hood, some puffing in through a vent near the glove box, the acrid scent competing with the fragrance of the plants.

"*Vut, vut, vut!*" The ork pounded her fist against the steering wheel, the horn sounding angrily and not subsid-ing. "Frag, frag, frag." The horn continued to bleat as the van plunged through the intersection, narrowly avoiding a construction truck lumbering past. "Somebody take them out, or I'm gonna!"

"Shut that horn off!" Sindje was doing her best to concentrate, trying to tap some magic to help. "Should have done this earlier," she hissed to herself. The van bounced over another pothole and the elf lost her balance, falling against a tray of plants but righting herself immediately. "I said shut that *cachu* horn off!"

"Drek, drek, drek." Max pounded on the steering wheel again, in time with her words. But the horn persisted, mixed now with the sound of a siren.

"Lone Star?" Khase wondered, a frightened look crossing his face. He saw flashing red lights out the back of the van, but they were too high for a Lone Star car or cycle. He caught a glimpse of a DocWagon cutting down a side street and moving out of sight in a heartbeat.

Max spun the van around again, careening off an old C-N Jackrabbit and losing the front bumper in a screech of twisted metal. The impact put the Roadmaster on a collision course with a building marked for demolition. Wrestling for control of the stubborn cargo truck, she whipped past the building, missing it by a hairsbreadth, and headed south.

"Head for Everett," Khase suggested. "Lose them in the boxy blocks!"

Sindje heard the DocWagon siren fading, heard the Roadmaster's horn still wailing, though softer now, as if it was losing its voice. She heard her brother polishing his role as a backseat driver, heard Hood gack up something as he brushed some dirt back into a pot. Then all she heard was her heart beating.

It was so difficult to concentrate with all the jostling, but somehow she forced it. For an instant, it felt as if she were folding in upon herself, becoming smaller and smaller and impossibly heavy. Of course, she wasn't physically changing, she was just focusing on her "center," as she called it, that part of her that burned with magical energy. She envisioned herself a sunlike ball, denser than anything, impervious to the gunshots that threatened to intrude and the shattering of more glass. It must have been the window in the back door that shattered, because she vaguely registered something stinging her face—like ice crystals in a winter storm. And she vaguely registered her brother calling to her in a worried voice.

Then she thrust all those small distracting noises away and ignored the sting of the glass slivers in her cheeks. There was only the bright ball she had become. Warm and strong, she coerced the psychokinetic force within it to come out and play.

Join me?

In response the ball burned brighter in the back of her mind.

"Where are you going?" This came from Hood. "Max, do you have any idea where you're driving?"

"At the moment, no. Past the park now. Chinatown maybe."

"No, I said lose them in Everett! North!" Khase had given up on bracing the plants and used his elbow to knock the last bits of glass away from the edges of the back window. "Down by the bay. Lots of little side streets there."

"I'm driving here!" The ork drummed her fist against the steering wheel. The horn still wailed.

Shall we play? Sindje suggested.

The elf's eyes snapped open, wide and glowing and searching the sidewalks behind the speeding van. She held the energy in her mind, sensing it crackle like a straining fire. Indeed, it was willing to play this very early morning.

Yes, I'll play, the ball crackled.

A moment, she told it, feeling it grow more intense. *A moment more.*

The cycles were catching up to the van again, which listed to the left as the rear tire, stressed beyond endurance, collapsed with a *bang!* The horn was still bleating, a whimpering sound now, almost mournful.

A moment.

The van was only a handful of meters ahead of the sec guards now, who were side by side again and conspiring.

Now!

"No!" Khase began crawling out the back window, monofilament whip unspooling from his modified glove. "The other two caught up with us again! All four are on our tail!"

Let's play!

Sindje formed the psychokinetic force into a lightning

bolt, invisible to all but her. It lanced from her mind and struck a streetlight a meter behind the van, shearing through it like a monofilament chainsaw would drop a tree. The pole tipped over and clanged into the street, throwing up a shower of sparks. Another bolt sliced through a light on the opposite side, sending down another barricade. It was called a powerbolt spell, the most potent magic she had mastered. It could have easily taken out the guards, but Sindje couldn't risk incapacitating the riders and causing them to fall from their bikes, or geeking them outright. Their team didn't kill—even accidentally. She already knew from this manic chase that the sec guards were skilled enough to stop the cycles before hitting the fallen streetlights.

They'd drive around the poles, she was certain. In fact, they were doing that just now, all four of them, riding up on the sidewalk, two on each side, swerving around streetlights, trash cans, a broken rocking chair and a three-legged table someone had set out for the garbage collector.

Added to the drain her earlier casting had taken out of her, the powerbolt weakened her considerably—the price one paid for using magic—but Sindje would have coerced the mana into action again had she not heard the roof creak above her. She twisted her head. No sign of her brother.

"Khase?"

"He went up top." Hood gestured with the tip of a horn. "Now how 'bout you make sure those plants don't spill."

She grudgingly took Khase's place, back up against a tray, chin tucked to her neck but eyes glaring up at the troll. "Some run. Some . . . ouch!" She bit her lip as the left rear rim ground against the curb, leaving a trail of sparks behind. The van jumped again when Max took a sharp right down Jefferson. Sindje looked to the back window, fearful Khase might be pitched from the roof and she'd see him fall.

"He's all right," Hood grunted. "You know this is a piece of cake for him."

On the roof, Khase kept his balance with ease, shifting his weight when the van turned, bending his knees as he moved to the rear edge. The rain had faded to early morning mist, though the roof was slippery with accumulated water. The street looked haunted, with faint lights glowing

from the windows of an office supply company, a large
furniture store and a bar making the pavement glisten
darkly. Loud music spilled from an open window, some
bluesy piece that he couldn't make out because of the
shrieking sound the rim was making and the whine from
the cycles. Above, a comely elf in a silky robe and nothing
else leaned over the railing of a third story fire escape balcony, watching the chase. Khase's deep green eyes met
hers, and he winked as the van rounded a corner into another block, this one darker and with fewer streetlights.

"Dear sister, what a fine idea you had to slow our pursu-
ers." Khase extended his monofilament whip to its illegally
modified full length of five meters. Stepping to the right
side of the Ares, he cracked it at an approaching streetlight.
The lightweight wire wrapped around the pole, with the
weight at the end hitting it with a *clank*. As soon as he
heard that, Khase pulled the monofilament back, the wire
biting into the pressed metal as the friction from its movement spun it through the pole. Cut through, the streetlight
toppled as neatly as the ones felled by Sindje's spell had,
hitting the street in the path of two of the cycles. The motion, coupled with the rain on the roof, almost toppled him,
and he crouched to stay standing.

One of the riders managed to jump the pole, but the
second was not so lucky. The front wheel ran into the improvised barrier, and he flew over the handlebars, tumbling
to a stop in the road. Khase cringed, but let out a deep
breath when he saw the man get to his knees and remove
his helmet. The second pair of guards farther back hopped
on the sidewalks and sped around the pole. One of them
gunned his Stealth again and drew up to the corner of the
van, the rider drawing a Colt Manhunter and aiming the
heavy pistol at Khase.

"Now that isn't very nice at all." In one fluid motion,
the elf reached down and grabbed the edge where the van's
back window had been, flipped over and landed on the
back bumper, which creaked under his feet, threatening to
tear loose. With his free arm he cracked his whip at the
approaching guard, wrapping it around the barrel off the
gun and yanking it out of his hand. Khase snaked the whip
out twice more. The first strike split the aerodynamic windshield of the Stealth in half, the second used the weight to

chop off the left handlebar. Two chunks of metal clattered to the pavement as the guard steadied his wobbling cycle while he reached in his jacket for another pistol, this one an Ares Predator IV.

In spite of the man's attempts to kill him, Khase admired his aptitude at managing the cycle with only one handlebar. *Let's see how well you do with nothing to hold on to,* he thought, flicking his whip out again and cutting off the rest of the steering mechanism. The bike wobbled and slid sideways across the street, fenders and wheels scraping and screeching, the rider rolling free and coming up with a shredded uniform and the Predator IV still in his hand. In obvious pain, he still tried to get off a shot at Khase, but the van lumbered out of range before he could fire.

Only two sec guards left.

The van listed farther over, riding completely on a rim now, the tire shredded roadkill strewn along the curb. The steel against the street made the sound of a muted chainsaw, sparks flying and sending up the scent of something that settled uncomfortably in Khase's mouth. The elf reeled in the whip, and grabbed the bottom of the open rear window with one hand, ignoring a stab of pain in his palm. Then he reached down and grabbed the rear bumper, wrenching it off its mount with a grunt. He looked up to see the third guard leveling a pistol at him.

Khase waggled his eyebrows at the guard and smiled. He was close enough to see the shocked look on the sec man's face before the adept launched the bumper into the air with all his strength. The guard tried to brake, but moving at eighty kilometers an hour, he had no chance of avoiding the missile. The bumper bounced into his Stealth's front wheel, locking it with an abrupt jolt. The rider pitched head over heels into the street, rolling to a motionless heap by the side of the road.

Three down, one to go, Khase thought as he retracted his whip. But the Roadmaster was severely disabled, and the lone cyclist was trailing it with ease, staying far enough out of range of the elf. "Max, you gotta step it up, or this guy's gonna dog us all night!"

"She won't go any faster—we're lucky to still be moving at all!" The ork yelled back at him.

That gives me an idea. "Gun it, and hit the brakes when

I say!" The adept tensed, readying himself. Somehow Max coaxed a burst of speed from the valiant Ares, and the cyclist accelerated to keep within range. The last guard drew his pistol and lowered it at the cargo hauler.

"Now!"

Max stomped on the brakes again, and the Roadmaster burned tread as it squealed to a stop. Caught by surprise, the guard braked as well, but not fast enough. The Stealth nearly stood on its front wheel as the street bike wobbled to a stop before it hit the rear of the van.

Gripping the window ledge with both hands, Khase whipped his legs out and back, extending his body to its full 1.8-meter length. The soles of his boots struck the guard's helmet with a satisfying *crunch*, knocking him off the bike and onto the pavement. The Stealth lurched to one side before falling over and spinning to a stop in the middle of the street. Meanwhile, Khase used the kinetic energy from nailing the guard to rebound back into the window of the Roadmaster, landing on his feet in one fluid motion.

"Perhaps there is such a thing as luck after all." Khase directed this to Hood, who was having a difficult time keeping the plants upright given that the van was now so off balance. "We're clear, *tad*."

Max grumbled something they couldn't understand, then she turned onto a recently repaved avenue, driving several blocks before finding a dark alley. Sirens erupted from not too far off, and she jumped out of the cab, motioning for Khase and Hood to come with her.

"You two, put your backs into it," the ork snapped, carrying an undersized spare. The troll and elf looked at each other, then each leaned against the corner of the Roadmaster and heaved up with all their strength, lifting the battered rim off the ground. Max went to work with a tire iron, spinning nuts off with ease.

"More than one." Max nodded toward the wailing sirens. "Four, I count. Not DocWagons, either. I'm sure it's Lone Star. We made enough of a ruckus for an army of go-gangers, and also drove by an open bar. Someone probably called it in."

Arms straining with effort, Khase thought about the woman leaning over the fire escape railing. *It's possible she reported us,* he thought, *even after getting a glimpse of my natural charm.* "They'll find us here. Easy to track the scrape in the street from the rim. Won't need tech to follow our trail."

"Van's totaled. Totaled, totaled, totaled." The words were a mantra. "My cut of this run won't replace her. Not enough nuyen by a long shot." The ork gestured to the right rear body fender, hanging loose and thoroughly pitted and dented, pointed to where the back bumper used to be, where bits of the window glass hung to the edges of the frame, bloody in one spot from where Khase had cut his hand. "Grill's gone, and the front bumper, too. Bullet holes everywhere."

"But none in us." Khase offered the ork a wry smile. The spare secure, Hood and he let the Roadmaster down, and the elf helped her tighten the bolts. He glanced at what was left of the original tire. "Rim's crooked. It's still not going to ride right."

"Never ride right again. Totaled, totaled, totaled."

Khase spotted a gleam in Max's eye, and for a second thought she might be crying. The stocky ork rose to her feet and stomped back to the driver's door.

"Get in, or get left behind."

The crippled Roadmaster limped down another alley, across two blocks, then down another. The sirens were louder, five or six of them screaming together from the sounds of it. Lone Star definitely, a DocWagon or two in the mix from the pitch of them, no doubt for the injured sec guards.

Hood put a hand to his temple, rubbing at the persistent ache there. He remembered a few gawkers . . . a dwarf had poked his head out of the bar, anyone in the cars they'd passed, certainly others they hadn't spotted because they were preoccupied with saving their necks and the plants. Some of the gawkers would describe the van; the elf like a circus performer riding on top of it, cracking his whip and bringing down light poles; the angry ork driving like a demon; bumpers and motorcycles flying every which way. Probably some security cameras caught them for good measure. *Anything but a simple job,* he thought with a frown.

"Have to ditch your van," Khase said, as Max pointed the Roadmaster toward a section of short blocks and alleys.

"Totaled, totaled, totaled. Totaled for a fraggin' milk run."

4

The occupants of the Roadmaster were wisely silent, the troll breathing as quietly as possible, and the elves sitting side by side against a tray of plants, Khase meditating and Sindje staring into the darkness.

One hand clenched so tight around the steering wheel that her knuckles were white, Max tapped a free finger against a tusk, glancing over at what remained of her side mirrors. She left Everett and headed back into Seattle, drove down a long alley, relying on a memory of a few years ago, since the navconsole had shorted out during the chase. The Alki suburb, sandwiched between Elliot Bay and the rest of downtown Seattle, wasn't a place she frequented. In fact, she'd been there only once before, and that was for a true milk run. They were going to the plush neighborhood now because Hood said he had a place there where they could hide the battered van; because the Johnson hadn't called yet with a drop spot; and because Lone Star would never look for a van like this in Alki.

Johnson should've called by now, Max fumed. *Should've. Should've called. Told him we'd be in and out of Plantech in twenty, thirty tops. Should've called by now to name the drop.*

The Roadmaster was on its last wheels. Smoke continuously puffed out a crack in the hood and in through the vent by the glove box. She waved a meaty hand to disperse the cloud out the open window. The engine rattled, belched and bucked, wheezing like an eighty-year-old narcostick addict. She held her breath for a moment until it smoothed out again.

Max dropped the finger from her tusk and twitched it, ticking in the numbers the Johnson had given them on her AR glove.

No answer.

She hit redial, then dialed from scratch in case she'd keyed a wrong number. No answer. No tone. Maybe the reception was lousy here, or maybe her commlink had been damaged, too. *It better not be,* she thought, *or I'll take my payment out of Hood's* buunda *hide, troll or no. Vut, vut, vut!*

No streetlights here, the alley was blessedly thick with shadows, and she relied on her low-light vision to avoid garbage cans, restaurant food crates and sleeping bums. Rats? Even though the downtown was clean, even the alleys, there were plenty of rats here, drawn by the restaurants—in one place so thick they looked like an oil spill oozing across her path. Lights would've frightened them, maybe. But she couldn't have used the headlights even if she'd wanted to; they'd died several blocks ago. The right turn signal worked, though, not that it would bother the rats. The vermin could decorate what was left of her tire treads as far as she was concerned.

Only occasional flashes of light intruded, these coming from third and fourth floor windows, home to young corporate go-getters, prepping to hit the office and get a start on their fourteen- or fifteen-hour day slaving for their corp. Max's lip curled in contempt.

The rain had stopped, though there were puddles everywhere, and water was still beaded up on her front windshield. It was the only window not shattered, but a spiderweb crack snaked through it from the upper right corner to the middle above the dash. She figured the entire window would smash to proverbial smithereens if she so much as huffed on it.

Smoke puffed steadily through the vent near the glove box by the time the van lurched into a cavernous parking garage beneath an apartment building in Alki.

"Pray to Ceres our cargo pulls through." Sindje slid out the back, tugging one of the trays with her. "Some of these twigs are already wilting."

"The smoke from the engine, the chemicals in it." Hood helped her, then off-loaded the rest himself while Khase and Sindje watched Max sadly inspect the van. "They'll be better inside."

The ork gingerly touched one of the bullet holes above a wheel well. The gesture was almost reverent. It was no secret that vehicles were her passion. "Can't afford one this nice for a while, not even a down payment with my share in this run. *Buunda* on the Johnson who hired us."

"*Buunda* happens." Khase borrowed the ork slur with a nod. "But you'll get another van. And a better run will come along and you can upgrade it."

Max took a step back and gave the van one last look. "I already had plans for this run's nuyen, and it wasn't to replace my wheels."

Khase arched an elegant eyebrow.

"I had me a dog reserved."

The eyebrow went higher.

"A designer dog, one of Tobias Vierheller's. You've heard of him, right? He's a genetic artist. Advertised these pug puppies that would never shed and that came already housebroken. Got a deposit with Vierheller's Renton breeder. Probably not refundable, just my fraggin' luck. Had a name picked out, too. Bought a dog bed two days ago, bowls, food, chew toys, a retractable leash."

The ork ground the ball of her foot against the garage floor and continued to mutter, switching to an odd language of snarls, grunts and clicks. Sindje joined Hood, making sure the last of the plants were out.

Khase glided away from the ork and from an acrid-smelling pool of dark fluid that was growing beneath the van. He took a good look at the garage around them. There were only a dozen luxury cars here, though he was certain there were more tenants, given the size and levels of the building above them. Maybe they were vacationing; if they could afford this neighborhood, they could afford multiple homes. Or perhaps the place was too pricey and some of it hadn't been rented yet. The cars—two of them vans— were either new or so well maintained that they looked fresh off the lot, all softly gleaming in the subdued ceiling lights. And had the ork's van not been producing the odor of burnt soybacon, the garage would have smelled like fresh-minted nuyen.

"Max's van . . ."

The troll growled. "Not to worry, Khase. I'll make a call upstairs and have it towed and compacted. Never be found. Let's move. Elevator's over there."

Hood popped the whisper-silent apartment door and ushered the rest of the team into a spacious, quiet living room with a chocolate-colored ceiling and a matching thick, soft carpet.

"Never pictured you in a place like this." Khase waved his hand at the opulence. "Too rich for my blood. Makes me itchy."

"Didn't hear you volunteer your place."

The elf drew his lips into a tight line. "We're mobile—more or less—at the moment." He shrugged, a thin smile on his lips.

Hood's eyes narrowed.

The high-ceilinged apartment was simply furnished. A low long table made of some no doubt expensive black wood was the centerpiece of the living room. It sat in front of a deep-cushioned couch and a matching high-backed chair, both troll-sized. Leather, Khase guessed, or something that imitated leather so closely he couldn't tell the difference. No other furniture in this room, though the elf spotted a huge bed through an open door to the right. It was covered with pillows and fake furs, and could have held Khase and three of his very best female friends all at once.

"So that's where all of your nuyen goes, Hood. On this place." Khase whistled as he watched the troll arrange the plants in the center of the room near the table. Sindje helped, although her eyes flitted about to take everything in. Max paced back and forth, still tapping a tusk with her finger and muttering under her breath.

Large fish tanks lined the walls, the water in all of them a brilliant, unnatural blue because of the lights and the backdrops. Ten tanks, Khase counted, each filled with what looked like goldfish and live plants. *Simple fish,* he thought at first. Then he looked closer.

In one tank, the fish were pearly white with orange head growths that looked like bubbles—or brains. Their tails were long and translucent, and their eyes were wide and blue. In another were dusky black ones—moors, he knew, from an article he'd read in a streetdoc's office a few months ago. The largest tank held an assortment: bulbous ones with scales that protruded from their sides; thin ones with globe-shaped eyes, one on either side of their heads; elegant ones that looked like pieces of lace floating in the water; disturbing ones because of the large ephemeral sacks that hung on both sides of their ever-moving mouths. For some reason the elf suspected that these were not products of a genetic artist, they were expensive originals.

"Celestials," Hood supplied, following Khase's gaze. "Those ones with the sacks. Have to be careful what I mix with them. They're slow eaters, can't see too well, can't compete for food."

"And on the fish," Khase added absently. "All your nuyen goes on this place and on the fish. No wonder you don't have a single chip in your head, no laced bones, no wires, no nothing. You can't afford it. And no magic, either, just what your genes gave you in the first place."

The elf moved to another tank, this one higher up on a stand. Smaller fish swam listlessly, larger ones nuzzled the loose gravel on the bottom in an effort to stir up something tasty that the filter hadn't sucked up.

"Those are ryukin. Just got them two weeks ago. One of them had ich, and I didn't notice it in time. Spread through the whole tank. Managed to get it knocked back, though. They're all healthy now." Hood was staring at the tanks with pride, and if Khase hadn't known better, he'd thought that the troll was talking about his children instead of a bunch of fish.

"Ich, indeed." Khase figured it was some fancy fish disease, but decided not to ask, as he wasn't particularly interested in an explanation.

In the gaps between tanks, and above some of the tanks, the elf saw holographic pictures of rainforests and deserts, and one lone picture of an icy shore where penguins moved in and out of the water and where the shadow of something big, perhaps a walrus, appeared and disappeared along the face of an icy ridge. There were a few large plants in the living room, one with leaves shaped like elephant ears, another with waxy-looking leaves outlined in yellow and maroon and with feathery spires that stretched to the ceiling high overhead. A spiky-looking plant was in the bedroom.

"Ick? Ick, ick, ick." Max dropped into the armchair. She wasn't small by a long shot, but the massive chair dwarfed her, almost swallowing her like she was a child. Her feet, which dangled off the edge of the chair, bounced up and down as if it was impossible for her to be still.

Hood settled himself cross-legged on the floor in front of the low table. He'd taken one of the plants off the tray and with surprisingly nimble fingers was tenderly brushing dirt off its leaves and making sure the roots were covered.

Khase hovered nearby. The elf considered Hood's gentleness incongruous to his monstrous form . . . but then this place didn't seem to suit the huge troll, either.

The plant the troll concentrated on looked like some kind of ivy, twisting vines spilling over the pot, the leaves a dark, dark green but covered with a fine, hairlike purple fuzz. The troll held the plant close to his wide face and inhaled, closing his eyes and not moving for several moments.

The elves and the ork observed him, the latter still swinging her feet, and now drumming two fingers against a tusk. Max snorted after a moment to get Hood's attention, but the troll's head didn't move.

Khase made a show of clearing his throat. "If you're so well off, chummer, and you obviously are, given all of this, why the low-end shadowruns? Like our little tour of Snohomish and Everett tonight?"

That caught the troll's attention. His eyes flashed wide, and his upper lip curled back, showing a row of glistening white, pointed teeth. "You going to help with these plants, Khase?" Hood used his thick fingernails to prune a broken leaf. "They need to be as close to perfect as possible, or we won't get paid."

"And you definitely need that, don't you? This place must set you back some."

"Like you said, Khase, I don't spend my take on wires and chips. I don't pay a soul to put me under the knife. Got better uses for nuyen."

"Fish."

"Yeah, Khase. Fish. I like fish. Now, are you going to help or keep flapping your lips?"

Behind Hood, Sindje was already working on the plant in the oval container, the first one to tip over in the van. It was not in good shape.

Khase rolled his head on his shoulders, working a kink out of his neck, and strolled to the other end of the table, sitting down opposite the troll.

Nearby, Max continued to tap and drum, pausing to twitch a finger to call the Johnson again.

"Nothing," she announced. "Doesn't work." Her fingers curled into a fist. "*Vut, vut, vut.* I can't get a line out of here. She paused for a moment, then her eyes widened. "That's some kind of jamming system you got online here. You folks must like your privacy at the top end of the money pool."

"Yes, we do. Try this." The troll pulled a compact earpiece from a front pocket and tossed it to Max.

Max inserted it into her ear. "That works." She spoke the Johnson's number. "Hoi, this is Max. We got everything, all the plants on your list. Nothing missed, nothing else taken. Just like you instructed. Where do we drop 'em?" She pursed her lips, and the wrinkles on her forehead deepened as she thought about her useless van, and about how they were going to get the plants to the drop now that they had nothing to cart them in.

As the Johnson kept yakking, she drummed her tusk harder. "What do you mean we can't drop them this morning? You have a meeting? Yeah, you have a meeting—with us. Another meeting?" Max cupped her hand over the tiny mouth mike and leaned forward. "Johnson says he's got an 'urgent crisis' to deal with." She leaned back and spoke again. "Well, we got a plant crisis to deal with. Plants all over the place. Dirt on the carpet. That means you've got a crisis too—late when? This *afternoon*? Fine, I suppose. Where? We are not happy about this—all right, we'll wait to hear from you."

Max wrenched out the earbud and slipped it in her pocket; noting Hood's eyes on her, she curled her lips back from her tusks, daring him to say a word. When he didn't, she addressed all of them. "Johnson says he'll call us on this line with a time and place for exchanging the plants

for the nuyen. Says it'll be late this afternoon, probably."
She snarled and tipped her head back against the chair.
"Lovely, lovely, lovely." The chair hummed, and rolling
servos kneaded Max's tight back muscles.

Sindje frowned, looking up at the rest of them. "I don't
like it, either. Holding this merchandise for any longer than
absolutely necessary is risky. Greater chance of attracting
heat from Plantech security, maybe Lone Star, certainly
something none of us can afford. I don't like it one infinitesimal bit."

Beside a fish tank set on a low pedestal, Khase's frown
mirrored his sister's. He stared at a lone calico-colored
goldfish the size of his fist as it swam through a stream of
bubbles. *No idea you're on display, living sushi platter,
stared at by everyone who comes to call. I know just how
you feel, since I also have no idea how many slags're gonna
be looking for us yet.*

Hood, however, had a serene expression on his warty
visage. "I don't mind it. Babysitting these plants for a
dozen hours or so won't be so bad." He returned his attention to something that resembled a philodendron, a smile
lighting up his craggy features.

Around him, the other three runners exchanged worried
glances. *Frag, frag, frag,* Max mouthed, Sindje and Khase
nodding in agreement.

5

"**I** do not fraggin' believe this." Roland Ators ran a hand over his bristly crew cut as he surveyed the greenhouse in the rising golden dawn. Although he spoke quietly, his tone made everyone within five meters look up with nervous expressions before returning to their assigned tasks with increased vigor.

"I want initial reports on everything here in the next thirty minutes, with follow-up every hour." He stalked to a window on the far side of the room and examined the epoxied bulletproof glass while activating his commlink. "Morgan, report," he subvocalized.

His lieutenant's voice answered in his head. *"I'm in the garage, overseeing the CS techs at the vehicle's parking space. Look, boss, I—"*

Roland cut him off. "Save your apology for the *sararimen*. Let's run through what happened again."

"Yes sir, I'm connecting you to Control's vidlink now. They hacked the exterior elevator cameras to play back an empty greenhouse entry on the sec feeds, but when the system reset at oh three hundred it started recording again. No audio or visual monitors in the greenhouse proper, so we couldn't get a look at the actual break-in."

A small window popped up in Roland's vision with a time date stamp in the lower left hand corner. It was a picture of the entry to the greenhouse, and the time was 0301 hours that morning. As he watched, four black-suited, masked figures clustered near the main greenhouse door, all of them hauling plants.

"Satshot confirmed a modified, unmarked Hughes Stallion in our airspace at oh two hundred and fifty-four hours; that's how they got on site. The suspects were well-informed about our security and knew exactly what they were going for. Probably knew we only had surveillance by the elevators."

A text list scrolled up next to the video feed, listing every missing plant. Roland's steel-gray eyes widened as he read it, and he looked out the window so none of the other Plantech employees could see his reaction. "Frag it, Morgan, this is practically everything we sold to Shiawase last week! The Jap execs are gonna fry all our hoops if we don't recover these plants ASAP."

"Believe me, I'm trying not to think about that right now—"

"You fraggin' well better! The biggest deal this agricorp has seen in the past decade, and now all of our careers are on the line 'cause a bunch of slags waltzed in and snatched our product from under our very noses! If we don't save this deal you and I will be doing mall patrol until retirement, overseeing a bunch of drones or chasing down ork hooligans in the Barrens!"

Morgan's tone was crisp as he continued. *"Yes sir. As I said, the suspects were not average smash and grab tech or info thieves. In fact, we might not have caught them at all if the internal alarm codes hadn't changed, thereby alerting us to the broken window."*

"Great, just what I always want to rely on for security— dumb luck." Roland grimaced and shook his head as his subordinate continued.

"My squad was on patrol, so we confirmed the intrusion and headed to level thirty. The greenhouse doors were supposed to be in auto lockdown, but one of the suspects cracked it, and they held us up at the elevator by shooting the door with an arrow—"

"With a what?" Roland frowned. "Repeat that last sentence."

A picture of a broadhead arrow, broken in two pieces, flashed up on his image link.

"Yeah, one of these jokers used a bow to shoot the elevator door so it wouldn't open. K-Tog overrode the safety

protocol and executed plan Beta to secure the corridor, but they were ready for us. Here's a feed from an elevator cam."

Roland watched the security feed from the cam, seeing Morgan's pistol slide free from its holster, chamber a round, and fire into the air. "Drekking mages. Still, they didn't shoot you when they had the chance?"

"No, strangely enough. It was a fraggin' good distraction, but my men responded exactly as they should have. K-Tog and Faraday turned to secure the area behind us, while Davis and Weiger stayed locked on the greenhouse doors. Unfortunately, one of the thieves was already in the hall by then."

Roland watched in silence as the unseen presence disabled the pair of point guards in under two seconds. "He's fast, whoever he is."

"And he never showed up on our helmet cams. Apparently there's a mage trick that can hide a person from cameras as well as people. And the little slag took out K-Tog, too; watch this."

The scene unfolded in front of him; Morgan, ultrasound optic down on his helmet, HK subgun snugged into his shoulder, aiming at empty air. A blur streaked in from the bottom of the screen and hit the weapon, knocking it off target for a second. As he struggled to bring the firearm back up, Morgan staggered from an unseen blow, while the troll was rocked back and forth from a series of impacts at the same time.

Roland paused the feed. "What the frag is this? Is he taking you both on at once?"

"No, the shot that took me out—what I remember of it—wasn't from a fist or a foot. It was like the air itself solidified and hit me in the face."

"I swear, drekking mages. And what's even worse, we can't even afford to hire one ourselves." The sec chief activated the playback again, and watched a lithe figure almost punt the troll's head off his shoulders before the camera went to static. He split his viewscreen and brought up the internal greenhouse view, an image from one of his men's helmet cams. Switching it to thermal sight, Roland spotted what he was looking for under a long table; a crouched figure looking like it was punching air at the moment when

Morgan got knocked into next week. "Both the mages are elven, one street mage, one adept, I'd bet your paycheck on it. Frag, with that kick, even for a troll, I'm surprised he's in one piece. How's our boy doing?"

"Heck, chief, you know K-Tog—he'd come to work with a broken jaw and no one would know until he ordered soup in the cafeteria. He'll be all right. Next, their hacker scammed the elevator camera and turned it off. The suspects then dressed in the guards' uniforms and brought their haul down to the main floor, where that drekhead Conner told them to go ahead and take the plants to the safe room. Instead, they took a different elevator and hauled hoop to the garage, where they had a cargo van waiting, and left by the main gate—"

"Hold up, hold up, one thing at a time. First"—Roland reviewed the video until he found what he was looking for, a shot of all four intruders by the greenhouse's main elevator door. He zoomed in on the troll's head, his face hidden by a mask, but his horns left uncovered—"this guy's horns sweep back, while K-Tog's point forward. Did Conner tell you how he missed that pertinent bit of info?"

"Yeah, I spotted that, too. He said the troll had me over his shoulder and passed me off to the Crashcart guys, and Conner was focusing on the intruders still upstairs. The guy also knew our sec regulation about securing all plants in the event of a penetration. Conner was about to order the fake squad back up with him when a request for backup came over our radios."

Another file opened up, and an audible readout line burst into a red zig-zagging visual of noise as Roland listened to the assistance request from Squad Two, complete with the background sounds of a pitched firefight. "So they hauled your out-cold meat down with them, then broadcast a false call for help?"

"Yeah, according to Conner it sounded like all hell was breaking loose up there, and without monitors in the greenhouse itself, it was a reasonable assumption. They headed up and found the rest of my squad down. By the time they scrambled guards to the garage level to intercept, the thieves were already gone."

"How in the frag did they get out of the garage when

you guys had a level-three lockdown on the entire building?" Roland tried to keep his subvocalized voice in check, but his anger came through loud and clear.

Morgan's tone reflected his utter confusion, but Roland took no chances, activating his internal voice-stress analyzer as his lieutenant answered. *"Boss, I wish I could answer that one. According to Central, I was the one who had his retina scanned at oh three hundred and seven hours, and the computer registered my voice responding to the system's query about the sec issue with an almost perfect accuracy level. Voiceprints have always been around, but we've only heard rumors of a ret-copy program for years. I didn't think anything of this high quality had filtered down to the street yet."*

The security chief checked the results of the program's scan: 98.6 percent chance that the sec man told the truth. "Well, apparently it has now—get someone on the matrix to check out who may have sold that program in the past month, and find out who the buyer was."

"Right, sir. The cycle teams already had been activated as per SOP, and they caught the target vehicle coming out of the garage, an Ares Roadmaster. Central records say the plate of the van was registered to an overnight repair crew, and was scheduled to be in the building until six this morning. I'm downloading the schedule file to you now."

Morgan sucked in a breath and continued. *"They gave chase and attempted to disable the suspect vehicle to save the plants, as per standard orders. Every rider said they beat the frag out of the Roadmaster, but the suspects disabled both teams—again, not killing anyone, although three of our crew suffered minor injuries in the pursuit—and escaped. We're negotiating to get the security cam feeds from the chase route, but Lone Star has been jacking us around—"*

"You leave them to me, I'll have that feed in the next hour." Roland tried to ignore the sinking feeling in the pit of his stomach. "What else you got?"

"The vehicle was traced to the Historic District, but vanished in the alley maze down there. Paint traces from a car the Roadmaster sideswiped turned out to be your basic primer coat. Tire remnants are also standard run-flats, you can buy them at any one of a hundred places in the city."

"Vehicle's probably scrap or a new reef in the bay by

now." Roland checked his list of salvage yards. "Still, have Conner begin calling the junkyards in every 'burb about a beat-to-drek Roadmaster in primer gray. Pass along the plate, for all the good it'll do. It'll probably be the last order he gets from me, and I want it to suit his abilities."

"Canvas teams in the area have turned up nothing so far—it's like the runners vanished off the map completely." Morgan's voice already held a hint of defeat, but he kept it together.

"And took the future of our company with them." Roland rubbed his goateed chin as he considered the slim list of options available to him. A small, blinking red light appeared in the upper right quadrant of his vision. *Frag,* he thought. *Well, like I didn't know that was coming.*

"All right, finish your sweep of the garage, then retrace the chase route—take the uninjured rider with you—see if you can pick up anything the teams might have missed. Get someone you trust to review the files on every employee. Look for anything unusual, high debt, repossession, medical bills, divorce, whatever oddities you can find."

"You suspect an inside job?"

"The way they penetrated our perimeter so easily, you bet your hoop I do. I gotta see the Old Man, so check in with me when you're done."

"Affirmative, and—good luck," Morgan replied.

"Yeah, luck to you, too." Roland walked through the foliage to the open elevator doors, ignoring the whispers trailing behind him. Inside, one button on the panel was lit. Roland pressed it. The doors closed with only a minor hitch as the arrow hole in the door appeared in front of him. Roland ran his fingers around the edges of the perforation, shaking his head as his other hand dropped to the butt of the holstered Browning Max-Power on his thigh. *Takes all kinds,* he thought.

The elevator stopped moving, and Roland stepped out, aware that he was now several dozen meters below ground, and never comfortable with the feeling. There was only one way to go, down a polished black marble corridor that led to a pair of closed double doors. The squeak of the sec chief's combat boots against the floor echoed in the passageway. When he was two meters from the doors, they swung inward without a sound. Roland kept moving, his feet now sinking into plush carpet. There was no natural light to be seen anywhere, but plants climbed all four walls, fed by artificial cold lights.

"Mr. Ators. Please, sit down."

Roland had seen the head of Plantech, Jefferay Siskind, about a dozen times during his ten-year stint as head of security, and had been in this office seven times, by his recollection. Jefferay always addressed everyone he spoke to formally; the sec men had a long-running bet among them that he even called his own mother Mrs. Siskind. But in all that time, Roland had never been invited to sit down. With a barely perceptible pause in his stride, he walked to a leather wingback chair and settled in.

Jefferay leaned forward, his paper-white skin, pale red eyes and pointed ears giving him the appearance of an elf that had just spent the past ten years in a snowstorm. A maverick among the rest of his kind, the albino had founded Plantech three decades ago to research and develop allergen-free foods, with a secondary goal of creating safer drought and insect-resistant crops. He was one of that rare, vanishing breed in the Sixth World—an altruist.

But even altruists have to eat, and pay salaries and fund R and D departments, Roland thought. Hence the deal with Shiawase, which had been very interested in some of the more exotic hybrids Plantech had developed during the past four years. They had made an overture toward buying the entire company, but Siskind had dissuaded them without either side losing face, an impressive accomplishment. Shiawase had contracted to purchase the plants that had been in the greenhouse. The same plants that had been stolen exactly two hours and seventeen minutes ago.

Siskind shot the cuffs of his beige linen suit and rested his forearms on the bare desktop in front of him. "There's no need to apprise me of the situation, I know exactly where we stand in regard to our missing product." Despite his appearance, the elf's voice sounded normal—polished and smooth, with a hint of British prep school in it.

Although Roland respected his boss—part of the reason he took the gig in the first place—he wasn't about to kiss his hoop, either. "Yes, sir. My report on the break-in will be ready for you in twenty—"

Siskind waved at him to be quiet. "Other than the immediate dismissal of Mr. Conner for his inattention to detail, there will be no disciplinary action against your security squads. I'm afraid that, despite their best efforts, they were simply outmatched. Assuming we come out of this intact, I'll expect your updated report on the feasibility of hiring at least one corporate mage for security. And maybe, just maybe, I will consider putting some monitors in the greenhouse."

Roland's fingers flexed on the arms of his chair, waiting for the CEO to continue.

"There is no need to embellish the situation, Mr. Ators. I'm sure you know that with the failure of the dwarf citrus tree program, combined with the Norwegian root blight that killed half of our foreign programs, along with the flooding on the African coast that completely wiped out our subsidiary and its dry rice project, this licensing deal with Shiawase was our last chance to keep Plantech in one piece. Although we have all the necessary data ready for them, the deal's conclusion is contingent on delivering live samples of every plant they had purchased. Without those, the deal is off, and without that payment, Plantech will go bankrupt, and I will have to sell off our assets and let everyone go. Or Shiawase might be bold enough to demand my company as restitution for the missing samples. Neither of these outcomes is acceptable."

Roland prided himself on keeping a straight face, although the sinking feeling in his stomach threatened to turn into a whirlpool of acid. *Good-bye stock options, good-bye pension, good-bye everything.* Plantech would be chopped up like a plump hydroponic carrot, its pieces thrown to a slavering pack of corps looking to profit off the dead agricorp's carcass.

"Therefore, the course of action is clear. You have approximately twenty-nine hours to track down and recover the missing plants. Naturally, Lone Star cannot be involved in this—if they were to get wind of the fact that biotech was loose on the street, even plants as benign as ours, their reaction would be very unfavorable. Do whatever you can to recover those plants, Mr. Ators. That is all."

"Yes, sir, I already have everyone on the problem. We'll do everything we can."

"I have no doubt you will. The very survival of our company rests on your capable shoulders. I've opened a private number on your commlink that will connect you with me at any time of the day or evening. Keep me informed of your progress."

Roland stood, knowing the meeting was at an end. "Yes, sir." He walked out of the dim, oppressive office, craving a breath of fresh air. The elevator doors opened for him, and he stabbed the lobby floor button, tapping his foot and staring at the ceiling. On the way up, he dialed a number on his commlink.

"Hi honey, it's me . . . yeah, we've got a situation down here at the corp . . . I know, I know, nothing usually ever happens here, but I've got to stick around for a while, make sure everything is taken care of. Um, I might not be home until late this evening, just wanted you to know. Yes, I'll grab something here. We'll have to review the plans for the cottage over the weekend. I know, I'll be there as soon as I can . . . I love you, too . . . see you later."

He killed the connection and dialed another number. "Could you patch me through to Sergeant Jhones Redrock? Yes, I'll take his voice mail, thanks. Jhones? It's me, Roland. I need a favor, and I want to discuss it face-to-face. Meet me at the diner at nine thirty this morning if you can, but call me only if you can't. I hope to see you there. I'll stick around for a bit in case you don't get this message right away."

Roland closed the commlink connection and walked into the lobby, heading for the elevators that led to his office on the twentieth floor. The sick feeling in his gut had been burned away by a cold ball of rage at the street slags that had done this to his corp, and jeopardized everything he and hundreds of others had worked so hard for. *One way or another, they're gonna pay,* he vowed to himself.

6

Hood looked around the kitchen, his three-meter-tall frame eerily reflected in the mirrorlike surface of the equally tall refrigerator. All of the appliances had brushed aluminum surfaces, thereby presenting various likenesses and angles of the troll. It reminded him of when he had visited a carnival house of mirrors in his childhood, and made him vow—again—to have a redecorator stop by. He wondered, for probably the millionth time, what he'd look like if he had been born human instead of one of the metatypes that had appeared when magic returned to the world.

"Certainly not as comely as my bumpy self," he said, also probably for the millionth time. Odd to think of himself without the magnificent, curled horns and impressive row of teeth, or the muscles upon muscles that strained the seams of his skinsuit.

He'd changed out of the tight black suit he wore during the early-morning run and now wore beige cotton trousers and a tropical print short-sleeve shirt, both on the baggy side and both more than a little worn from age. He fancied that the clothes made him look like a beach bum, but they were comfortable and he wouldn't mind getting them dirty from working with the plants. After today, though, he would throw them away.

He opened the fridge, grabbed a milk bottle and scowled. The holostamp showed that its shelf life had passed two days ago. He popped the top and sniffed, finding it not too objectionable. Then he grabbed a package of imported almond cookies from the top shelf of a cabinet (where he knew the others couldn't easily reach), and opened it, reading the package for a moment. "Suggested serving size: three cookies. My hoop it is." Shaking his head, he emptied the bag's entire contents into his mouth, and followed them with all of the milk, chewing noisily, then swallowing with a belch.

His hunger pang temporarily mollified, he turned to the kitchen's large, granite-topped island, where he'd arranged a half-dozen of the more interesting-looking plants. He started with the stunted vine with dark green leaves and purple "hairs" everywhere. Hood's fingers tentatively brushed the largest leaf, finding the purple follicles ever-so-tickling. He'd never seen such a specimen before, not even on any of the numerous nature trideo programs he owned, and he was fascinated by it. He bent down until his chin touched the hairs and inhaled deeply. The scent of the potting soil was predominant, a rich mixture that the common gardener probably couldn't afford—or find. It had egg-shell colored granules in it, a few of which Hood plucked out with his fingernails and made a note to study later.

The plant itself gave off the odor of fresh-cut grass, and he wished it wasn't so subtle. "I'd have me a few of these, I would." He raised an eyebrow at his comment, then raised the corner of his mouth. "Indeed, I think I will have one of these."

"What did you say?" This came from Sindje, who was somewhere in the cavernous living room.

"I was talking to myself." Hood knew the elf couldn't physically see him, but he suspected she was watching him magically. A whisper: "You're far too curious for your own good."

"What are you doing?"

He didn't answer that, certain he didn't need to. "You know what I'm doing, Sindje." He reached into a cabinet beneath the island and retrieved a salt-glazed ceramic pot, an antique from an old pottery sale. A sack of potting soil and a small box of rooting powder followed.

"You should leave the plants alone, Hood. You said they should be as close to perfect as possible for the Johnson. He'll know you've been tampering."

"He won't know. Why don't you relax, meditate with

your brother or something?" Hood measured out some potting soil and mixed it with a few pinches of the rooting powder, added some water and then took a cutting of the purple-green plant. He followed this with three cuttings from other plants he found interesting, and made a mental note to buy some more old, but pretty, ceramic pots in the event the cuttings prospered. Hood knew a fixer who could probably find a few salt-glazed containers that would come close to matching—and would no doubt set him back more than a few nuyen. "Be worth it, though, for displaying these beauties."

"What?"

"Still talking to myself, Sindje, nothing to worry about."

Hood placed the salt-glazed pot on the center of the island and turned on a grow light. The cuttings were small; he'd selected little more than healthy leaves with stems attached, and he knew the Johnson wouldn't have a clue the plants had been disturbed.

"One more, I think." A pause: "Still talking to—"

"I know." Sindje made a huffing sound. "Yourself."

The troll took one more cutting from the purple-green plant and put it in the salt-glazed pot. "Wonderful plants." *But just how wonderful?* he mused. Most of the varieties they'd snatched looked like run-of-the-mill houseplants. *Looked* like, he corrected himself. There were subtle differences. For example, the plant next to the purple-green vine resembled a golden pothos, and it also had some similarities to a common philodendron. It didn't look especially valuable. And even though the nuyen promised for this job was good, Khase might have been right, it was a little too good for . . . these plants.

"Or is it?" Hood carefully felt the stems of the one that looked like a pothos. It had heart-shaped leaves, jade mottled in places with yellow-white splotches. The leafstalks grew upright, straight as a candle, but the longest ones showed signs of drooping, like a pothos should, taking on the aspect of a vinelike houseplant. "Why does the Johnson want these?"

Sindje cleared her throat, that simple sound expressing a world of irritation. "It doesn't matter why the Johnson wants them, Hood. It never matters. You're the one who's always repeating that phrase like a Gregorian monk."

"Gregorian chant."

"Drekkin' whatever. What does matter is that you stop messing with them."

Hood peered around the corner and into the living room. Sindje was stretched out on the couch, appearing child-small on the massive cushions. She locked eyes with him. Max was still in the massage chair, his commlink plugged into her ear, and eyes staring into space—jacked into something or listening to gossip from one contact or another. No jumping eyelids, so the ork wasn't involved with Beetles. Hood would kick her back into rehab in a heartbeat if he thought she'd returned to her old addiction.

At first the troll didn't spot Khase, and he growled low in his throat. But another glance through the room and he saw the elf. Khase was indeed meditating, doing a one-armed handstand, legs tucked in a lotus position, neatly sandwiched between tanks of pearlscales and orandas. He might have been a decorative statue, he remained so still.

Hood returned to the plants. The pothos was a hardy plant, he knew, and a fast grower. It didn't require much care, just a reasonably warm atmosphere and moist soil. But what were these granules in the mix? And why did it matter what the granules or the plants were? And why was he "messing with the plants," as Sindje had coined the phrase?

Call it my need to know, Hood thought. He dampened a soft cloth and wiped the upper and lower sides of the leaves, leaving them shiny and healthy-looking. It was how one took care of such plants, he knew. He couldn't use the same technique on the purple-green vine with the "hairs," only on the plants with slick leaves. If he had a cosmetic brush, he could clean the purple-green plant, sweep away the loam that had spilled on them in the chase. Max wouldn't own such a thing as a cosmetic brush, and Sindje probably had one—but he knew better than to ask. So he gently blew on the purple-green leaves, watching the edges flutter.

"Fertilizer!" That's what the granules were. A mix of nitrogen, phosphorous and potassium, no doubt. Balanced, certainly, he decided, noting that the granules were larger and darker in the soil of the flowering plant. "Twenty-twenty-twenty in the pothos." Hood knew that was the best

percentage by weight of nitrogen, phosphorous and potassium in the fertilizer for the green plants. Likely fifteen-
thirty-fifteen for the plant that flowered. "Well cared for,
definitely, which is to be expected." Hood used a liquid
fertilizer for his houseplants, a costly mix made to his speci-
fications. He plucked out a few more granules and put them
in an empty food container, and used another container for
the larger crystals from the flowering plant so he could have
them tested later.

"Granules must be water-soluble and slow-release. Have
to be." Hood knew that if they didn't use something that
wasn't water-soluble or heavily diluted, the plants could be
subject to "fertilizer burn." So the people at Plantech knew
what they were doing. "But that's just it, what are they
doing?"

"What are you muttering about?" Sindje was on her feet
now, pacing across the chocolate-colored carpet and leaving
a trail in the nap as she went. "What are *who* doing?"

The troll released a great sigh and didn't bother to answer, though for a moment he thought about again telling
her to meditate with Khase. The elf was still in his one-
armed handstand, a pose Hood suspected he took up an
hour ago. Maybe Sindje would unwind a bit if she let the
blood rush to her head.

"Something about these plants. There's something special about them." Hood was referring only to the pothos
look-alike and the purple-green vine. "But what?"

"It. Doesn't. Matter." Sindje raised her voice.

Max's eyes refocused and Khase came out of his trance,
though he didn't alter his position.

"Doesn't matter one fraggin' whit," she went on. "We
were hired to steal them. We stole them. Now all we have
to do is wait for the Johnson to call with the drop spot.
You're not taking any more cuttings, Hood. Don't think I
don't know what you're doing in there. You're leaving the
plants alone. Understand?"

Khase moved while she spoke, leaning forward and landing silently on the balls of his feet, centimeters from the
edge of the low table that was covered with plants. Hood
sucked in a breath and lowered his head, glaring at the
female elf.

"You're not costing us any nuyen, Hood." Sindje stopped

pacing and continued her rant, ignoring her brother, who
moved up behind her.

"We don't have any nuyen yet, *chwaer*." Khase's voice
was calm as he tried to deflect his sister's ire.

"We will, assuming nothing else goes awry." Sindje
ground her heel into the carpet as Hood sucked in another
breath. She leaned over the tableful of plants. "Nuyen on
the table, right here. We'll drop these this evening—
provided Hood doesn't cut them all up into garnishes
first—get our creds and get onto the next run."

"Lower your voice." Hood was in the living room now,
staring at Sindje, whose nose brushed the top of what
looked like a calathea. It was a striking plant with pointed
oval dark green leaves with silvery stripes down the centers.
He noted a scalloped stripe on the sides of the leaves, near
the margins, a red tint on some of the undersides. "Shouting isn't good for plants. Besides that one's rather delicate.
You're blocking the light, and it requires about one thousand foot-candles for optimum growing conditions."

He came closer, and Sindje retreated behind the couch,
pacing again, her brother following. Hood looked down at
the calathea, noting a different mix of granules. "This one
should get fertilized about every other month. So I suspect
these constitute a very slow release mixture."

The air whistled out from between Sindje's clenched
teeth. She spun and would have bumped into Khase were
he not so nimble. He vaulted over the back of the immense
couch and landed on a cushion, legs crossed lotus-style
again and looking nonplussed.

"However, I do agree with Sindje, Hood. Please stop
messing with the plants. Stop jawing about leaf scorch and
potting media and humidity. I like it warm myself, *tad,* but
you've cranked up the heat in this place for the plants, and
I'm starting to sweat."

Sindje had a smug look on her face. "Doesn't matter if
you've got a drekkin' horticulture addiction, Hood. Probably what interested you in this low-end run in the first
place. What matters is—"

Hood made a fist, his thick nails digging so hard into the
palm of his hand that he felt it. "What matters, Sindje, is
that you and your brother beat your proverbial feet for a
little while. Your negative energy is not good for the plants,

especially the fancy-leaved caladium, the emerald ripple peperomia and the exotica perfection dumbcane. Now go, get out of here for a while. Buzz. Max'll let you know when the Johnson calls."

Color rose in Sindje's face, and she opened her mouth to protest. But Khase was instantly at her elbow and guiding her toward the door, snatching a keycard off the table as he did so. "I assume the doors are maglocked."

"They are. Don't go too far."

"We won't. Stairs go to the roof?"

Hood nodded and the door slid shut behind them. He then returned to studying the two plants he considered special. "All that negative energy, bad for the fuchsia, the Lagrimas de Maria, the injurious Amapalo Amarillo, and especially bad for me."

Max closed her eyes and leaned back, letting the chair massage her tense muscles. She'd thrown off the link she'd been perusing when Sindje went into her tirade. Time to go back for another look.

The ork drummed her fingers against a tusk, then picked at a piece of bacon caught between her teeth; Hood had the decency to feed them a little less than two hours ago. The bacon had tasted like the real thing, and she wondered what else "real" he might have in the refrigerator.

"Later," she muttered to herself. "Got things to do. Surf's up." Max took a deep breath and prepared to go back online. She imagined the commlink as an antenna, able to transmit and receive info to and from the matrix right from where she was sitting, with no one else the wiser that Max was doing anything, since the uplink she was using wasn't hers. The image made her feel secure and comfortable, the trickle of power was as soothing as the massaging chair. *Mebbe oughta get me one of these for sleazin' the matrix. Frag, I could get used to this.* The electrons danced in her skull and started spinning so fast, like horses racing at the Preakness.

The fingers of her right hand flinched and the electrons moved erratically. Her tongue tingled from the sensation and her eyelids grew warm. In her mind pictures flashed, advertisements and news stories, real enough to touch. Without leaving her chair, she walked along a street in downtown Seattle, looking up at billboards, glancing at placards in shop windows, deciding if anything caught her interest.

Nothing so far.

In her mind, she turned down another street, dark like the one from the early-morning chase, but there were state-of-the-art holographic projectors in some of the shop windows, one showing the site of a new building that was going up on Pier 63. Another held the image of the light rail system, the train frozen between University Street and Pioneer Square, where someone had been murdered. Not the news items she was looking for.

Max was in her element here, relating better to the matrix than to people. She spent most of her nuyen on advancements, the leftover on whatever she was driving at the time. Metal and wires were her friends . . . they couldn't hurt your feelings.

There was an alley to her mind's right, and she took a peek. A shadowy figure opened one side of his longcoat, neon-light threads of green and pink in the lining displayed his wares.

Chips.

Max swallowed hard.

Beetles. Better Than Life chips. Better-than-anything chips.

The fingers of her left hand tapped faster against her tusk.

They weren't the *real* chips, not the kind she used to slot, the kind that would take her . . . everywhere and nowhere. But what the shadowy figure offered would be close.

Just a taste.

One little taste.

Not the *real* chips, she told herself, not the ones you could feel in your fingers, ones that would take you to heaven before rudely depositing you in hell. But hell was a brief visit if you could get more chips. Not the *real* chips, so not the *real* danger.

But a danger nonetheless.

The figure beckoned with a glinting hand, arraying a vast display of chips in his nimble fingers.

She took a mental step in that direction, then stopped herself. *Mebbe later,* she sadly decided. *Mebbe when Hood isn't so close, and when the elves are out of sight. Mebbe not at all if I'm lucky and keep my head on straight.*

Max turned away from the alley and headed toward a large storefront that had lots of posters in the windows. She was here on a self-imposed mission, after all.

Things to do, news items to read.

The first poster showed a petite human woman in a tailored red suit. She was pointing at a map of the West Coast. As Max watched, little rain clouds appeared above Seattle, and curving lines with jagged teeth radiated toward the city.

"*Onara*. She's a fraggin' weather girl, and I ain't interested in the weather." Max shut out the petite voice and moved to the next poster and the next and the next.

The posters represented all the news broadcasts the ork was picking up through the commlink:

A fire in an abandoned apartment in the Barrens, declared arson-for-profit. *Like that's some news item.*

A Lone Star crackdown in a white-collar neighborhood in Bellevue near a metroplex.

Go-gang activity on Route 520 along the lakeshore.

A memorial at the Crying Wall in the Bickson Building in Tacoma.

Onara! *What the frag? Where are we?*

Max went from one building to the next, one street to the next—staying away from the temptations of the dark alleys. She looked through all the posters, up at the billboards, and was finally reduced to studying the little sheets of paper tacked to light poles and garbage cans.

We're not fraggin' mentioned anywhere.

The ork was certain she'd spent an hour searching the recent news files, maybe more. With each block she wandered she grew increasingly puzzled that she couldn't find a single mention of the early-morning theft from Plantech. Granted, they stole only plants, nothing very exotic looking, and therefore nothing seriously valuable. But with the chase through the streets and all the bullets and streetcycles flying, she thought she would have picked up *something* on the news.

She was at the same time relieved and disappointed— what they'd done apparently wasn't worth even the space of a classified ad. But the lack of news also meant they got away clean.

Safe.

Max retraced her steps down the streets, checking the news items one final time . . . just in case she'd missed something. The shadowy man was still in the alley, green and pink neon wares lighting up the grimy lane. She shook her head and focused on the plug in her neck and the electrons dancing in her head.

A moment more and she was staring at the table of plants and still feeling the soothing massage motion of the chair. Judging by the muttering and muffled noises, Hood was obviously still in the kitchen.

She felt a gentle vibration in her ear and activated the borrowed earpiece, adjusting it as she did. "Yes?" The corners of her bulbous lips turned down; she'd expected the Johnson on the other end.

"Who? Oh, you're looking for Hood. He's busy."

She paused and snarled, considered hanging up.

"No, I'm not his drekkin' secretary. No, he's not going to be here this afternoon." *We've got a Johnson to meet.* "No, I don't know if he's going to be here tonight." *Depends how long the drop takes.* "Yes, he's going to be out for at least a few hours. What's it to you anyway?"

Max disconnected the call, but kept the earpiece in place.

"Fraggin' Johnson better call fraggin' soon. Drek, drek, drek."

7

"Lone Star officers! Stop right there!"

Sergeant Jhones Redrock raced down the alley as fast as his short legs could propel him, his long, flame-red Mohawk fluttering in the breeze. A few steps ahead, his partner, Officer Simon Chays, closed the distance between himself and a pair of human go-gangers that had been roughing up a female elf in the alley. The two thugs split up, each veering in a different direction at a T-intersection. Redrock pointed his left hand, palm up, at the fleeing ganger, and a small dart flew out to tag his target. A blinking red dot immediately appeared in his vision, telling him that the punk had turned left a half-block up.

"Ma'am, please stay where you are, we'll be right back," Jhones ordered the woman upon seeing that she wasn't in immediate danger. *Take the left one, I've got his buddy,* he subvocalized to his partner, cutting down a narrow alley that paralleled the main passage his quarry had taken.

"Are you sure? Regulations say we shouldn't split—"

"Just do it, Chays. Loser buys breakfast." Jhones brought up a map of the area on his cybereye and watched the tagged human's blinking red dot as he cut back around the building, trying to get to a main street so he could blend in with the rest of the early-morning crowd. *Fat chance, slot-head,* the dwarf thought as he increased his pace. He wouldn't even need to draw his real pistol for this one. Although he had every confidence in his partner's ability to catch a punk low-life, he also kept a screen open on Chays, keeping an eye on the rookie in case he got into trouble.

Jhones approached the exit of the narrow alley and turned on his amplified hearing, filtering out the ambient noises of the alley to focus on one sound—the rapid-fire footfalls of someone running. A small screen popped up and displayed information about his target based on measurements of the force and width of his hurried steps:

Human Male
Height: 1.6 meters tall
Weight: 75 kilograms
Speed: 6.2 kilometers per hour
Distance: 30 meters and closing

Scanning the alley entrance, Jhones found a dirty dumpster set flush against the wall around the corner. It suited his purposes perfectly. He waited behind it, listening to the pounding footsteps approach, the distance counting down in the corner of his vision. *20 meters—15 meters—10 meters—5 meters—1 meter—*

Stepping out from behind the dumpster, Jhones pivoted on his heel and buried his fisted cyberhand between the human's legs. The go-ganger, who had been looking back for signs of pursuit, folded in half around the dwarf's stocky arm, paralyzed by the blow. The Lone Star cop shoved the human off his hand, sending him sprawling to the filthy plascrete, where the hood curled up in a fetal position and squalled in anguish, cupping his privates with both hands.

"Oy, I love being a dwarf. You humans keep falling for the *chamalyeh* every single time." Noticing a familiar gang symbol on the kid's synthleathers, Redrock nudged him over onto his back. "Troll Killer, eh, boychik? You're a bit far from your usual Wolf Bay hangout. *Nu,* maybe you're messing around up here in something you shouldn't be— besides beating up ladies of the evening? Bad for downtown business, but I guess you didn't know that."

"Jhones, I got the other one," Simons' voice said inside his head. *"But neither one of us smells too good right now."*

"Tackled him in a pile of garbage, eh? I like a cop who

throws himself into his work. Haul yours back to the elf, and we'll get a positive ID on these two before taking them in." Jhones flipped the punk onto his stomach and patted him down while scanning him with his cybereye for concealed weapons, finding a set of strap-on snap-blades on his right forearm, a dead shock glove on his left hand, and a Hattori YH-1 bowie knife in a spring sheath at the small of his back. He twisted the kid's hand behind his back while pulling out a pair of plasteel cuffs, locking them around the ganger's wrists and activating the heat fuser to seal them shut until the suspect could be booked down at the station.

Jhones leaned near the go-ganger's face. "On your feet, schmuck. And if you're thinking about legging it down the alley, I won't bother chasing you again—I'll just shoot you, and save us both the trouble." From the terrified look on the kid's face, Jhones knew he had gotten his point across.

He boosted the ganger up and marched him back to the alley where Simon, the other human banger and the elf waited for him. Simon was right, his collar and he both looked and smelled like they had rolled around in a Stuffer Shack's grease pit. The human's hands, wrapped in blood-stained rags, were cuffed in front of him, and Jhones arched a quizzical eyebrow at Simon, who shook his head.

"Later," he subvocalized to the dwarf.

The elf, her lacquered hairstyle in disarray and face smudged with dirt, had managed to regain some of her poise. Now that Jhones got a better look at her, he saw that she wasn't a prostitute at all, but a corp exec in a once-sleek Bodyline pantsuit, now torn and dirty, who had apparently taken a wrong turn while on her way to work.

"Thank you for waiting, ma'am. My name is Jhones Redrock, and this is my partner Simon Chays, Lone Star. I assume that you'll want to press charges."

"Absolutely. These idiots made me late for my morning conference." The elf's face twisted into a mask of hate at the two would-be criminals.

"Very well, let me record your positive ID of these two suspects, and then we can handle the rest of the report down at the station after your shift is over." Jhones activated his cybereye camera and recorded the exec's sneering identification of the two ruffians, along with her SIN, which would give him everything he'd need for further contact. "I'll be in touch with you to set up a time to stop in. Please let me know if there is anything else we can do."

The elf brushed ineffectually at her soiled suit and took a deep breath as she bowed to both of them. "Thank you for your assistance. Horizon Group will be very pleased that I am unharmed."

Jhones exchanged a covert glance with his partner at the elf's attempt to save face. *Sure they will, chummer-san. If you were a* shaikujin *worth knowing, you wouldn't be walking to work through these alleys, you'd be in an armored limo or rotorcraft.* Regardless, he bowed as well, his movement mirrored by Simon. "Just doing our jobs, Ms. Terakuna. May I say that I hope the rest of your day goes better than your morning. Would you like a ride to your corp—"

"No—no, that is not necessary, but thank you all the same. We're close enough to the main street that I will be able to get a cab without any difficulty. Again, I thank you." With that, the exec straightened her suit jacket, picked up her matching Bodyline leather soft-sided attaché case, now scuffed and wet, and walked out of the alley with her head high. Even mussed and shaken, she still managed to radiate a haughty arrogance.

"Maybe she's got a chance to climb the ranks yet," Jhones mused. "Come on, street rats, we got a nice comfy holding pen waiting for you at the Third Precinct." He yanked his collar toward their LS modified Ford American patrol cruiser, and put his man next to Simon's prisoner in the backseat. "What'd you find on the sprinter?"

Simon glanced at the filthy ganger as he got into the passenger seat. "My guy was armed for bear, or at least what passes for it here. Check this out." He picked up what looked like a normal riot baton from the floor of the car and handed it to Jhones, who weighed it in his hand.

"Hm, fraggin' heavy for a beatin' stick."

"That's 'cause it isn't. Put both hands at the end near that small button there, then hit it, but keep this thing away from your face."

Jhones did so, and the expected top spike popped out, but so did two other strange features, a pair of stained steel spikes, one on each side of the handle. The Lone Star cop zoomed in with his cybereye and spotted a glint of wire attached to the point of each spike and running back to the haft, forming two taut monowire blades.

"Slice and dice indeed. Let me guess, this explains his hands." Jhones hit the button again, causing all three spikes to retract back into the handle, and gave it back to Simon. He crossed to the driver's side and hopped up, the bucket seat and pedals conforming to his reduced height.

"Yeah, I cornered the guy in an alley, and he pulled this thing on me. While he was fumbling around with it, I grabbed the end closest to me—the correct end to hold, by the way—and hit the button by accident. He's lucky he didn't lose a finger or two, but he is cut up pretty bad."

"Oy, Chays. You do realize that we carry these things called guns, and that they can force a suspect to drop his weapon when used appropriately, yes?"

The rookie looked sheepish. "Sorry, I hit my wired reflexes, and grabbed it almost before I knew what I was doing."

Redrock shook his head. "Like a kid during Chanukah, you are. All right, since we're almost done with our shift, let's drop these two shlimazels off and handle the report—" Jhones broke off as a light flashed in the corner of his eye, signaling a voice mail message on his direct line. "Hang on a moment. Run it."

He listened to the message from Roland Ators, then ran it once again. "Look, boychik, I just got a message from an old friend of mine that he wants to meet me at the Anything Diner off Nineteenth. We'll drop this pair at the precinct—and give you a chance to change into something more suitable—then go have a nosh. How does that sound? Besides, you owe me."

"What, no way do I owe you anything. I caught my guy, too."

"But not first, *chaver*." Jhones tapped his head. "I was watching as you took him down. What is this when a dwarf can run down a mugger faster than a human? I have fifteen years on you, no less—"

"*Wakarimasuka*, all right, all right, you win." Shaking his head, Simon leaned back in his seat as Jhones merged onto Highway 5 and headed north, smiling all the way.

A half hour later, the two officers pulled into the crowded parking lot of the Anything Diner in a sleeper, or unmarked patrol car. Located on the Snohomish-Seattle border, the 24-hour restaurant was popular with a wide variety of clientele, both human and meta alike, for one particular reason that was its sole claim to fame.

"Ever eaten here before?" Jhones asked as he slid out of the car. He had changed into plainclothes for the meet, as had Simon, who had also grabbed a quick and necessary steamshower at the precinct.

"No, but I've heard about it. Is it true what they say about this place?" Simon wore a dubious expression as he looked at the dingy, faux-50s diner exterior of the restaurant.

"Let's head inside and find out, shall we?" With a wave of his hand, Jhones motioned for his partner to go first.

The interior of the diner was crammed to capacity, with every counter chair, table, and booth filled. A dozen conversations swirled around and through each other, from the deep bass voices of three trolls taking up an entire corner of the diner, to a family of suburban elves enjoying their breakfast. Orks and humans were also present, and everyone was tucking into what looked like huge golden omelets. As Jhones watched, a skinny man in a grease-stained apron wrote something on a touch screen, which also appeared on a screen above the counter:

ANYTHING DINER'S OMELET SPECIAL: 10 NUYEN
"YOU BRING IT, WE SLING IT!"
OMELETS SERVED IN THE PAST 24 HOURS:
RAT
SPAGHETTI
RADISH
GOAT'S EYE
BLOOD
EGGPLANT
FUGU
RUM & COKE
COCKROACH

"I think I'm going to be sick." Simon stared at Jhones in disbelief. "They're kidding, right?"

In answer to his question, a waitress brought out a steam-

ing platter to a table of orks who were definitely out-of-
towners, dressed in brightly colored robes, head wraps and
capped golden tusks. Hoots, cheers and catcalls followed in
the dish's wake.

As the platter passed the two cops, Jhones saw the look
on his partner's face. "Still had the legs on, eh?"

"You can't be serious—we aren't possibly going to eat
here?"

"Hey, one man's pleasure is another man's poison.
Relax, they serve normal fare as well. And no one has
gotten sick here in the last ten years. So the owner claims."

"Yeah, what about before then?" Simon shuddered.
"And what about the health inspectors? I'd think they'd
have a field day here."

Jhones patted him on the arm. "Oy, don't worry about
it, you'll be fine. Look, a counter chair just opened up, grab
it while you can. I just spotted my guy at the table, but
there's only room for one. I'll fill you in when we're done."

"Uhh—okay." Simon squeezed in between a dwarf who
looked like he had spent the past decade on the street and
a well-dressed elf shoveling down a heaping Denver omelet.
Jhones made sure his partner was reasonably comfortable,
then threaded his way through the crowd to the small table.

"*Hoi,* Roland, it's good to see you."

The sec man nodded, his face grave. "It's good to see
you, too, Jhones. Still clinging to those sergeant's bars, I
see."

Jhones grabbed a menu and scanned it. "Well, I didn't
frag off from my Lone Star tour of duty and take a lucrative job sitting on my hoop in the private sector like some
people I know." He waited for Roland to riposte with another verbal jab, but heard only silence. The cop slid the
menu down to peek at his companion, only to see the human's brow furrowed, obviously lost in thought. A waitress
sidled over, and Jhones set the menu back down. "Hummus
omelet, and realcaf, please."

"Just an English muffin for me, and realcaf as well,"
Roland said, running a hand over his cropped hair.

Jhones cut to the chase. "All right, *chaver,* what's got
you so *verklempt,* eh?"

Roland leaned forward over the table. "First, this has to

stay off the record. If you can't do that, then this meeting is over. I'm asking you as my friend, not as a cop right now, okay?"

Jhones had known the sec man sitting across from him for two decades, ever since they were both green recruits at Lone Star. Even after Roland had left the corp to go into private security, they had stayed in touch, helping each other numerous times over the years. In all that time, the dwarf had never seen the man like this. "No prob, boychik, just fill me in on what's going down."

Roland started talking, and when their meals arrived, Jhones let his grow cold as he absorbed the details of what had happened at Plantech earlier that morning. "Our CEO doesn't want to bring in Lone Star or UCAS especially; if they think rogue biotech is on the street they'll go crazy, tear us and the streets apart looking for it," Roland finished, his hands wrapped around his coffee mug.

"Plus, you wouldn't want Shiawase to get wind that their delivery has vanished, either, would you?" Jhones' smile never came close to his eyes. "That wouldn't help your bottom line if they got the plants first, eh?"

Roland sighed. "Touché. Look, I give you my word that none of the plants are dangerous, we just want the chance to get them back first. The team that swiped 'em is small, with at least two elves, an ork and a bow-and-arrow-wielding troll, which should stick out if they're all still hanging together. We're beating the street right now as it is, and with any luck we'll find them first. All I'm asking is if you get a line on these slots, you give me a holler first, okay?"

Jhones sipped his caf and leaned back in his chair. "I can't promise you anything, Roland, but you know I'll do whatever I can if these ganefs pop up on our radar. If we find them, as long as my partner and I can get credit for the bust, I think we can work something out."

"Thanks, chummer, I was hoping I could count on you." Roland pushed his chair back and stood. "I've downloaded the chase route to your personal account. I would really appreciate it if you could shoot over as many vid bytes as you can to me. I've already taken care of breakfast, and I've got to get back on site. Let me know if you hear anything, right?"

"*Nu*, what breakfast?" Jhones pushed his untouched plate away and swallowed the last of his realcaf. "You'll be the first one I call after backup." He slid off his chair and followed Roland toward the door, signaling to Simon as he passed.

"So what was that all about?" the rookie asked as they headed to the car.

"Pull up anything on an attempted break-in at Plantech agricorp this morning from our database," Jhones said as he climbed into the driver's seat just as his commlink went off. "I got another call. Bring up that file and I'll bring you up to speed." Then he turned his attention to his call. "Redrock here—yeah, I've got a minute—what? What do you mean you just sold me!"

8

Sindje fumed with every pace up the stairs. Ahead of her, Khase flitted from step to step like a ghost, leaving no sound in the stairwell.

Don't think I don't know why we're taking the stairs, brawd, she thought. The street mage knew her brother was hoping that the physical action would take the edge off her displeasure, but instead it fueled it even further. Cachu, *he knows I don't like to perspire!*

The two elves reached the top of the building, and Khase fed the card through the lock and popped the door. They stepped out, blinking at a rare sight for them: the morning sun. The apartment building was on the edge of a short peninsula of land that jutted out into Puget Sound, forming the bottom part of Elliot Bay. The rooftop gave them a gorgeous, unobstructed view of the sound and the naval traffic that plied the waterway. The sunlight glittered on the blue-green water as if a giant hand had cast a fistful of diamonds on the tide, almost painful to look at, yet hypnotic at the same time.

Khase stepped to the edge of the building, standing on the lip like he was waiting in line for a theater show, unaware of the stiff breeze blowing at this altitude. Sindje kept her distance, comfortable enough on the roof's broad plain, but unwilling to get closer than five meters to the edge. Above them, a dozen giant windmills sliced through the air, their whirling, broad blades providing power to the building.

"Beautiful, isn't it?" Khase shaded his eyes and gazed out across the sound. "Just think, this land, this water was all here before any of us were even a gleam in our parents' eyes. And, nature willing, it will still be here when all of us have returned to the dust from whence we came."

"Spare me your environmental raptures, will you?" Sindje paced the roof, oblivious to the stunning vista before her. "Drek, my bad feeling about this run is getting worse and worse. And what's with Hood playing Mr. Happy Gardener down there? I mean, I think he doesn't even know anything about the Johnson that gave us this gig. Frag, I think our Johnson doesn't even know anything about the plants, set it up for someone else and—"

"I agree, *chwaer*."

"And to top it all off, when I call Hood on what he's doing, messing with the drekkin' plants, he dismisses me like I'm a *roba*. You all but kiss his hoop while shoving me out the door. I mean, way to back me up in there, brother—"

"You are correct, something is off here."

"And another thing—what? What did you say?" Sindje halted her tirade in midsentence. "Did you actually just agree with me?"

Khase turned to face her. "Yes, I tend to do that once in a while, when you make a good point." Sindje's mouth hung open as he continued. "There are too many aspects about this supposed 'milk run' that have made me very suspicious indeed."

He leapt into the air, coming down on his hands and walking along the lip of the building's roof as easily as another person would walk down a city street. "I think that Max, you and I have already noticed the difficulty executing this heist in the first place—"

"Wait a sec, and get over here." Sindje tapped her foot until her brother ran, still on his hands, to her. She shoved him over while activating her mindlink spell with the push. Khase flipped head over heels and landed on his feet in a balanced crouch. *All right, let's continue this conversation this way—I'd rather take the lower chance of spirits listening in than satellites.*

However you prefer, chwaer. The adept ran straight at the base of a windmill, sprinting several meters up its side, then arcing off to flip through the air and land in front of Sindje. *As I said, besides the difficulty of pulling off what was supposed to be simple break-and-grab, then we come back to a triple-A neighborhood to hang out until the heat dies down. You can't tell me Hood actually owns a co-op like this, unless he's been seriously jacking us around about his real life—perhaps one that is completely outside the streets.*

Yeah, not that he's really told us all that much about his big, warty self. He knows far more about us and about Max, I'm certain. But what's really raising my hackles is the so-called delay by our Johnson, Sindje thought, turning to look at the tangle of skyscrapers, superhighways, and the bustling humanity of all kinds across the bay to the northeast. *This whole run has been a big load of drek from the start, and it doesn't look like it's going to get any better. Who knows what that Johnson is prepping for us at the drop? A full-bore sec team or two, with mages and elementals and frag knows what else? No thanks, Hood can jam those plants up his—*

Point taken, my sister. Khase rubbed his smooth chin. *I think it's time to bring in a little help—someone who can go places more easily than we can.* He walked back to the door and picked up the maintenance handset inside. "Max? Yeah, it's me. Why don't you come up to the roof for a minute, get some fresh air? Trust me, it will do you good to get a different perspective on things. See you in a few."

He strolled back to Sindje. *If I know our industrious little hacker, no doubt she's already been scanning the screamsheets, looking for any hint of interest in what went down this morning. If she has, then it will be even easier to have her poke around into Hood's life—if he really does own that condo. A troll like that has to have an electron trail, faked or otherwise. And I'll bet Max is just the person to find out.*

Interesting thought, brawd. *You have been thinking about this.*

More like letting it filter through my subconscious while I entered a higher realm of awareness. Really, sister, you should try meditation sometime, it would soothe—

The only thing that will soothe my mind at the moment is getting those plants out of our hands and getting the nuyen we're owed into them. Sindje brushed a stray lock of hair back from her face as she regarded her brother, choosing her next thought carefully. *That reminds me—how far are you willing to take this if necessary?*

Khase smiled, steepling his fingers as he considered the question. *Why, dear sister, whatever do you mean?*

Don't play fraggin' coy with me, slotter, you know as well as I do that we need this payoff—folks we owe aren't going to be as forgiving this time around.

Oh, that little matter.

Yeah, the debt. You know we were lucky to get out of New York in the first place. I still don't know how those enforcers from Tir na nÓg picked up our trail so fast. And after that scum Niswaters had the nerve to claim that we hadn't paid him after we dropped the money off.

Don't forget our little adventure trying to switch planes in Detroit, either. Khase's handsome features clouded as he considered past events. *Don't worry, Niswaters will get his, one way or another. But his boss is still saying that we owe that debt—including the vig, which is racking up even as we stand here—so we need all the jobs we can get to get out from under his wide thumb.*

No kidding. My question still stands.

Let's just say that in the event of complications—which I am expecting, by the way, I am prepared to take any measures necessary to ensure our payment. Provided those measures don't jeopardize the team or bring the heat down on us.

Does that include geeking? You know how our tad Hood frowns upon that.

Which, as I recall, we have had no problem with either. Unlike many others who think that life of any kind is cheap and easily sacrificed if it interferes with their goals, I know we aspire to a higher standard—

But?—

But if push came to geek . . . well, I haven't come to that point in any of our runs yet, but one never knows—

A heavy hand slapped at the rooftop door, and Khase sprang over to open it. Max stomped out, squinting in the bright sunlight. "Fraggin' Hood keeps it like an oven down there for those plants."

"He didn't notice you leave?" Sindje crossed her arms.

"*Vut,* that loco troll was elbow deep in potting soil, last I saw of him. But what I wanna know is, what's so all-fraggin' important that you two gotta drag me out of my comfy chair up to this bone-cold rooftop?"

Sindje grinned. "Tell me, Max, anything seem—weird—about this run to you?"

"Anything? Don't you mean everything?" The ork snorted in disgust. "Besides the small army dogging us through that agricorp—an agricorp, for drek's sake!—the loss of my Ares RM, our kickin' it in these plush digs . . . and here's something you didn't know: there hasn't been a peep in the newsvids yet about our run—nothing, not even on the police blotter. So far I haven't found anything that jives on this run yet. This smells . . . major *kusatta.*"

Told you she'd been working, Khase thought to his sister. "We surmised you might be feeling that way, since it's the exact same conclusion we arrived at during our rooftop constitutional." He sank to the roof in a perfect split that would be the envy of any gymnast, his legs pointing straight north and south. "The question is: what should we do about it?"

"Bottom line, Hood knows more than he's telling, and we want to find out what's up." Sindje resisted the urge to rub her hands together.

"And you want me to snoop around, and see what I can see, eh, chummers? Dig into Hood's background? Haven't known him all that long. Been on . . . what . . . four runs with him? All lucrative, though." A cunning look appeared on Max's rough features as she tapped a tusk with one finger. "What's in it for me?"

"What's in it for you? What's in it—" Sindje's eyes glowed all on their own, she was so apoplectic.

The hacker remained unfazed, crossing her arms. "Don't think I need to remind you two who lost both her ride and her gonna-be brand new pug puppy on this run. Cut's not even gonna cover my expenses, and my skills don't come cheap. Both of you are asking me to risk my hoop doing a look-see into Hood. A *zakhan* like him I do not need."

Khase feigned a cough. "Not just Hood. The Johnson as well."

"How did I know that was coming?"

Sindje's gaze narrowed. "Most likely 'cause you already thought of it yourself."

"So you also want me to really risk my hoop in a sneak and peek on our Johnson, which normally wouldn't be an option, 'cept my gut's telling me something's definitely *kusatta* in Seattle."

"Kusatta?" Sindje ground her heel against the roof and put on a false look of disbelief. "Really?"

"Bottom line, *cerri,* as you said earlier—no pay, no play." Max stood like a rock, waiting. "A girl's gotta make a living any way she can. I'm already in the red on this deal, so let's get to it."

Sindje looked to Khase, who was standing on one leg on the corner of the roof, arms outstretched, doing a Sumatran kick kata with his other leg so fast his foot blurred. Without pausing, he shrugged. *No reward is more generous than that for a spy. Your call.*

"Fraggin' lousy son-of-a-slitch fraggin' frag!" the mage muttered under her breath, then turned back to the ork. "Five percent of mine and Khase's share."

"Twenty."

"Seven."

"Seventeen."

"Nine."

"Fourteen."

"Eleven."

"Twelve."

Sindje thought about pushing for the extra half-percent, but decided not to bother, sticking out her hand instead. "Twelve, but only if you get something concrete on both the Johnson and Hood. No pay for wasted time."

"Pointy, in the 'trix, my time is never wasted." Max grinned, revealing more tusk than Sindje was comfortable with. "I'll even round down to the nearest second for you. Ooh, look at the time. Well, since I'm on the clock for my new gig, let me see what I can dig up."

"Yeah, you do that." Sindje watched the ork slip back downstairs, then turned and kicked the plastic windmill housing several times with her booted foot. "Frag, frag, frag!"

9

Belver Serra was a remarkable looking woman, exquisitely fine-boned, standing nearly two meters tall and appearing at least a decade younger than her forty years. She prided herself on "being natural," as the only "enhancement" she'd undergone was a simple surgery to have her nose straightened, and that was shortly before her fourth birthday. Her parents paid enough for the operation that all record of it was expunged; no reason for the world to think that a Serra had ever been born less than perfect.

Her peach-pale skin was smooth and unblemished, the only hint of age being miniscule wrinkles at the edges of her ice-blue eyes, and these were covered by the smallest dabs of concealer. Her makeup was professionally applied at a shop in the New Century Square Hotel two blocks away; she stopped there every morning before coming to work. She had her hair done there, too, today wearing her short inky curls fanned back and up to halo her oval-shaped face—a professional style that was more alluring than the tight, twisting buns favored by several other women executives with the corp.

Her lips were tinted "vibrant salmon no. fourteen," precisely matching the color of her tailored faux-silk suit, which gleamed softly in the noon light that spilled through the conference room window. With her broad shoulders, made more pronounced by her narrow waist and hips, she cast a shadow that looked like a dagger—a hard, dangerous image that matched her demeanor.

And perfectly matched the keen edge in her voice.

"This merger was supposed to go down smoothly, gentlemen. In your report, Melton, you said three days." Belver stepped to the table, leaning between two young men sitting in swivel chairs. She clicked her manicured fingernails against the black-mirrored surface and let her breath hiss out between clenched teeth. Her gaze held the three men on the opposite side of the table in place. "Three days has turned into thirteen."

The man in the middle on the opposite side nervously tugged at the collar of his shirt. Sweat beaded up on his forehead. "There have been complications."

"There are no such things as complications, Mr. Melton. Only opportunities."

"We've made considerable progress in the past few . . ."

"Progress is not a closed deal, Mr. Melton."

He swallowed hard. "But we will close it. In fact . . ."

"Close it?" Belver stepped back from the table, her dagger-shadow pointing straight at Melton. "This afternoon?"

He shook his head.

"Tonight?"

Another shake. "We're close, though. Very. I think . . ."

"Think? If you were capable of thinking, Mr. Melton, you would have closed the deal ten days ago."

Sweat trickled into his cybereyes.

"Still, the fault is not entirely yours, Mr. Melton."

A measure of relief crept onto his face.

"And not entirely the fault of your team." Belver circled the table now, each step measured and deliberate, her spiky heels leaving deep divots in the carpet. "I hold some of the blame, gentlemen."

One of the men released a breath he'd been holding.

"I selected you, after all. I named Mr. Melton lead negotiator. I erred in my judgment, and therefore I must count myself culpable."

Melton made a move to rise, but in a heartbeat she was behind him, the mere touch of her index finger on his shoulder sinking him deep into the cushion of his chair with a soft *whoosh*.

"So I accept a measure of the fault." She brought her lips to Melton's ear, her breath misting on the datajack in his neck. "And therefore I will not have you fired. I will, however, put this failure on your corporate record."

Melton tipped his chin up, his jaw quivering ever-so-faintly. "This merger with Gaeatronics, we can still close it. We can . . ."

She swung away from Melton and made another sweep around the table, a shark circling prey. Then she was in the doorway, her dagger-shadow looking menacingly long and dark because of the angle of the sunlight. "I will close the deal myself, Mr. Melton. This afternoon, or perhaps this evening. Then tomorrow I will find something else for you to handle, something more suited to your"—she icily stared him down, enjoying the way he withered under her gaze—"abilities."

Belver left the conference suite without another word, leaving the underlings to fumble their way out of the room. The understated perfume of Europa's new BodyChrome eau de toilette, which wasn't even available on this continent yet, surrounded her as she took the hallway to another conference room. The gleaming stainless steel double doors swung open as she approached, and the exec crossed to two women studying a holo-image model of a housing development reactor. "Ready to present to the client?"

"Of course." The reply was practically in unison.

"For the two o'clock meeting?"

Twin nods.

"Very good." Belver watched the holo-image shift to a cutaway, showing a bank of circuits and wire-feeds. "I've scheduled Room C for two hours. I trust it won't take longer than that."

The pair shook their heads. "Absolutely not," one replied.

"Excellent." The word was a purr. "I've something else to tend to late this afternoon, and I'd hate to miss it because your report was not concise."

Belver stopped in two other rooms, checking on the progress of a lawsuit and another merger. In three more years she might move far enough up the corporate ladder that she'd have underlings supervising concerns such as these.

*Three more blasted years. Should've been on the board
already. Get my blasted father off my back.* She downed a
protein drink before stepping into her office. *Should've had
one of the top corners last year.* Still, she did have a corner
office, midway up the corp tower. She had a view of the
Seattle Art Museum, the building itself a bit of a relic with
its curving bone-white façade, and a view of the more impressive Washington Mutual Tower, which had held its age
better and reflected her own corp building in its myriad
windows. Belver loved seeing what she was aiming for
every single day.

She watered a spider plant that had sent runners down
the side of her desk, then contacted her secretary on her
personal commlink. "Darla, cancel my personal trainer
today. I've two meetings this afternoon, and then I'll be
leaving for an appointment off-site."

"Very good, Ms. Serra. Should I reschedule your trainer
as well?"

Belver sat in her ergonomic leather chair and rolled herself back from the desk. "Tomorrow would be fine, Darla.
Anytime after my nine o'clock conference." She made a
move to disconnect, but the secretary chirped:

"Three . . . ah . . . gentlemen are here to see you, Ms.
Serra. They've been waiting some time. Shall I reschedule
them, too?"

Belver sat straight and pulled herself against the desk.
"Send them in, Darla." She activated several more programs, setting in motion a personal holo-recorder and shutting down all monitors connected to the corp security
systems.

Two of the men were young and likely brothers, their
builds similar, their jaws square and their eyes the same
steely gray. The third was on the far side of middle age
with a face pockmarked from what was likely a childhood
disease. His gray-streaked hair was pulled back in a braid
that hung down to the middle of his back. All were in
slightly out-of-date suits, but were clean and could have
passed for salesmen of some kind.

"Don't like to be kept waiting." The pockmarked man
was obviously the spokesman. "Our time is valuable."

Lacing her fingers together, Belver steepled her thumbs
and silently regarded them for a few moments. The quiet

didn't rattle the trio, which impressed her. Finally: "I'm paying you well enough to wait. Is everything in place?"

A nod from the pockmarked man.

She reached into a drawer and retrieved a credstick. After another few moments of silence, she slid it to the far edge of the desk. "Then be about your business. I've no time for further pleasantries with you. Today is tight, and no matter what you may think, my time is certainly more valuable than yours."

One of the brothers grabbed the credstick and read its side, then passed it to the pockmarked man. "Hope to do work for you again, ma'am."

The three tipped their heads and left her office.

Belver rested her chin on her hands and closed her eyes. One of those damnable sinus headaches was starting, the kind that settled in when there were drastic changes in the temperature. It had been so pleasantly warm until the cold front moved in yesterday. This chill fall day made her worry that Seattle might actually have a winter this year.

A little pill would make the pain melt away, but it would also numb her senses. *A little pain might be helpful,* she mused, *sharpen my edge.* Help get her through the rest of the day. At least until dinner that evening. With her father.

She opened her eyes and called another number.

"Yes?" The voice was husky and accompanied by hoarse breathing.

Belver picked a dead leaf off the spider plant. "Those runners you hired for me . . ."

"For the Snohomish job?"

"Set up the meet with them, my dear Mr. Johnson. Make it for . . . four should be good, I think. I've some things to take care of this afternoon, then we will conclude our business. Even with traffic, four will work just fine." *Everything should be wrapped up before dinner at seven.*

Then she cleared the call and called yet another number. The individual on the other end was slow to answer.

"Good afternoon, Ms. . . ."

"No names."

There was a faint crackle of static that made Belver frown. *Recording me?* she pondered. *With cheap equipment, no less? Not that it matters. I'm above the law on this.*

"As you wish."

"That—employee—you're arranging for me. Is he on board?"

"Reluctantly. Unhappily."

"But he is . . . arranged?"

"Most definitely. He has no choice."

"I'm looking forward to making his acquaintance. You've made me most happy this afternoon."

"The pleasure is mine."

Belver pushed back from her desk and gripped the arms of her leather chair. The sinus headache became inconsequential. The last piece of the deal of a lifetime had just fallen into place. And it was all hers.

But first, one more call. For insurance.

10

Max stared at a bank of never-ending file cabinets—all gun-metal gray, all reaching to the ceiling, which was out of sight, all stretching to her left and right and fading to the horizon. More rows of file cabinets loomed behind her. File cabinet drawers made up the tiles under her feet. She swore she could smell the metal and paint and could hear papers rustling, could taste the fusty folders.

Frag, frag, frag. Bleah.

She was jacked in, her body feeling the motion of the massage chair in Hood's condo, her mind deep, deep in the matrix, trying to find any interesting scrap of information about the troll who invited them on the plant run. So far, after over two hours of searching, she'd found nothing.

"Hood," she muttered. *"A street name, not a real name. Never asked his real name. Never had cause to ask. Probably would never answer if I did ask."* She'd certainly never give the troll, or the keeblers for that matter, her real name. And none of them had the digital savvy to go digging.

He can't be without a SIN, she thought. *Not if he owns a condo like this. But I don't have a real name, and I've found very little on a troll using a big fraggin' bow. Linked to a few high-end runs, nothing concrete. Doesn't mean there isn't anything substantial on him.* Just meant she hadn't found anything. Neither had her contacts proved useful, and she'd called all of them, plus a few the keeblers provided. Something he said once made her think there were records on him. Why couldn't she remember that tidbit he mentioned? It might help her pick a file drawer.

She wasn't really surrounded by cabinets, they just represented endless data streams she sifted through. Max could go deeper, but she suspected she'd already spent enough time on Hood, and there was the Johnson to consider. He'd be the one exchanging nuyen for plants, and so he was the one she should be devoting her time to.

Vut, vut, vut! Max cursed herself for trying to find out about the troll when she should have looked to the Johnson first. *Always follow the nuyen, they say on those police trivids.*

But the troll . . . what was he up to? *One last quick look before the Johnson dive,* she decided.

Max stayed connected, feeling the electrons dancing just inside her skull, sensing the power that pumped through the commlink. But a part of her returned to Hood's condo. The heat of the place hit her like a wall, and she sniffed the air. The scent of the plants was strong, as was the scent of her. The heat—the impromptu greenhouse he'd created—made her sweat and stuck her clothes to her body.

Be good to hand these plants over to the Johnson and get our nuyen. Get more nuyen if I can find out something juicy about Hood and the Johnson. Was it fifteen percent she'd negotiated? No. Twelve. But that was pretty good from the elves; she knew they owed someone and so nuyen was precious. *Precious to me, too. Get me that pug puppy with that twelve percent. Something beyond metal and wires to come home to.*

Max stuck out her considerable lower lip and blew upward, her breath cooling her face. She shifted in the chair slightly, so she could see a corner of the kitchen where the troll was hovering over the island, still studying the plants.

Not all of the plants, Max noticed. Two of them. One all green and purple, looking unnatural in the color combination. The other something for the house you could pick up in a grocery store—right next to the balloons and birthday grams.

Something special about those plants, Max decided. *Hood knows there's something special or he wouldn't be obsessed with them, especially with two of them. So they're not run-o-the-mill houseplants like they appear, at least not those two. So they're valuable.*

Real valuable, she guessed.

She let out another breath to cool her face, then put her connection on hold. Edging out of the chair, she went into the bathroom, certain the troll was either oblivious to her movements or didn't care.

Closing the door, she made a call. Max faced the far corner, talking softly and into a towel.

"Johnson?"

She wiped the sweat off her chin with a white hand towel edged in lacy trim—something else that didn't fit Hood.

"Yeah, I drekkin' know you didn't want me to call. But I don't drekkin' want to wait. Got something to discuss with you."

Max let him blather on for a while, thinking he was scolding her, then she continued: "The nuyen we're 'sposed to get for these plants. Ain't enough, *ujnort.* Not near enough."

She listened to his tirade, which was not as bad as she expected—but then they held the plants, and therefore all the proverbial cards.

"Lost my van. Totaled, totaled, totaled in this milk run of yours. Lots of security for a greenhouse. Lots of bullets flying around. Totaled, totaled, totaled my Roadmaster is." A pause. "Yeah, I want my van replaced. No, that's not what this is all about. Listen, I figure these plants are a whole lot more valuable than we were led to believe. We didn't hose nothing, not me, the troll or the two dandelion eaters. We did just what you asked, and if you'd handled the exchange a few hours ago like we had originally agreed on, then the price wouldn't be rising with every minute ticking, ticking, ticking by. Got me?"

Max squared her shoulders, pleased with how she was conducting this. Good time to take a chance.

"We've been babysitting these plants, Mr. Johnson, keepin' them all nice and toasty warm. Feedin' them their special plant food. And we've also been giving them a close looksee. We know all about these plants, Mr. Johnson. And we know they're worth far more than you said you'd pay. Yeah, I'll wait."

She tapped the earpiece to disconnect, then reached for a larger towel and dabbed it all over her face, neck and arms. "It's a drekkin' greenhouse in here." She glanced around the bathroom . . . a troll-sized toilet, sink, a shower that looked like a spa she'd once seen an ad for when she was perusing notices in the matrix.

Shower'd feel pretty good right now. Lookit that fancy soap, like something you'd snatch from the Hotel Nikko or the Lucas Palace. Smells like oatmeal. Quick shower. Hood won't mind and . . .

The earpiece vibrated in her ear. "Yeah? That was pretty fast, Mr. Johnson. We must have moved to the top of your inbox. You got an answer for me?"

Max rummaged in the linen closet while she talked and spotted two new bars of the oatmeal soap. These she thrust in a pocket, followed by a vial of designer shampoo.

"Yeah, I want double the original fee. Won't take a nuyen less. You heard me, double."

There were small packets of bath salts, one with purple crystals that caught her eye. This, too, she pocketed.

"Good. The run's easily worth double." She was angry she didn't ask for more. The Johnson agreeing so fast meant she could have got it. "Now, you got us a meet set up yet? I bet you want these very special plants as soon as possible. Good, good, good. We'll see you there." The ork tugged the earpiece out, glanced in the mirror above the sink and straightened her untamed mass of dreads, then returned to the living room.

Hood was waiting for her, hands on his hips, looming above the low table covered with plants. At first Max thought he'd overheard her conversation, but he was looking at the plants, not her.

"Find anything interesting about any of those?" Max well knew that he'd found something; she was just making conversation to distract him from her bathroom trip. Without waiting for Hood's reply, she touched her comm and called the elves. "You wanna jander your skinny hoops down here? Got some news."

It wasn't the news they were expecting—no tidbits about Hood or the Johnson. *No twelve percent,* Max mused. But she'd be making more than that, now that her share had been doubled. All of them would be making more.

Max delivered the news as soon as Sindje and Khase came through the door.

"Double?" Sindje's smile reached her eyes. The ork had never seen her so happy.

"Well done," Khase pronounced.

"Fragging idiot." Hood's reaction was not what Max had expected. His entire face darkened with anger, and spittle flecked at the edges of his lips. He was breathing faster and deeper, the exertion fluttering the hem of his gaudy shirt. "The Johnson contacted me. I set up this run. I called you in to share the work and the pay."

"We're a team. What's the old saying, no 'I' in team?" Khase's flippant remark went ignored.

"And you go around my back, Max. Fragging idiot ork! Go around my back and negotiate with the Johnson. It wasn't your deal to negotiate, Max. It wasn't your Johnson to play with."

The ork didn't wither, just clenched her fists and puffed out her chest. "No pay, no play," she growled.

"You want to negotiate, Max, you can find your own Johnson. You can broker your own deal. You can do that all by yourself. But not when I'm calling the shots."

"Wait a minute." Sindje glided to Hood's side, her delicate fingers fluttering up the troll's arm. "Max didn't mean anything wrong. In fact, doubling our nuyen . . . you should be praising her, not ripping her up one side and down the other. Shame, Hood."

The troll's eyes continued to glow, but his breathing slowed. He shrugged off the elf's arm like it was a bug. He saw Khase tense on the other side of the room, just the slightest bit. "You working magic on me, Sindje?"

"Wouldn't think of it." Her fingers continued to flutter.

"You try this again, Max, you go around my back, and I'll find me another hacker."

Max raised her upper lip, displaying her tusks. "Double the nuyen, Hood. I didn't hear you upping the payment any."

"That doesn't matter. My deal, my Johnson."

"If the nuyen doesn't matter to you, *tad* . . ." It was Khase, somehow he'd ghosted around his sister to stand at Max's side. "Why not just throw in your share of the take?"

He gestured to the opulent condo. "You're doing well for yourself, neh? Very, I'd say."

"My deal, my rules," Hood repeated, somehow looking even larger and more menacing than he had a few seconds ago. The other three runners exchanged glances, all of them thinking the same thing. None of them had ever seen him this angry before.

The four metas stood staring at each other, nobody willing to give a millimeter. The tension in the troll's living room was so thick Khase doubted he could cut it with his monofilament whip. *I wonder if Max has finally bitten off more than she can chew?* he mused. *And if it comes down to it, can the three of us take down big and warty here without getting geeked ourselves?*

11

"**H**oi, Jagyar? Yeah, it's Roland. Listen up . . . have you got wind of anyone trying to sell some kind of plants? No, not the recreational kind . . . just—plants. You know, decorative plant-type plants . . . sort of like ferns, I guess. Stop laughing! Look, all I need to know is whether you've heard of anyone on the street looking to unload some green . . . no? All right, fine. If you do hear in the next dozen hours or so, get in touch with me *rapido,* understand? Yeah, the usual fee applies, with a twenty percent bonus if you get me something in the next six hours. Thanks, Jag."

Roland disconnected the cell and clenched his hand, resisting slamming his fist into the roof of the Honda sedan.

Drek idea in the first place, he thought, *but I had to try.*

There was almost no chance that the runners who broke into Plantech were trying to fence the lifted flora on the street. But during the past few hours he had called all of his contacts in downtown, and even visited several anyway, hoping against hope that someone with their ears to the ground might have heard a whisper about the runners or the plants.

Nope. Whoever's got our cargo already has a buyer lined up, I'll bet. Could be that the plants are already gone, that the runners made the drop and have melted into the cityscape. He slammed his fist into the roof. *Can't think like that, there's got to be something I can do. Even if they got rid of all the greenery, I'll bet we can convince them to give up the name of their buyer. If we can find them. The proper persuasion—like avoiding prison—should work nicely.*

Most corp employees accepted shadowrunners as a way of life in the Sixth World, but Roland's view of them was Lexan-clear; they were the enemy. Oh, occasionally he'd seen newsvids with runners prattling on about their so-called "noble" aims; trying to stick it to the man by undercutting the corp arcologies. But to him, they were criminals, plain and simple. Not only criminals, but hypocrites as well, since they would accept jobs from the very people they claimed to be working against—if the nuyen was right. Nothing but a low-rent army of paid mercenaries, many of whom would no doubt turn on their employers if offered better deals. Nobody he wanted to do business with, that was for sure. Send the whole lot of them to prison. Forever.

Finally, to add insult to injury, a group of them had the nerve to hit his corp, an agri that wasn't doing anything bad to anyone, much less destroying the planet in its wake. His corp was even trying to do some good in the world! And now, because some drekhead thought they just had to have what Plantech was working on, three hundred and fifty people could be out of work in the next day or so—including himself. As he drove, Roland realized that although he wanted those runners, he was just as interested in the suit that had hired them in the first place. Who wanted the plants? And why?

Maybe Jhones will let me look at their interrogation vids once they're nabbed. Or even better, perhaps he'll give me a little alone time with one of them. I'm sure I can shake the info loose, one way or another.

In the corner of his vision, a chronometer steadily ticked off the seconds down to the deadline. Right now he had about twenty-one hours and twenty minutes left until the end of Plantech.

By tomorrow afternoon everything Siskind and his people have worked toward for the past three decades will be destroyed.

Although his boss had absolved Roland and his team, the sec chief still felt responsible. Roland's people had failed to stop the intruders, and therefore, by extension, *he* had failed to stop them.

He floored the accelerator and sped up the on-ramp to the interstate. His commlink chimed with two separate tones, indicating that both a text message and a call were coming through. "Download text and file to both car screen and office and answer call. Ators."

Morgan's voice filled his head. *"Roland, can you get back to HQ right away? I think there's something here you're going to want to see."*

"Only thing I want to see right now is the plants."

"I'd hurry."

"I'll be there ASAP. Discon. Play text file."

The small screen built into the dashboard of the Honda lit up, displaying a message on the heads-up windshield so Roland could still drive:

> *Hoi, Roland, got the vidfiles of that chase this morning for you—pretty wild stuff. These* ganefs *look like they might know what they're doing. Real pros. So watch your step, and remember—don't forget to cut your old* chaver *in on the bust, neh?*

"Jhones, if you can give me any clue as to who these guys are or where they went, I'll give you what's left of my pension," Roland muttered as he brought the file up, watching the chase as he drove. He saw the light poles break as if by, well, magic, his lip curling as one of his men went down on the street. He watched the elven adept rock and roll on the van roof, graceful as a zerodancer as he took out the cyclists.

Frag, I didn't think a monofilament whip could do that much damage. This guy will have to be taken out hard when we find him. The archer too; no need to have K-Tog get beaten up twice in one day. Stun weapons should do the trick, maybe break out those new Fichetti nonlethal systems we got. Unless they have the plants with them, then all bets are off.

Roland pulled up to Plantech's security gate, which was manned by four guards instead of the usual pair. He submitted to the retinal scan and full palm ident, knowing that no one, even the CEO, was above these rules. They raised the gate and waved him through.

Inside, Roland headed straight for the security offices, a

room that was off-limits to the rest of Plantech personnel. His eyebrows raised slightly when he saw Morgan, K-Tog and several other guards clustered around a short woman with a thick braid of long, salt-and-pepper hair. She was dressed in a white lab coat and, from Roland's vantage point, appeared to be waving a short wand around at the men.

Roland cleared his throat. "I trust that all of you have a *very* good reason to be standing here instead of working at your stations!" He stalked toward the group, most of the guards scattering like Barrens roaches under a microwave light.

Morgan straightened up and gazed past the diminutive scientist's shoulder, causing her to turn around.

"Morgan, you know that no one besides security is allowed in this room except on my say-so." Roland rested his hands on his hips and waited for an answer, but the one he got was a surprise.

"Calm yourself, Commander Ators, I requested access." The woman's voice was crisp, with more than a hint of a German accent. "My son created this little device, and when I heard of our company's problem, I thought it might be able to help you."

She stepped aside to reveal a small box with a handle on the top that looked for all the world like an ancient Geiger counter. Roland didn't move, except to raise one eyebrow. "And I suppose you're going to help us solve the theft with that? Your son's toy?"

The corner of the woman's mouth quirked up in a crooked smile. "I hadn't mentioned yet that my son is currently studying at a Yamatetsu entrance college. He's thirteen years old. His expertise runs more to the mechanical. This is a project he created in the fourth grade. It utilizes some old micro-cantilever TNT sensors that he modified to pick up anything they get a sample of. It's several million times more sensitive than the best cyber-olfactory suite, and can pick up thirty picograms of any substance, which, as I'm sure you know, is a very, *very* small amount."

"All right, let's say I sign on to this possible wild rat chase. What will you be tracking?"

"Commander, several of the stolen plants contain pollen for reproduction. A few of them are wind-pollinated, meaning they leave a trail behind them. We have samples of all of the plant pollens. For example, this one is from the *Esculenta Mays* hybrid, our corn-manioc blend."

She inserted a small chip into a reader at the side of the box, picked it up and walked to the door. "Follow me, if you please."

Roland nodded to Morgan and led the other man out of the security room, following the scientist to the elevator. In front of the one they knew the thieves had used, a small light began to flash on the box. She opened the door and stepped inside. The light grew brighter.

"Going down." Roland and Morgan crammed themselves into the elevator as the doors began to close. The scientist hit the button for the garage level, the light blinking all the while. When the doors opened, she followed the invisible trail to the space where Roland knew the runners' van had been.

"Not bad, but as you can see, they took wheels out of here," Morgan commented.

The scientist's mouth quirked again, and she swung the wand around, heading toward the exit. "The signal is a bit fainter here, but it still can be picked up. Now, out on the street, that may be a different story given the traffic and weather conditions, but unless you have a better idea . . ."

Roland bowed. "I apologize for my earlier reaction, madam. In fact, you have me at a disadvantage. I do not even know your name." He could have gotten it from the Plantech database, but in some ways Roland was still a gentleman at heart.

"Biogeneticist Lilith Chalmers." The older woman regarded the sec chief. "What happens now?"

"Now—" Roland paused while he turned to Morgan and subvocalized: *"Scramble Teams One and Two in heavy gear and two transports to garage level three immediately."* He turned back to the diminutive scientist. "If you please, you will accompany us as we go hunting."

12

For several seconds, the only sound heard in the room was breath—the light, feathery, almost imperceptible purrs from Sindje and Khase; the angry wheezing from Max; the even angrier huffing coming from Hood that practically drowned them all out. For several moments they faced off, the low table filled with plants between them.

Then the furnace kicked on again, with its faint hiss promising to add to the humidity and misery.

It was Khase who tried to diffuse the situation. He spread his hands in a gesture of peace and gave a slight bow to Hood. "All this negative energy, it can't be good for the plants, neh?"

Hood's eyes darkened even more for a moment, then seemed to return to normal. "The mission was more dangerous than expected, I will concur. Therefore, the payment amount agreed upon was less than satisfactory." Max and the elves raised their eyebrows; the concession was uncharacteristic of the troll. "However . . ." His heavy brow creased. "Max was also out of line with her little side negotiation. If she—if any of you—pulls a back door deal like that again, I won't be working with you. With none of you, understand? If you don't like the way I do business, just say the word and you'll all be free to find runs on your own."

Sindje opened her mouth, but a glare from Hood kept her quiet.

"You could have talked to me about wanting more

nuyen. I wouldn't have had a problem with going to the Johnson for more . . . given the circumstances. But it was *my* run, and *my* call. You getting the pay upped, great. Double the fee, great. Me finding out about it after the fact, that's not right, Max, and you know it. Not right at all. It's pure deep and ugly drek."

Max shook her dreads, the metal tabs on the wires clacking together in denial. "Not right? Getting more nuyen for riskin' our hoops for a bit of foliage isn't right? You can say that, Hood. Look where you're living. You can say anything isn't right. You didn't lose a Roadmaster."

"I'm not going to say it again. If anything like this happens again—if any of you do something like this again—we're done." Hood stooped and adjusted a plant on the table so its vine wouldn't hang to the floor where it could be stepped on. "And, yeah, I'm comfortable, Max. And, yeah, Khase, maybe I don't need the nuyen from this gig. So I tell you what—I'll donate my share to the lot of you . . . since you all seem to be so hard up."

Hood picked up a plant from the center of the table and carried it to the kitchen island. "When's the drop, Max? And where? I figure you've got that all worked out with the Johnson."

"It's at four, so we've still got a few hours to kill." Max muttered the address, an ethnic neighborhood across town. Then she returned to the roof with Sindje and Khase, where the cool air would dry the sweat off their faces.

Hood was oblivious to the trio's departure. He forced down the rest of his anger with another package of cookies, a block of cojack cheese and a jug of peach nectar. He sensed that he was on the edge of some great discovery, feeling anxious, feeling like a thousand gnats were dancing on his warty hide. Some piece of knowledge was just beyond his grasp.

The ring on the drekking merry-go-round, he mused. *And I have to get it.*

"What's this?"

The plant from the table he'd just pulled, the one that resembled a ti from the tropics. Pronounced "tea," Hood knew they were thought to bring good luck and long life, true romance to the very fortunate. Hardy, they could grow indoors or out—though not outside in Seattle's chilly fall and winter climes—and thrive in sun or shade. In decades past people in the islands placed it just to the left of the entrance to their homes in an effort to ward off evil spirits. Hood made a mental note to ask Sindje if the plant could indeed do that. The root could be made into an alcoholic drink, the stem ground up and used in candy. Above all of that, it was said to have medicinal value.

"Medicine." He returned to the living room and gave the plants another exhaustive study. The largest was three-quarters of a meter tall, and he knew that a full-grown ti could reach two meters. These plants were all "babies," and most of them could be used in various medicines. "Interesting."

He returned to the kitchen and brought his face down to the tropical plant. It didn't just resemble a ti plant, it *was* a ti plant. But it was also more than that. Why hadn't he noticed that it was special when he first ogled the lot of them? He admitted that he'd been so focused on the purple-green vine and the golden pothos look-alike, that this beauty had escaped him.

The leaves on the ti were larger and thicker than the other two plants, so he could better manipulate them with limited risk. Too, the stems were suppler and bent farther without bruising or breaking. The potting soil mix was different, the fertilizer crystals glabrous. And the mix smelled—

"Metallic." He tasted the dirt to confirm. "Definitely metallic."

"Just what is . . . by the Green Mother." He let out a breath so intense it caused all the leaves to quiver. His eyes opened wide, like a child with a pile of birthday presents in front of him.

"Incredible. Fiber-optic veins." He looked around the corner of the kitchen, wondering if the others heard him and not seeing any of them. "Wonderful. Now where did they go?" Not far, he knew. There was the drop in a few hours—no, less, since they had to make a stop along the way now. A digital chronometer on the stove told him he'd spent a half hour studying this plant.

"So this one's been bioengineered. But to what purpose?"

If he had a datajack like Max—and countless other tech

junkies—he could jack in and delve into the collected wisdom stored in bank upon bank of horticultural research. He could consult biologists in universities throughout the world. He wouldn't have to rely on the memories of his own studies. And if he had chips and wires embedded in his flesh, like the fiber optics were embedded in these plants, he could better smell them, better see them, perhaps run an analysis as if he were a walking laboratory. For a single moment, he regretted not using some of his nuyen on enhancements. The Green Mother knew Max had likely spent every last cred, and then some, on bioware and whatnot . . . when she hadn't been spending it on Beetles. She was a fraggin' cyborg, no doubt, spending too much time in the matrix for her own good.

"Too hard on her, maybe." But then Hood pushed all his regrets aside. *I don't need chips and wires. My brains, my skills, my arm, my aim. My own flesh and blood, not some techno-whiz's cyberware fabrication. Nuyen's better spent on things that matter.*

Another half hour melted away as Hood carefully examined all three plants, finding fiber optic veins coursing through them to the very tips of their smallest leaves. "This had to have been done when they were seedlings, some kind of cellular graft or manipulation. Maybe they introduced the tech in an embryonic form, to sprout and grow with the plant itself. Amazing. Still . . . to what purpose?" He took four cuttings of the ti and added them to his others. Then he carried the salt-glazed pot into the bedroom, past a large window that provided excellent light for a dwarf acacia. He opened his walk-in closet, only half of which was filled with clothes. The rest contained plants under a grow-light, cuttings he'd made from a visit to the Japanese gardens in Portland. He arranged these new cuttings so they couldn't easily be seen. He didn't want the elves and Max to know just how many cuttings he'd made—not that it was any of their business.

"So you didn't find anything juicy about the Johnson?" Sindje had asked Max the same question three different times since they'd come up to the roof. The elves exchanged worried glances.

The wind was colder than it normally was for this time

of year—especially given that the sun was out and reflecting harshly on buildings that appeared to be made entirely of glass. An architect's palette, the skyline of Seattle, Sindje had said. A nightmare to more refined senses, Khase had corrected.

"*Vut, vut, vut.* Nothing, nothing, nothing." Max was alternately thinking about that massaging chair and about that troll-sized spa that would feel so good. *Maybe the troll's onto something with a pad like that,* she thought. *Maybe I shouldn't be downloading every nuyen I make right into my own body.* But right now, the greenhouse-that-was-Hood's-condo was stifling. She shook her head, returning to the conversation at hand. "Not much about Hood, just some scattered reports of a troll runner with a bow on some high-end jobs. Our contacts are pretty much useless on all of this."

Khase strolled along the edge of the roof like it was a tightrope, hands in his pockets, paying no attention to how narrow the ledge was or how high up he was. He watched Sindje as he went; this was his eleventh circuit of the large building. She sat next to Max in the center of the roof, where the housing for the elevator and stairwell offered a little shelter from the chill breeze.

"An omen, sister, this wind?"

Sindje shrugged.

"An omen of this curdled 'milk run?' Or perhaps just a hint that winter will be harsh?" He walked on his hands now, then his fingertips.

"*Kichigaijimata!* Doesn't he ever get tired?" Max stuffed a fist in her mouth in a failed attempt to stifle a yawn. "Been up going on twenty-four hours."

Sindje yawned, too. "Hood's bed looks real inviting, neh? If it wasn't so warm in there, I might have tried to grab a little shut-eye. I think he's got the heat cranked up so high just to keep us out."

The ork raised an eyebrow. "It is hotter down there than I remember Plantech's greenhouse being. In fact . . ." A trilling in her pocket stopped her. She retrieved the earpiece and opened the connection, thinking it might be the Johnson. It wasn't. "I done told you that Hood's busy." It was the same man who had called earlier looking for the troll. "And he's going out, like I told you before . . .

Now . . . He's going out now, so you're out of luck . . . How long?" Max sputtered. "A while . . . He's going to be out a while . . . And, yes, I'm going out with him . . . What's it to you? . . . A while, I said . . . He's going out for a while . . . I don't know for how long . . . Hours, mebbe . . . Probably . . . Didn't you hear me the first time you called?" She severed the connection. "Drekkin' stupid trolls . . . Had to be a troll, voice like an old capo on serious 'roids."

Sindje seemed to be studying the toes of her slippers. "You could try again, you know, to get something on the Johnson and Hood."

"For twelve percent of our double-pay? The idea's appealing, keebler, but I don't got the time anymore. Spent my time talking to the Johnson to up our pay. And drek on Hood for getting bent about it."

"Speaking of time . . ." Khase vaulted off the ledge, flipping twice before landing crouched on the balls of his feet. "We're a handful of hours away from the drop, and no wheels to carry the plants. I'd like to know that we won't be carrying pots in our hands when we go to meet the Johnson."

Max snarled, getting an instant picture of the truck towing what was left of her van out of the parking garage. "Frag, frag, frag."

"We could rent a limo," Max suggested. "After all, you probably have the nuyen to cover it." The ork was chest-to-chest with the troll, looking up into his dark eyes. "Because we ain't got a way to get to the drop, Hood. And I don't think the light rail is a good idea." She waved a fist toward the plants Sindje and Khase were arranging on the carts.

"It's state-of-the-art transportation, the rail. And part of it's historic." Hood took a step back and glowered down at the ork. "A lot of folks' taxes went to pay for that system."

Sindje frowned. "Drekkin' funny, Hood. A lot of folks also ride it every hour of every day."

Hood grabbed a keycard and nodded to the other three. "Let's take all of this to the garage and get going. I've already got us a ride."

3:27:50 P.M.

The elves and Hood loaded the plants into the back of a Ford-Canada Bison, a gleaming black RV that was at least ten years old, judging by the model style, but looked as if it could have come straight off a lot. It was a little larger than Max's Roadmaster, with a better suspension, judging how the plants and the elves didn't make the rear dip a hair's breadth.

"Three times as much as my van, that's what this cost." Max couldn't take her eyes off the gleaming machine.

"When it was new." The troll pulled a handkerchief out of his breast pocket, blew on a smudge above the fender and gently wiped it off.

"So why didn't we take this on the plant-grab? Why my ride? Why ruin my ride?" Max was staring at the spot where her van had been, the only hint of its passing being a patch of oil that hadn't yet been cleaned up. "This's bigger, would've been better. Could've ruined this instead of mine."

Hood wiped at another smudge and stared at his bumpy reflection in the mirrorlike finish. "This is more noticeable. And a model in this shape would cost too much to replace."

"I'm driving." Without waiting for an answer, Max got behind the wheel. The leather upholstery was easy to slide across. It smelled new inside, the result of an air-freshener poised on the dash. She studied the dials and levers and made a few adjustments so she sat higher and could easily reach the overlarge peddles. The forward seating and wrap-around windshield made her feel like she was in a fixed-wing cockpit. Max took another deep breath, breathing in the alluring, indefinable scent of major nuyen dropped on the RV.

"Any other of the vehicles in this place yours?" She made the question soft, though she was certain the elves could hear her.

Hood didn't answer.

The troll had changed clothes again, wearing loose gray trousers, a pale yellow linen shirt open halfway down his chest, and a black blazer with buttons that were made from the horn of some animal. Around his neck was a bolo tie, the fob a piece of silver decorated with a chunk of turquoise. His bow and quiver were nested in the center of the backseat.

"Has armor plating, doesn't it?" Max continued. "Concealed, but it is there. I can tell 'cause the doors are so heavy."

Hood took a look around the garage, the hairs on the back of his neck up. There wasn't a sign of another soul; Sindje had astrally perceived and taken a quick jaunt around to confirm that the garage was empty before they came down. There also wasn't a sign that the other vehicles had been disturbed. The tow truck had left hours ago. He shrugged off the bad feeling and slid into the passenger seat. The RV dipped only a little.

"Definitely a wiz suspension." This came from Khase, who was settled face-to-face with Sindje on the floor of the cargo area. Their backs were to the plant carts, as a precaution, and his hand was extended against the third. "Wiz ride, *tad*. Nothing like heading to a drop in style."

Sindje yawned. "Max, make a pass through a Nukit Burger, will you? I need a jug of soykaf."

"And don't forget about the other stop we have to make as well." Hood glanced back to make sure their cargo was secure. "Regardless, we should be there in plenty of time."

The ork edged the RV out of the parking garage, at the same time pleased and livid that the vehicle operated so quiet and smooth.

13

Jhones' hands were rigid on the Americar's steering wheel as he weaved in and out of traffic, driving almost on instinct. He had tasked Simon with reviewing everything Lone Star had on the Plantech break-in, and sent a copy of the file to Roland, tagging it as part of an ongoing investigation so his superiors wouldn't get their boxers in a knot. Then he and Simon had driven the entire chase route twice, looking for information or any clues as to the whereabouts or identity of the perpetrators.

But all the while as he drove, he kept replaying the conversation he'd had a few hours ago in his mind:

"What do you mean, you just sold me?" Jhones was so furious he barely remembered to subvocalize.

He still remembered the bookie's matter-of-fact tone. *"Sorry, chummer, but the Azatlan-Kenya game cleaned me out. Who'd have thought those squat little muchachos would whip tail on the Afriques, knowhutimsaying? Anyway, I got overextended, and your chit was up. So I made a deal."*

"Nu, you know I'm good for it, I always have been. With the playoffs coming up I'll get back out, you know that."

"Hey, you aren't the only one owes money, you know. I got my own problems to deal with, and as of ten minutes ago you aren't one of them anymore."

"You sold out a Lone Star, you fraggin' son-of-a-slitch!"

Jhones' bookie tittered. *"Calm down, it's not like it's the first time that's happened. Anyway, your new holder will be calling in his marker sometime soon, I expect. Sounded like a suit, so I imagine you won't be asked for too much, maybe a bit of bodyguarding on the side, impress some locals. Who knows?"*

"Frag it, Hollander, I'm not going to do anything this meshuggener wants. If I ever find you on the street—"

"You won't do a thing to me, Redrock, and you know it." The bookie's voice turned ice-cold. *"And you are going to do whatever this exec wants, you putz, because if word got out that you not only welshed on your vig, but also hauled in your bookie, the street would drop you like yesterday's fashion. Face it, Jhones, you'll square this, and in a few days you'll be back for more. You can't help it. Gambling's in your blood. You got into this mess, and now you can get yourself out of it. Now be a good copper, and handle this like an adult."*

Hollander rattled off a cell number, which Jhones recorded. *"You can reach the exec at this number. They said to call after three this afternoon. Be smart, and be in touch before the end of today. You just tell 'em I sent you, and the exec'll take care of the rest. Sayonara, chummer."*

With that the bookie broke their connection, and although Jhones had been trying to reach him for the past ten minutes, he got no answer. *I can't believe it; the fragger sold me out.*

Jhones knew he had a gambling problem. Indeed, he had no problem admitting it, but that didn't mean he was going to stop, either. Four years ago, he had gone on a spectacular seventy-two hour wagering spree, only to flame out at the end. That had cost him every nuyen he had, as well as his wife and family, his home and almost his career. Only a lot of fancy footwork had prevented his getting fired, and the fallout from the cloud still hung over him, limiting his advancement opportunities. That was fine with Jhones; he loved being on the street anyway. After the maxed-out meltdown he had even kicked the parlors for a while. But the boredom crept up on him, and before he knew it, he was devouring trid and matrix odds reports, getting back up to speed so he could get back in the game.

Despite those odds, and the thousands of other variables that could play a part in any match or race or game, Jhones usually took only a cursory look at all of that when he wagered. He bet because deep down in his psyche, so deep that he would never admit to it, he felt he shifted the universe in some small, unexplainable way every time he put his nuyen down on a team. Somehow, he equated the act of placing a bet with shifting the odds in both his favor and the team's as well. It made absolutely no sense, and indeed, if a person ever asked Jhones about his habit, he'd just say he gambled for the thrill. But it went much deeper than that.

And now I'm in way too deep, he thought. Jhones had never considered himself a schlimazel, or unlucky person, but this last run just hadn't been up to his usual standards. First the Packers had dropped what should have been a cruising win to, of all teams, their longtime rivals the Bears, then the Oakland Terminators had lost half their team in the Urban Brawl semifinals. And now, when what even he admitted was a risky trifecta in horse racing had failed to pay, he was tapped out. More than tapped out; combined with his previous debts, he was fifty thousand nuyen in the hole.

But he had been in similar situations before and had always managed to either pay or bet his way out. Now, however, faced with this completely unknown variable, a person who doubtlessly knew he was a cop—for it couldn't have just been the money this exec was after—the game was skewed heavily against him.

No, tsuris like this I do not need right now, he thought as they pulled into the basement of the 3rd Precinct house. A persistent mumbling noise in his right ear made him realize that Simon was saying something.

"Yeah, boychik?"

"Geez, Jhones, are you all right? I've been trying to get your attention for the past fifteen minutes."

"Yeah, yeah, I'm fine, just a message from an old friend earlier. Got me a little distracted, that's all. What's up?"

Simon tapped the vidscreen of the Americar as Jhones pulled into a parking space. "I've reviewed the chase vid and the patrol report on the Plantech break-in, and I've got some ideas on how to follow up our crime scene investigation. You want to talk about this inside before shift change?"

"I'd love to, kiddo, but I've got some things to take care

of that can't wait. You get your facts together, and we'll connect around dinnertime, okay?" Without waiting for an answer, Jhones slid out of the driver's seat and headed for the elevator that would take him outside, walking as fast as his legs would take him. He felt Simon's eyes watching him with every step, and he didn't breathe easy until he was in the elevator and the doors had closed.

What can I do? These ganefs have me hanging over a barrel, he thought. *I have no choice but to see what this* macher *wants. But it has to be a one-time deal; no stringing me along, frag it!*

Simon Chays shook his head as he watched the thickset dwarf almost run to the elevator. His partner's increased heartbeat, pulse and breathing rate, all of which had started after that meeting with the guy at the Anything Diner, meant that he was nervous about something. The sinking feeling in Simon's stomach intensified, but he activated the security system on their cruiser and headed for the central elevators.

Upstairs, the 3rd Precinct was the usual bustle of afternoon activity: suspects being booked, streetwalkers shuffling in and out, and officers and detectives at desks everywhere, catching up on the endless flood of electronic forms that had to be filled out on a daily basis. *Privatizing the cops certainly didn't change much in that regard,* Simon thought as he stopped by his desk to download his own reports. That done, he headed for the CO's office and knocked on the door, glancing around to make sure that no one was taking more than the usual interest in him.

"Come in."

Simon slipped inside and shut the door behind him. The 3rd Precinct commander, Carson Tallfeather, sat behind a desk completing several cyberforms that swirled around him. Like many career officers, Carson was uncomfortable with jacking in and preferred using holograms to do his work, either filling them out verbally or poking at the forms with a finger to fill in the blanks. He looked up at Simon and waved the officer to a chair while he kept talking.

"Resume dictation— Therefore, it is imperative that the budget outlined in form BUR-nine-three-five remains at the indicated request levels for the next fiscal year. Please let me know if you have any questions. End dictation, and send to stated address list." The CO leaned back in his chair. "What's on your mind?"

Simon rubbed his chin then looked up. "Are we in the bubble?"

"You're new to IA, aren't you?" Carson grinned. "In here, we're always under the bubble."

Simon's answering smile was weak, but he mustered it anyway. He knew a lot of cops didn't like what he really did. And ironically, the street also looked down on Lone Star Internal Affairs as well, figuring them to be one more rusty point on a bent star. But the lanky human believed in a real, true concept of law and order, one that was fair and just, which is why he signed on with Lone Star Internal Affairs when offered the chance. Fortunately, Commander Tallfeather shared his attitude, which had certainly helped during Simon's first tour of duty. But when he spoke to the chief, they always made sure that the protective shield against both magical and cyber-eavesdroppers was securely in place. "I think I might have something on Redrock."

"Do tell."

"Who's assigned to the Plantech break-in?"

Carson brought up a translucent duty roster, the hologram casting a blue sheen on his handsome Yurok features. "According to the report filed by the beat patrol, Plantech said the thieves were interrupted before getting away with anything, and the corp wouldn't be investigating any further. Wait a minute, here's a note from Redrock himself, saying he's following up."

Simon brought up the matrix access log from their cruiser. "Jhones met with a guy I didn't recognize at a diner near Snohomish this morning. I couldn't catch their conversation, but on the way back I ran his face through the SINID database. He's Roland Ators, the sec chief for Plantech. Anyway, afterward, we drove the route the shadowrunners took from Plantech—twice, and took our time looking for any evidence as well. I think Jhones will either be investigating further under our jurisdiction, doing it on his own time, or the sec boss has something over him and is pressuring him to help out with a private investigation of some kind. Here, you see Jhones downloaded the vidfiles of the chase scene to Ators. Why would the sec man want it if his own corp wasn't going to pursue the matter?"

The CO canceled the report and frowned. "Good point, and also why is Jhones following up what appears to be a nonevent? But if he was going to some kind of meet, why take you along in the first place?"

Simon leaned back in his chair. "What better cover than to have a by-the-book rookie partner to watch his back and attest to what happened if necessary? It's possible he wants to use me as his alibi. But Jhones didn't know I had my cybereyes installed before I came to the Third. Doesn't know I can watch real close, and record. After breakfast, he also got a personal call that really shook him—I could barely get his attention on the ride back. Whoever he spoke to, they delivered some drek news, that's for sure."

"Interesting." Carson thrummed his fingers on his desk. "You've ridden with Jhones for what, two months now? What's your impression of him?"

Simon thought for a moment before answering. "By everything I've seen he's an excellent officer, great clearance record. If it weren't for that gambling problem a few years back, he could be gunning for an admin position . . ."

"But?"

"But he wouldn't, sir. Jhones loves his job and the street. You can see it when he's out there. There's nowhere else he'd rather be, that's obvious. He's one of those officers who would wither and die behind a desk."

"Or if he was off the force completely."

"If that happened, he'd probably eat his gun in a month." Simon tapped his fingers on the arm of his chair. "My gut says he's not dirty, but the evidence is too strong to ignore. So that's why I'm here."

"Well, for all of our sakes, I'm hoping there's no dirt on him. Jhones is one of our best, but I'm not going to cover for him or anyone else on the take. All right, stick with it, and let me know what you uncover. But for frag's sake, watch out for entrapment. Say the wrong thing while on the wire, and he could skate off scot-free."

Simon rose and headed for the door. "I understand, sir, and I'll be careful. And thanks—for what it's worth, I hope I don't find anything, either."

14

Roland tried not to fidget as Morgan guided the Mitsubi-shi Nightsky Limited through the late afternoon traffic. As the sleek limousine wove in and out of the lanes on Interstate 5, he silently prayed that his lieutenant wouldn't put a scratch on the luxury vehicle. For the tenth time, he thought about checking his cell messages, but knew there would be nothing there. *Jhones will contact me when he's got something.* And all the while, the countdown kept shrinking in the corner of his vision. *Twenty hours left until Plantech is history.*

The sec chief also tried not to appear nervous in front of the other two passengers in the opulently appointed rear compartment. Sitting across from him was Lilith Chalmers, who had traded in her lab coat for a subdued, dark gray, three-quarter-length trench coat. Her attention was concentrated on the sniffer she held, a small wire leading out to the window, which was cracked just enough for the sensor to be slipped outside.

Next to Roland sat a man that just made him plain uncomfortable. He looked like a well-heeled Japanese *shai-kujin* in a razor-pressed, lapel-less Wellington Brothers suit that cost more than the sec man made in three months. He had short, styled hair that lay immaculately in place and smelled faintly of ginger. Kenji Hiyakawa, however, was anything but a corp suit. The short Asian was a shaman, and from what Roland knew, he took great pride in not conforming to the stereotype of the traditional unkempt, tattooed, grunge-wearing spirit summoner.

As Roland had been rounding up his sec teams to go hunting, Siskind had sent Roland a message that Hiyakawa would be joining the recovery effort. Roland didn't protest, as he had been trying to add a mage to security operations for months now, and was certainly willing to accept any help to save the company.

Hiyakawa had been escorted to the greenhouse, where he had summoned a city spirit and had it search for the combat mage's astral signature. He had locked on to it, and the spirit had tracked her to an alley in Everett, but another hour of searching by it had drawn a blank. Roland had suggested that he, Lilith and Hiyakawa go to the site and look around, just to be sure.

Behind the stylish Nightsky rumbled two Renraku Typhoon RVs, containing the rest of Squads One and Two. Roland had planned to have his group ride in the same vehicle as his men, but when Hiyakawa watched the RVs pull to a stop in front of him, the distasteful expression on his face had said a few thousand words on the subject.

Roland usually turned his nose up at the obsequious hoop kissing that happened every day in the corps, but he also knew when a VIP had to be pampered. Stepping forward, he spoke before the shaman could leap to the right conclusion. "Our transportation will be arriving shortly, Hiyakawa-san. These vehicles are for the rest of the team." As he reassured their freelancer, he activated the number for Siskind's office.

"Yes?"

"Our shaman has requested—more suitable transportation."

"Of course he has. I'm sending a more appropriate vehicle now. He may avail himself of anything inside, naturally. Please express my gratitude again that he has agreed to assist us."

"Yes, sir."

When the Nightsky rolled up, Roland had quickly looked down the street to hide his surprise. In all his time with Plantech, he had never been inside the corporate limousine. Hiyakawa waited for the chauffeur to open the door and slipped inside like he owned it. Roland nodded to Morgan to take the wheel, ignoring the almost imperceptible stiffening of the driver's spine at the blatant commandeering of his vehicle. He had then entered the plush passenger area, sinking into a silk-soft, real leather seat that cradled his tense muscles. Hiyakawa shot his French cuffs and perused the dry bar with barely a sniff of his upturned nose, selecting an unopened bottle from inside an authentic oak box.

"Glenlivet 1962. I was unaware any of these still existed. You'll join me, of course."

It was anything but a request. Despite the pressure Roland was under, his mouth watered in anticipation of tasting 101-year old scotch. "It would be a pleasure."

That's the trouble with cat shamans, he thought. Fastidious in the extreme, they expected their surroundings to be as spotless and perfect as they thought they were. And heaven forbid they ever got dirty, then all bets were off. The other problem with the shaman was that whispers on the street said he was one of the best. Unfortunately, Hiyakawa knew this, and charged accordingly. *We'll either be broken up for scrap or go broke feeding this snooty guy's appetites. Ah well . . .*

"My employer wished me to express his gratitude for agreeing to assist us on such short notice." As he said this, Roland bowed in his seat.

The shaman acknowledged his deference with a curt nod as he broke the seal and unscrewed the cap, breathing in the heady aroma that wafted from the bottle. Roland snatched three small snifters from a rack built into the door and extended one to Hiyakawa, managing to deliver the glass and take the cap without touching the shaman. The Japanese man nodded again, longer this time, and poured the scotch.

Roland glanced at Lilith, who smiled and shook her head. "*Domo arigato,* Hiyakawa-san, but I am afraid that I must decline. Alcohol does not agree with me, unfortunately."

Unfortunate, indeed, Roland thought, letting the amber liquid settle in his glass as he leaned back again, not daring to try it just yet. Hiyakawa sipped appreciatively and sat back as well, swirling his glass around in deft, economical movements.

"We're coming up on Washington Street now." Morgan

spun the wheel and the Nightsky floated around the corner, the epitome of smooth grace. "Cameras in the area show the thieves' Roadmaster turning into an alley somewhere around here."

Roland regarded Hiyakawa. "I don't suppose that spirit is still around here, is it?"

"Unfortunately, no, he had fulfilled his duty, and has discorporated again."

"Start cruising, and I'll see if we get a hit." The biogeneticist leaned over the sniffer and waited. Roland nodded to Morgan, who turned the limousine down the first alley and slowly drove down it, alert for anyone who might be foolish enough to make a move on the car.

Roland took a swallow of the Glenlivet, feeling the warm, smoky burn slide down his throat. Then he set the glass in a small recess in the armrest, promising himself that he would finish it only if they got a solid lead on the runners. All three of them waited silently, Hiyakawa barely concealing his distaste for their surroundings as the Nightsky traversed the alleyways, up one and back down another.

A flash of light from the scanner lit the interior of the limo. Then another. Lilith looked up, a smile on her face. "Got it. Keep going in this direction, the trace is getting stronger."

"Take it slow, Morgan." Roland loosened his Browning in its shoulder holster as they eased down the neglected alley. The flashing increased as they came to the end of the narrow lane.

"Pull over. It looks like there's some kind of deposit here."

"Maybe they stopped for a moment." Roland reached for the door handle. "Let's take a look."

"Unless you need me, I'll remain in here," Hiyakawa said.

"As you wish." Roland, Lilith and Morgan got out of the limousine and began searching the alley for any kind of clue. To his credit, Hiyakawa lowered the window and watched the three as they perused the ground. His apparent squeamishness surprised Roland. The alley wasn't *that* dirty.

Lilith swept the alley with the sniffer, pausing near a

large puddle of oil and other less identifiable fluids. "Looks like our quarry did stop here for a bit. I'm getting a high concentration of pollen, most likely adhered to the ground. In fact, didn't you say they had lost a tire?"

"Yeah." Morgan walked over and looked at the ground, seeing nothing out of the ordinary.

Roland pointed to a fresh scrape line on the concrete. "This is probably their rim mark. However, it stops here, and a tread drives away through this puddle, which means they changed it and—"

"—If they pulled back out onto any main thoroughfare, that machine probably won't be able to pick up any kind of signature after the morning rush hour, right?" Roland rubbed his temples at the thought of being so close to their quarry, only to lose them again.

Lilith stepped to the mouth of the alley, waving the sensor back and forth. "No, I'm not getting anything here now. The air movement would have scattered all trace of the pollen hours ago."

"When science has failed, then there is only one thing left to do—use magic." Hiyakawa opened the Nightsky's door and stepped out gingerly, his nose wrinkling. "My, you people certainly take me to the most interesting places."

Roland took a few paces back and watched the shaman look around, his narrowed eyes taking in the alley in one pass. Hiyakawa stepped over to the puddle of oil and nodded to Lilith.

"If you would be so kind as to give me a bit of room."

She did so, shooting a puzzled glance at Roland. The shaman squatted near the pool and stretched out one hand, the sleeve of his suit riding up to reveal a TAG Heuer 9000 titanium chronometer on his wrist. Hiyakawa slowly turned his arm so that the crystal face caught the rays of the late afternoon sun and reflected it onto the puddle. The rainbow-swirled surface of the pool rippled for a moment, then an amorphous face appeared in the sludge, with crude, pupil-less eyes and a mouth that was little more than a wavering hole in the water.

Hiyakawa kept the light playing over the face while he spoke. "*Kónban wa,* spirit. Tell me everything you know about the vehicle that stopped here at—" The shaman glanced up at Roland.

"Around four this morning."

The shaman repeated the time to the city spirit. Its answer sounded like the creature was speaking through a mouthful of water, gurgling and bubbling as it formed the words.

"Fooouuurrr beings stopped here this moooooorning. Right in my pudddddle, spppplashing it everywhhhwhere. They sssssspoke to each other, then leftttt that wwwwway." A black finger extended out of the pool and pointed toward the street that Lilith had confirmed as the most probable escape route.

The shaman leaned over to peer at the tire tracks. "They took some of your puddle with them, *hai?*"

"Yesssss . . ." Roland thought he actually saw the city spirit's face frown at the thought.

Hiyakawa rose slowly to his feet, keeping his hand above the puddle. A small humanoid form, black as night, formed out of the viscous fluid as the shaman straightened. "I want you to find the rest of your puddle, then come to me and lead me to that place. Can you do that?"

"Yesssss . . ." The city spirit ran to the end of the alley, then turned left. Hiyakawa smoothed his suit jacket and turned to his companions. "Shall we wait in the car?"

Lilith shook her head in admiration. "Please excuse me, Hiyakawa-san, but I have rarely had the opportunity to see magic performed up close. May I ask a question?"

"But of course."

Roland thought he saw the Asian man actually preen at the older woman's deferential tone. He exchanged a dismissive glance with Morgan as they got back into the limo.

"I was under the impression that some theorists believe spirits are created by a shaman when needed at a particular moment, but do not otherwise exist or have any contact in this reality. However, you brought one forth that could recall events of this morning. I assume then, that you do not believe in the instant appearance of a new, so to speak, spirit when it is summoned?"

Hiyakawa had picked up his glass of scotch and sipped again before replying. "For someone who does not practice, you are well-versed in magic theory, Chalmers-chan. Although there are those who believe the theory you have stated, I believe that spirits are much more than random accretions of mana in a particular area. If a spirit was created, then we would say just that—it was created anew from the nearby ambient mana energy, not that it was summoned. The latter implies it was brought to this plane from somewhere else. The very act of summoning brings the spirit into existence on this plane, but it—and every other spirit in the Sixth World—is all around us, all the time. When properly asked, there is practically no limit to what they can do."

Roland had been listening to the conversation, but now he shifted uneasily in his seat as he considered the possibility of hundreds, maybe thousands of unseen eyes watching his every move wherever he went. *Fraggin' mages.*

15

"Turn here." Hood jabbed Max in the shoulder. "Two more blocks and take a left."

The ork snorted. "That'll take us near the old neighborhoods of Everett, Hood, quite a bit out of our way. We're 'sposed to meet the Johnson at a dead end in Ballard." Still, she made the turn when the troll's eyes narrowed again.

"Just a quick detour," he said. "We've got plenty of time and you know it."

Close to an hour later, the Bison headed along a street that ran parallel to the bay. The late afternoon sun hit the water and turned the chop a shiny vermillion, making it look like the sea was on fire. Gulls drifted down, searching for small fish in the surf. Max was alternately wistfully glancing at the birds and keeping an eye on traffic.

"Lovely time the Johnson picked for this meet." Max kept one hand on the wheel, the other arm was propped out the window so the sun could tickle her skin. "Just when lots o' places are closing up shop for the day, he decides on the exchange. Roads are gonna get stuffed real quick."

"As *tad* rightly pointed out earlier, most people downtown take the rail," Khase offered from the backseat. He had his window down, too, his head stuck out and tipped back so the wind would play across his face and shaved head. Directly behind Max, the elf was on the oceanside, enjoying the offshore breeze. "The light rail's fast, and the riders don't worry about finding a place to park by the downtown corps."

"And you'd know this why?" Max shot back. "You haven't worked a regular job in your life."

Khase didn't bother to answer. Eyes closed, the elf took the salt-tinged air deep into his lungs. "It's sweetest here by the ocean, Sindje, like the odor of the city stops right at the last curb."

"Yeah, and the stench of rotting fish and dead seagulls starts." Sindje rolled her eyes and made sure her window was all the way up. Then she settled back in the leather seat and adjusted the safety belt off her shoulder.

They drove past the Federated Boeing Shipyards. The noise of the gulls and the traffic was instantly drowned out by ships' bass horns and the clang of metal echoing from the shipyards sprawled along the coast.

"Fraggin' eyesore." The ork flipped a finger at the twenty-story building perched on the edge of the west waterway. "Hydroplanes and hovercraft for the military, Boeing makes with our tax money. Like Boeing needs more money. Like the military needs more fraggin' hovercraft."

"Makes them for the Salish-Sidhe Council, too," Hood added. "And ferry companies, various corps, Lone Star, Ingersoll and Berkley, Aqua Arcana, Ares. . . ."

"Like you know everything." The ork snorted.

"I'm not going all pedantic on you."

"She doesn't know what that means." This came from Khase, who still had his head out the window. Max hit the electric rear window control on her armrest, and the adept got his head inside just in time to avoid being choked by the rising safety glass.

Sindje gave her brother a pained look. "You don't know what that means, either."

The ork snorted again. "Look, Hood, all I'm saying is that the Boeings have nuyen up the ying-yang. People's taxes go to the fraggin' Boeing plant for the military. Taxes that could be better spent on . . ."

It was the troll's turn to snort in derision. "You don't pay taxes, Max. You're SINless, remember. You live under the city's radar. It doesn't affect you. Why are you so worried about taxes you don't pay?"

"It can still bother me, neh? And if by chance I paid

taxes, it would bother me a whole lot more." The ork continued along the coast, closing in on the Ship Canal and then turning onto a residential street. "Ballard. This is it."

The homes marked it as an upper-middle-class neighborhood, and the businesses proclaimed its Scandinavian extraction. Along a side street decorations were strung between houses and streetlights, holo-projectors spaced irregularly on several of the strings. Larger holo-projectors were mounted on the roof of a manor house, and a stage was set up on a corner lot.

"Gonna have a party tonight?" Max pointed to a woman who was trimming an evergreen tree with silvery ribbons. The trees were planted against the corners of a house made fancy with holotrim. Across the front was a row of bushes cut so perfectly they looked like military helmets. "And she thinks that's pretty, I'll bet, those helmet bushes. Makes it look like she had her yard landscaped at a drekkin' convenience store or maybe one of them military surplus places. Looks plastic and cheap. Probably got her ribbons there, too."

"They always seem to have some sort of festival going on in this neighborhood." Hood nodded to an elderly gentleman blowing grass shavings off his walk. "Swedish and Norwegian celebrations, mostly. A lot of the older folks living here emigrated from the territory after the Treaty of Denver was ratified. Crime rate's low here, relatively speaking. Not a bad place to settle."

"Mebbe. But there's a gang." Max seemed proud that she could provide a bit of trivia about the neighborhood. "The Berserkers. Make themselves up to look like Norse gods and warriors, and they leave other gangs alone, relatively speaking."

The troll continued: "Yeah, but the Berserkers supposedly have ties to smugglers."

"I know that," Max countered. "The smugglers take a minor route from SSC territory across Puget Sound and into Seattle. That's where the smugglers meet up with the Berserkers and conduct their biz."

Khase leaned forward. "And you'd know all about these smugglers why, Max?"

The ork pointed down another side street, this one with

no decorations. "Johnson's directions say at the end of this street."

The street was narrower than the others and led to an older section where the houses were not as well maintained and where sections of the sidewalk were cracked and buckled from tree roots. There was one exception to the rundown dwellings, a big place with a wraparound porch and a small balcony on the second floor. Max slowed the Bison to ogle it. The house was painted canary yellow and had green and red piping around fish-eyed windows. There were two columns at the top of steps that led up from a red brick walkway; the trees were far enough back so their roots didn't threaten the walks. Clearly visible at the tops of the columns were security cameras and uplink boxes. A small placard at the base of the steps warned intruders of a direct connection to the nearest Lone Star precinct. The grass was meticulously kept.

"Kentucky-Seven." Hood gestured to the lawn. "Grows seven centimeters high and stops. Expensive stuff."

"Bet there's motion sensors in the lawn, all around the place. Need the security for a historic home like that on this block." Sindje pointed to the balcony, where two more security cameras were perched. "It's the only house I'd even think of living in around here. You sure this street is still in Ballard, Max?"

"The edge of it."

"Wonderful, most likely the bad edge. The Johnson picked a great spot, neh?" Sindje fiddled with her seat belt again. "But not as bad as the drop two runs ago. Barrens after dark. Never again, I say." She shivered, wrinkled her long nose and noted that the faint hairs on her arms were standing up.

"This street make you . . . itchy . . . *chwaer?*" Khase shot her a sly look.

Sindje chewed her lower lip. "I watch the newsvids, Khase. Something you might try instead of inspecting your eyelids all the time. Berserkers might run Ballard, but there's a splinter group roaming the edge—the Wild Hunt, they call themselves—from the Ancients elven go-gang. And while the Berserkers are into protecting their turf, the go-gang is into picking fights. News is they go after outsid-

ers. You and me, Khase, we'd be all right. But"—she nodded at Max and Hood in the front—"the big 'uns here
might attract unwanted attention."

The slim elf waved a hand at the crumbling block, her
eyes narrowed in a frown. "And the houses here are falling
apart, like the city's already forgotten about this block. You
take a good gander at this street and tell me you aren't
itchy, too. Yeah, plenty itchy. And this whole run, I guess
that's made me itchy bad. Babysitting plants, that's just
drek, *brawd*."

With another wave of her hand, she spoke directly to
Khase's mind. *And maybe I'm just fuming because we
should've been at this drop more than a few hours ago. We
were to spend this day paying off a debt, remember? Not
babysitting plants. Not stranded on the roof of that condo
watching you turn somersaults while Hood played with the
foliage and turned his place into a hothouse. I was waiting
for him to say "ferns are my friends." Sheesh. Drekkin'
wasted day.* Aloud: "Frag it!"

Max cleared her throat. "Double the nuyen. Don't forget
I got our fee bumped, keebler." Hood and Sindje both
scowled at the ork as she parked against the curb on a
cul-de-sac where the rundown street ended, but the troll
said nothing.

Sindje, however, wasn't done by a long shot. "An itch
like this isn't worth ten times the payment." She rubbed
the palms of her hands against her knees. "A dead end
street. One more thing I don't like about this. And that
house, ugh. Truly itchy, *brawd*. A real piece of drek. Max,
make sure we're pointed away from the house and back
down this skidsville street. Just in case we need to get
out fast."

The ork didn't argue. No one did. They had run with the
combat mage enough to know when she was talking sense.
This certainly seemed like one of those times.

The house Max parked the Bison in front of, with the
RV's nose pointed back the way they'd come, had been
regal once. That was evident from the shabby, carved wood
cornices and shattered sections of latticework that ran beneath a massive porch and up the sides of an attached
gazebo. It had been white. Through the decades it had also
been blue, green, pale orange and drab yellow, the latter

of which was the most predominant in places. Where the wood was bare, it was painfully weathered, looking like a corpse's ashen complexion. Eaves sagged, the steps were crooked, the roof seriously bowed and the entire building looked exhausted, ready to give up one big sigh and fall in.

"This beauty's not going to stand much longer. See, by the front steps?" Max got out of the Bison and waggled a finger toward a window displaying a holo-sticker marking it for demolition.

"Just needs to stay up for a few more minutes. We get in and out." Hood got out of the Bison and stretched, his bunched muscles cracking as he worked a kink out of his neck. He opened the door for Sindje and reached around her to grab his bow and quiver.

"Expecting trouble?" Khase asked the troll.

"Hope not. But I'm not leaving these in the Bison. Not in this neighborhood."

Sindje continued to wrinkle her nose. "Better than the Barrens. Still, even for us, this is low class."

Khase was at her elbow. "When was the last time we made a drop in a swank place? Never ever. This isn't the worst. Far from it." He glided to the back of the Bison and popped the hatch. Reaching in, he pulled out a plant that Hood had called a philodendron hybrid. "Besides, I think this house has . . . oh, I don't know . . . a pleasant touch of ambience. Character."

Sindje's expression said it all: *Oh, please!* "Hold up, Max." The ork had just planted a boot on the sidewalk, which was seriously buckled from the thick root of a huge half-dead elm. "I want to do a little scouting first, 'kay? Don't need any more surprises on this 'milk run.' "

Sindje closed her eyes and leaned back against the Bison. Hood hovered in front of her, hands out in case it looked like she would fall. There was a faint smile on her face, and the slightest sheen of sweat appeared—evidence that the magic was taking a physical toll on her. She swayed back and forth, balls of her feet on the curb, heels hanging over. Then her lips parted and she started humming something soft and dissonant.

The elven mage felt herself floating, becoming an elegant apparition that rose above her corporal self and the Bison like a piece of lifting, incorporeal fog. A moment more and she was a meter above Hood and Max and her brother. She knew the wind had picked up since they'd entered the neighborhood; it made the dead branches of the elm clack together like the beaks of hungry crows. But she didn't feel the wind, didn't *feel* anything, not exactly. In this form she only watched and listened.

The old homes on this street looked no better from above. Some had actual shingles that long ago should have been replaced with scalloped plastisheeting. The home the Johnson had selected sported a hole in the back of the roof, where it looked like a tall tree in the backyard had dropped a branch. The backyard was small compared to the front, all of it taking up about three-fourths of an acre. The grass might have been that Kentucky-Seven Hood mentioned, as it was still reasonably short and even. But other plants had found their way into the weave—ugly like the rest of the places along this street. There were a few suffering, green patches of grass left, but these would eventually be choked off by more aggressive flora. A fine crop of weeds grew along the back line of the property, the fall not cold enough yet to turn them brown and brittle. Behind them stretched the parking lot of a small grocer's.

A smattering of vehicles was scattered throughout the lot—a few recent-model Americars, a large gray van, gleaming with fresh wax, that Max would covet. The van was parked against the weeds; its windows tinted dark, and therefore sending a shiver down Sindje's astral spine.

Don't like the looks of that. But then, it might be the Johnson's mobile. Probably is, she decided. *Too well kept for around here. Let's take a little look inside the house and see if he's waiting for us.* She'd seen him at the meet and memorized his features—handsome enough for a human in his middle years, well dressed and well-spoken, someone she might fancy spending time with between runs. Sindje knew she wasn't really attractive by elven standards, but many humans still had a thing for the exotic, and pointy ears and almond eyes usually fit the bill. Cozy up to him after this, and perhaps he'd come up with a run lucrative enough to wipe out all of her and Khase's debts. He'd probably want to get to know her better for the thrill of it, and an artful spell here and there would ensure the deal.

So they'd use each other for a time. No prob, as long as the bills got paid. Just the cost of doing business in the Sixth World.

She drifted down toward the porch, insubstantial feet dangling just above the weed-pocked Kentucky-Seven. Up the steps, she spread her arms for an effect no one would notice and then floated to the large front window. Despite the abysmal shape of the soon-to-be-demolished house, most of the windows were intact, a testament to the manufacturers of bulletproof glass.

Dark inside. Wait, there's a light in the back.

Her diaphanous fingers touched the window, then the tips reached through. *Knock, knock, Mr. Johnson, I'm coming in.*

Max paced back and forth on the sidewalk. Her palms grew moist as she anticipated the credstick filled with double the nuyen. It was nuyen she had brought in; not Hood, not the keebler twins. *That was all me.*

She felt a tingling in her pocket and for a moment didn't recognize what it was. "Oh." She pulled out the earpiece, stuffed it in.

"Yeah?" She let out a snarl. "No, Hood ain't home . . . I told you he was going out this afternoon . . . What? . . . No, I'm not going to let him talk to you . . . He's busy, I'm busy . . . Sure." She let out a louder snarl and stuck the earpiece back in her pocket. "Hey Hood, some guy named Sasa-something said to tell you he had visitors."

She noted the troll's raised eyebrow and opened her mouth to ask a question. But the earpiece tingled again. "What?" She half expected it to be the troll calling again for Hood. "Oh, Mr. Johnson . . . Yeah, we're outside . . . I understand . . . Don't need the neighbors to be gawking at us . . . The troll does stand out a bit . . . Upstairs? . . . The front door's open? . . . Be right with you." Max turned to Hood and tapped him on the elbow. "Gotta go. Johnson says we're eyesores out here on the curb. We can worry about your friend's visitors later."

Hood growled from deep in his chest, and hit the catch that opened the top of the quiver on his back. "Sindje! We're moving."

In a heartbeat the elf was back in her body, the humming

stopped and her head shaking to clear her senses. "I didn't get a chance to take a look inside, *tad*."

"We'll all take a look together." Max motioned for the others to join her, as she hurried up the steps.

Khase held the plant in one hand, and took his sister's arm with the other. "Shall we?"

"I wanted to look inside astrally, *brawd*."

Hood nudged them forward. "I'm going up that porch last. Just in case the steps won't hold me."

"Lovely." Sindje frowned as she did her best Max impersonation. "Lovely, lovely, lovely."

16

The sleek Nightsky, with the two Typhoons trailing it like a pair of looming pit bulls, pulled up to a gleaming apartment building in the suburb of Alki, surrounded by perfect green lawns irrigated with unobtrusive sprinklers that cost a fortune here or anywhere in the Seattle area. The limousine looked as if it belonged in the tony neighborhood; the Typhoons, not so much. But Roland was less concerned with either of those facts than with how he was supposed to get two sec teams, a scientist and a shaman into what was no doubt a building protected by a state-of-the-art security system.

"Ah, now this is more like it." The shaman refilled his glass as they gazed up at the skyscraper from behind the relative safety of the Nightsky's tinted windows.

Roland frowned. "You're sure your little oil slick is right—this is the place?"

Having already dismissed the city spirit, Hiyakawa regarded the sec chief over the rim of his glass with cool eyes. "Spirits interpret their commands to the best of their ability, often literally. If it says that the rest of its pool is here, then that is the case."

"Something's not right—how could runners afford a place like this?" Roland rubbed his chin at the incongruity of it. "I mean, they drove a POS Roadmaster, for drek's sake. It doesn't add up."

Lilith nodded, a slight vertical line above her nose the

only physical evidence of her concern. "We can confirm at the garage entrance. If the truck stopped for the door on its way inside, then there should be more trace pollen there."

"Which leaves the small matter of getting inside the building without tripping alerts. We are more than a bit out of our jurisdiction, you know," the sec chief muttered.

Morgan contacted Roland from the front seat on the commlink. *"Sir, you know Trevor is back at HQ and just waiting for the word. He's always wanted a crack at one of these Triple-A 'burbs."*

"Well, get him online, because he's about to get his chance today. But you let him know that the second any IC gloms on to him, he evacs pronto. No grandstanding, no flashy heroic stuff, just go. And tell him to be sure to reroute his sleaze through at least six links around the city. I'm sure he'll do it anyway, but I just feel better saying it."

"Yes, sir, I'll make sure he reads you loud and clear."

"And make sure our boys are ready to move at a moment's notice."

"Affirmative."

"So, what is your plan?" Hiyakawa asked.

Roland settled back in the leather, throwing his arm across the top of the seat as he tried to conceal his satisfaction that the mage had no idea what was about to happen. "We're going to wait for that underground door to open, and when it does, we'll just drive right in."

"This I look forward to seeing," the shaman said.

Yeah, me too, Roland thought, tipping his glass back and pouring the scotch down in one smooth gulp. He knew Trevor was good, but also a bit of a risk-junkie, and he didn't want the hacker getting in over his head. *Angie would not approve,* he thought with a pang of guilt, followed by the realization that he hadn't called his wife since that morning. *In fact, she wouldn't approve of this whole mess. But when it comes to bending a law or two or seeing my corp wiped out, I know which choice I'm taking.* Still, he couldn't help feeling as if he had sunk a little closer to the shadowrunners he despised. *Frag that, they put me into this mess. Can't take the time for a warrant. Even Jhones*

*can't help me out here. It's not his jurisdiction, and I'm not
gonna get him in trouble. No, this is the only way.*

"Boss, we're on." Morgan put the Nightsky into gear as
the building's door rose. The limo cruised toward it, RVs
close behind.

Roland opened a channel to both teams. "Squad Two,
establish a position on the outside perimeter. Squad One,
follow us inside. Both teams lock and load and go to
overwatch."

The garage level was eerily silent as the two vehicles
pulled in. There were no obvious human guards at a place
like this; it would have been gauche. Still, Roland couldn't
help feeling that they might be heading into a dangerous
dead end.

Lilith pulled her sniffer out as they cruised into the garage level, and almost immediately got a hit. "This is the
place. Strong trace—stop right here!"

Morgan braked the limo, and Lilith got out and walked
in front of the car. "Very heavy pollen count—looks like
it leads back to the elevator."

"Morgan, if Trevor hasn't already, cut the garage and
elevator feeds."

"One step ahead of you, Boss."

"Good man." Roland switched to the common channel
for the rest of his men. "Squad One, we are go, repeat, we
are go. Squad Two, maintain surveillance on perimeter."
Roland got out of the limo and went to the trunk of the
car. Opening it revealed several weapons and three sets of
body armor, including helmets. Slinging on a vest, he
jammed a helmet on his head and then picked up an HK
227X subgun, slapping in a magazine and chambering a
round. He hurried to join Lilith as Morgan turned the car
around in the parking lot, backing into a space for an easier
escape if necessary. The second in command got out, armored up, and grabbed his own weapon as the rest of the
squad piled out of the Typhoon and clustered around
Roland.

"All right, the plants are somewhere in this building. Ms.
Chalmers, I cannot order or ask that you come with us, as
we have already violated several laws, and are about to put
the screws to a whole bunch more before this is done."

"In for a penny, in for a pound. If I were going to bow out, I wouldn't have come in here in the first place." The older woman shrugged. "Besides, this sure beats twelve-hour shifts in the lab any day."

Roland's eyebrows rose in surprise as he pulled on a pair of custom-fit gloves. "Very well. Hiyakawa-san, the same goes for you as well."

"We are already here, so let us pursue this matter to its conclusion." The shaman smiled. "I would hate for anyone to say I do not earn my fee."

"All right, since the pollen trail has been working so well, we'll stay on it. Dr. Chalmers is going to sniff each floor to find out which one our plants are on. We find their hideout, bust it, and recover our flora, but leave them alone. Anyone in the room resists, subdue if possible, take them down only if necessary. Everyone clear? If this goes red, you are to clear out as many team members as possible without endangering yourselves. Primary escape route is out the lobby and to the Typhoon in the parking lot. Backup is the garage level, and pray that Trevor can get that door cracked in a hurry again."

The five team members nodded, and Roland turned to Lilith. "I'm afraid that you will have the point, ma'am. May we at least offer you a vest?"

"No, thank you, Commander." The older woman drew her trench coat closer around her and held up the sniffer. "I'm ready when you are."

"Okay, we'll have to check every floor, since we have no way of knowing which one they're on. Visors down and let's move, people." The group hustled to the elevator, which was open and waiting for them. Everyone squeezed in, the fit made more difficult by K-Tog and his pair of short-barreled Remington Roomsweepers in a custom harness mount. Once on board, Hiyakawa closed his eyes and concentrated, while Roland stabbed the lobby button, and Lilith readied the sniffer.

Up they went, the elevator doors opening on each floor, Lilith getting a reading as quickly as possible, then shutting the door again and proceeding to the next floor. They ran into trouble only once, when a well-dressed man and his wife on floor three tried to get on. K-Tog reached out with a huge hand and shoved the man backward, his wife flailing alongside him as they staggered away.

On the eighth floor, Lilith got a hit, and stepped out into the marble-tiled hallway. Roland was right behind her, muttering into his commlink to confirm that Trevor had overridden the hallway cameras. The rest of the team fanned out, taking their assigned positions in a standard sweep-and-cover leapfrog formation. Roland gave the scientist the sign to move forward, and she did just that, following the blinking light. They passed five doors before Lilith held up her hand and pointed at the next one on the left. Roland immediately moved to the opposite side of the door, signaling for Morgan and the rest of the team to take up their positions for a door-knock.

Trevor fed Roland camera feed from inside. Through the wall of the condo he spotted three figures—two the large, distinct forms of trolls, with another person that might have been a big ork. Roland held up his hand with three fingers out. *Three suspects.* He pointed to Morgan, then the door, then made a typing motion with his fingers. Morgan nodded, and they all watched the red light on the door for several long seconds. It flashed once and then returned to the steady red glow. Roland gritted his teeth as he waited for the door to change. Even with K-Tog here, he doubted they could break the maglock. And if Trevor tripped the alarms—*that would be all she wrote.*

He heard a faint click, as the light changed from red to green. Roland motioned to the troll, who reached out with one hand and slowly eased the door open on its rollers, a Roomsweeper in his other hand to cover the short hallway inside. Roland gestured for Morgan to lead, then himself, then K-Tog, with one man to sweep the rest of the apartment and two to watch the hallway. He counted down on his left hand, right curled around the grip of his HK. *Three . . . Two . . . One.*

Morgan stormed the hallway and burst into the living room, shouting: "Freeze! Nobody move!" Roland was right behind him, subgun tracking the three occupants. K-Tog's basso growl reverberated around the room, and the twin autoloader shotguns, their muzzles as big as cannons, issued their own undeniable orders.

The three people in the room froze in various positions, expressions of surprise and fear on all of their faces. Two were certainly trolls, and the third person also looked like troll as well, but on a closer look, Roland saw she was a huge human woman, easily two meters tall and bulging with muscles. *Muscle enchancement and plenty of it, gotta be.* All of them were in various stages of undress; the women grabbing pillows to cover themselves, the troll straightening up and wearing nothing but a huge toga and laurel wreath.

Despite the strange scene, Roland issued orders. "Everyone just stay where you are. Keep your hands in plain sight, and you'll be all right."

Voices in his head confirmed their sweep of the apartment. *"Bedroom clear."*

"Bathroom clear."

"Kitchen clear."

"What the frag is going on? Who are you people, and what do you think you're doing?" Despite his outlandish outfit, the troll radiated a mix of haughty arrogance and glowering menace.

Roland pinned the guy with his gaze before answering. "You two"—directed at the women—"stay right where you are. Sir, do not move or make any otherwise threatening gestures"—*besides just standing there*—"and if you surrender the stolen property you have in your possession, we'll be out of your hair in a few seconds." He certainly couldn't bust the guy, since they had already executed an illegal enter-and-search. Now he would be happy just to get the plants back and get the frag out of there.

However, the troll, who was rapidly turning from surprised to indignant, was having none of it. "Do you—people—have any idea who I am?"

Roland's voice turned steel hard. "Right now, you are a suspected criminal in possession of stolen property. If you give me a few minutes, I'm sure I can come up with several more felonies to charge you with."

"What? First, you did not identify yourselves as enforcement officers when you rudely invaded my home. Second, the lack of identifying insignia on your uniforms means that you're probably not Lone Star, so therefore you're a corp security unit, here for some reason I cannot fathom. And last, and certainly not least, I have absolutely no idea what 'stolen merchandise' you're referring to."

"Sure you don't—wait a minute." Roland opened up his subvocal channel to his team. *"Tell me someone saw a bunch of little leafy plants in those rooms?"*

A chorus of negatives answered him. Roland glanced at Lilith. She held up the sniffer, its light strobing like crazy.

Roland's stomach plummeted between his feet. "Where were you between oh three hundred and oh six hundred hours this morning?"

"Hmm, let's see—oh yes, I was returning from Edinburgh, and my vacation, in my private jet." The troll gestured toward the bedroom. "If I am allowed to get my passport, it will confirm what I have just told you." The troll's eyes were filled with anger. "Shall we?"

"Morgan, Choi, escort him to the bedroom and verify his story." After the two sec men flanked the troll and saw him into the bedroom, Roland turned to K-Tog. "K, please tell me you have some kind of idea who the frag we're dealing with here?"

The troll cast a worried glance toward the bedroom door. "Uh, I think that's Sasalga Ottod, an up-and-coming Seattle politician. Street word is that he is working to bring the orks and trolls together downtown, create a meta coalition that will actually make some changes around here." The troll craned his head around Roland, peering at the women on the couch. "Don't know those two."

Yeah, like I haven't heard that *before,* Roland thought. "Hey, eyes front, officer. So he's connected?"

"Yeah."

"Perhaps I might be of some assistance here?" Hiyakawa appeared at Roland's elbow.

"Anything would be appreciated right now." Roland had a brief vision of himself patrolling a Snohomish strip mall, but he banished the thought and tuned back in on what the shaman was saying.

"—sure that the pollen trail led here?" the short man asked Lilith.

The scientists nodded. "No doubt."

Hiyakawa looked around. "Then let's ask the one being who would know for sure." He settled on the kitchen, and walked into the area, the lights coming on automatically as he entered. The mage placed his hand on the marble counter, and then brought it up like he had in the alley. As he did so, a small creature dressed in the latest Bodyline fashion—a band-collared white shirt, close-fitting black pants tucked into knee-high leather boots, and ink-black, square eyeglasses perched on his nose—rose from the stone surface to stand in front of them, arms crossed.

"And what do you want? Tracking in dirt and mud all over my clean floor? Bad enough the mess *he* makes." The hearth spirit gestured toward the bedroom with a sniff, his accent pure British butler.

Hiyakawa placed his hands together and bowed. "*Sumimasen*, good sir, I apologize for disturbing you. In fact, I believe we may be able to help you. Tell me, if you would, were there some plants in here earlier today?"

"*Some* plants? The place was like a bloody jungle, with flowers here and fronds there! Then hornhead cranks up the thermostat like it was the blooming—pardon the pun—Amazon! All that hot, moist air is not good for the inlaid teakwood accents, I'll have you know. And the dirt! Fortunately my domain has a good central cleaning system, but it doesn't activate until tonight—"

Roland broke in. "Wait a minute, you said horns—that troll brought the plants in?"

"No, not him. The other one." The spirit shook its head sadly. "Terrible dining manners as well. What a glutton. Cookie crumbs all over."

Two trolls. Roland thought, just as his two men came out of the room, leading a smirking Sasalga, who rubbed his large palms together as he muttered something about making the lot of them street sweepers.

Morgan commed in. "*Sir, his alibi checks out—even had a flight plan.*"

"Okay, anyone got any ideas?" Roland's temples felt like they were about to implode.

"Actually, I do." This came from Lilith. "Hiyakawa-san, can this spirit find things, like the other one did?"

"Within its domain, yes."

"Even better. May I speak to him?"

"By all means." The shaman gestured to the spirit.

The scientist leaned over until her face was a few inches away from the diminutive spirit. "Good day, sir."

"Well. Someone else with manners."

Roland stole a glance at Hiyakawa, then realized the implied insult was more likely directed at him.

Lilith took out a small datapad. "If I show you some pictures of plants, can you find any of them that might be in this apartment?"

"Anything to get you all out of here," the spirit replied. Lilith selected the file that detailed the stolen plants and set up a quick slide show for the spirit.

"Look, I don't know what drek you're trying to pull, but I want you all out of here now!" Sasalga raised his voice in a tone of command. "Sec—"

Five small, unwavering red dots appeared on the troll's chest as every Plantech man in the apartment pointed his weapon at the politician. Over the stock of his HK, Roland addressed the seething meta. "We're gonna need a few more minutes. Sit down. Now."

The troll's lips skinned back from his teeth in a fearful grin. "I'm going to find you, sec man. There isn't anywhere in Seattle that will hide your stink. I'm going to find you, and bury you so deep the worms won't be able to get to your carcass."

Roland ignored him, nodding to Lilith instead. "Please continue."

The spirit blurred out of the kitchen with Hiyakawa, Roland and Lilith right behind. It streaked into the bedroom, heading straight for the walk-in closet and running right through the closed door. Roland held up his hand to the shaman and scientist, and signaled K-Tog to back him up. Stepping to one side of the door, the troll ready in front with both Roomsweepers leveled, Roland nodded and pulled the door open.

Inside, the closet was warmer than the bedroom, due to the several heat lamps shining on the floor, and the various transplanted cuttings that sat there. Roland looked at Lilith, who waved her scanner at them.

"These are some of them. Cuttings. Just pieces. There are some cuttings from other plants that must have been taken from elsewhere."

Hiyakawa bowed to the spirit. "*Domo arigato* for your assistance. You are free to go."

The spirit sank back into the floor, fixing them all with

a beady glare. "As are you—and take all of those blasted trolls with you!"

Roland signaled to his men to stand down and enter the bedroom. "Take every cutting down to the van and prep for evac. We'll be joining you soon."

K-Tog, his brow furrowed in thought, holstered one of his Roomsweepers, then snapped his fingers. "Boss, I know what isn't right about this!"

Roland looked up at his crewman. "Besides everything? What are you talking about?"

The troll leaned down and put his lips to his boss's ear. "That troll woman—that isn't Sasalga's wife."

"Are you absolutely sure?"

"Yeah, I actually shook her hand once at a meta rally. That's how I know."

"Oh really?" Roland grinned, and the sinking feeling in his gut floated away as if on a cloud. "K, why don't you wait outside with Lilith and Hiyakawa-san for a minute? I'll be right out."

He walked over to the troll slouched in the massive leather chair, keeping his subgun at port arms, and leaned over to whisper into a pointed ear. "I'm only going to say this once, drekhead, so listen up." The troll stiffened at the insult, his nostrils flaring even wider than before. "When we leave, you are not going to call building security, or Lone Star, or anyone else regarding this little incident. If you do, and they somehow manage to pull their heads out of their hoops and find me, I'll be spilling my guts about how I recorded Sasalga Ottod in the middle of a little ménage a troll with two women, neither of them his wife. Are we clear?"

The troll sucked in a breath, but remained silent as Roland kept going. "That's right, chummer, I've got your big, tanned cojones in the palm of my hand. However, you keep quiet about this, and I'll do the same. You have my word on it." The troll didn't know that Roland would have had an impossible time using any of their evidence in court after what they had done to get it. *But what he doesn't know won't hurt me.*

Roland straightened and waited for the troll to look up at him, eyes burning with fury. Sasalga's breath whistled as he tried to contain his rage, but he had no options, and they both knew it. Finally, he dropped his head in a single nod.

Roland smiled at the two women, who hadn't uttered a peep. "Ladies." And with that, he walked out of the apartment, accompanied by the sound of something large and heavy being hurled across the room to shatter against the wall behind him.

17

On the ragged border between Snohomish and Redmond, Jhones pushed open the doors of a small bodega that remained in operation by the grace of the local Lone Star precinct and walked in, each footstep weighted with worry. With a nod to the proprietor, he headed for the ancient, small vidbooth in the back and closed the door. After scanning it for trace programs and cyberbugs, he blanked the screen, took a deep breath and dialed the number Hollander gave him.

Advertisements started scrolling, extolling the upcoming weekend of football games on a direct feed trid. Even as Jhones waited to talk to the person who might destroy his life, he scanned the messages, calculating the bets he could put down on each match through another bookie he knew.

There was a faint click as a connection was made. As a matter of course, Jhones tried to trace the call, but the originating numbers came up empty. *Pretty high-tech stuff to fool Lone Star gear.*

"*Yes?*" the voice was neutral, neither male nor female. The dwarf recorded the call anyway, hoping to get some kind of clue as to who his blackmailer was.

Jhones wasn't in the mood to play around. "Hollander gave me this number."

"*Ah, yes, it's a pleasure to make your acquaintance, Sergeant Redrock.*"

"Yeah, well, the feeling is anything but mutual."

The voice made a tsk-tsk sound. *"Now, now, that isn't very polite."*

Jhones gritted his teeth, feeling acid squirt in his stomach as his rage swelled. "Look, I don't have time to waste here. You've got something that needs to be done, and you also have something I need taken care of. Let's get down to business."

"My, my. You're so direct. I like that. Perhaps I could look into making this arrangement more—permanent."

"That's never gonna happen. Listen, *pisher,* you got five seconds to start talking, otherwise I hang up and walk away."

"The street wouldn't like that at all, but very well. The task is simple. In sixty minutes, you are to go to the following address"—the voice rattled off a street that Jhones recognized as part of the north downtown neighborhood of Ballard—*"and arrest a group of four shadowrunners. You will be able to charge them with murder."*

"How do you know all this?"

The question went unanswered.

"There is another part to this little caper, however, Sergeant. These criminals should be in possession of quite a few plants. You must recover the plants, and keep them from entering evidence. There is a chance the plants won't be with the runners, but I'm sure you can get them to admit just where they are stashed. When you have these plants safely stored—a warehouse or something similar should be acceptable—you will call this number again, and I will have them collected. Once the flora is in my possession, your debt will be discharged, simple as that."

"Really?"

"Absolutely."

The chutzpah these ganefs have, getting me to do their dirty work, he thought, leaning his head against the grimy wall of the booth.

"Are you still there? Remember that this deal is nonnegotiable."

With a sinking feeling, Jhones realized he was trapped. "No drek. All right, I'm in. I'll call you when I have the plants."

"Excellent. I look forward to hearing from you very soon."

"Yeah." He cut the connection and walked out as if in a daze. The dwarf took the light rail for a while, letting the people and city flow around him while he rode the main circuit, trying to figure out what he was going to do.

On the surface, the task the Johnson had requested of him sounded perfect—too perfect. Jhones knew there wouldn't be a problem detouring the plants out of evidence—the officer in charge of that department owed him several favors. And as it was likely the plants would need to be kept alive, someone would have to drive them to a Lone Star-owned greenhouse for safekeeping. Jhones would just make sure he was the one doing the driving, and switch the plants out on the way. With Simon along for backup that evening, the bust would go down perfectly, Jhones would square his debt and life could continue as usual.

Except for Roland, Jhones thought.

Even Simon would realize that this had to be tied into the Plantech heist that morning. It stank of it. It was at that point that Jhones realized why this person who had bought his marker needed a cop. Something had gone wrong with the original shadowrun—the perps had wanted more money, the exec's black ops budget had gotten cut and he couldn't pay—whatever, and now the hirer wanted the runners out of the way. The ganef who held his marker had to make sure the law would be there to bust the runners—*or kill them, more than likely,* he thought—and recover the plant cargo intact. The runners wouldn't be able to tell Lone Star who had hired them, and would be left twisting in the breeze, and the exec or whoever had set them up could sleep easy that evening—assuming the plants were recovered intact.

Which leaves Roland and his corp out in the cold.

The thought made Jhones' gut clench again as he realized the double-bladed decision he faced. *Some choice—betray my chaver so I can keep dancing with the devil. This tsuris I do not need.* And yet he already felt that undeniable gambling need growing stronger deep inside. Jhones had tried to log in to a few virtual betting sites that morning, but the whispers had already spread about the deal Hollander had cut, and no action would be available to him until they got word that he had done the job. As he scanned the sites,

Jhones hadn't been too surprised to find that a small pool had formed among the bookies he knew—all betting on an anonymous person in a hypothetical situation, of course, but it was obvious who they meant—over whether he would actually do the deed or not. The current odds stood at 5 to 3 that he would square his tab.

These zhlubs know me too well. But Roland asked for my help, too. Still . . . if I don't do this, everyone on the street will know I welshed—I'll never be able to place a bet in this town—or anywhere—again. It will be over—forever.

The rail car zipped around another corner as it started its circuit again, an apt analogy for how Jhones felt at the moment—running around in circles. *Oy vey, what choice do I have? I've got to look out for number one right now. If IA got wind that a corp exec had leverage over me, I would be lucky to be busted back to foot patrol. No, they would boot me in a Seattle second. That cannot happen. I'll just have to find some way to make it up to Roland, that's all. The way he talked, it didn't sound too terrible for Plantech, just that the deal with Shiawase would sour. They'll survive. They've been around a long time. I'm sure it'll all be fine.*

His mind clear, but with his gut still roiling at the choice he had just made, Jhones waited for the stop closest to the precinct and got off, scanning the street for the nearest Nukit Burger. *A bite to eat, that's what I need. Then I'll collect Simon and head to Ballard, get this whole thing over with.* The rookie wouldn't be a problem; Jhones would just have him take care of any suspects they captured. If they had the plants stashed someplace else, he'd cull one from the group and go collect the plants. From there it would be smooth sailing, and he would be free of this drek he had found himself in once and for all.

As he walked, Jhones did his best to ignore the small, incessantly gnawing guilt that had started in his gut over what he was about to do to his best friend. *A man's got to look out for number one; that's the rule on the street, always has been, always will be.*

For the twelfth time in half as many minutes, Simon wished he had gotten the cyberears mod first, instead of the eyes. Granted, the visual suite implanted in him was unbelievable, but right now he'd give it all up if he'd been able to record the conversation between Jhones and Roland at the diner that morning.

One thing's for sure; I do not have a second career ahead of me as a lip-reader, he thought as he stopped the data file and massaged his temples. He had been trying to make out what Roland said to Jhones, but the sec man watched the table or looked down at the dwarf. Simon had only gotten snatches of words, none of which made any sense. Even filtering them through a language program that analyzed the known data and extrapolated possible sentences hadn't gleaned anything.

Unless someone can make any kind of sense out of "Theme wipe dam is mail, with yeast twelves, nark atoll." Simon leaned back in his chair, yawning and stretching as his vertebrae popped from being hunched over for the past hour. A loud burst of chatter caught his attention near the door, and he glimpsed what looked like a trio of dwarf street hustlers being herded right into booking. *Must be sweeps week already.* The holding pens were already filled to capacity, but when the brass had to look good for the quarterly reviews, woe be to the street people caught just about anywhere for anything. *That's the risk you take running outside the law.*

The use of their constituents to make quota was only one aspect of law enforcement that Simon wasn't happy with. *Still, I wouldn't be anywhere else,* he thought. Simon's father, who hadn't been able to pass the physical for Lone Star due to trauma he had suffered in the UCAS military during the Night of Rage, had instilled the need for order in his son at a very early age. *"Society can never reach its potential until those who would transgress against others are brought to heel."* It had been one of Thomas Chays' favorite sayings, and he had clung to it until the day he died.

Ah, what happens when the transgressors use the law as their shield? That had been the fundamental problem Simon had realized as he went through Lone Star's cadet training, and witnessed the minor graft the cops were tempted with every day, which would eventually lead to bigger and bigger graft and offenses. At graduation, he had made a solemn vow to never become a cop on the take. To insure that, he had joined Internal Affairs as soon as possible, knowing that because he was policing other cops, he wouldn't be as likely to fall from grace himself.

Simon realized from the start that if word leaked out about his real job at the precinct, the others would band against him, the so-called "Lone Star Shield" would go up and he'd never be able to work there effectively again. But he didn't care; he was working for a higher purpose. He was there to try and insure that these officers, still servants of the public trust despite the private contract they had with the city, were not above the law. *The police still need policing, and if not me, who?*

On that question, Simon's thoughts turned to his partner. *I know there are badder apples in the Third's barrel, but for better or worse, Jhones is the one they wanted looked at first.* Simon suspected that several of the officers were protecting a large fencing operation for a slice of the profit, but he hadn't been there long enough to get close to them. Jhones' gambling problem had spiked on LS's monitoring radar, which was why Simon had been paired with him. But Simon also knew there were other reasons. *For all Jhones' bluster, he's an easy case. He actually believes that he's staying one step ahead of everyone else, poor guy. The brass is watching me on this one, to see how I do, and if I can be trusted to handle bigger jobs.* And Simon had every intention of coming through.

A stubby hand slammed down on his desk, jolting him from his reverie. "Ah, boychik, you look like drek warmed over. Didn't you get any sleep yet?"

Simon scratched his head as he realized the obvious truth. "Uh, no, I got caught up in that Plantech data, so I was going over what we had one last time, trying to see if anything was missed."

"I like that energy, it's good, 'cause you're gonna need it." The dwarf pounded him on the shoulder. "Let's go, I got a line on those runners that lifted the plants."

Simon frowned. "You do? From where?"

Jhones tapped his temple. "My years of experience on the street, knowing just what rocks to look under, just what folks to ask the right questions—"

"Okay, okay, *omae,* I believe you." Simon cut the dwarf off before he could pontificate about his prowess any longer. "Lead the way, I'm all yours."

18

"**P**lace is just as dumpy on the inside. Bet it was really something once, though." Max stood in the living room, hands on her hips, shaking her head in dismay. "Shame that someone let a house like this fall apart. I had a house like this? It'd be in tip-top shape."

"Maybe you can buy it from the city. Bet it wouldn't cost you more than a few thousand," Sindje said as she scanned the corners of the room.

The large living room had a raised ceiling with a ledge running around the walls just below it. A rusted, broken antique train hung half on, half off a track on the shelf. Miniature trees and faded, mildewed signs and railroad workers decorated the rest of the perimeter. Shreds of wallpaper clung below that in places, featuring washed out designs of old locomotives and whistle stops, giving the place a forlorn, haunted look. Remnants of charred furniture were piled in the center.

Max sniffed the musty air, the filtration system she'd bought with her trachea replacement picking up traces of old sweat, rancid soyjerky and an assortment of other unpleasant things she elected not to take the time to identify. "Homeless have been squatting. Probably come in here at night and set a fire to keep warm. Been chilly." Her face was a mask, showing no compassion or disdain for the unfortunate vagrants. She pointed to some discarded food wrappers. "Dumpster diving, most like. 'Spose the Johnson needed to meet with us before the sun went down and the bums crawled back inside."

"Makes me feel fortunate for what I have." Khase looked to his sister, who wriggled her nose as she made a concerted effort not to touch anything. *Debts and all,* he mouthed. She glanced around, and he knew she was weighing whether sustaining a levitation spell would be worth keeping her feet out of the mess on the floor.

"Yo, Mr. Johnson!" Max cocked her head, waiting for an answer. "He told us to find him upstairs." She tromped through a doorway and entered what used to be a dining room. There were more bits of railroad memorabilia there, namely smashed china plates and cups, the fragments of which showed old-time engines circling the rims. The dining room table had been hacked up and used in another bon-fire. "Surprised this whole place isn't ashes, what with the firebugs everywhere."

Stairs rose off the dining room, thick with shadows be-cause the side windows had been boarded up. Through a listing archway was the remains of the kitchen, the appli-ances long gone, and remnants of chairs, pots and smashed canisters scattered and broken on the tile floor. There was more of the railroad wallpaper, it faring slightly better than what clung to the living room.

"Mr. Johnson, we're—"

Sindje put a hand on the ork's shoulder. "Real itchy about this place, Max. Let me take a better look around first, 'kay? Then when I'm satisfied, we'll all go upstairs. Something just isn't sitting right. But at least I don't sense any spirits here."

"No boogga-booggas peeking at us?" The ork put on an impatient look and tapped her foot. But she didn't make a move for the stairs, just watched them, her eyes picking through the dark with her thermographic vision and seeing spiderwebs artfully hanging from the railing dotted with the husks of long-dead insects.

"No boogga-booggas, Max. Still. . . . Keep me up, Khase. I am not sitting on this floor."

Khase thrust the philodendron at Hood. "*Tad,* if you please."

Then Sindje was softly humming, inharmonious, but so muted it wasn't jarring. She became an elf-shaped piece of fog again, glancing in the kitchen, flitting down the hall and peering in bedrooms, where it was very obvious vagrants were staying. Then she floated up the stairs, marveling for just an instant at the banister, carved to look like a railroad track. Maybe because it was so intricate and made of a beautiful dark wood that the bums had left it alone—their small measure of respect for the crumbling house. Or maybe they simply hadn't yet run out of other things to burn. She sadly suspected the latter.

The stairs turned at a landing, then angled up to a short hallway cut by four doors. All of them were closed.

Odd that the Johnson wouldn't have met us downstairs, she thought. Odd that since he decided to handle the trade upstairs, he also didn't leave the door open so he could see them coming. The Johnson had no magic, she would have sensed this at the first meeting, and so he couldn't watch them with a spell.

Odd indeed. Sindje tried scratching her arm, only to remember she was still astral. *Duh.* The itching had now settled in the back of her mind, sending prickles of unease through her.

She ghosted through the first door to find an empty room thick with dust. The second showed the same. The third had been a nursery with an attached bathroom, with pink ducks painted on the wall and a bassinet and crib burned for another campfire. The last room contained a man—face down on the floor in a still-spreading, red-black pool of blood. Not the Johnson; in fact, she'd never seen this man before.

Recent. Very recent, all wet and shiny. Maybe the vagrants did it. Maybe not.

She knew the body was warm, though she couldn't touch it. She stared, though she told herself not to. The man's brown hair was mussed, the ends of it touching the blood and drawing some of it up like an antique quill pen might. His fingers were curled, one hand in the pool, the other clutching at a tattered throw rug, likely a reaction to the pain he'd felt in the last seconds of his life. His face probably evidenced the hurt and shock, but she wasn't going to float down into the floor to confirm it.

Sindje wasn't panicked, and she wasn't surprised to find a

corpse. As she'd already suspected, something was terribly wrong in the house. Too, she'd had a niggling feeling ever since they had left Hood's condo that the entire run was botched. Hood would want to know about the dead man, and naturally who killed him and why. But Sindje wasn't going to waste precious time looking for any more clues to make the troll happy. She'd not spotted bullet holes or burns on her quick look-see. If she was in her physical body, she'd have searched the man for a credstick or two, wanting something out of this soured milk run. But she wasn't going back to get her physical body . . . not to come up here.

So where was the Johnson? He'd called Max. But he didn't call from this house, as he led them to believe. A shiver raced down her insubstantial spine.

Time to leave this rat hole.

First a look out a window, though, that wasn't boarded over. It was at the back of the house, facing the suffering lawn, stripes of weeds and the grocer's parking lot. She floated above the dead man and let her face pass through the filthy bulletproof glass, wincing as she did so. Sindje spied the large gray van that had bothered her earlier. Two men, no . . . three, were getting out. All of them were in black pants and shirts, stocking masks on their faces. One had a long ponytail sticking out below the mask, and he carried an Uzi IV machine gun. The others had short-barreled assault rifles slung over their shoulders, and all of them had Ares Viper sliverguns holstered on their belts.

Gonna rob the grocers? No. Too much firepower for a register takedown.

They looked to the back of the house, the one with the ponytail pointed her way and said something. Then they started jogging toward the decrepit mansion.

Frag! Major setup!

Her ghostly image flowed back under the door and across the hall floor, running fast down the stairs like rushing water and pouring into her body, which Khase was holding up.

"Out of here now!" Then she was pushing away from her brother and heading into the living room, nimbly stepping around the furniture campfire and heading toward the front door. "It's a trap! There's a dead guy upstairs. And there's a team coming in the back to send us to the hereafter!"

In a heartbeat she threw the door open and stood in the frame.

"Ah, frag! More coming in the front, too! We're cut off."

19

The Nightsky slipped through the streets of Ballard like a gray wraith, the blocky Typhoons following on its flanks. Inside, Roland watched beads of sweat form on Hiyakawa's forehead as he concentrated on the spell he was maintaining.

After they had left the troll politician fuming in his plush apartment, Roland had requested that the shaman summon another city spirit and request that it search the area to find the pollen trail and lead them to its source. Hiyakawa had also wanted to keep an eye on the spirit as it looked. As he was doing so, the sec chief's commlink hummed, indicating an incoming call.

"This is Roland, go."

"Chief, get ready to be happy." Morgan's jolly voice said in his mind. *"Tell him, Trevor."*

"Hey boss, while I was in that apartment building's sec system, I 'borrowed' the last twenty-four hours of camera footage on the garage door, and this is what I found."

A window opened and showed three still shots from a security camera. The first was a familiar, battered Ares Roadmaster entering the underground garage. The second showed the same Ares, now being towed by a heavy-duty GMC 4201 that had been converted into a wrecker. The last shot was of a clean and shiny Ford-Canada Bison RV, complete with license plate. The time stamp in the bottom right hand corner showed that the two vehicles had come and gone about twelve hours apart.

"Now, these are the only two vans or RVs that have entered or left the premises in the past twelve hours. I'll bet my next paycheck that our runners—and the cargo—are on that Bison."

"Trevor, if you're right, you're getting Morgan's job." Roland had cut his connection over his lieutenant's squawk of outrage and nodded to the shaman. "I've got something better than the pollen for your spirit to track." He linked into the flatscreen monitor in the backseat of the limo and showed the Bison. "Have it look for this vehicle, as fast as it can, starting with the downtown area first."

That had turned out to be very fast indeed. The spirit had easily outpaced the Nightsky, disappearing into the urban sprawl in a twinkling. Hiyakawa had suggested cruising Highway 5, which bisected Seattle proper from the University to downtown, figuring the runners wouldn't want to set the deal up too close to where their safe house had been. Meanwhile, the shaman would maintain a view one hundred meters above them, so that he could see the spirit as soon as it came back.

Roland had set it up, informing the Typhoon drivers of the plan, and they had settled in for the most nerve-wracking twenty minutes of their lives. As the Nightsky slipped in and out of the late afternoon traffic, he tried not to think about the precious time slipping away. But the readout in the corner of his vision wouldn't let him. Nineteen hours and six minutes left until his corp and his world crumbled underneath his feet. *That is not going to happen on my watch, not without one fraggin' huge fight.*

To distract himself, he had run the Bison's license plate through the DMV database, but come up with nothing. The RV was registered to the company that also owned the Alki apartment building, which had all the earmarks of a shell corp. Roland didn't have the time, skill or inclination to poke deeper, but he had sent a note to Trevor to dig around and see what he could find.

As he had finished the message, Roland's commlink rang with a different chime, and he smiled as he realized who was on the other end. He turned to Lilith, who was watching the shaman work with the intensity of a BTL addict, and touched her on the sleeve. "I've got a call I have to take. Let me know if he comes up with anything, all right?"

She had nodded and returned to her study of the mage while Roland slid over to the other side of the limousine and established his connection. "Hello dear . . . where am I? Well, you're probably not going to believe this, but I'm sitting in the company limousine on Highway Five. What did I do to deserve this? I'll tell you later tonight over dinner. Yes, I should be home, assuming all goes well this afternoon. Yes, I'm still pursuing that business I mentioned before. No, no, of course it's nothing dangerous"—he stole a glance out the back window at the twin Typhoons trundling along in the Nightsky's wake—"You know I'm always careful. Oh, you have been thinking about our vacation . . . good, keep your list handy, and we'll narrow down where we'll be going when I get home. I'm looking forward to a peaceful night in, too. Thanks, sweetheart. I love you, too. See you soon. Good-bye."

Roland disconned just as Hiyakawa came out of his spell-induced trance. "The spirit is returning." As he spoke, the translucent head of the watcher spirit popped through the window, searching for Hiyakawa.

"Found it, found it, found it, yes I have, yes I have." Its voice was high and squeaky and childlike.

The shaman bowed to the small figure. "If you would be so kind as to take us there."

"Follow, follow, follow me." The spirit flew ahead of the Nightsky, and Roland lowered the barrier between the front and back compartments. "Morgan, follow Hiyakawa-san's directions to the letter."

Minutes later, their small convoy pulled onto the Ballard street, and Morgan pointed ahead of them. "Got a Bison parked on the street near that old house there. License is a match. No one outside, and thermal registers that there's no one in the vehicle."

"Try scanning the house, but keep it on quiet," Roland ordered while opening a channel to the squads in the Typhoons. "Gentlemen, we have our suspects' vehicle in sight. On my command, and only my command, execute Drill Echo Three. Try to take the suspects alive, but use deadly force if necessary, copy."

Each squad leader confirmed the orders. Roland turned back to Morgan. "What you got?"

"Walls are run down enough that I get a read on four in the house—a troll, an ork and two humans or elves. I think this is our crew."

"All right, get ready. We cut off the Bison, disperse in standard flanking formation; One right, Two middle, Three left, and take them as they're coming out. Morgan, when we hit the street, your only job is to tag that Bison with a homing beacon, then regroup with me." Roland picked up his helmet and grabbed his HK, hauling back the cocking lever to make sure a round was seated in the chamber. "Once again, Lilith, Hiyakawa-san, I cannot ask you to accompany us on this mission."

"In for a pound, in for a ton," Lilith said.

Hiyakawa nodded. "I believe you had mentioned that at least one of them is a mage. If so, my services will probably still be needed."

"Thank you both. I would suggest that you stay close to the limo, just in case things get hairy." Roland opened his channels again. "Squad One, Squad Two, Squad Three, Drill Echo Three, execute!"

With a throaty roar the Typhoons accelerated down the street, screeching to a halt as they boxed the Bison in between them. Morgan brought the Nightsky up, everyone in the limousine watching as the Plantech security forces spilled from the side doors of the RVs and spread out across the lawn, subguns at the ready.

"Here we go." Roland popped the door and paused at the opening. "Please keep your heads down and stay close to me. Let's move!"

20

"**D**rekkin' lovely!" Sindje stood in the doorway and motioned frantically to her brother. "I said there's more of 'em coming at us from the front! A lot more. They're armored. They got guns—lots of 'em. They've got us ringed in here!"

Hood let out a roar loud enough to rattle the windows. "No geeking, understand? No geeking!" He swept the bow off his back in one fluid movement and took the stairs two at a time to the second floor, each step screaming in protest at his weight.

"Frag it, *tad*, we need to be getting out of here, not deeper into the house!" Khase thrust the philodendron at Max. "Here. You hold this. You don't have a weapon." He unreeled his monofilament whip off his wrist and raced to the kitchen's back door, nimbly hurdling what was left of the table and chairs and clearing a narrow breakfast bar in one smooth leap. As soon as his first foot hit the floor, he pistoned his other one into the door, slamming the first intruder square in the face. The man, on the far side of middle age, had just come up a short flight of crumbling cement steps and now tumbled back down them. The submachine gun he had leveled at the door flew from his hands and clattered on what was left of a backyard sidewalk. The safety off, the impact caused the Uzi to fire a burst—bullets striking the back of the house and sending chunks of wood flying at the two black-clad men who had been close behind him.

The two were so similar in build and mien that Khase guessed they were brothers. Their lips curled in unison, and one of them barked: "Give up the plants, elf, and you might live."

"Only brought a little one with us." Khase flicked his wrist and the whip snaked out in threat. "*Tad* thought we should stash them someplace else for insurance. I guess we really needed that policy."

The men dropped back a few more steps, standing shoulder to shoulder, knees slightly bent and guns pointed at Khase's chest. The adept imagined he felt the red dots from their laser sights centered on his chest, but that was unimportant right now. He was as calm as ever, centered in the moment.

"Tell us where you've hidden the plants and we can all go our separate ways." This came from the man whose eyes were darker blue, the same one who'd spoken a moment before.

"Like I believe that." Another flick of his wrist and the elf sent the whip forward, the tendril glimmering in the late afternoon sun. Khase had intended to catch both men's guns and shear them in half. But they surprised him, springing forward like gymnasts as they ducked under his attempted strike. Before he could curl the whip around again, they had grabbed their fallen comrade and pulled him out of harm's way. All while they kept the guns pointed at Khase.

"Awakened," Khase muttered. "Adepts. But I doubt very good ones, or you wouldn't be toting guns to a fight." He could tell by the way they moved that he faced two men with skills vaguely similar to his own. "Not wholly skilled, and certainly not on my level."

"Marty's out cold!" Dark Eyes hollered. "Take him!" He raised his gun a few centimeters and fired at Khase. The elf sidestepped the bullet and vaulted down the steps toward them as more siding splintered away and pelted his shoulders.

"Not supposed to geek them, remember? Boss said just keep 'em here," the other one, bent over their unconscious third, said.

"It's okay to waste this one. There are three more inside who'll talk. We'll keep them three here until Lone Star arrives."

There was another burst of gunfire, but this came from the front of the house. It was followed by another, this one deeper and more sustained.

"Sindje!" Khase feared for his sister and half turned back; the instant of panic giving the two men an uncommon moment of advantage over the elf. Dark Eyes fired again, aiming for a kill shot in the chest, but even distracted the adept twisted out of the way, the bullet catching him in the left arm.

"No geeking, eh?" Khase's eyes narrowed to needle-fine slits. "We'll see about that, Hood."

Inside the house Max looked uncertainly between the plant in her hand and Sindje at the front door. "No weapon, Khase said. Nope, didn't bring a gun. Don't like using 'em." Softer: "All I got in my pocket is some shampoo and two bars of oatmeal soap."

She set the plant down and headed behind the stairs, spotting a door that took a strong tug to open because the wood had warped in the frame. A rickety set of steps stretched into the shadows.

Didn't bring a gun. But I never come to a party unarmed. She tapped her finger to her temple and quickly but gingerly went down, ignoring the little voice in her head that pointed out if things went to drek, she could be trapped down there. *I'll just have to make sure that don't happen.*

At the small window near the front entrance, Sindje watched a familiar-looking troll and what looked like two squads of men pour out of three vehicles—two of them dark green Renraku Typhoons with small, tasteful Plantech logos on the side doors. The other was a current-year Mitsubishi Nightsky Limited. The people getting out of the limo included a frumpy-looking woman in an ash gray trench coat; a large, older man in a Plantech uniform, body armor, and helmet; another man similarly dressed beside him; and a smallish, impeccably-dressed Japanese fellow.

"Fraggin' shaman," Sindje hissed. "Smell the magic in him from here. But how did they find us?" She stared incredulously as she counted twenty-one in all. "A small drekkin' army. Didn't know we'd stirred up that much trouble." Then she forced her fear and anger aside and felt for the mana that coursed through her.

"No geeking, huh?" Sindje slammed her eyes shut and felt her mind wrap around the blue-white ball of mana she gathered to her. The process seemed to take minutes, but it was actually instantaneous. Her thoughts held the ball suspended in front of her, hands rising until her fingertips touched the underside, feeling the peculiar, arcane sensation against her skin. She balanced the ball on her index fingers, rolling it back and forth, tossing it ever-so-lightly and catching it again and again, as all the while it grew larger and brighter and crackled with an energy she supplied.

At the same time, the Plantech folks assembled on the front lawn. They looked pro, spreading out to cover the left and right flanks, each man ready to advance with his sec brothers.

"All right, Hood. No geeking."

They were close enough for Sindje to hear the command. "Advance on the house." This came from the big man who had climbed out of the limo. A dark object whirred down to land on the lawn, and the combat mage ducked, knowing what was about to happen. There was a loud series of bangs, and white light glowed for several seconds outside. It was Hood's signal.

Time to get this started. As the men closed, Sindje straightened and used her mental fingertips to shove the ball forward, like a child would throw it to a playmate.

"Mage!" shouted one of the men near the shaman. "Incoming!" The rest of his words were lost in the pulsing hum of the energy ball that grew even larger as it struck the man's armored chest. The ball became translucent, still faintly blue with motes of white light sparkling like the sun hitting water. It was so large now it enveloped the man, motes sparkling on the exposed skin of his face, and it also expanded to encompass the surprised shaman, her real target.

The shaman had started casting a spell, and Sindje was pleased that she had been able to keep him from getting it off. The man next to the shaman slung his gun and tried to break free of the energy; his arms waving furiously at first, then slower and slower. He crumpled in a heap as the energy ball doubled in size, then doubled again, the blue-white sphere giving off enough light to illuminate the entire block. The frumpy woman dropped right away. The older man had dived away and rolled, coming to a stop near the Nightsky, his subgun still out and trying to find a target. The ball continued spreading outward, swallowing five more of the Plantech guards before they could evade it, including the troll she remembered had been called K-Tog. It rendered them all unconscious.

Sindje's stun ball spell physically and mentally drained her. She likened releasing one to running a twenty kilometer race. Normally she'd rest after calling forth such taxing magic, but there was no time now. She reached inside herself and began manifesting another blue-white ball, feeling the slow burn as drawing the mana so soon again began exacting its price on her.

Upstairs, Hood kicked in the first door he came to. It was empty. He'd hoped to find the corpse Sindje mentioned, but he'd look for that later. First piece of business was to see just who had come to pay them a call. The floor creaked in argument as he stomped to the window that overlooked the front lawn. It was one of the bulletproof glass windows not boarded up, and Hood rammed his elbow against it—hard. The window cracked, but didn't shatter, and it took a second hit to get it to pop out of its frame and fall to the lawn below.

The troll immediately spotted the two Plantech Typhoons; they had his Bison sandwiched between them, so it wouldn't be able to get out. He whistled in appreciation at the Nightsky.

"Now how'd they find out about us?" He forced down his curiosity and anger. "Doesn't matter. They're not going to catch us." He reached over his shoulder, thick fingers dancing across the tops of his arrows, the fletchings telling him which one he wanted. He pulled one out, nocked it to his bowstring and fired.

The arrow landed near the sidewalk, in the heart of the throng of men, and set off a sun-bright explosion of light, a deafening noise and the thick stench of sulfur. It was meant only to blind and deafen the men and make them sick, and thereby gain Hood a small measure of time to get a better position.

He held his bow out the window and then squeezed himself out the frame, cursing as jagged splinters of wood shredded his blazer. Shouldering the bow, Hood dug his fingernails into the siding, clawing his way up the house and onto the roof. As he hoisted himself up, he knocked the gutter loose in the process, and felt the edge of the roof sag beneath his feet, but it didn't give way.

From his lofty vantage he could easily see the men in the front yard, though he couldn't tell if any had made it under the overhang and onto the porch. He counted twenty-one, then spotted a shimmering blue-white globe appear and disappear, leaving six men, a troll and a woman lying stunned across the Kentucky-Seven.

The troll grunted in satisfaction. "Good work, Sindje."

The rest of the men wore body-armor uniforms just like the Plantech security guards had, and they toted identical submachine guns, with various models of pistols in holsters at their sides. Half of them were wearing visors, which rendered them immune to the light of Hood's flare arrows. One man stood back by the limo, an older human with a riot helmet and a subgun in his hand. He pointed up at Hood and barked orders at the men, one arm gesturing to his left to get them to spread out.

"I'd say you're in charge. And that makes you my target."

The troll selected an appropriate arrow and fired, just as the Plantech security forces opened up on the house.

In the basement, Max relied on her natural lowlight vision. Faint light spilled in through a couple of window wells, but it wasn't enough, given the depth of the basement and the curtains of spiderwebs that hung from every rafter. She wasn't worried, however, moving easily through the dimness like it was daylight.

"Vut, vut, vut." She moved aside one mass of webs to find sticky tendrils still clinging to her arm and dreads. Shaking her head and spitting to get the webs away from her mouth, she made her way to the nearest wall and started looking.

"Buunda! Gotta have a power box, a mainframe, something. Don't care how old this place is, it's gotta have something."

She heard bursts of gunfire coming from the back of the house, shouts coming from the front. From high overhead she heard the creak of wood and, based on past runs, figured it was Hood moving around.

"Fraggin' troll chews on me for getting our pay doubled. Chews on me! Should've been down on his knees saying 'thank you, ma'am.' Should've been tripled, our pay. No, four times the original offer. Five, mebbe." She moved quickly over a hard-packed dirt floor. "Frag, this place is older than cement."

Rats squeaked, and she heard faint scratching sounds as they scurried to the far corners. Max was so intent on searching the walls she nearly stepped on a dead rat the size of a small house cat and stumbled over a broken workbench.

"*Buunda, buunda, buunda!* Place smells worse than I do." She sniffed under her armpit, made a gagging sound and mentally shut down her olfactory boosters. "Should've done that the second I hit the bottom step. I'm gonna borrow Hood's fancy shower when this is through." She paused and pawed through another veil of webs. "Provided we manage to live through this—ah, here's what I'm looking for." A pause: "But not what I wanted to find."

The ork frowned as she popped open the metal plate on the house's mainframe. It was at least twenty years old, making it way outdated, but still the most modern thing she'd spotted in the house so far.

"Hmmm, expensive for the time. But a piece of crap now." She noted a charred spot along the right edge, a panel blown. Her eyes glimmered in the dark as she reached into the pouch at her side and pulled out a cable. With a flick of her wrist, she threaded the plug on, then slipped one end into the lowest slot of the mainframe, and the jack behind her ear. "Hate these antique things that use wires."

She felt a faint tingle of power.

"Let's give you a little boost." She pulled a thin splicer cable from the pouch and tugged one of the wires free that tied her hair. As the crackle of gunfire continued outside, and Hood kept creaking around upstairs, she threaded the cables into her deck. *Frag, they're gonna bring Lone Star down on us in spades, they keep this up.*

The tingle of added power grew stronger, and she felt the electrons start their merry dance along the inside of her skull. She imagined they were getting ready for a race, all jumpy and straining at the gate. The Belmont Stakes waiting to be played out at this little run-down mansion at the tip of Ballard.

"And they're off!" Max leaned against a mold-speckled,

water-stained wall, oblivious to a veil of spiderwebs she knocked free that fluttered down around her, draping over her back like a gossamer-thin fairy cape.

The gunfire continued.

The roof high above creaked.

The rats squeaked and scurried in the darkest corners.

And Max strained, via the house's old mainframe, to find the vehicles outside the house. She knew better than to connect to the city's grid-link street system with its Black Ice. Not enough time, and not with this old equipment.

Through her decksuit she pulled down a schematic of the neighborhood, crossing it with a quickly borrowed real-time satellite image. It was as good a picture as she could have received if she had been floating over the house like a Sindje-apparition. No, a better and more reliable picture, she told herself, as it was provided by technology rather than magic. Her view let her get a good look at the vehicles outside.

Max loved vans and RVs—because her father taught her about engines, and he'd been her one fond memory of childhood. She liked vans especially because of the roominess, the versatility for different runs. She liked the power of the engines, whether they ran on the city's grid or guzzled a gas-mix. And there were four RVs near this house, all of them with computer-assist engines.

Hood's big Bison was easy to pick out. There were two other RVs near it, Typhoons wedged so close that the Bison wouldn't be able to move unless it muscled its way out. She figured the Bison had the power, but the bumpers and fenders wouldn't fare well, and that would be too heavy a loss for such a beautiful machine. A gleaming Mitsubishi Nightsky next to the RVs made her breath catch for a moment, but she forced herself to move on. There was another van behind the house, in the nearby supermarket parking lot. It had its motor running, and she would contend with it first—easier.

Max had the latest model vehicle control rig implant and could hack just about anything with wheels with it. And though it worked best when she was jacked directly into a vehicle, she had picked up a few modifications that let her do some driving from a distance.

Her fingers typed air, sending directions through her

commlink and into the house's system. In an instant she was connected to everything—to the Typhoons, the Bison, the limo that she was drooling over, her thoughts finally activating the gas pedal of the gray van in the back parking lot as she put it into reverse. She maneuvered it out of the parking space, then drove it off the lot and down a side street past the grocer's for several blocks. It was a clumsy effort, for even with the satellite image she couldn't see all the obstacles. Once Max thought the van had hit a tree or a signpost, and decided that she had taken it far enough, quickly pulling it to a curb and turning off the engine.

Perhaps Hood would let her take the Bison through that neighborhood when this was all over. Cruise past that new gray van. By now it was likely that the men who'd driven that van here wouldn't be capable of driving it for some time. And it would go a long way in replacing her demolished Roadmaster. Now, on to the matter of the two Typhoons and the Mitsubishi limo. No worry about parking one of them someplace else to retrieve later. She had her heart set on that streamlined, dolphin-gray beauty.

"My new ride," Max purred.

21

"Hey, our van!" One of the brothers facing Khase glanced over his shoulder in time to see their gray van back out of the grocer's parking lot and trundle out of sight.

The moment of surprise was on Khase's side this time, and he blurred into motion. His honed body moving almost by reflex, he flipped toward and over both men, extending his legs like he was coming off a vault. At the same time he retracted his whip and drove his arms down, fingers stretching toward the guns. He grasped only one barrel, which he wrenched up and flung away. As he completed his arc, his heel slammed into the head of the man with the lost gun. The whip would have been easier and allow him to keep a distance, but it was also much deadlier— more than capable of slicing a man in two and injuring himself in the process.

"No geeking," Khase said under his breath. "On my part, anyway."

His other target was far more dexterous, leaping away and bringing the gun up to sight on Khase's head. The elf tracked the barrel movement as he flicked his left arm out, his mind shunting the pain away as his monofilament whip hissed out and curled around the assault rifle's banana magazine. He pulled, and the magazine casing fell apart, bullets clattering to the pavement. The sudden jerk also yanked the rifle off-target, and the thug squeezed the trigger in reflex, the lone bullet in the chamber firing harmlessly into the ground.

The wanna-be adept didn't give up, however, flipping his rifle up and grabbing the barrel. He stepped forward and swung it like a baseball bat, clipping Khase's leg. Then he threw the rifle at the elf, and while Khase ducked, he pulled a pistol, firing it and grazing the elf's already-wounded arm.

The elf didn't flinch, but his ears twitched when he heard a noise behind him. He turned his head just enough to keep the two thug brothers in his peripheral vision.

The brother Khase had just kicked was on his knees, palm pressed against the side of his head, free hand reaching for another gun. Before his fingers could close around the pistol's butt, Khase launched himself, extending his leg in a ballet leap he had seen on a trivid last year. The toe of his boot clouted into the man's forehead, dazing him. Landing beside him, Khase chopped the weaving pistol from his grip with one hand as he grabbed the punk's jacket with his other. He spun around, hauling the man off his feet, shoving him through the air and into his brother. The two men collided, and Khase heard a loud crack as bone met bone. The men collapsed in a heap, a pistol flying as the second one dropped to the sidewalk, out cold.

"Two down." Khase landed in the grass, crouched in a deep knee bend, arms straight out to his sides and seemingly oblivious to his own injuries.

The first man pushed himself to a sitting position, pointing a shaking finger at Khase. "You're dead, elf. We went into this knowing we were only supposed to detain you. But the boss said it was okay if we had to geek one or two to get the job done. That makes this a wetwork job as far as I'm concerned."

Given their recent performance, Khase wasn't too worried, although he was aware of the trickle of blood running down his arm. "Kill me, and where will you sit with the plants?"

"Just fine." The man nudged his downed brother with his shoe, relieved to hear him groan and know he was alive. "Like I said, there's three more of your gang in that house. I'll get the plants from one of them."

"Eron, you got to get to the ones in the house now!" This came from the first man Khase had struck, the older one with the long ponytail. Apparently he'd woken up. "You'd be deaf not to hear that."

They all paused, hearing more gunshots coming from the front of the house.

"Don't know what that's about," Ponytail continued. He tried to get to his feet, but couldn't manage beyond making it to his hands and knees. "Thought we were the only team on this. Maybe the boss sent in backup."

Khase instantly thought about his sister again. He wasn't completely worried—in many respects she was far more formidable than he. But he was at least curious. *Should see what's going on out front. Have to end this fast.* He sprung straight up, angled his body like a high diver and aimed for the man with the ponytail. The elf's torso cleared the man's head and then Khase brought his legs down, both knees striking the man in the side of the skull and rendering him unconscious again. Khase landed on his hands, ignoring the flare of pain from his wounded arm and pushed off again, spinning in midair and coming down on the balls of his feet directly in front of the remaining man.

"Like I said—*Eron*. Two down."

"Khase! Khase, you got him, neh?" It was a bellow, coming from the roof of the house.

"Null sheen! This piece of nutrisoy drek's got nothing, Hood!" Khase glanced up to see the troll head toward the front of the house.

"Null sheen?" Khase's last opponent gave him a malevolent sneer. "I won't go down easy, elf. In fact, I won't be going down at all. And, yeah, I'm awakened." Of the three of them, he had looked the most adroit. The man raised his hands in a defensive martial arts pose, shifted his weight on the balls of his feet and locked eyes with the elf. "Shouldn't have brought the guns in the first place." He didn't blink as he started circling Khase. "But my mother gave them to us. Sometimes we use them out of sentimentality." He snapped a leg up and lashed out at Khase, striking the elf in the hip and sending him back a step.

He followed through immediately, darting in and chopping at Khase's wounded arm. Then he jumped back, circled again and came in from the other side with a roundhouse kick that the elf blocked on the thigh. Again the man retreated, staying out of Khase's reach. Twice more he successfully used the roundhouse and moved away.

Khase stayed on his feet and nodded, mentally upgrading his adversary's ability as he studied the man's moves. He considered the whip for a moment; his left arm was burning, his hip and leg ached, and the whip was looking lethally appealing. "Who hired you? Who's this boss you talk about?"

The man waggled a finger and made a tsk-tsking sound. "Mom taught me never to tell."

"Sure don't think a lot of the guns she gave you." Khase glanced at the weapons strewn all over. The chatter bought him time to further study his opponent and push his pain to the back of his mind.

"I'll pick 'em up and polish 'em later. Mom'll never know." He winked at the elf, the gesture meant to unnerve him.

It almost succeeded. The muscles in Khase's legs bunched and he made a move to spring, but stopped himself. Eron had shifted position, and wasn't holding his hands in any of the usual martial arts postures Khase recognized. Looking closer, he spotted a thin, almost invisible wire stretched between the man's hands. A monofilament garrote? Khase touched his neck and shook his head.

"Oh, mom'll know you've been careless all right, *Eron*. She'll have to pick up you and your brother . . . and your snoozing playmate with the ponytail."

"My uncle," the man said. "Mom's favorite brother. I'll use your face to polish his boots when I'm finished with you." Then he was in the air, leading with a flying kick aimed at Khase's chest. He was fast, the air whistling around the material in his pants, the late afternoon sun gleaming off the metal plate on his boot heel.

"That'd hurt if it connected." Watching the man tense, Khase stepped aside as the boot shot past his face, the material in his skinsuit making a shushing noise against the man's pantleg. In the same motion he raised his wounded arm and brought the edge of his hand down in a knife-hand blow against the man's abdomen. Khase connected. The elf struck with all the strength he'd gathered, no longer worrying if he accidentally geeked his assailant, and stopped the man cold in midair, following through to slam him down on the ground. He felt flesh and bone yield under his strike and sensed that he'd fractured several ribs and ruptured the man's spleen, maybe a few other organs as well. All of it was treatable, but he'd never be as good as new. Eron's face froze in shock, and only a slight mewling noise could be heard as he slipped into unconsciousness.

A feral grin on his face, Khase held his wounded arm and loped across the grass, following the ornamental sidewalk that would take him to the front of the house.

Sindje released another stun ball, this one targeting four men running toward the north side of the house, their subguns chattering in short, controlled bursts as they peppered the windows and roof as they advanced.

"Mustn't let you sneak up on us." The ball caught the four and dropped them in a heap.

Then she focused on the man who was shouting orders, and was now standing by one of the Typhoons. She'd heard someone call him Mr. Ators. The name wasn't familiar, but she figured he was in charge, and he presented a risk by his authority and by that linked smart gun he was toting. He'd be the better shot among the security guards standing, and so he must be dealt with now.

A variation of the stun ball, she decided, as she focused on her heart, each beat fueling the globe of mana burning brightly in her mind. The globe suddenly appeared hovering in front of her face, her fingers reaching up to tickle its surface and to find pleasure in the energy that crackled wildly inside of it. One more heartbeat ticked off and she mentally hurled the energy at the sec leader, the globe turning into a shimmering stroke of ephemeral lightning that shot unerringly at him even as he tried to roll out of the way. A stun bolt would do nicely, particularly since Hood demanded no fatalities.

The bolt struck him squarely in the chest at the same moment he was bringing up the big subgun to fire at her . . . and at the same moment an arrow arced down from the roof to land at his feet, releasing a sticky net that trapped his legs and brought him to his knees. Pitching forward, stunned from her magic, he landed face-first in the gooey net mass.

"Like a bug in a spider's web. Oh, he'll have bad dreams for weeks. And his boys'll never let him live it down." Then Sindje was instantly serious again as several remaining members of the Plantech security force started firing at her. She hit the floor as streams of bullets chewed into the door-frame and walls. She heard excited voices outside talking to each other.

"Boss said try to keep them alive, 'least 'til we get the plants back!"

"The boss is down! Maybe dead!" someone shot back. "I ain't risking my neck for a few ferns just 'cause Ators said no killing! 'Sides, if we don't geek that mage, we don't stand a chance. All units open fire!"

A second volley completely shattered the doorframe, and a high-explosive round cut through the front of the house, sending a belch of plaster dust and flame into the air when it impacted on the wall behind Sindje and blew a second opening into the dining room. The model train high on the living room shelf tottered and fell.

Duckwalking, Sindje crouched behind the picture win-dow, only half of which was boarded up. She'd momentarily lost her focus amid the hail of bullets, but she was at it again, nurturing her magical spark and calling up another spell—the one she'd used on the streetlights in the early hours of this morning. If the Plantech security guards were playing with deadly force, she had no chance but to match them. As the mana grew warm, spreading from her chest down her arms and to the palms of her hands, she visual-ized twin globes forming. Aimed right, they'd take out the rest of the force, very likely killing the weaker men because of the jolt it would give to their hearts. The magic would take her out, too, as she was putting everything she had into it. She knew she could well be useless after this, but she had no choice.

As she peeked up through the window to spot her tar-gets, her breath caught. One arrow after another lanced into the lawn, Hood rapid firing from the roof. The first was another flare arrow, meant to blind the rest of the men without visors. The second, third and fourth were more of the sticky nets that held them in place. A fifth struck the limo; it had an explosive head, and as the arrow tip pene-trated the metal hood, it detonated. The resulting blast rocked the cul-de-sac and spun the Plantech men's heads. Pieces of the car rained down on the guards Sindje'd stunned and the ones netted by Hood's arrows.

That bit of pyrotechnics gave Hood and Sindje another precious few moments. More arrows thudded into the ground—more nets, more flashes. A concussion grenade followed, and another that emitted a greenish-gray smoke followed close behind.

Screams cut through the air—not from the men Sindje and Hood were dispatching, but from neighbors who were standing on porches and sidewalks, pointing and hollering, too afraid and too curious to run.

"Didn't know *tad* packed munitions. Thought he was all peaceable and drek." Sindje took a deep breath and let the globes dissipate; she didn't need the lethal spell anymore. Her energy started to return, but she was still weak. Pressing her palms against the windowsill, she eased herself up, brushed the plaster dust off her shoulders and walked to the shattered doorframe.

"Call Lone Star!" Someone across the street shouted.

"I already did!" This came from a woman standing under a gaudy string of decorations on her porch. "They're on their way."

"You okay, Sindje?"

The elf shuffled out onto the porch and looked up. Hood was on the edge of the roof, staring down. She nodded and mouthed: *Fine and double-dandy.*

"I'm gonna check on that body you saw. Then we have to get out."

"And quick," she added. She carefully picked her way down the front porch steps and onto the walk, not wanting to get caught in the sticky nets, turning when she heard Khase's feet slapping against the sidewalk. "What the? . . ." She faced the street again when she saw the Typhoon in front of Hood's Bison peel away, scraping against the burning remains of the Nightsky and knocking over a trash bin as it went speeding down the narrow street. "No one's driving it."

Inside, Hood turned the body over with the tip of his boot. An older man, human, eyes slanted just a little to hint at an Oriental parent or grandparent. The death had been painful and came as a surprise, judging by the expression on the man's face. Fingers not calloused, but stained faintly green.

"Ah, if I had cybereyes." Then he'd be able to record an image of the corpse and consult some databank to glean an ID. "But I have a good memory." He stared long and hard at the face so he could describe it to Max, who could look through records stashed in various corners of the matrix. Or Sindje could maybe magically pull a picture from his mind if that didn't work.

Hood knelt, just beyond the pool of blood, and spotted dirt on the man's shirt. Rich potting soil from the look of it, with a few of those crystals the troll had noticed in the plants they stole. The troll wanted to examine everything more closely, but there wasn't time. He closed the man's eyelids, rose and glanced out the window into the yard, seeing the three men Khase had taken out, one lying at an odd and disturbing angle. They weren't dressed like the men in the front, though that alone didn't mean they weren't Plantech security.

"No, definitely not Plantech," Hood decided after another moment, catching sight of the gray ponytail. He knew a trained security force likely wouldn't allow a hairstyle like that. All of the other men had high and tight cuts. Besides, he doubted the Plantech force would have sent only three to the back of the house—and without the body armor the rest of them were wearing. "So who?"

He'd puzzle it all out later. Now they had to get out of here. He knew Lone Star was coming in answer to a neighbor's call, and Plantech had probably called for backup, too. He started down the stairs, just as he heard Max racing up the steps from the basement.

"Vut, vut, VUT!"

The ork had extended herself into the Typhoon in front of Hood's Bison, her mind—through her implants—manipulating the starter. The engine purred to life, and for a moment she reconsidered. Perhaps she would indeed take this one down a side street and come back for it later—come back for it *and* the gray van, repaint them both and start her own little fleet. After all, she had such trouble holding on to vehicles; maybe a backup would be a grand idea.

Then the Nightsky exploded, the flare as it went up painting a bright red-gold dot on her satmap as the lustrous limousine disintegrated in a fiery ball of wreckage.

"Aww, now who did that?" She mentally punched the pedal, and through the mainframe saw the city's grid and drove the Typhoon along it. *A little too fast,* she scolded herself, as it didn't handle quite as smoothly as the gray van. The Typhoon scraped the remains of the limo and hit something else. A trash bin? A motorcycle? She couldn't get a clear enough image from the uplink. Then she took it straight down the street, past that big fancy yellow house with all the security systems and the fisheye windows, past the buckled sections of sidewalk. When she spun it into someone's driveway, missing the intersection she'd aimed for, she released the pedal and turned off the engine. Maybe she would come back for it, if possible.

"Now we've got a little room to move." She tried to turn over the engine in the Bison, get it ready for their exit, but her mind couldn't manipulate the controls. Too many safety measures, and one of them might give her a backlash if she wasn't careful. "Fine, Hood's got the key. He can start it."

Max pulled the cables, took a last look around the basement and through a veil of gossamer webs spied something a few meters past the mainframe.

"What?" She tugged down the curtain, sputtering when some caught on her tusks and left a horrid taste in her mouth. "What in the name of. . . ." She stared at it for exactly one second—at a box on the wall, at the pale blinking lights at the bottom of the console, nearly invisible before she pulled down the webbing. The lights were blinking faster and faster now.

Her eyes grew wide with the realization.

"Bomb!" She hurled herself toward the basement steps, taking them three at a time as she raced for the upstairs. "Bomb! A very big bomb!"

She nearly plowed into Hood as she turned the corner and headed into the dining room. The troll had just cleared the last step from upstairs.

"Bomb!" Max hollered again. Then she was tugging at

Hood's arm, then running past him. "Bomb! Bomb! Bomb!"

The troll hesitated only for a heartbeat, and then he was on her heels, his footfalls thundering across the floor. He kicked aside scraps of furniture and stepped on a rusted toy boxcar on route to the front door, crushing it flat as he ran.

Max waved her arms as she jumped down the front steps and did her best to avoid the sticky nets and fallen, groaning security guards. "Bomb, keeblers!" She shot toward the Bison, the elves picking up the pace behind her. "Hurry! Go, go, go!"

Hood was behind her, grabbing the fallen Plantech men that were closest to the house and, therefore, in the most danger. He scooped up two under each arm and tossed them toward the curb, then went back for four more. The sticky nets yielded to his massive strength as he piled the men like raked leaves behind the remaining Plantech Typhoon. He was heading back for another armload when he saw a pillar of flame shoot out the roof and every window of the old house. It was accompanied by a deep rumbling sound that rattled the vans and sent the neighborhood gawkers finally fleeing back into their homes.

The rumbling gave way to an explosion that sent what was left of the roof a dozen meters into the air, burst out all the bulletproof glass windows and turned the wooden siding into slivers. Shards of the house flew over them as Hood, Max and the elves dove to the ground. Once the flaming maelstrom had subsided, they popped up and ran the last several steps to the once-perfect Bison. It was scratched and dented everywhere, with bits of flaming wood on the roof and windshield. Hood threw open the back door and motioned the elves inside. Then he hurried to the passenger door and opened it.

"Max?" Hood turned to see the ork sprawled facedown on a buckled section of sidewalk, wood shards still falling out of the sky on her. "Max!"

"Drive, Hood! I'll get her. Move, *chwaer*!" Khase pushed Sindje into the back of the van and rushed to the ork's side.

Max wasn't moving. She outweighed Khase by at least a hundred kilos, but the elf gritted his teeth and pulled her up. "C'mon Max. We gotta move!"

But Max didn't budge, just hung off the adept, dead-weight, and Khase saw a blossom of red growing against her back and chest. A glance over his shoulder revealed the culprit. One of the Plantech guards lying on the ground had a pistol out and aimed at the two of them. He squeezed the trigger again, but a piece of flaming wood fell off the still-burning house and thudded to the ground right next to him, spoiling his aim and causing the bullet to thunk into the Bison's side panel.

Shielding the ork's body with his own, Khase pulled her to the van and thrust her at Sindje, then jumped in and slammed the doors shut just as the Plantech man reloaded and started firing again.

"She's not breathing!" Khase hovered over Max, stretched out in the back of the Bison.

22

Jhones felt strangely calm as Simon and he traversed the downtown traffic to where the shadowrunners behind the Plantech heist might be. A small voice in the back of his head was busy chewing him out for selling out his best friend, but the dwarf found it surprisingly easy to tune out the niggling bit of conscience, preferring to focus instead on the bets he planned to make once he had gotten this small matter of the job at hand out of the way. *Quit worrying about Roland, he'll make out. My old* chaver *always has, always will.*

In contrast, Simon seemed ill at ease, tense in the passenger seat of their patrol car. Jhones' eyes flicked over to him again, seeing the rookie chew on a ragged fingernail. "*Nu,* boychik, what's the matter? You look like someone ran over your cat."

Simon started as he turned to look at the dwarf. "Oh, nothing, it's just—I don't know, I just thought that working for Lone Star would be more—"

"Exciting? Glamorous? Worthy? Lucrative?" Jhones took an exit off Highway 5 and began navigating the streets toward Ballard. "Kiddo, I've heard just about every 'should have been' from rookies for the past ten years. Lone Star is a job, just like any other. It has its good points, one of which is that you get to help people. And its bad points, one of those is that often you will be shot at, or a drunken troll will try to use you as a projectile in one of their silly games."

"You don't mean—"

"*Don't* say it, chummer." Jhones turned a hard eye on his partner. "Just because those *chazerai* like to play their games doesn't mean my kind goes along with it." *At least not usually,* he thought. "Anyway, my point is that everyone in this business—and no matter what anyone tells you, it's a business, mark my words—gets into it for a reason. Me, I like to help people, and Lone Star is the best way for me to do that." He glanced over again to see Simon regarding him with a strange look on his face. "What?"

"You gotta be kidding me! You joined Lone Star, take crap from just about everyone, from the corps to the dregs of society, just so you can help people?"

"Absolutely. Look, society cannot exist without laws, and those laws must be enforced by someone. Granted, having the police be a private company instead of a public trust is not exactly what a lot of people want, but here it is. And now there's only the 'how do we all work best together?' details that have been worked out."

"But what about the rampant corruption in the system?"

"And that's different how from any other corp, or different back when the police was government run?" Jhones snorted. "It's intertwined with the history of humanity, meta or otherwise. There are always those who seek to better themselves at the expense of others. And those people have to be found and brought to justice, no matter what ideal or system they hide behind." The dwarf frowned as he considered his partner. "What's with all the deep philosophical statements today, huh, *chaver*?

Simon squirmed in his seat. "I don't know—I see corruption all around us—the corps taking everything they can, and leaving the pickings for the rest of the have-nots, and I wonder sometimes if it's all worth it, you know?"

Jhones shook his head. "Actually, I don't know. But the one thing I do know in this world is that everyone, no matter how low or how high, is entitled to justice. That elf we saw this morning deserves it, and so does the lowest street person. It's as simple as that."

"But what if a person goes outside the law to get their own justice? What then?"

"Why the twenty questions? What is up with you today? Look, we're getting close to the address my informant gave me. Now, we're going to chase down that lead on the Plantech robbery, and we'll pick up this conversation later, okay?"

"Okay, Jhones, fine by me." Simon was more confused than ever. Jhones had sounded like he embraced law and order with as much zeal as he did. *Then what is going on with Ators and Plantech? Is he just helping out a friend off the clock?* Simon hadn't even gotten a chance to bring up the potential for illegal activity in Lone Star; he was afraid that the dwarf would take his head off. *Surely I couldn't have been mistaken, could I?*

As they turned down another street, they heard the faint sound of automatic weapons fire just as their commlinks came to life:

"All units in Ballard vicinity, all units, multiple shots fired at Ballard address. Requesting all units converge on the area immediately. Backup is en route." The address was the same one that Jhones had mentioned earlier.

"Drek!" Jhones slammed his hand against the steering wheel. "Some overzealous beat cop probably stumbled across our bust. Frag it!" He hit the sirens and lights and floored the accelerator, sending the Americar shooting forward.

Simon's hand went to his pistol as he checked the semi-automatic's load. *That was an odd reaction for what should be just a simple bust.* He looked over at his partner, seeing him hunched over the steering wheel, muttering under his breath. *His pulse has accelerated again, and he's certainly not his usual calm self. Maybe I'm not so far off after all. I'll just keep watching and see what happens.*

Jhones rounded a corner just in time to see the sky several blocks ahead erupt in a huge fireball, with pieces of something raining down onto the rest of the neighborhood. Simon's eyes widened, and he and his partner both had the exact same thought, and expressed it with the exact same word:

"Drek!"

23

"Well, make her breathe!" the troll shot back. "I can't help you with that! I have to get us out of here!" He stomped on the pedal, the Bison accelerating down the narrow street, minor explosions going off behind it as the old house continued to erupt. He wrenched the wheel hard right, taking them down an alley and careening into a line of garbage cans as he went, spraying refuse everywhere. Leaning over the front passenger seat, he popped open the glove box and retrieved a spongy package. He tossed it over his shoulder to Khase. "Trauma patches in there. Use as many as you have to."

There was a siren—Lone Star by its whining pitch. It sounded like only one vehicle . . . at the moment. It had gotten here awfully quick, from the time of the nosey neighbor's announcement. Hood knew there would be more coming, as the rent-a-cops usually traveled in packs.

"Make her breathe, I said! Khase, Sindje, use the patches."

Khase didn't reply. His hands were over the hole in Max's chest, trying to staunch the blood. The Bison hit a pothole, momentarily sending his palms off the wound. Blood gushed out, a miniature fountain.

"I don't recall anyone requiring a medical degree for this run. She's dead." Sindje looked at the ork's face, dreads splayed out and coated in blood. "So much blood. It stinks." The fresh coppery smell was overpowering, and coupled with the stench from their sweat and the odor of the plants that had been in here, Sindje had to concentrate to keep from gagging.

"Do something." Khase shot her an angry, desperate look. "Please try to do something. Go ahead, use a patch."

"Dead is dead." Sindje scowled at the blood, cringed when she knelt next to Max and got her knees in the pool. "She's not breathing, Khase." Still, she leaned over the ork. "If this was me laying here, and Max looking down, bet she'd be thinking 'where are we gonna drop the body,' and 'one less share to divvy of the nuyen.'"

"We didn't get any drekking nuyen on this run to divvy. Just shut up for once and do something now!" Keeping his hands on the ork's wound, he twisted and picked up the packet with his teeth. "Mmmph pachem."

"Shhh, Khase. I don't need your noise." Sindje curled her mouth into a grimace as she gingerly touched Max's chest, near where her brother was continuing to put pressure on the wound. "Let me see if maybe I can breathe for her. Those patches are dangerous. They go right over the heart and mainline the medicine straight in. I don't like them."

Khase opened his mouth and dropped the packet. "I'd say we're at that last-ditch measure, *chwaer*."

"Shhh!" Sindje closed her eyes and started humming, not because the spell she was casting required the tune, but because it helped shut out the ragged breath of her brother, the muttered curses of the troll and the clanging of garbage cans the Bison continued to bowl over on its frantic course down the alley.

"Khase, how's she doing?" The troll risked a glance over his shoulder, frowning to see all the blood.

"Not now!" Khase drew his lips into a needle-thin line, met Hood's stare and then turned his attention back to Max and Sindje.

Sindje somehow found her magical spark, though it was barely an ember after all the stun balls and bolts she'd cast at the Plantech security force. She felt her heartbeat and focused on it, coaxing it to pump strength into her mana force. Her heartbeat sounded loud in her ears.

"I don't practice this sort of magic. Been so long since

I've used it. Years." She was talking to herself as she continued to ply the mana. "Not sure I remember how. Good at hurting people, though. I'm pretty good at that." She smiled at the thought of taking out more guards than Hood did. Then she frowned. Had she been just a little better at it, or had she used the lethal force she was considering, Max wouldn't be spilling her smelly, slippery ork blood all over the back of the Bison.

It was tradition, touching the person you were attempting to heal. Sindje wasn't sure if it was necessary, but she remembered studying the programs and listening to her teacher from a decade or so back. So she ran her fingers around Max's chest, then up to the ork's face, lingering on the craggy forehead. *Detox.* Now that was a medicinal spell that quick came to mind. She'd used that one on herself and several of her friends numerous times in her school years after their late-night club flings. Accidentally, she started to work the tendrils of the detox spell into Max.

"Idiot! Sloppy." It was nerves, she knew. "Concentrate!" Stabilize, that was the name of the magical spell she needed. Never used it, only practiced it once or twice when she was learning to manipulate the mana under a teacher's petulant gaze. She understood all the principles, though. "Stabilize, Max. Breathe."

The ball of mana she'd formed in her mind was orange, like the smoldering remains of a campfire. It warmed her, and as it grew more potent, it sapped more of what little strength she had left. It wasn't a large ball, and she envisioned cupping it in only one hand. That's what she did now, held her right hand out, letting the ball manifest itself. The fingers of her left hand walked down from Max's face, across her neck and up her chest and over Khase's hands that still applied pressure to the wound.

The pool of blood had grown beneath Sindje, and this surprised her because Khase seemed to have stopped most of the bleeding.

"Bullet went all the way through her," she heard Khase say.

So she was bleeding out the back, too.

Great. "I can't save her." But she tried anyway. Sindje dropped the orange ball of mana, opened her eyes and watched it fall onto Max, its glow fade into her slippery chest. A moment more, and Sindje closed her eyes again and imagined herself following the ball.

There were so many wires inside Max! A cyborg, Hood had called the ork on numerous occasions, and the troll was certainly right. Max had so much hardware and bio-ware laced into her system that she had to have spent weeks recovering from the extensive surgery. All the metal and plastic made it difficult for Sindje to find the ork's real veins and organs, like sifting through a carton of soycereal to get the holo-toy surprise. Still, she persevered and eventually found her way to Max's lungs. That's what the bullet tore through. Sindje hadn't needed her spell to tell her that; it was obvious from the hole in the ork's chest. And the hole was why Max wasn't breathing. The ork's injured lung was filled with blood.

"So much blood, Khase. An ocean of it. She's drowning in it."

Sindje thought she heard her brother say the ocean had spilled into the Bison. It felt that way, as wet as her knees were.

She sent the orange ball of mana into the wounded lung, pushing more and more of her waning energy into it. She gave the ball a greater presence, a palpable thickness and merged it with the tissues of the ork's lungs and filled the holes left by the bullet. It seemed like she spent hours doing this, and in truth Sindje wasn't sure how long the spell was actually taking, as she'd drawn herself completely away from her body now and could no longer feel the jostling of the Bison or hear the Lone Star siren. She was amazed at her own ability to work this spell! Exhaustion crept in, and her vision started to cloud and turn gray at the edges, but she bared her teeth and kept going, sending what little mana she could gather into the hacker.

As she continued the healing, Sindje marveled at the threadlike wires that ran in the lower part of the ork's lungs and wondered what use they might have. Certainly nothing to aid in Max's visiting the Matrix. Perhaps she'd ask just what all of this implanted tech did—if both of them got through this. Sindje focused on all the blood in the lung, pushing it out to make room for air and sensing that Max had started to cough. To breathe! The elf was so excited she nearly lost the spell, and it took all her mental prowess to draw herself back to the task. Max might be breathing again, but she was still critically damaged goods that had poured out an ocean of blood.

"Too much blood."

Sindje's magic couldn't replace the blood loss, which would be a problem all its own soon, but it could cut the pain Max felt, which she imagined was considerable. So at least she could ease Max's suffering. She directed the mana to cocoon the damaged lung, then to pull away and to mend the shattered main arteries and start on the holes in the ork's chest and back. She shivered—those Plantech men had been shooting at her, too, and she could have easily shared Max's fate. Then both of them would be dying, as Khase and Hood hadn't the skills to save them.

Khase? She thought he was wounded, too, saw blood running down his arm. *Should've tended to him first. Family, after all. Max will probably die anyway. One fewer share to worry about from that pile of nonexistent nuyen. Should have worried about my brother first.*

"Our debt. Too much debt."

That debt wouldn't be paid off today, that was for certain. If the man they owed the nuyen caught up to them, she and Khase would be as bad off as Max. Or worse.

The ball of mana grew hotter under her direction and became a magical soldering iron that closed first the hole in the ork's chest, then the one in the back. It returned to the lungs, cauterizing the twin spots from the bullet, then went on to repair muscles and tissue threaded with wires, moved past something that might have been some kind of internal generator and headed toward the ork's large heart. The mana cooled now and became soothing, and Sindje's humming grew louder and less dissonant. She urged the ork's heart to beat stronger and to pump the blood faster again. At the same time she worked to further cut the pain, taking some of it into herself and feeling a white-hot burning sensation in her chest. She gasped and redoubled her efforts, not having felt this kind of pain in a long time.

"Oh, for some little white pills right now. That'd set Max and me up."

The light from the orange ball faded, diffusing through the ork's wire-ridden body. Sindje was too weak to keep the magic together anymore. She'd spent her last measure of strength, and she collapsed across the hacker.

24

Roland's eyes fluttered open when he heard the first sound of faint sirens, an alarm clock he couldn't find the shut-off switch for. His mouth tasted of smoke and plastic, and somewhere during the fight he had lost his helmet. He tried to find his subgun while rising to his feet, but his legs refused to obey the insistent commands from his brain. Clawing for his pistol, he drew the Browning Max-Power and cocked it. It was only then that he noticed the sticky threads attached to his arm as he managed to get to his knees.

A thick, gooey puddle surrounded the ground around him for a meter in every direction. Roland tensed his legs and tried to get up. The polymer that glued his legs to the street flexed, but didn't budge.

"Oh, frag." Roland saw a war zone surrounding him. The two-story house was gone, reduced to rubble and charred slabs of broken wall. Several meters away, what little was left of the Mitsubishi Nightsky lay on its side in the street in a charred puddle of rubber from its melted tires, a blackened mess. *Well, scratch one limousine.*

His squad lay in various positions on the lawn, but amazingly, a quick scan with his cybereye revealed that most of them were relatively uninjured. Sure enough, armored men began to stir as whatever effect the mage had put on them began to wear off. A few meters away, Morgan sat up, rubbing his forehead with a dirty hand. A guard he didn't recognize headed toward him. Even K-Tog showed signs of life, the huge troll rising like a mountain in the darkness.

The sirens were getting closer now, the deep howl of local fire departments counterpointing the shrill wail of what might have been either Lone Star or Knight Errant squads, and probably a SWAT unit or three given all the pyrotechnics that had just gone off. *Think, fragit! They're maybe four, five minutes away. We can still get out of here. But we have to move now!* "Morgan, find Lilith and Hiyakawa, make sure they're all right! K-Tog, get your hoop up and get all of our men that you can find into the Typhoons right now! Police the area; we evac in one minute!" He returned his attention to the gelatinous, gray mass that had him firmly imprisoned in its sticky grip.

"Sir, I've located Lilith and Hiyakawa, they're both all right."

"Sir, I have information—"

"Just a moment, Officer—Thaddeus. That's good, can you bring them over here? Perhaps one of them knows how to remove this drek that's all over me." Roland leaned back on his knees and looked up at the guard, who must have been hired just out of the Academy, he couldn't have been a day over twenty-two. "Report!"

"After the mage took down half of Squads Two and Three, we tried to concentrate our fire to keep her head down and unable to cast. However, the troll archer on the roof incapacitated the majority of our forces with some kind of strange incendiary arrows, and others that burst into that stuff"—he waved at the goo enveloping Roland— "I think I might have been the only one conscious when the four of them came out the front door. Typhoon One might have gotten a good shot off them, I think. Anyway, the ork came out screaming something about a bomb, then the troll, then two elves. They headed for the Bison, and I saw my window and took it. I fired, hitting the ork in the back. One of the elves got her into the Bison before I could shoot again, and they took off."

"So they weren't the ones that blew up the house? Stranger and stranger." Shadows fell over him in the flickering firelight from the remains of the derelict house, and Roland looked up to see Lilith, supported by Morgan, with Hiyakawa close behind, the shaman's eyes glittering with anger. "I don't suppose either of you can help me with this, can you?"

The shaman drew himself up to his full one-point-four meter height. "Of course, Ators-san." With a wave of his hand, the gunk fell away from Roland's body, squelching into sticky, rubbery piles on the ground. Not only that, but the soot, dirt, and sweat that covered his jumpsuit also disappeared, leaving the uniform as clean as if it had just been washed. In fact, his body felt the same way, from teeth that now felt clean and shiny to his hands and face, which were scrubbed, all traces of dirt gone.

In moments the cat shaman was immaculate once more, and wearing a different, completely new suit that he had magicked out of his old dirty clothes. The sec chief bowed, following street protocol even as his mind registered the sirens getting much louder. "*Domo arigato,* Hiyakawa-san. Now, if none of you object, we should be leaving the area."

"One more moment, if you please." Hiyakawa summoned another city spirit and whispered instructions to it, then sent it into the wreckage of the house. "Since we are not able to investigate here, I have taken the liberty of sending in someone who can."

"An excellent idea, Hiyakawa-san." Lilith said from the Typhoon's doorway. "Now, those fire engines and cop cars are going to be on top of us any moment now, so—"

"Very well." The shaman stepped inside, once again wrinkling his nose at having to be crammed in with a dozen other sweaty, exhausted men. Roland was the last one in, and he found himself next to K-Tog.

"Morgan, signal the driver of Typhoon Two to head north, and stick to the speed limit. We don't want any more attention then we've already got. We're going south. Please tell me you got the transponder on the Bison?"

"That's affirmative."

"That's my boy. You get to keep your job for the next week. Let them know they should be able to track our suspects. Lock and load and move to intercept. We will coordinate and serve as backup. Roland out."

He turned back to K-Tog. "Give me the bad news."

The troll shrugged. "Actually, boss, other than the Nightsky, we came out pretty primo. Three of the guys have flesh wounds from the house exploding, and Sleath and Hannigan ended up stuck together when one of those gooey arrows landed between them, but there were no serious injuries."

"So you're telling me these guys fought us to a standstill, but didn't take out a single one of my men?"

"That's right, sir."

That's twice now they could have geeked my men, but they didn't. Roland shook his head and connected to Morgan again. "You got a signal for us?"

"They are heading south toward the Queen Anne district."

"Once we're out of Ballard, step on it." *They haven't gotten away yet,* Roland thought, his fingers curled around the butt of his pistol as he imagined taking a bead on the huge troll's face. *And they aren't going to, either, not if I have anything to say about it.*

25

"Max is breathing, Hood!"

Khase slid to his sister, his skinsuit's legs slick with blood. He pulled Sindje back and stretched her out next to Max, noting that both women breathed in unison now.

"M'all right, *brawd*." Sindje's eyes fluttered open and she offered Khase a weak smile. "Gotta take a little nap, 'kay? Get Hood to drive slower so I can sleep. No more potholes. My best magic ever and I'm not going to be awake to catch yours and Hood's praises." She didn't wait for a response, just let out a deep sigh and matched Max's breathing again.

"So Max is going to make it?" Hood's voice came from the front again.

Khase shrugged. "Lots of blood, Hood. Don't know. But she's not dead yet. Breathing good, looks like. Sindje will be fine, too, by the way."

"How're you?"

"Shot." Khase looked at his arm, then tore his sleeve off and began wrapping it. "I'll take care of it proper when we stop."

"I could call a DocWagon."

Khase offered the back of Hood's head a glare. "You and I both know that's simply a great idea. Doc gets me, traces my picture and I'm away for a long time."

"Just offering." The troll swung the Bison hard left. "The Plantech guards . . ."

"The guys in the backyard weren't Plantech."

"I know. I saw the ponytail."

"And they were talking about their boss. Didn't sound like they were working for a corp."

"So who were they working for, neh?"

Khase didn't answer, his ears picking up the growl of engines instead. He rose on his knees and looked out the back window. "Hood, we've got . . ."

"Yeah, I know. Company."

"Another Plantech van, one of them pretty Typhoons. Should've taken out all their rides. Shouldn't have left them one."

"Twenty-twenty."

"Huh?"

"Hindsight, Khase. It's twenty-twenty." In the rearview mirror Hood saw Khase cock his head. "An old, old expression. Perfect vision."

"Should've taken out all their rides the first time. That would've been perfect." Khase gripped the door handles when Hood sped around a corner and jumped the curb. "Easy, think about Max and Sindje!"

"I am thinking about them." The troll let out a long growl. "I'm thinking that if we don't lose those security goons, Max, Sindje, you and I will be spending a long stretch of time in a small cell."

"A very, very long stretch of time for me, *tad*," Khase said so softly the troll couldn't hear.

The Bison jumped another curb, the fender brushed a street sign, and Hood growled again. "Should've rented a van and ruined someone else's machine."

Khase checked on his sister. "Hey, Hood, you got a blanket or something in here?"

"Lower cabinet, to your right."

The elf found a neatly folded coverlet, which he stuffed under Sindje's head. Then he returned his attention to the back window. "I could use my whip again, like this morning."

Hood shook his head. "Let me try to lose 'em this way. Don't need anyone . . . anyone else . . . getting hurt."

Khase shrugged. "As you wish." Still, he made sure his monofilament whip was ready and eyed the side window; it was plenty wide enough for him to climb out. Hood may have wanted no one else hurt, but the firefight and fiasco at the house, not to mention Max getting shot, had turned Khase into a realist. *If the choice is between them and us, I'm choosing us.* He looked back at the troll. "Speaking of hurt, Sindje said there was a dead body upstairs. You get a look at it?"

"Yeah. Didn't recognize him. Memorized the face, though. When Max comes to I'll give her a description and she can go snooping to get an ID."

"*If* Max comes through."

"*When.*" The troll's voice was firm.

"Fine. When Max comes to she'll get you an ID."

"And then we can figure out who'd try to pin a murder on us."

Khase turned away from the window. "Excuse me?"

"I figure there's a good chance whoever geeked the guy will try to blame us. The question is who is the guy? And what did we do to stir someone up?"

"We stole houseplants, Hood. Drekkin' houseplants. We made the creator of Miracle-Gro tremble in his grave."

"Hang on!" The Bison shimmied and leapt forward as Hood gunned the engine, his huge hand slamming down on the horn. Khase looked up to see a massive Conestoga Trailblazer semitractor entering the intersection ahead of them, hauling three long cargo trailers. The gap between the Bison and the freight truck dwindled.

Their stoplight at the intersection was blood red. *Perfect,* Khase thought, throwing himself across the ork and his sister. *I can't watch.*

The Bison slewed to the left, then heeled over hard right as Hood fought the RV's inertia, wrestling the shuddering steering wheel with every muscle he possessed. The heavy-duty runflats howled in protest, and Khase felt the vehicle start to tip over onto its three left wheels.

"Khase, ballast!" Hood shouted.

"Sorry, *chwaer.*" The adept grabbed his sleeping sister and hauled her over to the right side of the RV. *Frag, I hope this is enough to do it,* he thought, throwing himself against the wall as hard as he could. The Bison groaned as it absorbed stresses above even what its rugged frame was built to handle, and for a moment it was touch and go as the RV balanced on its wheels for another second. Then Hood, with one hand still on the wheel, scrambled over to the cockpit passenger's seat, his several hundred kilos making all the difference.

With a thunderous crash, the Bison came back down on all six wheels, the front undercarriage shrieking as it slammed into the pavement. Khase took a moment away from thanking the capricious gods of luck, fate, the universe and anything else he could think of to peek out the rearview window.

The Conestoga's driver had hit his brakes the moment he saw the Bison barreling toward him, but the thirty tons of whatever he was hauling hadn't stopped quickly. The tractor-trailer caravan had squealed to a halt right in the middle of the intersection, completely blocking the cross-street traffic in both directions. He heard an angry horn blast from the other side, followed by furious shouting.

Khase's mouth dropped open in astonishment. *He did it. If I hadn't seen it, I wouldn't have believed it, but the son-of-a-slitch did it!* What came out of his mouth, however, was much more restrained. "Nice driving, *tad*."

The troll found a side street and slipped down it. Five more turns and three klicks later, Hood doubled back into the neighborhood and headed down another alley, and then another. One more cross-street, one more alley, and he pulled in next to a big garage shaded by a massive maple. The rest of the block consisted of light industrial buildings, small manufacturing shops and storage warehouses, every onc lockcd up for the night.

"Lost them." Khase's shoulders relaxed. He knelt next to Sindje and smoothed the tangled hair away from her face. "Didn't know she was so powerful, Hood. I mean, the magic is strong in our family—my *chwaer* and I are two of the most powerful—but I had no idea she could do that kind of magic. Very powerful."

"How's Max?"

"Still breathing. Needs a hospital, though."

Hood shook his head. "Can't take her to a hospital. She's got a warrant on her; ripped off a corp a few years back to finance a Beetle habit. She was crashing, got careless, and the security cameras got a good look at her. That was down in Portland, and she moved here 'cause the shadows are thicker."

"So, that was Portland. She needs a hospital."

"And you could use a DocWagon, or maybe a hospital yourself."

Khase shut up and adjusted the makeshift pillow under Sindje's head. "I'll be fine, just need a few hours to hole up. Besides, after what Sindje did for Max, my arm should be *plentyn*'s play."

Hood shut off the engine, rolled down the window, leaned his head out and took a deep breath of air. There was a Lone Star siren off in the distance, but it was muted, at least a klick away. A barking dog was closer, and also nearby came the sounds of a band tuning up and then breaking into a number. They weren't parked too far from that stage they'd seen earlier.

Neither talked for several minutes. They listened to the neighborhood and watched for the Plantech Typhoons or any sign of Lone Star. The band finished a lengthy medley, and applause erupted, muted because of the distance and the garage. They delivered a few jokes about Norwegians and drifted into a classic ballad. After a pause, the lead singer started another tune with an a capella intro.

"Sounds like their festival is going well." Hood tried to recall the name of the tune the singer was belting, something popular about love and loss from a few years back. "Wonder what they're celebrating?"

"Wonder what's so special about those plants that people are willing to kill for them?" Khase helped Sindje to sit up. She was coming to and had her hand on her forehead, inadvertently smearing it with blood.

"Migraine city. Hood knows, don't you? What's so special about the plants. Arrgh, it feels like an earth elemental tap-danced on my skull, then sat on me." Sindje leaned over Max. "My patient's still with us. I was pretty amazing there, wasn't I?"

Khase nodded, pride evident in his voice. "Yes, you were." A pause: "Do you, Hood? Know what's special about the plants?"

The troll let out a great sigh that steamed the front window. "They're laced with some sort of bioware. That's all I know for sure. Don't know what it's made of, or what it's for. Haven't had time to puzzle that out."

"But you'll have time now, won't you?" Khase helped

Sindje to her knees, then opened the rear door and lifted her out. "I want you sitting up front."

The elf tried to wipe the blood off her skinsuit, and only succeeded in smearing it around. "Fine." She got in next to Hood. "So fraggin' tired." She tried to brush off her brother as he buckled her in, but to no avail.

"Yes, I'll have some time." Hood answered Khase's question. "Good thing we didn't bring the plants with us, though."

Khase nodded. "Yeah, *tad*. Good thing you stashed them, just in case. We going back to get them?"

"Right now."

Khase jumped back into the van, taking a vigil next to Max. Hood started the engine and eased back into the alley, driving slow toward the far intersection and away from the heart of the festival.

"Hood . . ." Sindje put a hand on the troll's shoulder, startling him. "Max needs a hospital."

The troll and Khase exchanged glances. "She can't— she'll be busted once they get a look at her." He filled Sindje in on how Max had come to be in Seattle.

"That can't be helped right now," Sindje said, a trace of her steel reasserting itself. "There's no time to find a street-doc, and she is going to die if she doesn't get help. She won't rat us out, I'm sure of it."

Khase came up behind them. "It's the only way, *tad,* we all know it."

Hood opened his mouth as if to argue, then saw the looks on the two elves' faces, and nodded. "All right. There's one on the way to where we're going. We'll drop her off there. At the very least I'll see what I can do to get her a good lawyer."

They'd cleared three intersections and were heading back toward the bay when the Plantech Typhoon and a single Lone Star squad spotted them at the same time.

26

"Drek." The word came out in unison from Sindje and Hood.

"Floor it!" Khase scrambled out the side window, monofilament whip free, his other hand anchored to what passed for a luggage rack. A moment later he stood on the Bison's roof, legs bent to keep his balance, as Hood sped down the residential street.

"No geeking!"

"No kidding, Hood! Just get us away from this stuff!"

"Can't kill a Lone Star," the troll growled to Sindje, "or one of those security guards. Then we'll be in shoulder-deep drek with no prayer of getting out. Nothing would make us Seattle's Most Wanted faster than killing a rent-a-cop."

Sindje's voice was as dry as the desert. "Gee, *tad,* thanks for the shadowrunning lesson, I had no idea it could be so dangerous."

They cleared the south end of Ballard and were streaking down the main road parallel to the ocean. It was risky, fleeing in the open like this, with the chance more Lone Stars could join the chase, or even worse, call some backup rotorcraft into the fray. If that happened, Hood knew he might as well plow the Bison straight into Elliot Bay and have them all swim for it. But then Max wouldn't make it for sure. With the workday over, traffic was thin going into the heart of the city and the Bison had plenty of room to swerve around the few cars it came up on.

"This is a drekload of work, Hood, for no nuyen so far." Sindje's face was a mask of fury. She thumbed the button to take down her window, unhooked her safety belt and leaned out as far as her waist. Then she searched for her inner spark, a daunting task given all the mana she'd already expended today, her features contorting with the effort. "Nothing there! I've no magic!"

"Fortunately you've still got me, *chwaer*." On the roof of the Bison, Khase lashed out with his whip, catching the front bumper of the Plantech Typhoon and slicing the chrome in two. Sparks flew across the road as the split bumper fell, and the van ran over a piece. Khase lashed out with the whip again, cutting the grill in half and tearing it away, adding more sparks on the road. The Typhoon pulled back, and the side door opened, revealing the huge troll K-Tog leaning out, a shotgun every bit as big as he was in his hands.

"Hood, incoming!" Khase tensed, unsure if the guard would try to nail him or the RV. *Just my luck, he'll go for both.*

Hood increased the speed, reaching under the dash and flipping a switch. The engine whined, revving hotter now, and he put a little more distance between the Typhoon and the Bison.

"Wiz ride indeed," Sindje said. She was still hanging out the window, she and her brother drawing the attention of motorists as the Bison sped by. She gripped the edge, so tight her fingers turned bone white, and she squinted when strands of her hair whipped in her face and stung her eyes. "Let's see if I can find juice to take care of their tires."

"Don't push it, *chwaer*," Khase's voice came from up top.

"You worry about your own pretty head, *brawd*, and let me worry about mine." Somehow, Sindje found a shred of mana lurking, and stoked it with the full measure of her concentration. As she reached deeper and deeper into the magic inside her, she became oblivious to the traffic and the speed, to the sirens—three Lone Star cars trailing them now, the horrid salt air with its dead fish smell and the slashing hums of her brother's whip. She saw only the ball of energy, and she pictured it streaking toward the Plantech Typhoon.

The energy formed at a spot between her eyes and struck out like a bolt of lightning to the front left tires. Though they were run-flats, she shredded them in a heartbeat, the Typhoon swerving over the median as the rim screamed against the road, sending the troll tumbling back inside the cargo area. It stopped in a lane of oncoming traffic, flashers going to alert other motorists. The pack of Lone Star squad cars swerved around the accident in progress and kept coming, their lights and sirens flashing off the scraped and dented Bison.

"Am I something, or am I something!" Sindje beamed and looked to the lead Lone Star vehicle. "If Max were up she could tap into the engines or something." She plopped back into the seat and clicked her safety belt around her waist. "My battery's burned out. Sorry."

Hood didn't offer a reply, all his concentration focused on putting more distance between the Bison and the rent-a-cops. The sun was dipping toward the horizon, but it would be at least an hour before it set. And the shadows wouldn't grow thick until some time afterward. Hood wanted the shadows so they could hide and think.

"Who was the dead man, Sindje? Got a clue?"

She shrugged. "Didn't get a look at his face. Wasn't the Johnson. I figured it would have been. Just one more thing going wrong with this caper."

"I think he worked for Plantech." Hood had decided that upstairs in the house, the dirt and the green fingers being a giveaway. "Why would he be at the house? Was he behind our Mr. Johnson?"

She shrugged again. "I'm more interested in how you're going to lose the Stars, *tad*. Yeah, you've got a lead, but I'm sure they've called ahead and have some more cars waiting for us."

Hood slammed his open hand against the steering wheel, bending it. "Of course they do." A glance in the rearview mirror, and a look to the oncoming lanes on the other side of the median. "Khase! Hold tight!" Then Hood punched another button under the dash and the Bison growled like an angry beast and lunged forward. He turned the wheel hard left, jumping the median and scraping the undercarriage and throwing the Bison on its three left wheels again. It hung poised for only a moment this time, then dropped down with a crunch and he sped across three lanes, whipping the wheel back and forth to avoid the stream of cars and vans coming straight at him. He cut east, taking a main street then swerving into the first alley he came to.

"You're getting pretty good at taking out trash cans, Hood." Sindje looked over her shoulder and winked at Khase, who had climbed back inside.

"Hood! This jostling can't be good for Max." Khase knelt next to the ork again and was stuffing the bloodied blanket under her head. "Take some care, willya!"

Hood's growl matched the noise the engine was making. The Bison roared through the alley and turned left at the next street, cruising past a row of trendy boutiques and a posh hotel. The sun's rays struck the shop windows, making fun-house mirror reflections of all the vehicles going by.

Sindje frowned. "Where are you going?"

"Frag!" Hood slammed on the brakes and hung another left. He lost the car that was tailing them, but he picked up two more Lone Stars, a traditional Ford Americar with a dwarf driving, and a van with a spread of lights on the roof.

Khase let out a breath he'd been holding and climbed out the window again. He was a little slower this time, the ache in his arm a dull, persistent throb that was finally getting to him. Once more riding the top of the van like he was a surfer in the bay, he balanced himself and cracked his whip.

The businesses they passed were closing down for the evening, save the scattering of restaurants and bars they whizzed by. There were people out on the sidewalks, heading to the nearest light rail stop and to parking lots, most of them pausing to stare at Khase, but only few of them seemed really curious.

"Hood! Look lively!" Khase watched as the van pulled even with the Americar, and as a hatch opened on top. A man's head and shoulders appeared, and he brought a missile launcher with him, steadying it against the roof. "Frag, Hood! Heads up!"

The elf crouched and flicked his whip forward, not quite able to reach the car or the van. That situation was remedied a moment later, as both Lone Star vehicles sped up and the man with the missile launcher took aim.

Khase's left arm cocked back, about to snap his whip toward the rocket launcher. Out of the corner of his eye he saw the officer in the passenger's seat of the American stick his pistol out the window, aim at his head, and fire. Without thought, the adept brought his hand up in front of his face, the bullet smashing into the monofilament whip mount and shattering it into a dozen pieces.

"Kutabare!" But Khase didn't let himself dwell on his lost whip. He took two giant steps and propelled himself off the Bison, hands outstretched and pointed at the missile launcher. His keen eyes saw the man's finger tense on the trigger, and then his own fingers closed on the end of the missile weapon, yanking it out of the man's hands and hurling it away as he came down. Khase landed with a bone-jarring thud next to the hatch, and reached in to pull the Lone Star officer all the way out. He grinned before punching the cop's lights out, turning the man upside down and flinging him back down into the interior of the speeding van. "Hope that didn't hurt too much."

"Sindje!" Hood hollered a second time to pull her attention away from the rearview mirror and her brother. "Take the wheel." The troll reached behind him and grabbed his bow and quiver. Then he squeezed himself out the driver's side window, ripping his clothes, scraping his skin and cursing with each centimeter he gained.

"I don't have a license, Hood."

"Like a legality would stop you. Fragging small window."

"I don't know how to drive this behemoth."

"Gas pedal, steering wheel. Keep it going straight down this street. That's the five second course."

Hood somehow scrambled on top of the Bison, kneeling and reeling as he slung the quiver on his back and tried to take aim at the Lone Star American. He didn't hear Sindje's reply, though he heard the squeal of the Bison's tires as she pushed the pedal down, and he nearly fell off the roof as the RV picked up speed.

"How the frag does Khase do this?" He took a different tactic, lying flat against the roof of the Bison, head and arms dangling over the back. It was awkward, aiming and drawing the bow this way, but he angled it sideways and selected an arrow. He couldn't risk a shot at the van, not with Khase now locked in a struggle with another officer on top of it. So he kept to the Americar, sending a dikoted arrow through the grill and into the engine. He saw a hand with a pistol snake out of the passenger side, and shot an arrow that starred the windshield, making seeing though it impossible. He followed that arrow with a third and a fourth, both aimed at the engine again, and grinned when he saw sparks fly from underneath and the car drop out of gear and begin slowing down.

"Khase! Quit fooling around and get back here!"

The second officer lying unconscious next to him, the elf had pulled a third officer out of the van and briefly struggled with him before head-butting him across the bridge of the nose and dropping him back inside. A fourth officer now leaned out the passenger window and aimed a subgun, while the driver had a Predator IV pointed at Hood.

The troll drew another arrow and let it loose at the man's gun hand. The arrowhead pierced the officer's wrist up to the fletchings, the gun falling from his grasp. The man screamed and the van swerved into an oncoming lane, falling farther behind the Bison.

"Sindje, slow down. We have to get Khase back. Sindje!"

The Bison smashed against three cars parked in a line outside a bar and grille. Hood was nearly thrown from the roof, and as he dug his fingers into the metal his bow clattered onto the street and was run over when Sindje, gears grinding, accidentally threw the Bison into reverse. The RV lumbered across the center lane as she tried to regain control of it. Then it struck the stopped Lone Star van, which had braked to a halt in the middle of the street.

The impact sent Hood sliding off the roof and onto the van, knocking the wind out of him. Dazed, he looked over to see the remaining uninjured officer climbing out the passenger side.

"Lone Star, don't move! Don't give me an excuse, troll. Don't twitch a . . ."

A shadow appeared, and the officer and Hood looked up just as Khase pile-drove both his legs into the officer's back, effectively ending the order and the man's consciousness in one blow. The elf stepped off the cop's motionless body and helped Hood down from the Lone Star van.

"And you," Khase directed this to the officer who'd been driving. The man cupped his wrist, with Hood's arrow still protruding from it. "You don't move from your seat." The elf reached through the window and smashed the communications panel with his fist.

Then he and Hood hobbled to the Bison, the elf climbing into the back, where he could again nursemaid Max. The troll glared at Sindje, who glided into the passenger seat.

"Told you I didn't know how to drive." The elf flipped her hair back as she settled herself.

"Max's still breathing," Khase reported.

"It's a wonder any of us still are." Sindje's sarcasm was left hanging as Hood punched the gas pedal. The Bison didn't budge. He reached beneath the dash and turned a knob, pulled a wire free and thumbed something. The RV grated to life, its engine missing on at least one cylinder, and limped away, accompanied by the distant sound of more sirens. He took the first street to the west, followed it and then went north. The buildings and businesses appeared little different here, though decorations in some of the windows looked exotic, with a definite nature theme; and the holo-images of girls dancing outside the strip clubs were definitely elven.

The Bison died at the far south end of the neighborhood.

"We're on foot from here," Hood announced. He got out of the Bison and gave the tire a solid kick. "RIP, old friend."

"More sirens. Closer now." Khase slid out the back, cradling Max in his arms. Despite his injuries, it didn't look like her weight bothered him.

"Ow. Frag, frag, frag." Max raised her head to complain, then drifted off into the blackness again, her eyes fluttering closed.

"That's the understatement of the year," Sindje said. They hadn't taken more than a dozen steps before she collapsed.

27

Two blocks later the high-pitched whine of cycle engines reverberated off the walls of the alley they had just ducked into.

"Great. Now what?" Sindje's voice carried none of its customary sarcasm, which told just how truly strung out she was. She was cradled in her brother's arms.

Hood was carrying Max. All of their recent exertion, combined with the past twenty hours of no sleep, was starting to wear down even the indefatigable troll, and his steps were plodding rather than quick.

"Looks like a go-gang out for kicks." Khase said, noting the single halogen headlamps that strobed the entrance of the alley. Hood and Khase scanned the length of the narrow lane, but there was no other way out, the path terminating in a solid concrete wall.

"Hoi, chummers, you look lost!" The innocuous comment was followed by laughter and the sound of revving engines. "Maybe we can help you find your way out of here."

"Is that a troll? No wonder they're lost. Fraggin' metas never could read a map!" This ember of wit brought howls of laughter from the group behind the bright lights.

Hood snarled and turned to face them, but was stopped by Khase's nudge. "This one isn't your fight, *tad*. Besides, once I start the distraction, only you can carry my sister *and* Max."

The adept handed off Sindje, who groaned and reached for her brother with trembling hands. Now both she and Max were in Hood's huge arms. "*Brawd . . .* what are you . . . doing?"

Khase kissed her on the forehead. "Just got to take care of some business, *chwaer*. Don't you worry, I'll be right back."

"Don't . . . get . . . killed," the mage mumbled as her head lolled back.

"Not today." He nodded at Hood, his eyes flicking toward a nearby loading ramp and the steel fire escape above the troll's head. "Make sure they get out of here. Get to the roof if you can. I'll catch up sooner than you think."

"Khase—be careful."

"How one can make the enemy arrive of their own accord—offer them advantage. Watch and learn, brother." With that the elf jandered down the alley toward the men clustered at the far end, raising a hand in a casual wave, as if he were greeting a group of friends instead of thrill seekers.

"Hoi, chummers." Khase's shoulders slumped in relaxation as he got closer, his voice carrying back to the troll. "And here I was worried for a second. I thought you guys might have been the Halloweeners, or another gang I'd actually have to worry about."

Hood's jaw dropped at the open insult. *Did he get hit on the head during the chase, knock his brain loose?* Apparently the elf's words were having the same effect on his audience, for only shocked silence greeted him.

Finally, a wiry Japanese with green and black kanji tattooed in vertical rows down his face, revved his bike long and loud, the tires screaming on the pavement. "Brave words from a *baka-gaijin* with no wheels!"

"Well, perhaps you'd let me borrow yours, then?" Khase was the picture of studied innocence, as he clasped his hands behind his back. Hood was so flabbergasted by the elf's performance he almost didn't notice the elf's slim finger jabbing at the air. *Is he flipping me off?* The finger pointed again, and Hood looked up at the fire escape again. *Oh, right!*

"What did you just say?" the gang leader moved his bike closer. "Go on, say that again, you *chikushome.*"

The elf remained unruffled, and put his unwounded arm on the handlebar of the sleek cycle. "I said, maybe you'd let me borrow yours."

Oh drek, I hope he knows what he's doing! Setting Sindje down, Hood hoisted Max over a shoulder, stepped up onto the slanted ramp and grabbed the rusty ladder with one hand, praying the structure would hold both Max's weight and his. The old metal creaked alarmingly, but seemed to be solid. Hood kept an eye on Khase, then he grabbed Sindje, put her over his other shoulder and started to climb, praying all the while to the Green Mother that the bolts would hold.

"Frag, this *baka yaro* got a slottin' death wish!" the leader said. "Okay, *henjin,* you're on. We got ourselves a duel!" The cycles all revved at once, the noise of their engines a howl that shattered the night.

Hood reached the top of the three-story building, and he laid Max and Sindje on the roof, the ork moaning softly as she hit the pebbled surface. He crawled to the edge of the roof and peeked over.

The street was deserted at this time of day, with the families that worked in the sweatshops locked inside, sewing or weaving or performing any of a hundred other chores for their taskmasters—heartless criminals that thought nothing of enslaving their own brethren to accomplish their criminal goals.

The rest of the gang had lined up on one side of the street, their idling bikes in a neat row. The leader had just finished heading down to the end of the street nearest to Hood's vantage point, and did an endo to turn his heavily modified Mitsuhama Blaze around. He twisted the handlebar, revving the engine to the red. His left hand snapped out to his side, and the troll spotted the gleam of stainless-steel triple-spurs flick out of his hand.

I do not like the look of this. Shaking his head, Hood looked down at the other end of the street, already knowing what he was going to see there.

In the middle of the lane stood Khase, beaten and bloody, his left arm hanging loosely at his side. Hood started to rise, unwilling to let the elf get sliced to bits, but as he did so his eyes met the adept's, and he froze.

Khase locked gazes with Hood and ever so slightly shook his head. Then, before the troll could do anything else, he raised his right hand, and made a "bring it on" motion.

The leader was enthusiastic, Hood had to give him that. Screaming like an *oni*, the punk revved his engine in first until the back tire was a blur, lost in a cloud of white smoke. Then he popped the clutch and rocketed forward, lifting the front of the bike in a smooth wheelie as he roared down the street, hand spurs extended, ready to slice and dice right through the elf.

Khase remained motionless, waiting. Not a muscle twitched, the elven adept didn't even blink as the man sped directly toward him. The cycle hit fourth gear, doing at least ninety kilometers an hour. When the cycle was about fifteen meters from Khase, the rider's mouth opened in a silent scream, and the adept burst into action.

Crouching, Khase sprang forward, aiming to fly not past the bike, but directly at it. Arms locked in front of him, the elf jabbed his stiffened fingers into the leader's face, who was gasping in shock as he realized what was about to happen. The blow snapped his head back, and his hand popped loose from the handlebar. The adept's forward motion carried the biker off his ride and into the ground, the elf landing on top of him and skidding to a stop. The modified racing cycle careened out of control down the street, tipping over in spray of sparks as it crashed into a building.

Khase rolled off the bloody, unconscious ganger, bowed to the rest of them, and ran like hell for the alley. There was a moment of shocked silence, then two thugs raced for their leader, and the rest revved up and headed straight for the elf. Khase hit the alley with not a second to spare, arms and legs pumping as he ran up the loading ramp and leapt for the fire escape ladder. The bikers were right behind him, with one of them actually riding his cycle up the ramp and launching himself into the air, hoping to knock the elf off his perch. Khase heard him coming, however, and lashed out with a booted foot, hitting the man's shoulder and sending him flying—but not before his bike smashed into the fire escape framework, snapping bolts and making the whole thing sag a few inches lower.

Khase shot up the stairs. He hit the top, and didn't even have to say a word to Hood, as the troll was already working on levering the fire escape away from the side of the building with a long length of steel pipe he had found on the roof. With a screech of metal and grind of steel on steel, the entire framework peeled away from the building to collapse in the alley, burying the three gangers who weren't lucky enough to get out of the way fast enough.

Khase didn't spare them a second glance, trotting to Sindje and picking her up again. "Let's go." The two leapt over alleys and across the roofs of the close-packed buildings, leaving the cycles howling impotently behind them.

The first thing Sindje became aware of as she returned to consciousness was that she reeked like nothing she had ever smelled before. *Cachu, what is that stench?* Opening her eyes, she looked down and saw that the front of her skinsuit was covered in muck and grime that brought with it the unpleasant odor of—

"Good thing we found that big sewer grate." Khase squatted next to her, holding out a steaming plastic mug of soykaf. "Who'd have thunk that gang would have found us again so quickly? Although I would have thought we'd need to grease Hood's sides to get him through it. Sorry about the mess, by the way. We uh, sort of dropped you on the way down." Khase smelled of gas and exhaust, and his clothes were a little more shredded than she remembered before she had passed out.

Sindje wrapped her hands around the mug and sipped the hot liquid. "What happened to you? Where are we? And where's Max? Is she all right?"

"Well, all right is a sort of optimistic term, but she's still alive, so that's a good thing." Khase shifted his weight and looked over his shoulder at a rough pallet where the hacker lay, breath whistling in and out of her mouth. "Snores like a herd of, well, orks, I guess. We're in the basement of an old church—"

"Khase, slot and run, we gotta move!" Hood's voice carried to them across the room.

"*So ka,* I'm there in a flash. Listen, *chwaer,* we need to go get the rest of the plants, so please keep an eye on Max. We'll be at some place Hood calls the Historic Everett Theatre. We'll be back for the two of you ASAP, okay?"

Still too tired to protest, Sindje nodded. "Be careful out there, *brawd.*"

"Hey, it's me, remember?" The adept stood and stretched, then loped off to join Hood at what looked like a large sewer grate. They slipped through it, then a large arm drew the grate closed, leaving Sindje alone with Max.

The mage took a minute to drain the steaming cup, uncaring about the slight burns she gave herself as she drank, then tossed the cup away. Testing her arms and legs, she thought, *Okay, everything works, now let's put it all together and stand up.* She used the wall for support as she dragged herself to her feet. Swaying a bit, she made her way over to the ork, who was still encased in her decksuit. *Good thing the bullet entered low enough to miss her mainframe, or we'd have one angry ork on our hands when she wakes up.*

Sindje leaned against the wall as she tried to sort out everything that had happened in the past couple of hours. Although she wanted to sit down again, she knew she'd just end up falling asleep. *Think, who's trying to turn all of us into cold hash? And who was that stiff in the house? Did our Johnson slip a shiv in our collective backs? No, that doesn't make any sense. He still has to get the plants; without us, he's got nothing. But how did the Plantech sec find us in the first place? And what the frag is up with those plants anyway? I'm too shagged out to project, but I need a way to find some intel, and my best source is out cold . . . unless. . . .*

Sindje searched deep inside herself and found a flicker of mana glowing there. *I never thought I'd have to use this spell, but here goes.* She coaxed the mana up, whimpering as she broke through a field of strong resistance, and feeling a bit more energy leach from her body. It took longer than she would have liked, but eventually a shimmering golden haze sparkled in front of her eyes, and Sindje took the phosphorescence in her hands and covered Max's face with it. She wished the ork had only stun damage on her, then a stim-patch would have worked. But there was still physical damage to be dealt with.

The effect was immediate, as the ork's eyes snapped open. "Bomb. Big bomb. We gotta move now—"

Sindje clapped her hand over the hacker's mouth. "Ssshh, Max, it's all right, you're safe, we're out of Ballard completely."

"What the frag happened? Did we meet with the Johnson?" The ork tried to rise up off the pallet, only to groan. "Ow, I feel like a truck hit me. Hey, did we get paid?"

"That's our hacker, always a one track mind," Sindje smiled through her pain before turning serious. "Look, I'll have to explain what went down later, 'cause I don't know how long you'll be awake. I need you to hit the matrix and find out if there is anything on the newsgrids about the Ballard explosion and a body they found inside."

"Oh, drek, is the Johnson dead? *Buunda, buunda, buunda*. Did the house blow up?—"

"Max!" the elf's old irritability surfaced again. "I just told you practically everything I know. Now, if you please, sleaze around and see what you can find out, okay?"

"Okay, okay, I'm going, sheesh." The ork looked around. "I hurt all over. I suppose a power source would be too much to ask for."

"Um, look around, and you tell me." Sinjde waved her hand at the rotting boxes and stacked piles of moldy wooden pews. "I'm not sure this place ever moved beyond candlelight. Or the twentieth century, for that matter."

"All right, all right, close your trap, kcebler, I got enough of a headache already." The ork shut her eyes and twitched her fingers. "Great, just great. Let's find a hotspot—ahh, there we go. Hmm, let's see what the screamsheets have to say. This looks interesting—house destroyed in Ballard blaze."

"Skip the newscaster drivel and summarize it, 'kay?" The spell Sindje cast had returned Max to full consciousness, but it wouldn't last very long. She tapped her foot and tried to conceal her impatience.

"Ah, here we go, info on the body. Whoa, what's this? 'The body found in the remains of the house has been identified as Dr. William Nansct, the head scientist for Plantech, one of the leading small-cap agricorps in Snohomish. What the frag was he doing there? He wasn't the Johnson."

"No drek, genius. But he was there for a reason, and since he was dead on the floor before we arrived, I smell a setup." The elf's brow wrinkled in thought. "But by whom?"

"Not much else here, but then—" As quickly as she had come to, Max winked out again, falling back unconscious like someone had flipped a switch on the back of her neck. Sindje wasn't worried, as she knew the hacker had protocols that would jack her out of the matrix if she ever fell unconscious while inside.

Her fatigue forgotten, the elf paced the floor, muttering to herself. "Plantech showing up to recover their own guy? Perhaps, and taking us down for a very long count as well. A sting operation—no, Lone Star hadn't even shown up yet, and beside, the corp sec would want to take care of this internally, so no mess would be made public."

On her next pass across the room, she slapped the wall in frustration. "*Cachu*, I've got more questions than answers here! And where the frag are Hood and my itinerant *brawd* right now?"

28

Dressed up in rose and violet neon and draped in necklaces of golden lights, the Everett neighborhood sprawled its gaudy, noisy self just north of the city's dark heart. It doused itself in the cloying fragrance of Asian cooking spiced with smoke and sweat, and sprinkled its windows with images of coiling, sequined dragons with wide eyes that met the stares of tourists. Neon signs flashed in various languages, but in keeping with tradition, painted caricatures announced the businesses' names and wares in Japanese, Chinese and Korean. The words proclaimed mahjongg parlors, hotels, pleasure houses, restaurants, beauty salons, grocers, biotech dealers, storefront temples, smoking emporiums and more. And they touted fried rice, tattoos, "barely legal" girls, imported art, tealeaf readers, sages, sake, rooms by the hour and all manner of medicinal herbs, legal and otherwise.

Delicate strains of *shakuhachi* music warred with blaring rock music and with sidewalk peddlers barking to passersby—selling food, trinkets and, in some cases, themselves. The occasional blat of a car horn intruded, and beneath that the melodic hiss of the light rail provided the chorus to the overture. The conversations of people walking this chill fall night were a constant buzz, and from open windows old women hurled down curses at the young plying various dubious trades.

Khase and Hood stood beneath the awning of a closed

fishmonger's shop. The lights didn't reach them there, so they could anonymously absorb the night scene. The troll nudged the elf.

"I see him." Khase talked in a whisper, though it was unnecessary.

Across the street a muscular mafia soldier leaned in the doorway of a mah-jongg parlor, scanning the block and looking bored.

"There's another one down the block."

Khase stifled a yawn. "The mafia run this part of the city with a tight fist. You should know that, Hood. The soldiers are pretty good at keeping the peace. I lived here for almost a year when I had a falling out with my family. Easy to lose yourself here . . . if you keep to yourself."

"Like you did with that go-gang?"

"Hey, they wanted to start trouble, and I wanted to finish it. Still, we shouldn't hang around here any longer than necessary, you dig, *tad*? The problem with these folks is that they have long memories."

Most of the residents in this particular neighborhood were from China, Korea, Japan and Southeast Asia. And though there was a scattering of elves and dwarfs on the street, the vast majority of the populace was human.

"Like your folks? I thought you had patched things up with your family."

"And I went home again for a time."

"Then Sindje and you moved out together."

"Yeah. A year or so later, when our parents went to Denver. We decided to stay in Seattle and pursue . . . various contracts."

"How are they, your parents?"

Khase shrugged. "All right, I suppose." He studied the tips of his boots. "The mafia shouldn't bother us."

Hood nodded. "They could care less about plants."

"Not about the kinds of plants we have anyway."

Still, they waited until the soldier went inside the mah-jongg parlor, and the other one down the street moved on. Then they waited a few more minutes before strolling toward a large movie theater. It was incongruous to most of the businesses in the block, which had renovated their storefronts to keep pace with the times. The theater looked like an antique, with the original brickwork and trim dating back to the early 1950s—so read a historical marker bolted near the cornerstone. It was called the Historic Everett Theatre, and even the neon lights displaying the name were original.

Posters behind bulletproof glass announced an upcoming martial arts marathon of films from the previous century . . . though now in trideo format. An elderly Japanese woman sat inside a ticket counter, stoically regarding Hood and Khase. The troll gave her a wink and ushered Khase inside.

The elf had seen the place only from the outside when Hood dropped the plants there this afternoon before they headed to the ill-fated meeting in Ballard. He didn't bother to hide his amazement at the lobby. Care, along with considerable nuyen, had gone into restoring and maintaining the old theater. A candy counter had been meticulously rebuilt to its original condition, a black and white photograph of which hung on the wall. An antique popcorn popper was hard at work, scenting the air with a pleasant buttery aroma. Another elderly Asian woman stood behind the counter, scooping popcorn into cartons and selling them to four teenagers, who quickly shuffled into the auditorium.

Columns rose in the center of the lobby, looking like something Khase remembered on Greek history trivids; along their tops cherubic faces gleamed down from between security cameras. The carpet was thick and dark to help hide the dirt tracked in by the patrons. The edges were frayed, and the wood floor that poked through between the carpet and the wall looked . . . old. Posters of movies from a hundred years past ringed the room, with placards below them giving a brief history of the films and principal actors. Sonny Chiba. Jet Li. Bruce Lee. Chow Yun-Fat. A wide circular marble staircase swept up the side and led to a balcony.

Hood started up the stairs and Khase took another long glance around the room before hurrying to catch up.

"This place is more like a museum than a movie house." Khase saw more posters on the second floor, three of them heavily yellowed and chipped and showing various scenes featuring a human in green tights with an English longbow. The elf stepped closer and read the placard. "Errol Flynn in *The Adventures of Robin . . . Hood*." He raised an eyebrow and regarded the troll. "Hood?"

"So I have a thing for old movies. Last time I checked that wasn't a crime." The troll pushed open a door at the end of a hall and started up another flight of stairs, this one narrow and obviously not intended for the public. Hood's broad shoulders rubbed against the walls as he climbed.

"Maybe not legally, but in taste—that's another matter." The elf grinned as he followed the troll up the stairs.

At the top was an equally tight corridor, the paint dingy and chipped, the carpet so worn through the burlap nap showed. The hall was dimly lit by exposed light bulbs that hung from century-old fixtures. Two doors bisected it, the first leading to a projection booth that was in the midst of being restored.

"Pan." Hood opened the door and spoke softly. "I've come for those plants."

"Ah, Hood-san. *Kochi koi-yo!*" An old Japanese man, looking similar to the woman behind the candy counter, stood and beamed at the troll. *"Kochi koi-yo!"*

Hood complied and walked close, and the old man affectionately wrapped both hands around the troll's forearm. "I was not here this afternoon. I was at the station, getting a new shipment of holovids and colorized. . . ."

"It was of no consequence, Pan, I was in and out quickly." Hood turned to Khase. "Pan Geng, this is my . . . associate . . . Khase." A respectful pause. "Khase, this is my friend Pan Geng. He and his wife and his sister run this theater."

Khase bowed deeply, keeping eye contact with Pan. *"Kakkoii,* Pan."

"The plants are up one more flight, Khase. You're welcome to stay here with Pan." Hood gestured to a window that looked out over the auditorium and the screen, where a 3D adventure film was showing. "Watch a bit of the movie while I see to our cargo. I'll be back in a bit." Hood didn't wait for the elf's reply. He left the projection room and creaked his way down the hall.

In his wake, the elf studied the room. A rusted, dented projector sat in the corner. The modern projector consisted of three small computers that sat on a table beneath the window. A shelf full of movie chips and other equipment was against the wall just inside the door.

"Come. Sit?" The old man motioned for him to come inside.

Khase bowed again. *"Domo arigato gozaimasu."*

"You are friends with Hood-san? A long time?"

Khase shook his head on both counts. "We work together, is all." He let a few beats pass. "You work for him, don't you, Pan-san?" The elf's intuition was buzzing, and he decided to see where it led him.

The old man smiled warmly, numerous wrinkles crinkling at the corners of his gray eyes. "Hood-san says it is my fault he likes old movies. I introduced him to an ancient series of movies of old England. Robin Hood. And then I made him watch the films of Lee and Li."

"Do you own this theater, Pan-san? Or does it belong to Hood?"

The old man pointed at the window. "A new movie is just starting. This one should particularly interest you. The original came out in the 1970s, I believe, and it was derived from a stage play. Humans put grease in their hair back then, to get it to lie flat—hence the name of the film. But it was redone about twenty years back as an elven musical. This is the most recent film we've shown here in some time. We tend to like the older pieces."

Khase stared in disbelief as a male elf decked out in tight, black leather pants and a matching leather jacket floated above a sparse audience and crooned to a female elf wearing a short shimmering pink dress who swooned to his every word. *Whoa, I can't believe I'm related to the folks who made this travesty.*

Hood checked the thermostat at the top of the stairs, making sure the heat was high enough to keep the top floor hot. The plants were arranged on battered card tables that sat beneath a large skylight. He flicked on an antiquated switch, and a light overhead flickered a bit before staying on. The room was too large for it, and so the shadows stayed thick around the walls. The troll liked it that way.

He carried a large stool over to the closest table and sat.

"Khase can cool his elven heels for a few minutes." He brought his head down to the purple-green plant that had fascinated him in the apartment. "Cruel what they did to you." He reverently touched the hairs on one of the larger leaves. "Why can't they leave things be? God never intended people or plants to be filled with chips and wires."

Still, Hood wondered; if he had a few chips and programs floating around inside him, could he study these plants better? Could cybereyes see things that much clearer than his normal eyes? Could a computer-assisted brain fathom their function more readily?

He slammed a fist on the table and upset a few of the plants. Cursing, he righted them, carefully checking to make sure none of the leaves or stems were bruised.

"My hands, my brain, my ability." It was a mantra to him. "I can think this out on my own." His tongue was between his teeth in concentration. "Why would anyone graft bioware onto a plant? For what purpose? It's not natural. Not right." He noted again, on the purple-green plant and on six others that the graft had to be done when the plants were seedlings and that the tech grew with the plants. "Ahhhhhhhhhhh. So that's it."

He hunched his shoulders as he leaned in closer, his chin brushing the top of the one that resembled a golden pothos.

"Clever indeed. Microphones."

Four of the thickest, largest leaves were indeed microphones, apparently omnidirectional, and the seedpods served as a kind of recording sensor that could be harvested.

He rose and stretched, unsuccessfully fighting a yawn. "How many hours have I been up? Too many." He shook his head, then strolled to the west wall, where the shadows were the darkest. A large cot was made up with military precision, tempting him for just a second. On one side of it was an old wardrobe, on the other a shelf stacked with small bins. Hood shrugged out of his shredded blazer. The shirt and pants quickly followed. He wanted a shower; he hated feeling dirty. But he didn't want to take the time. He retrieved a dark green pair of trousers from the wardrobe and selected a heavy charcoal gray shirt. Then he pulled one of the bins down from the shelf and went back to the plants.

"It's only you six." He spoke to the plants with the bioware as if they understood him, and who knew, maybe they did. "You're the ones the Johnson really wanted. The rest were cover, a ruse to hide the real target."

He selected a few tools from the bin, picks so slender it

was difficult for his thick fingers to manipulate them. But he persisted, and after several minutes he managed to dissect one of the seedpods.

Inside was an odd-looking bioware chip.

"Could be slotted into a computer for downloading. Could be. Could be." Hood scratched his head. "But downloading what?"

29

6:58:10 P.M.

Belver Serra stood at her living room window, staring across the street and down at a sprawling department store. The front of the old building was lit by the dull olive glow of security lights, which made the A-line dresses behind the glass look eerie and more abysmal than they probably were. Some distance beyond that, when she pressed her face close to the glass and looked between a gap in the skyscrapers to the northwest, she could see the night-black water of the bay. A full moon hung low in the cloudless sky and reflected on the chop. The tankers that she could see were indistinct, slashes of charcoal on a gray canvas drawn by an artist of no great skill. Her lip curled up in a distasteful sneer. Belver didn't mind an ocean vista—in fact, she wanted a better one. And if there was to be a store across the street, let it be a chic, upscale boutique, not a bargain-basement agora that catered to the masses.

Her apartment was a reasonably posh place by most standards, taking up a good portion of the building's seventh floor. It was more than she could comfortably afford on her salary, but less space than she desired and certainly not in a location that she coveted. Someday she would own an entire floor of one of the ultra-pricey condos in some enclave—perhaps the top floor with wraparound balconies encircling the perimeter. She had brochures listing such properties, and in rare moments daydreamed of what it would be like to live there. Until then, this place would have to suffice.

But soon things would be getting much better.

"Very soon," she purred.

She couldn't hear the traffic below, or her neighbors; the walls, floor, ceiling and windows were soundproofed. But the fact that there was this amount of traffic in her neighborhood at this time of night, and the fact that someone lived in an apartment on the other side of her bedroom wall terribly irked her. Belver shuddered and turned away from her far-from-perfect view.

"Dear heart, join me?" The speaker was human, a little more than half her age and not quite as handsome as she preferred them. He'd arranged his lanky frame in the center of her couch, no doubt thinking she would be forced to sit next to him.

As she silently regarded him, he opened a bottle of wine and poured two glasses. He was too young and inexperienced to let it breathe first, or to even pretend to sniff at the cork or taste it for her. But he was useful for—other things. She offered him a coy smile and slipped toward him, the toes of her bare feet sinking into an ivory-colored carpet that wasn't quite thick enough. He thought he was taking a shortcut to climbing the corporate ladder by creeping his way into her bed and her confidence. But he was just a tool, to be used and discarded at her whim. So far, he had proven up to the task, but if things kept going awry, he would also be her fall guy, too. Still, he had a ruthless streak she admired. *Maybe we will continue this relationship if this current mess pans out.*

"It's an Aussie Merlot, Bel. I saw it in the window of the shop on the corner. It was expensive, but I couldn't resist." He extended a glass to her.

She took it and held her nose over the rim and raised a laser-trimmed, pencil-thin eyebrow, surprised that it had an acceptable bouquet. "From—"

He looked at the bottle. "Nowhere truly exotic, dear heart. Canberra, Nicholson Wineries."

She sat next to him so their legs lightly touched, exulting in the thrill that ran through him.

"I thought the wine might help your mood. You said you had an early dinner with your father."

She furrowed her brow at the comment, thin nettled lines hinting at both her years and his constant annoyance.

"And before that things didn't go well in Ballard, I realize. A bad day, dear heart."

Belver stiffened and took a deep swallow of the wine. "The runners I hired . . ."

He drew his face in close, encouraging her to continue.

"The runners were at the same time too good, and not good enough." She quickly finished the glass and let him refill it. The wine settled strongly on her tongue and had a slightly woody flavor. Whatever the year, it wasn't the best one. But it was drinkable; at least he had gotten that right. "I told you I hired them to break into Plantech and steal all manner of things from the greenhouse. I gave them quite the list, wasn't even sure the greenhouse had some of the things I named."

"A ruse."

Yes, not completely obtuse. "Of course it was a ruse. Oh, I wanted plants, but only six of them."

"And they got those, I trust?"

"From what I understand they got everything on my list."

"But they didn't bring plants to the house in Ballard. I was watching from a neighbor's yard."

She wetted her index finger and ran it around the lip of the glass. It gave off a faint humming sound, showing the goblet was lead crystal. But not a top brand, not Baccarat. She couldn't afford that yet. "If I'd only listed those six plants I wanted—instead of giving them a shopping list so long they could scarcely fit everything in their van—they might have gotten overly suspicious."

"And you couldn't have that, Bel."

"Suspicious enough that they might have inspected them, learned they weren't just . . . plants. That they were unique, the only specimens of their kind in this world." She set the glass down on the coffee table and dug her fingers into her knees.

"But what's so special about a half-dozen plants?"

She edged away from him, turned and drew her right leg up under her, catlike in the slinky way she moved. She reached for the glass again and took only a sip this time.

"Unique in all the world, and only in that greenhouse—where Plantech conducted its most clandestine meetings."

It was his turn to raise an eyebrow.

"You see, pet, the Plantech board of directors, and the officials from whatever other corps they were meeting with, believed their conversations were safe in that greenhouse. Plantech designed the greenhouse so there wasn't a single piece of surveillance equipment inside; no little spy-eyes, nothing to record their precious secret words. Protected from the outside as well, no laser-reading of conversations there, everything scrambled once it hit the glass. A safe house of sorts."

She lapsed into silence for a few moments, sipping some more of the wine. Her shoulders rounded slightly.

"Granted that you're powerful, Bel, and that you've fingers in lots of interesting pies. But if these plants are so . . . unique . . . how did even you find out about them?"

Belver drained the second glass in one long, unladylike pull. "I was in one of those 'clandestine meetings.' And a few days after that meeting, a Plantech biologist contacted me. Yes, I'm powerful enough to have caught his attention. He tried to blackmail me."

The young man poured her another glass and added a little more to his. "This would be the biologist we took care of in Ballard this afternoon? He tried to blackmail you?"

Belver shook her head. *If I didn't know better, I'd think he was wired.* "What do you think? He'd developed the six specimens in the Plantech labs, under the noses of the corp execs and his fellow biologists, grafting bioware into the seedlings and growing microphone pods. He was secretly recording the meetings held in the greenhouse, and he intended to sell the transcriptions and files to the highest bidder. He was looking for a lot of nuyen for those recordings." She let out a deep sigh. "Doesn't everyone in the world need more nuyen? In any event, I let him think I'd meet any price he asked."

"That important, eh?"

Another nod. "I couldn't let the transcripts get out. I couldn't let my present employer discover I was working against his corp's best interests. As I said, I was . . . in a meeting in the Plantech greenhouse . . . I was negotiating to turn over some of my corp's proprietary information to Plantech or Shiawase . . . whichever would pay more. And I was working to negotiate a much more lucrative position with whichever one of those corps would hopefully be my new employer."

The young man gave a low whistle. "You would've been meat if those transcripts got out. But why have me geek the biologist?"

"No loose ends, pet. You know I don't like loose ends. The biologist—Dr. Nansct—was a greedy man. The nuyen we settled on for the transcripts *and* the plants, and which I truthfully had no intention of paying him, apparently wasn't going to be enough. The greedy, greedy fool. He was going to sell me the transcripts all right, but at the last minute he changed his mind and decided not to part with the plants. He was going to tell his boss at Plantech about his creations, reveal them at a board of directors meeting, gave me some line about being able to save the company. Scrounging up a last vestige of corporate pride, I guess. He wanted nuyen both from me—and from them. No doubt he was angling for a promotion of some sort, too. And now he has nothing, not even his pitiful life, and his family probably doesn't have enough of him to bury after that fiasco."

"It was quite a painful death, Bel. Find some solace in that."

"The runners were to find Nansct's body at the house in Ballard, which they did." Her voice dripped bitterness. "And they were to be framed for the murder."

"Which they weren't."

She shook her head, her eyes daggers pointed down her nose. "Oh, you did your part, Pet. But others failed me."

He leaned closer still and tenderly brushed his fingertips against her cheek. "Tell me the rest, dear heart. You promised to reveal it all. Let's have no secrets between us."

I know what I told you, but that doesn't mean it's the truth, my pet. Still, what would it hurt? The evidence linking him to the Ballard affair was ready to be planted, and the more information she gave him, the deeper the hole he'd dig should all of this ever come to light. "I'd hired three men to keep the runners in the house until my Lone Star puppet arrived. The runners were supposed to be caught red-handed, charged with Nansct's murder and put away for a very, very long time. The loose ends all neatly tied up."

"But what about the plants?" The man seemed truly curious and concerned.

"Oh, I knew the runners wouldn't bring the plants to the drop. At least not all of the plants. Nor would they talk about the heist to Lone Star . . . why tack more years on to their sentence?"

"So how were you going to get the plants?" He shook his head as if to correct himself. "How *are* you going to get them?"

"I had every confidence that my Lone Star puppet would winnow the location from the runners and recover them for me. What I didn't count on was a sec team from Plantech showing up and turning the entire plan into a steaming pile of drek."

The man swished the wine around in his glass and took a swallow. "Which is why, Bel, when I saw the Plantech squad swarm the house, I hit the remote timer on the bomb. You told me if anything went wrong . . ."

". . . to blow it all to hell. Like I said, you performed your part admirably, Pet. Would that I had a few others like you, there would be no limit to what we could accomplish."

He swelled at the accolades she tossed his way. *Men, so easily brought under sway for a bit of flattery*. This one was no different. *No, I'll continue with my original plan.* She stood and rolled her shoulders, finished the contents of her glass and took it to the kitchen, removing the temptation to have anymore at the moment. "As I said, you did your part, Pet. The rest couldn't be helped."

"I just wish things would have went well all the way around."

Belver returned to the living room with a plate of beluga caviar, a spoon and a stack of petite crackers on a Brazilian hardwood tray. She set it on the coffee table, directly in front of her.

"I don't like loose ends, pet."

He eyed the plate, but did not make a move to take any. "I tied up three more of those loose ends for you before I came over, dear heart."

"The brothers?"

"They let me in their hovel, thought I was settling up the rest of their payment for the botched Ballard job. They didn't suffer terribly long. Not as long as I would have liked. But I was in a hurry to come here."

Belver smiled, pleased at the news. *Yes, he certainly does do some things right.* "And their uncle?"

"I visited him first, in the hospital. There'll be no questions. It looked natural—poor fella, his heart just—gave out."

"Good." She edged the plate toward him. "Imported and pricey. I'd intended us to celebrate with this—after I'd received the plants. And while I've nothing to celebrate just yet, there's no reason this should go to waste."

He was quick to help himself, and to wash it down with more of the wine. "Delicious. Join me, why don't you?"

"No, you enjoy it, I'm just not in the mood. I don't know where the runners are, pet. Or what they did with my plants." Her fingers were digging into her knees again. "I want those plants. I want to hire my own biologist to create more and more and more. I want to ride that fool's creation to my own corner office at Shiawase, or any other megacorp with the brains to realize what I'm offering them. And to take you with me."

Belver had given the matter considerable thought. She intended to send the enhanced plants to corporate executives throughout the city and lift the pods at her convenience to learn what was transpiring in their offices. Either she'd sell the secrets to the highest bidder, or, in the case of more personal information, blackmail them at her leisure, raking in more nuyen than she could manage to earn with the highest-ranking corp position.

"The plants will be my perfect surveillance system. And with them I can spy on the competition and gain their secrets anytime I desire. The perfect, untraceable crime."

He slipped an arm around her shoulders and tried to move closer. Belver would have nothing of it and got up. She started pacing on the other side of the coffee table, alternately glancing at her manicured toenails and fingernails and at the young man. She watched him eat another cracker smeared with her expensive caviar.

"You understand I'm not in the mood for anything tonight, pet. I'm out of sorts over all of this."

"I understand." He paused and ate still more of the caviar. "Is there anything I can do, Bel?"

She stopped pacing. "Ah, pet, you've already done more than enough. If you don't mind. I need . . . to think. I need to be alone."

One final cracker dripping with caviar and he reluctantly got up from the couch and smoothed his shirt and pants. He reached for a long coat he'd draped over the arm and eased into it, drawing the hood over his head. "You'll call me tomorrow?"

"Of course. In the afternoon, probably late. And perhaps I will have learned something about those runners by then that will put me in a better mood. If so, I may have another task for you."

"And we'll need to do something about those plants."

"I hope so, pet. I hope so."

He was slow to make his way to the door, keeping his eyes on her with each step. "And those runners . . . I'll tie up those loose ends for you when you give the word. When you find out where they are, you let me know."

"You're very good about my loose ends." She kissed him on the cheek and let him out, locking the door afterward. Then she hurried to the window and looked down toward the storefront. A few minutes later the man crossed the street, his cloaked form softly lit by the olive security lights. He glanced up at her window, then headed down the block toward a parking garage. Belver never let him park close enough so the doorman would recognize his car, and he always wore a hood pulled up so no one would get a good look at his face.

Not that it mattered, she knew. She was careful and wouldn't be connected to him. All of her crimes were perfect and untraceable. The poison she'd laced into the caviar was virulent, but slow acting. He'd be halfway across town before he realized what she'd done. And he'd be too far gone at that point to do anything about it.

"I hate loose ends, pet. And you were certainly a loose end."

She closed the drapes and retrieved the dish of caviar, washing it and the rest of the poison down the disposal.

Then Belver took a long shower, hopeful the hot water would wash away some of the day's disappointment and help relax her. She wrapped herself in a thick terry cloth robe, took down another glass and returned to the couch to finish the last of the acceptable Merlot. When she sensed her tongue starting to feel thick from the alcohol, she reached for her commlink. She needed to make the call now before the wine made her too numb.

Frag, got his voice mail. Will have to be careful about this. "Jhones," she began. "Things didn't go at all well this afternoon." Belver continued, concentrating to put an edge to her voice. "I need things to go much better from now on, understand? Get me some results before the sun comes up. Otherwise, you will go the unfortunate way of all the others who've displeased me. Get me what I want, or I'll have your sorry hide."

30

"Come on, answer. These corp Johnsons are practically chained to their desks. Where the frag is he?"

"Hey, calm down, you don't want to reinjure yourself, do you?" For a moment, Sindje felt just a hair disconnected with reality. *Since when have I ever been the voice of reason?* She shrugged off the odd sensation and looked over the ork with a critical eye. "Look, I'm not really sure how well that spell is gonna hold you together, so you really shouldn't be pushing yourself."

"Hey, I'll relax when the *buunda* Johnson answers his cell, and we can get paid, and get the frag out of here— Hello?" Max tossed Hood's earpiece to Sindje as she got an answer. The elf fumbled it up to her ear just in time to eavesdrop on the conversation. Max had modified her commlink to also accept the call.

"Things have been a bit hectic around here, I'm afraid."

"Things been hectic around you? Man, you have no idea what the word even means!" The ork took a deep breath. "Look, the meet was blown six ways from Sunday, and the place it was supposed to happen in ain't even standing anymore, you hearin' me?"

"Loud and clear. Did you happen to go inside?"

Max looked at Sindje, who shook her head no.

"Frag, no, chummer, the Plantech sec forces were on us like Bodyline silk on a executive's hoop. We had to split

while they put on their own little Ballard fireworks
display."

"Hmm, that is unfortunate—"

"Yeah, I can hear you crying in your '45 Cabernet Sau-
vignon." Max winked at Sindje, who rolled her eyes and
motioned at the ork to get on with it. "However, because I
know you're gonna ask, your precious plants are still safe."

"Now that is very good news."

"Maybe for you, but I don't know how much longer
they're gonna stay that way, you know what I'm saying?
This deal has got to go down, and the sooner, the better."

*"Believe me, there is nothing I want more. The only trou-
ble is, you were not the only ones double-crossed at the
meeting site earlier today. The Plantech security was tipped
off that the meet was going down by someone—"*

"And the next words out of your mouth better not be
that we did it. I took a bullet trying to get out of there,
and I'm sure the newsvids are running full-holo of the chase
out of Ballard—"

*"Calm yourself, runner. Why would you set up your
own meet?"*

"Hey, who knows how you Johnsons think?

*"I think very much like you—when I am crossed, I won-
der why, and by whom. I have the answers to one of those
questions, if you're interested."*

"I haven't hung up yet."

*"You run with two elven siblings, a matched pair of
magic-users that go by the names Sindje and Khase,
correct?"*

Max's brow furrowed in a frown. "Maybe we did some
scores in the past, so what?"

*"If by the past you mean this morning, and by scores you
mean the Plantech building, then you're right. The point is,
the two elves owe people money. Serious people and serious
money. Those people got tired of waiting, and decided to
liquidate their assets, so to speak."*

Sindje's face had gone pale as she digested this news.
Max reached out with a big hand and steadied the shaking
elf, mouthing *he's talking out of his hoop.* "Why would they
do that? Then they'd never get the money back."

*"Like you said, who knows how criminals think? Maybe
they wanted to make a statement on the street to the rest of*

those who were reluctant to pay up. Nevertheless, it was these
people who tracked you all down and sent Plantech after
you. The elves are liabilities, but if we can complete our
original deal, then the four of you can vanish into the city
to your heart's content."

"Nice try, Johnny-boy, but you're still paying our increased fee, or we take those plants out to the forest and
make our own nice little garden. Who knows, maybe next
year you'll see them in pots at the corner store." Max let
him stew on that for a moment. "Look, the point is, each
of us has what the other wants. Now, since your great idea
for a meeting site blew up in our faces—literally—I'm
gonna choose the meeting place this time. Hold on a sec."

She did something to put him on hold and waved at
Sindje. "Hey, I need you focused now."

The elven mage was mumbling to herself, "How did they
find us . . . we were clean through Detroit and Denver . . .
who ratted us out?"

"Sindje!" The ork snapped her thick fingers. "What's the
name of that place?"

"The—Historic Everett Theatre."

"Thanks." She took the Johnson off hold, ignoring the
flashing red sign in the corner of her vision that warned
her the power was almost drained. "Okay, thanks for holding, *omae.* We want to meet you, and only you, at the
Historic Everett Theatre in a half hour. I'm gonna repeat
it for the cheap seats; come alone, and bring the magic
credstick. Oh yeah, and bring a truck, cause we'll supply
you with all the plants, pots, and soil you could ever want."

"Thirty minutes. I'll see you there."

Max didn't bother to reply, but hung up, muttering, "Not
if I see you first." She activated her commlink again, trying
to contact the Historic Everett Theatre, but got a recorded
message instead: "Thank you for calling the Historic Everett Theatre. Due to our desire to recreate the old time
movie-watching experience, commlinks and other transmis-
sions are not allowed in our theater. Please send a text
message—"

"Frag that!" Max disconnected in a huff. Taking a deep
breath, she hoisted herself to her feet, clenching her teeth
as a wave of agony crashed down on her. "*Buunda,* that
hurts. Come on, keebler, the theatre is only ten blocks from

here—we gotta get a move on. If the Johnson shows up before we do, Hood is liable to chew him up and spit him out, and then we'll never get paid." *Although that would be fun to watch,* she thought.

Sindje came over to Max and inserted herself under the ork's arm, supporting her as they moved to the basement stairs. The two women looked up at the flight stretching before them and both sighed together.

"Man, next time let's hole up in a five-star hotel." Sindje wrinkled her nose as she took one last look around their squalid surroundings.

"I'm with you. I hate, hate, hate this kind of filth." Max took a tentative step onto the stairs. "Let's get our hoops out of here." She paused and sniffed. "Keebler, what did you roll in?"

31

"I do not fraggin' believe this! We had them, we were right behind them, and this *momzer* troll pulls out a bow and shoots arrows at us! Arrows! And then they escape, poof, just like smoke they are—not a trace to be found. Oy *vey*, I cannot think of a worse thing that could have happened."

Simon looked over at Jhones, who was practically bouncing up and down in his seat with irritation. He had been so upset that when their replacement car, an LS modified Honda 3220 Turbo, had arrived, the dwarf had waved impatiently at Simon to drive. The IA officer had raised his eyebrows, but said nothing, just slid behind the wheel. He was glad he had. Compared to their Americar, which was a perfectly satisfactory vehicle, the Honda was a huge improvement. Quicker acceleration, a more powerful engine, and the sleek ride handled like it was on rails. *Maybe if I get a bust out of this, I can upgrade my street vehicle to something like this.*

Unfortunately, it looked like that bust might just come at the expense of his partner. Jhones looked like he was coming unglued, his eyes wild and staring, the Mohawk that was his pride and joy was limp and bedraggled, hanging over his face every which way. His fingers twitched in his lap. He had been of little help during the past half hour, during which they had cordoned off the accident area, reported in, and requisitioned a new vehicle. Beat cops had arrived to take statements and police the area, and Simon and Jhones had hit the street to try to pick up their quarry again. But as Jhones kept muttering under his breath, the *ganefs* had simply up and vanished.

Let's see if we can get this back on a more productive course, Simon thought. "All right, let's take it from the top. We know that a shadowrunning team that engineered the Plantech heist was meeting with someone—to sell back the plants? Maybe they were receiving a payoff for recovering them from the thieves—"

"No!" The dwarf's cyberhand slammed down on the dashboard hard enough to dent it. "The runners were there to get their payoff from whoever hired them to steal those plants, I know it!"

"Okay, okay, let's work off that for a moment. Plantech security tracks them down and tries to neutralize the team and recover the plants. Now, Lone Star arrives on the scene and arrests three other men, local 'talent' who were at the house as well, all injured, one severely, and each one smoldering from the explosion. Their initial statements claim no involvement in the action that went down in Ballard, but the shell casings recovered at the scene are probably going to pop that alibi like a balloon."

Simon turned north again. "So, Plantech is there to recover the plants, but why are these other guys there? Spoilers for the original team? Are they supposed to hit the Plantech security after they have the plants. No, that's drek, three against twenty? Highly illogical."

Jhones, his arms crossed, rubbed his beard thoughtfully. "Maybe they were sent to watch the drop go down. You know, provide backup?"

"That's a possibility. However, the drop goes to drek, and the scientist gets geeked. The three men engage the runners just as Plantech pulls up, and a three-way firefight ensues, with the team caught in the middle. They manage to get their hoops out of there—"

"And onto the freeway, where we managed to catch up to them. But now, somehow, they managed to *pffffttt*"— the dwarf blew air through his teeth—"and they're gone."

Simon's commlink vibrated in his jaw. "Maybe not just yet. Patch through to vidscreen and play."

"File transmitted, Officer Chays," the computer voice said in his head.

"I tasked an LS computer to monitor the radio airwaves in downtown and look for the words 'Bison,' 'plant' or 'Plantech', and 'Ballard' within thirty words of each other in a single transmission. Looks like this is our best match. Play."

Static filled the Honda's interior. *" . . . Sir, we've located the Bison. Looks exactly like the one that was in Ballard earlier. Plate match and everything. No sign of cargo or of any thermal signatures inside."* The disembodied voice gave an address.

Jhones snorted. "That's just what we need right now, involvement from the mafia."

"Let's not jump to conclusions here; they may have just ditched the vehicle." Simon held up his hand for silence as the conversation continued.

An authoritative voice replied: *"Do not engage. Wait for reinforcements. If they do move, stay on them at a safe distance. We'll be there in six-point-four minutes."*

"Time of intercept?" Simon queried even as he pushed the accelerator, the Honda's powerplant ramping up with hardly any additional noise. Almost before he knew it, they were traveling 170 kilometers per hour, but the car handled like they were doing a sedate 90. *Frag, I gotta get me one of these!*

"Time of communication intercept: 1919 hours," the computer replied.

"About five minutes ago." Simon checked the distance to their target area against where they were. "Assuming traffic is on our side, we should be there in a bit under six minutes—just enough time to catch the sec team in the act of raiding a private vehicle. Then maybe we'll finally get some answers if we haul the lot of them back to the precinct."

Simon looked over and got the satisfaction of seeing Jhones squirm in his seat. *Anything you'd like to add, boychik?* But the dwarf remained silent.

Simon sideslipped across two lanes, the Honda ghosting through the area like a black mirage. A klick later, and they turned down the street where the Bison was. Simon looked over one last time, but Jhones stared straight ahead, his impassive features looking like they might have been carved from steel for all the emotion he showed.

All right, looks like we do this the hard way. In the gathering dusk, Simon hit his cybereyes and saw two Typhoons clustered around a parked vehicle. He hit the red-and-blue strobes, then the halogen spotlight in the front of the car, lighting up the entire group of armor-clad, sub-gun toting guards around the RVs. Simon announced through the loudspeaker, *"THIS IS LONE STAR! NOBODY MOVE! KEEP YOUR HANDS WHERE I CAN SEE THEM!"*

Let's see how your good buddy likes this, he thought as he got out of the car, his Ruger Thunderbolt held down at his side.

"Oy, boychik, you certainly know how to get people's attention." Jhones shook his head as he got out of the car. "Perhaps I should do the talking."

"Sure, start reading them their rights. Operating out of their corp's jurisdiction, endangering public safety, destruction of private property, obstruction of justice. Heck, let's throw attempted murder in there. I'm sure we can put a case together—shall I go on?"

"Just hang back a bit, will you?" The dwarf walked forward, his stocky body silhouetted in the halogen light.

A helmeted man in a crisp black jumpsuit stalked forward, seemingly unaffected by the bright glare. "Jhones? Is that you?"

"Hoi, Roland. Why don't you and I take a little walk? Simon, make sure none of these 'suspects' tries to 'resist arrest'?"

Simon whirled on his superior, about to read him the riot act, but the words died when he saw the look of pain on the dwarf's face. He clamped his mouth shut. "Okay, you get five minutes, that's all."

Jhones nodded. "That'll do. Then you and I will have a little talk ourselves."

Slottin' right we will, Simon thought as he leaned against the Honda, heavy pistol still in hand, his cybereye recording the face of every sec guard there, particularly that of their leader, Roland Ators.

*   *   *

Roland kept a wary eye on the human near the Lone Star car as he walked away with Jhones. "What's up with your partner back there?"

The dwarf rubbed his forehead. "Oy, rookie fever. The justice bug is chomping his nads, that's all. Speaking of fever, *chaver,* why am I finding you out here, not even in Snohomish, busting a private citizen's vehicle? On top of that, we've got about a dozen witnesses who cannot only place your teams at that house that went up in flames in Ballard, but also several cops that will swear they saw a couple of Typhoons that look remarkably like these ones chasing that Bison all around downtown. That's breaking about a dozen laws just off the top of my head. If you have *anything* to say in your defense, now would be the time."

Frag, it's a good thing he doesn't know about the Alki apartment raid, or my hoop would be in the drek for sure. Taking off his helmet, Roland ran a hand through his crew cut and regarded his friend with a deep sigh. "All right, I was hoping we could have resolved this quietly, but these fraggin' runners keep slipping through our fingers." He went on to fill Jhones in on exactly how important the stolen plants were to his corp.

"So if we don't get them back and consummate the deal, Shiawase will either absorb us, or we'll go belly-up and the sharks will start biting off chunks." Roland looked down to see the dwarf gritting his teeth, his fists clenched at his side. "Hey, you all right?"

Jhones poked him in the stomach with a thick finger, his face flushed with anger. "Oy, Roland, you're killing me here. Why didn't you tell me this in the first place? You know I would have made it a top priority."

"Whoa, I'm sorry, *omae,* I didn't think it was that big a deal, at least not for you. Besides, we were—and still are—worried about the brass at Lone Star or UCAS getting wind about rogue biotech loose on the street. You know they're a lot more paranoid about this stuff nowadays. I was trying to minimize your involvement."

"But still hoping I might find a tip to help you out, eh, boychik? Well, now I don't know if we can keep this off the official report. The best thing to do will be to find these runners and locate the plants ASAP, then we get them back to you and write up the report as a fait accompli after the fact. All right, all right, let me think a bit. I'll go calm down Mr. Excitable over there, and you guys head back home while I call in a Crime Scene team to police the Bison. Do me a favor—make sure none of your boys left any trace of themselves in there, willya? Meanwhile, let me poke around and see what I can uncover. This whole thing is smelling fishier than Elliot Bay in July, you know?"

"Don't worry, we were just about to move on the vehicle when you arrived. We'll get out of your hair, but call me the instant you've got something, okay?"

"Okay, keep a channel clear. As soon as I have something solid, you'll know it. Now get out of here already."

Roland and Jhones separated, and the sec chief walked back to his crew. "All right boys—and Doctor—we're done here. The Bison is in Lone Star's custody now."

"We're not just going back to the corp, are we, boss?" K-Tog asked.

"Yeah, for now that's exactly what we're doing. We've bent and broken enough laws for one day, and I've pushed our luck as far as possible. I will not risk getting any of you in any more trouble today. My friend over there is going to see what he can find out, and he'll be in touch. You guys have all done a great job, and if anyone wants to clock out now, you can head out with my blessing."

Everyone looked at each other, but no one said a word. Morgan piped up on one side. "If it's all the same to you, boss, we'd rather know how this turns out instead of sitting at home waiting for a call."

Despite his weariness and frustration, Roland felt a swell of pride at their determination to see this entire mess through. "All right, then, let's head back to the corp."

He turned to the shaman, who was conversing with Lilith off to one side, and bowed deeply. "Hiyakawa-san, I thank you again for your invaluable assistance in this matter."

The shaman returned Roland's bow with one of his own. "Your courtesy is appreciated, Ators-san, however, we still have not accomplished your objectives."

"Nevertheless, that is out of our hands at the moment. I would be happy to take you wherever you wish to be dropped off, and the rest of your agreed-upon payment will be forwarded to your account immediately."

Hiyakawa and Lilith exchanged glances, and the shaman

bowed again. As he did so, Roland noticed that the Plantech biogenetist was also clean as a whistle, her gray coat spotless, and her hair looking freshly-brushed. His eyebrows rose, but he didn't say a word.

"*Domo arigato,* Ators-san. However, I think I will also accompany you back to your headquarters. I agree with your lieutenant in that I would like to see how this turns out. Besides, Chalmers-san and I have been having a most interesting conversation about flora and mana combinations, and I would hate to cut it short."

Roland rubbed his cheek and regarded the short woman for a moment, who was busy watching the men filing into the Typhoons. *Am I hallucinating, or is she blushing?* "Very well, please come with me."

Roland walked to the RV and glanced over at the Lone Star patrol car as he stepped up into the front passenger seat. The dwarf and his partner appeared to be deep in conversation. *Jhones, I hope you can pull something out of your hat this time, otherwise I might be applying for a job with* your *corp soon.*

Jhones trudged back to the Honda and got in the passenger seat, feeling Simon's burning gaze on him the entire way. The human got in the driver's side, but didn't start the car.

"All right, sergeant, what the frag is going on here? It's obvious you know the head of security at Plantech, one Roland Ators. Now, faced with blatant evidence of a crime in progress, as well as our own eyewitness account from other Lone Star officers about Plantech vehicles being involved in a high speed chase earlier this evening, it seems we're not going to arrest them. We're letting them go on their merry way."

Jhones watched the Typhoons pull away from the Bison and head off. Simon sounded like he was chewing on a mouthful of red-hot nails, he was so angry. "What kind of drek does this guy have on you, Jhones?"

The dwarf looked at Simon, his eyes wide. "What kind of—you think Roland's been blackmailing me?"

"What other conclusion am I supposed to draw? You meet him this morning at the diner, and immediately afterward you start sniffing around the Plantech break-in, which the corp itself said wasn't an issue. Now why would you do that? Only if someone asked you to."

Simon stared out the windshield at the now deserted Bison. "Look, I haven't known you long, but the one thing I do know is that you're a damn good cop. Now tell me what's going on, and let me help you, or so help me I'll haul you in right now and throw you to the chief."

"You—a still-wet-behind-the-ears rookie—are going to help me?" Jhones asked.

"Hey, I was the one who got us here, wasn't I?" Simon waved at the silent RV.

"Yeah, yeah, maybe I haven't been giving you enough credit lately. Okay, the first thing you need to know is that Roland isn't blackmailing me—we've been friends for the past twenty years. He did ask for my help with this incident. It seems that these runners got away with a bit more than the corp is willing to admit publicly. In fact, the corp's entire bottom line—its soul—is riding on getting these plants back."

"Okay, that may be, but your interest in this is way more personal than helping out an old friend. My guess is that it has something to do with that call you got after our meeting in the diner this morning."

Jhones looked up at the human, surprise again flitting across his features. "*Nu,* you bucking for my job already, *boychik?*" He took a deep breath while he gathered his thoughts, trying to decide whether or not to tell the kid. With a deep sigh, he realized that all of this had been weighing on him like a lead suit ever since the Johnson's call that morning. "All right, here goes. . . ."

He told Simon everything: the gambling, the marker, and what he was supposed to do about it. "But when Roland told me exactly what was riding on this, I saw red. I may have my own problems, but it burns me up that some corp suit wants to use me to burn my best friend, destroy his company, and advance their fraggin' career while they enjoy the sushi sampler platter at Oghi Ya's tonight without a care in the world for the lives they've just destroyed. That I cannot stand. So, there it is, *chaver,* any ideas?"

Simon let out a gusty sigh of relief. "Well, first of all, I'm very glad you haven't actually broken any laws. As for this problem you have, the best advice I can give you is to do what you know is the right thing—recover the plants and get them back to Roland's corp. Maybe sign up for Gamblers Anonymous or something."

"But what about my marker, and the suit?"

"Like I said, Jhones, I know you're a good cop. This gambling bug is the only monkey on your back that I know of, but it's a huge one. The best way for you to get it off once and for all is to make sure you can never bet again." Simon leaned back in his seat, letting the dwarf figure out the rest.

"Are you saying welsh on the marker on purpose? But no one would ever take a bet from me on the street . . ." Jhones trailed off as the implications of the solution sank in.

"Why view that as a negative thing? Instead, turn it around, use that to your advantage. It's the only way you're going to be truly free of this thing, and I think you know that. Lone Star needs every good officer it can get, and I don't want to see your career terminated before its time."

"Oy, I'm not sure if I'm sitting here with my partner, the police shrink, my rabbi or a combination of all three." Jhones stared out the window for a moment, gathering his thoughts. At last, he nodded. "All right, let's do this. Besides, if I let Roland down, every bet I ever made from now on would be like I was stabbing him in the back all over again."

"Good point." Simon started the Honda and pulled away from the curb. "So, where do we begin?"

"Well, we've got a ton of vid and stuff on the Bison and the team inside. I would suggest that we review that and try to get a fix on them—hold on, I'm getting a call on my private line. Go."

Jhones' eyes widened as he heard the voice in his head. "Yes, this is Officer Redrock. He looked over at Simon and mouthed *It's the guy that has my marker.* "How can I help you?"

32

The elf in the black leather pants and jacket was singing about a wiz convertible that glowed an electric cherry red. He had a good voice, clear and deep, and it was coming at the sparse audience from all directions. The voice had elven nuances, but Khase wondered if it was really the performer's or if it had been augmented or entirely replaced. Perhaps it wasn't really a living man's voice at all. So much of the entertainment industry was digital smoke and mirrors, they could create practically anything they wanted, and often did.

"Ah, Khase-san, that *is* the actor." Pan looked out the window in the projection room, too, and spoke as if he could read the elf's mind. "I heard him on stage some years back, and we have other musicals in our library that feature him. Some things in this world are still real, and we prefer to show pictures that are for the most part . . ." The old man paused, scratched his head and searched for the right word. "Authentic. The old movies, even the remastered tridee ones, remain as true to the original as possible."

We, Khase mouthed. *And just who is "we?"* He had a sneaking suspicion that this wizened human had been around movies for so long, he might have lost a bit of his grip on reality.

Pan continued to talk, Khase having missed some of it. ". . . like William Shakespeare's *Hamlet* and *The Dirty Dozen.* Kenneth Branagh and Aristotle Savalas, now they could act. I study the notes on each film before I order it. Nothing that was produced in the past decade . . . unless it is a remake of an old, old film."

"So why not just show the original? Not remastered. Not redone." Khase watched the singing elf seem to come out of the screen, dancing over the heads of the people in the first few rows. After the chorus, he leapt back to the hood of the car on the screen.

"Sometimes we do. Often, in fact."

"Flat movies? Flat actors? No special effects? No orbital sound?"

The old man smiled. "The Everett tries to cater to the 'Bs and Cs' as we call them. We fill a niche."

Again and again the "we." Khase pursed his lips and raised both eyebrows. That question was an itch that needed scratching, and the elf knew if he just let the old man talk, it would be.

Pan was quick to answer one of his unspoken questions. "Bs and Cs. For the film buffs and connoisseurs. There are a good number of people in this city, and down in Portland, who want to see unaltered films and will pay good nuyen for that privilege—especially to see them in such a fine theater as this. We don't have the actual celluloid, but we've recorded chips that are almost as good as the original. We even have more than a few silent films. *Wings* is my favorite, about two pilots from World War I. We are only one of three theaters in the northern hemisphere to possess that movie . . . and the Smithsonian, of course. We show a double-feature of *Wings* and *Dawn Patrol* with Errol Flynn every year at the first of December. The latter is a 'talkie,' but it is black and white."

Khase was watching the elf on the screen again. He'd been joined by two humans and a dwarf—all of them in black leather jackets, and they were all still singing about the ridiculous car. The dwarf floated above the center of the auditorium, waving an oversized spark plug in his hand. One of the humans pulled him back to the screen. "No sound in a movie? I find that hard to comprehend. It would be . . . boring. Utterly boring. I couldn't sit through it. I do not mean insult to you or your theater, but I would have far better things to do."

Pan sadly shook his head. "These films are a part of our history."

"Not a part of mine." Khase watched the singing elf leap into the car, his three fellows cramming themselves into the backseat. The elf ended the musical number and revved the engine, as the car zoomed across the audience and disappeared in sparkling motes of gray-white lights.

The image on the screen shifted to a bedroom decorated in pink ribbons and lace. The female elf lead was the target of a pillow fight. Another song started, this one syrupy and with nonsensical lyrics.

Khase stepped back, losing interest. "It appears that not many in this neighborhood enjoy this sort of entertainment, either. There are more empty seats than full ones."

"It is a slow night," Pan admitted. "We've shown this picture too often, I think, in the past few years. But we will have quite the crowd tomorrow night for our Rodgers and Hammerstein revival."

Khase didn't pretend to know whom he was talking about. "I like movies well enough, Pan-san, but I have little time to see them. My sister now, she likes the ones with lots of pyrotechnics and exceptional effects. She likes action movies that speed by so quickly you feel like time has melted and you have been cheated of the ticket price."

"And what kind of films do you like, Khase-san?"

The elf regarded the old man for a moment. "*Yojimbo. The Seven Samurai. Ran. Kagemusha.* Even that old pulp show *Throne of Blood.* Stories where people actually made a difference in the world."

"Ah, you should be here next March, when we run our annual Kurosawa film festival. Then you find the theater packed with attendees. Twenty-four hours of the master's films. You come back, I get you in."

Pan's eyes twinkled. "The old movies, they have action, too. But you feel the action better because the actors ran under their own power, and they sweated under the lights of the cameras. The old movies, they are art, and they are more intense than the ones of today that merely overload your senses."

Khase shrugged, not feeling the need to continue the discussion. When it came down to it, movies, whether old or new, flatfilm or tridee, were just that—movies. Something to escape reality for a little while. *Reality is much different—stark, dark and painful,* he thought as his injured

arm twinged again. He wanted Hood to hurry up with
whatever he was doing upstairs with the plants. He wanted
to be out of here and back with Sindje and Max. He stared
at a shelf full of chips. There was a musty smell, and Khase
realized it was coming from the wall behind the shelf. There
was a mildewed strip that ran from floor to ceiling.

"Old building."

"Very," Pan said. "We are quite proud of it."

"We? You and your wife."

"Yes."

"And your sister, too, of course."

"Yes, of course. My sister loves this theater."

Khase pretended to study the chips on the shelf directly
in front of him. "And Hood. I'll bet Hood is proud of this
place, too." He turned to see Pan nod.

"Hood-san is most proud of this building."

"And loves the flat movies, neh?"

"It took a while for him to appreciate them. But now he
prefers them to new releases."

"The Robin Hood movies . . ."

"Are his favorites."

"Of course they are."

Pan moved to the end of the shelf and picked up a large
chip made for an old computer-projector. "This film is of
the saving of the Everett, a documentary we had made
when the theater was purchased and the renovations
started."

"And that would have been when?"

The old man's face was relaxed and his pupils wide. It
was clear he enjoyed talking about the building. "Well
more than a hundred and fifty years ago the Everett was a
theater for stage plays and vaudeville and sometimes children's magic shows. It was converted into a movie house
when live performances became too expensive and were
not so popular anymore. It started showing silent films.
There were relatively few Asians in the neighborhood back
then." He carefully placed the chip back in the rack. "I
could show you the documentary. We have a small screen-
ing room upstairs."

"I'd rather hear all about it from you."

This seemed to please Pan even more. "The theater was
closed in the mid-2010s, and reopened years later when a

local industrialist thought it might help revive the neighborhood. But it didn't last long. The theater closed again, and the influx of Koreans brought in new businesses, including a new tridee theater two blocks west. The Everett opened again twice more, with varying degrees of success. But it could not compete with the new and bigger theaters."

"Until Hood bought it." Khase took the shot, figuring he had to be close. "And until he decided not to compete but to create his own . . . niche."

"Yes! Eight years ago Hood-san bought the theater and began making repairs. I had managed the Everett the last time it was opened. I was young, then. But when I saw the work crews, I came to watch and admire. And I met Hood-san."

"And Hood hired you."

"That very day." Pan's smile reached his eyes. "He wanted to learn about how this place was supposed to look and what it used to show. And so I taught him about all the old, wonderful movies."

"And about Robin Hood."

"And his band of Merry Men. Little John, Friar Tuck, Marian, the Sheriff of. . . ." Pan stopped when he realized the names were lost on Khase.

"How long after that did our troll friend start calling himself Hood?"

Pan drew his face forward until it looked pinched. "These are things you should know already, if you know Hood-san well."

"Oh, I know him very well," Khase lied. "Hood doesn't bring just anyone to his place at Alki or to here." His voice was mellow, the words slow and smooth. It was something he'd learned from his sister. And though her words could have real magic behind them and be hypnotic, his were at least convincing. "But I never asked his real name. Never thought to." He waved around at the theater. "Still, someone who's restored this old lady to her former grandeur, well, it would be nice to know the real person behind an act like that, not just a street handle." He focused with all of his charisma, trying to find that chink in the other man's armor.

"Darkren." Pan was caught up in the power of Khase's act. "Darkren Boeing."

The last name hit Khase like a fist, but he managed to keep his composure. "Ah, the aircraft family. Impressive."

"And the shipyards."

Khase remembered driving by the shipyards this afternoon. *No wonder he defended them.* "He doesn't seem like the freighter type."

"The last true Boeing, they say, ended his association with the aerospace company far back in the 1930s. And the family lost influence. William Boeing did have a son, however, and down the line and after some decades passed, the family regained control of the company. It has only been in the past thirty years that the Boeing name has regained prominence in this area."

"Interesting bit of history," Khase said. "So my pal's important."

Pan's face took on a sad cast. "Khase-san, didn't Hood tell you? His family shuns him, has ever since he—changed—as he was growing up. So while he is still of their blood and holds their name, he was forced to distance himself. He built his own fortune, with a little seed money from his father. Darkren Boeing, and Hood, keep low profiles to appease the family. He is a very private man out of respect and necessity. He owns a few of his own corporations in this city and elsewhere on the coasts, though he operates them through other individuals. He owns several businesses and . . ."

"And the Historic Everett Theatre."

"And the block it sits upon." Pan adjusted a tray of chips on the shelf. "He funnels some of his profits into continued renovations. As you can see, we still have some work to do here." He pointed to the mildewed strip.

"I didn't think this place could financially support itself."

Pan frowned at Khase's comment. "Our revenues are improving. Hood has made this building sound and fashioned apartments upstairs for me and my wife, my sister, and built a workroom for himself. And he has installed the latest technology for security to protect against vandals and treasure hunters. And to block tech."

"Block tech?"

"Broad spectrum jammers. So the patrons in the audience are not disturbed, we have jammers to prevent signals from coming in."

"No phone calls."

"Except in the lobby."

"Impressive and expensive."

"Hood-san can afford it." Pan returned to the viewing window, just as the elf in the black leather outfit was singing on a carnival ride that spun away from the screen. "His industry ventures . . . and some of his other undertakings . . . do well."

"Other undertakings? His runs? Do you know about those, Pan?"

The older man didn't answer.

"And does he rob from the rich and give to the poor?"

"He does have several charitable projects in the neighborhood." Pan watched the film's closing credits, and thumbed a switch to slowly bring up the house lights.

Khase got a good look at the auditorium now. It appeared new and old at the same time—seats he thought he might find in a museum upholstered in dark red velvet, walls papered in something flecked with maroon and gold, and wood trim everywhere meticulously painted a creamy off-white. He imagined that it would be comfortable to sit and watch a movie there, and he decided he would come back some time and do just that—without Hood knowing, of course. Perhaps he would take in one of those Robin Hood tridee festivals, and perhaps he could talk Sindje into coming along. No flat movies, though. Well, except for the samurai feature Pan mentioned. That would be excellent.

"I worry that I have spoken too much about Hood-san." Pan was readying another set of chips to cue up the next film.

"I don't recall a single thing you mentioned about our troll friend." Khase's voice was again smooth and reassuring. "Besides, like everyone else on the street, I've secrets of my own. Maybe I'll tell you a few someday to even things out." The elf bowed formally to the old man and slipped out of the projection room.

Khase quietly closed the door behind him, listening as the opening theme music swelled and the same elf's voice started singing again. This time it was some foolish tune about staying alive.

My friend, you have absolutely no idea what you're talking about. Then he padded down the hall and to the other door, taking the creaking stairs up to the next floor.

*   *   *

"Sophisticated recording devices." Hood was studying the purple-green plant. "Six of them, all thick with bioware, all undetectable by virtually anything because the stems and leaves mask the vein-wires so thoroughly. Wildly valuable." He whistled appreciatively.

He quickly culled as many of the recording seed pods as he could find, wrapped them in a large handkerchief and put them in his front shirt pocket.

"So our employer wants only these plants, and probably because they recorded something very interesting."

"Or very incriminating," Khase said in the doorway.

33

Jhones disconnected his commlink, a stunned look on his face. "That Johnson who owns my marker just dropped the runners in our laps. He said they're holed up in the Historic Everett Theatre right now. Drek, the address is only two dozen blocks from here. I think we'd better get some backup over there pronto."

Simon hit the lights on the Honda and traffic magically parted for them as the interceptor sped down the narrow street. "You gonna let Roland know?"

"Not this time, he's taken enough risks for one day." The dwarf activated his commlink. "Precinct Ninety-Five, Precinct Ninety-Five, this is Three Romeo Three, requesting backup at the Everett Theatre to assist in apprehending suspects in the Plantech agricorp heist. Three Romeo Three is en route at this time, and as investigating officers will coordinate operations on site."

"Three Romeo Three, backup en route to Everett Theatre. Officers Redrock and Chays are commanding officers on scene," the computer's voice confirmed.

Jhones switched over to his private line. "Hoi, Roland? Tell me, just how did you track the runners to Ballard? . . . Shaman, eh? . . . Did they go anywhere else besides there? . . . An apartment building in Alki? . . . You saw them there? . . . trace physical evidence, I see. Hmm, I might have something, but we need to check out a lead first. I just needed to know if these guys had been anywhere else recently . . . yeah, yeah, you'll be the first to know after us. I'll be in touch."

Simon glanced at him as he pulled around a Seattle MTA bus. "ETA to The Everett four minutes. What was that all about?"

"Something that's been bugging me since we got wind these guys were running around in the first place. Assuming their Roadmaster was trashed, which, judging by those camera shots, it was, they managed to put their hands on that Bison—an expensive piece of machinery—in about twelve hours."

"Okay, so why were you calling Roland?"

"I wanted to see where it had come from—it is one of the best leads we have on these guys."

"Is that all? Well, let me run that plate I recorded on it." Jhones and Simon waited the standard twenty-five seconds for the Seattle DMV mainframe to give them the information. "Hmm, registered to Lakeshore Gardens Condominiums on Elliot Bay."

"Corp-owned, eh? So who owns the corp?" Jhones asked. "Let's see—a holding corporation called Baysound Real Estate Development—that's original—which, as I suspected, is a holding company owned by—Debarring Keno Enterprises, and that in turn is owned by—"

"ETA to Everett, one minute." Simon palmed the steering wheel as the Honda slipped around a corner. "Hope P-Ninety-Five is glad to see us."

"*Sha,* hold your fire a minute, will you, I've almost got it—*b'emet*? It says that Debarring is controlled one hundred percent by the Boeing Consortium."

"Boeing owns that real estate? Okay, that makes sense, maybe their corp suits stay there."

"Maybe, but if I cross reference the Everett Theatre with that real estate corp, I get—the exact same match. Either these runners are from Boeing, or they're working for them. Either way, this will be one very interesting interrogation."

"Look sharp—we're here." Simon unsnapped the restraint on his Ruger as he looked out the window. "Hey, that vehicle isn't Lone Star."

Jhones peered out as well, seeing a large RV disgorging

heavily armed men in riot gear and full face helmets. "What the—Who the frag are these guys? And where's our backup, this is Ninety-Five's backyard, for crying out loud!"

"I don't know, but they're armed for bear. What do you want to do?"

Jhones pulled back the slide on his Browning. "Let's give them sixty seconds, then we roust the driver. Hopefully our backup will show, and we can take the team when they come outside. For now, all we can do is wait and pray no one inside does anything stupid."

34

"**H**ood-san, a war has come to us!" Pan squeezed through the doorframe, brushed past Khase and went straight toward Hood, moving remarkably fast for a man his age. "The theater, Hood-san. We are under attack! Just like in the *The Killer!*"

Hood darted to a cabinet and pulled out a bow. It wasn't as large or well made as the one he'd lost on the road this afternoon. In fact, in his huge hands it looked like a toy or a flimsy stage prop. He reached to the bottom of the cabinet and came up with a quiver. Not near so many arrows as he usually toted around. He shouldered the bow and quiver, then he looked to the elf, but Khase was already gone.

"Hood-san, they are out front."

"What gang?"

Pan shook his head and nervously wrung his hands. "No gang, Hood-san. The Red Army has come! These are professionals." Then he was hurrying from the room. "I must see to my wife and sister."

Hood grabbed a chair and poked it at the skylights to break the old glass. Then he reached up an arm, grabbed the edge and pulled himself up. He climbed out onto a roof covered with finely pebbled tarpaper. The soles of his shoes slapped against it as he raced to the edge of the building, fitting an arrow.

He paused at the edge, looking down on the neon-speckled street and searching for his first target. The sounds of traffic drifted up, accompanied by loud jazz music from the bar across the street. There was also the sound of men hurrying, the Red Army Pan mentioned.

"In the name of the Green Mother, what?"

A truck was double-parked in front of The Everett. It looked like military issue, save it was a shiny maroon with white letters and a logo on the side. The last few members of a private security team disgorged from the back. Hood couldn't read the truck's logo from his vantage point, or the small logos on the breast pockets of the sec team's maroon body armor jackets. But they were as heavily armed as the Plantech force had been, carrying a mix of shotguns, assault rifles and submachine guns. But these weren't Plantech, and they weren't an arm of Lone Star. They were all humans that he could see. Hood wasn't sure of the number, but the back of the truck could easily carry two dozen.

His mind churned. How could anyone have traced them to this theater?

Hood was a private man who kept his properties as secret as possible. Too, neither he nor Khase had bugs or electronic hounds on them that he could tell—certainly not on himself. He'd changed clothes often enough he would have found something. The Everett was filled with security devices so the patrons would not be interrupted with calls and other nuisances. So no one should have been able to find them here with sniffers—particularly a private team that hadn't been at the house in Ballard and hadn't chased them through the city streets to get a clue where they were running.

Hood fired an arrow near the truck's front tire. The head dug into the street and emitted a high-pitched shriek. The sound attracted the attention of three sec team members who left the front of the theater to investigate. A heartbeat later they were splayed on the asphalt, as the arrowhead erupted into a cloud of sleep-inducing gas.

"Teach 'em not to wear breathers," Hood muttered. "They're issued breathers, they should use 'em. Standard operating procedure." Two more arrows followed the first, one with another sleep-gas canister. The second produced an acrid tear-bringing smoke that the troll could smell three stories up. The sickly green cloud spread out under the marquee and across the street to the bar. Curious customers had spilled out onto the sidewalk, all of them gawking at the Everett and the security force. The green cloud gave them coughing fits and forced them away. Hood considered another arrow to drive them back farther, but he hadn't many in this quiver and so had to conserve them.

"Frag it." He pictured his expensive bow ruined on the street, and the quiver of arrows he'd thoughtlessly left behind when he abandoned the Bison. One last look below, eyes picking through the tear gas and the sleep gas and seeing only a few of the maroon-clad men moving sluggishly. No one he recognized. "Frag it all to the bottom pits of hell."

He turned from the edge of the roof and jumped through the closest skylight, wincing as the glass sliced into his legs and arms and groaning when he hit the bed, which broke below him. He was up on his feet, glancing at the table of plants he'd nearly come down on. Then his feet were pounding across the old wooden floor, carrying him out the door and down the hall, past three other doors and down the narrow stairway. Running down the second floor hallway now, he paused only to look in the projection room and make sure Pan wasn't there. A movie was still playing; Hood caught a glimpse of an elf in a white suit whirling on a multi-colored dance floor that flashed in dizzying patterns. The troll's frantic footsteps matched the beat of the music as he spun down the curving marble staircase that took him into the lobby.

Now Hood could see the insignia on their uniforms, but it still didn't make sense. What would Keashee Corp be doing here, and in force?

The Keashee sec men had already swarmed the place. The three who were leveling Uzi IVs at the old woman quivering behind the popcorn machine were soon gagging and rubbing their eyes—Hood had shot another one of the green-gas arrows at their feet. The old woman was succumbing, too, but the troll knew she wouldn't be seriously harmed—and it would be better than getting shot. The green gas continued to spread.

Khase occupied four men by himself, twirling and lashing out with his feet and hands, all hints of his fatigue and pain gone. He was holding his own, but the Keashee men were doing their best to contain him. Because of the way they were arranged, however, they couldn't shoot him for fear of hitting their own men. More sec men rushed by the elf, two of them charging Pan, another two coming at Hood, and a half a dozen heading into the auditorium, leading with their shotguns and Uzi subguns.

"Fools!" the troll bellowed. "This is private property!" Hood shouldered his bow again and slammed his fist into the face of the nearest sec man. Bones cracked from the impact, at the very least a broken nose. The man dropped just as his companion swung his own Uzi up and fired at Hood, the slug missing its mark and only grazing the troll's cheek. "Kill me for plants? For plants!"

Hood bellowed like a rabid beast and threw himself at the sec man. Another round went off, and another, one finding its way deep into the troll's left shoulder. Hood felt a hotness, smelled his own blood. Mixed with the scent of fear and tear gas and popcorn it was nauseating. The troll felt bile rising, but managed to keep it down as he drove his fist into the sec man's chest, breaking his ribs and pushing him back into another man who had charged forward.

"Khase?" Hood shouted over the screams that were coming from the auditorium.

"I'm fine. I'm handling these. And just who are they?" Two men were crumpled at the elf's feet, though another two had moved up to take their places. "Do these goons want the fraggin' plants, too? How could . . ." The elf started coughing, the green gas reaching his feet. Still, he kept battling with the men, whipping one leg out in a circle kick that shattered a sec guard's visor and sent him flopping to the floor while straight-arming the second guy who had tried to rush him. Khase used the human's own momentum and sent him sailing over the concessions stand to thwack into the wall behind it and slide out of sight. He waited a moment, but the man didn't get back up.

"Pan?"

"I am fine, Hood-san. See to our customers." The old man was not as fast as Khase, but seemed to be just as skilled. He was artfully dancing with his opponents, managing to disarm them and keep them away from his wife, who stared in disbelief from the corner.

"Mei sei go ah?" Pan spat at the taller of his foes. *"Seung sei ah?"*

"No geeking, Pan! You either, Khase!" The troll rammed his elbow into another sec man, caught him in the jaw with an uppercut, then picked him up and tossed him against the nearest wall. Without looking to see if the man was getting up, Hood barreled into the auditorium.

It took a moment for his eyes to adjust. The screen was bright, but the rest of the immense room was dark. Shadows ran along the aisles, patrons fleeing in panic from the sec men waving their guns. At least the security force wasn't firing at innocents; Hood had to give them that. Still, they were inflicting enough mental terror on people who would never come back to this precious place. That last thought further incensed the troll.

He leapt over the back four rows of seats and hurtled toward the center of the auditorium, waving his big arms and avoiding the aisle where the patrons ran. "Fire exit!" he bellowed, the words not meant for the sec men. "Go out the fire exit!"

Another four rows and he caught the armored jacket of one of the sec men, picked him up as if he weighed nothing and tossed him over a broad shoulder. He heard the clatter as the man collided with seats. Another two rows and Hood had another one. He yanked the shotgun from the man's grip and dashed it on the aisle again and again until he heard the butt splinter, then he threw the man down and in anger kicked him in the ribs, the guard grunting in real pain. Hood cursed his strength and moved up to grab another and throw him against the back of a seat.

The sec men had stopped chasing the patrons and turned their attention to Hood. Elven and human dancers spun above their heads, leaving the screen to gyrate madly in three-dimension to a pulsing, monotonous beat. Light beams spit out from their fingertips and momentarily distracted a few of the sec men—the show of sound and colors making it difficult to focus, the screams of the still-fleeing patrons adding to the cacophony.

Hood fired another tear gas arrow and dropped down on his hands and knees, crawling between a row of seats and away from the bulk of the security men. He reached a far aisle, and cut down it, still crawling, hands and knees growing sticky from food and drinks that had been spilled throughout the day. The smell of stale butter, popcorn and other dropped food made him gag, and the pain in his shoulder grew hotter.

He came up behind one of the smaller security men, his back crisscrossed with two rifles and two bolero packs no doubt filled with extra ammunition. Hood stretched up an arm and pulled him down so fast he couldn't cry out, his helmeted head cracking against the floor. The troll waited a moment to make sure the man was unconscious, then he fumbled in the shadows for the man's Predator IV and squeezed it until the slide cracked.

Hood hated guns, and he made quick work of the rifles, the sound of the metal barrels breaking drawing the attention of the rest of the force.

"Yeah, I'm over here," Hood called. "Come and get me."

"Where is he?" This came from a man fanning at his face, desperately trying to peer through the green gas cloud. "Where is . . ." He doubled over, retching, the gas doing its work.

"Ohhhhhhh, I am staying alive!" The elf in the white suit flew off the screen and started pirouetting above a spot near Hood. The elf sang in a falsetto voice that the troll found incommodious. "Ohhhhh, yes, I am staying aliiiiiiiiiiive."

"Ain't showing that fraggin' picture again. Ever." Hood charged through the image of the cavorting elf, arms extended and effectively clotheslining two of the sec men. Another brought a subgun up, which Hood spotted out of the corner of his eye. "Keashee doesn't issue those," the troll growled. "Not that I know of."

The subgun spit flame and bullets in a wide spread, nearly catching Hood as he dove between a row of seats. The projectiles sprayed into the screen, putting holes in the dance floor. Another burst and part of the screen was sheared away. The sickly green gas cloud expanded, stretching up toward the elf dancer and his chorus and toward the remaining sec men.

Hood screamed in rage and rushed the man with the subgun, ignoring the pain that cut into his leg when the man fired again and nailed him. The screams of the patrons stopped, the last of them spilling out behind the theater and leaving Hood alone with the security men.

"Kill me for plants?" The troll's fingers closed on the stunted barrel of the subgun and he flung the weapon toward the ruined screen. "My theater! What in the name of the Green Mother are you doing?" He picked the man up and shook him, tossed him into another man and howled his rage at two security men who fled up the aisle and out of the auditorium. Only one sec man still stood, and the troll churned toward him before he could flee, too.

"What are you doing in my theater?"

The man tried to draw a bead on Hood, and fired off two rounds before the troll was on him. Hood caught another round in the shoulder, his left arm useless and feeling like a fiery deadweight as a result. He brought his right fist up and pounded it into the man's stomach, pulled his hand back and snatched the gun from his fingers.

"What are you doing here?" Hood's eyes burned as the green gas billowed around him. Tears streamed down his face from the acrid chemical. The man in front of him was faring worse. He fell to his knees, coughing, and Hood dropped the gun and picked him up, dragging him to the back of the auditorium, where the gas hadn't yet reached. "I. Will. Not. Ask. Again." The troll pulled the man up until they were eye to eye. "What are you doing here?"

"Orders," the man managed. "Following orders. S'posed to retrieve some plants stashed in this theater."

"And you brought guns for that?"

"Had the go-ahead to geek anyone who got in the way."

Hood shoved him against the wall and brought his warty face up against the sec man's. "And the patrons? You needed to threaten them? And the sweet old woman selling popcorn and candy . . . was she getting in the way? You needed to threaten her?" Hood set the man down and tore the ID patch off the armored vest, then stuffed the patch in his own pocket. "Who's your chief?"

The man defiantly shook his head.

"Who?"

"Doesn't matter. Another truck's on the way. They'll take your warty hide down."

Hood growled and jammed his right knee into the man's leg, so hard the bone broke. "Let's hope a DocWagon comes with that truck. You're gonna need one."

The troll looked over his bloody shoulder at his auditorium. Rows of seats were ruined, the screen so damaged it would have to be replaced. News would spread about this night, seriously hurting attendance.

"Someone's gonna pay for this!" The troll raged. "Pay hard!"

The doors burst open as Hood pushed into the lobby. Ten security men were sprawled unconscious between Pan and Khase. The green gas had dispersed. The elf still fought with a pair both disarmed, but putting up a struggle with their fists and feet. The glass on the antique popcorn machine was in slivers, the frame twisted. Candy from the broken counter was scattered on the carpet.

"These two are mine to finish," Khase called to the troll, catching one in a joint lock that left him on the ground, holding his frozen arm and gasping in pain.

"Then hurry up." Hood leaned against a pillar, feeling a wave of muzziness crash against him. He looked at his shoulder, the shirt red and sticky with his blood. His trousers were bloody, too, and he could hardly stand on his right leg. The adrenaline rush gone, he was feeling every bit of the pain the Keashee men had dealt to him. "Hurry, Khase. More of these goons are on the way."

35

"*Yat-zeu!*" Pan shook his fist at the second Keashee corp truck pulling up outside the theater. "*Yat-zeu!*"

"Get your wife and sister upstairs. They'll be safer there than down here. Bet they got another truck out back." Hood had three arrows ready. His left arm was practically useless, two bullets in the shoulder and blood continuing to flow, another bullet or two in his right leg. Somehow he managed to bring the arm up just enough and steadied the bow, gritting his teeth through the pain. His eyes flashed between the front door, which had been shattered by the earlier Keashee crew, and Pan.

The old man shook his head and motioned to his wife and sister, who were already halfway up the stairs. "My home, Hood-san. I'll fight for it."

The troll grinned and fired the arrows just as security men started pouring out the back of the truck. Green gas billowed around the tires, but this time the men ran through it, all of them wearing breathers.

"Drek!"

"Yeah, drek!" Khase started coughing. "Drek on us!" The elf did a back flip away from the windows and toward the auditorium doors. "This was bad enough the first time. We have to take this fight away from that fraggin' gas you shot off!"

Pan held his breath and leapt behind what was left of the candy counter, coming up with an antique pistol.

"No geeking!" Hood drew two more arrows and let them fly, these emitting a hurtful *boom* at the theater entrance. The noise immediately stunned three of the men, and brought another three to their knees. The sound was painful to Hood, too, but he, Pan and Khase were out of range of the worst of it—and it was nothing next to the ache in his shoulder and leg. He bit down hard on his lower lip, tasting blood, and reached for another arrow. "Only three left." *Probably can't shoot even one more of 'em.*

Pan drew a bead on the closest sec man and fired, but the bullet bounced off the body armor. *"Sei chun!"* He aimed again, this time shooting the Ares Predator IV out of the man's hand. "Better!"

"Into the auditorium, Pan! With Khase! Move it! We can't defend the place from here!" The troll drew back and this time launched a heavy, metal-tipped arrow that found its way through body armor and deep into a sec man's thigh, sending him collapsing to the floor. Hood howled from the effort and watched Pan and Khase run into the auditorium, then he started backing after them, fitting another arrow and praying he could get his arm to straighten out one more time.

Max and Sindje could have passed for drunks, weakly stumbling along the sidewalk. It had taken them a long time to get this far, stopping every half block for a breather. Max had almost collapsed at the top of the stairs, and Sindje had blown what little mana she had managed to regather on stabilizing the wounded hacker. The elf was so mentally and physically exhausted from healing the ork she was oblivious that all the other pedestrians out this night were coming toward them, and in a hurry. However, a scream that cut above the clack of heels against the plascrete drew her attention.

"Max, what in. . . ."

The ork had been looking down, concentrating on putting one foot in front of the other. She looked up and her mouth dropped open. Her eyes widened.

"That ain't a good sign."

People were shouting and running toward them, a green cloud billowing in the background in front of the theater.

Across the street were braver souls, who stood and watched, one of them a tourist taking pictures with what appeared to be a wide-angle attachment to a cybereye. The ork leaned away from Sindje and against the side of a smoke shop.

"Keebler, that ain't Plantech up there. Or Lone Star."

Sindje was humming, moving toward Max and propping herself up against the ork and the wall. She sagged, and now it was Max who managed to keep her from falling. A few minutes later she was back in her body.

"Maroon goons." Sindje was in the center of the sidewalk again, staring at the theater. "Side of the truck says Keashee. The guys have Predators and rifles mostly, and they're wearing breathers and goggles. A bunch are already on the ground, must have been the first wave. There's a lot of them, more than came at us in Ballard. Wanted to take a look inside, but I just don't have the energy. Surprised I was able to ghost at all."

"Keashee? What the frag is that?"

Sindje shrugged and pointed to an alley that ran between the theater and a tailor's that was closed for the night.

"Can't you just cast one of your spells and take 'em all out?"

"No more spells. No more anything. Hard enough just standing here, Max. 'Sides, there's too many of them. Didn't see Hood, but I only took a quick look-see. Let's head around back, maybe get in that way and see what's going on."

The ork let herself be prodded down the alley. It was relatively clean along the side of the theater—the tailor's side was another matter, with crates and trash cans in a row and rats staring out between the gaps. The deeper they went, the darker it got, the glow from the streetlights not reaching far enough.

"Lovely, lovely, lovely, Keebler. I hate rats."

"Just move it, willya?"

Max shuffled at too slow of a pace to suit Sindje, but the elf knew the ork was hurting, and certainly should be resting, not running around near a firefight. Sindje offered her shoulder for support, but Max shook her head and tried to move faster.

"Wonder what will happen when our Johnson and his boss show up, hmmm?" The ork stiffened. "And just what is Keashee?"

Sindje looked over her shoulder at the thinning cloud of green gas stretched to the end of the alley. She saw the faint shapes of gawkers across the street through it.

"I could use my commlink, see just what Keashee is, and . . ."

"I think I know what Keashee is, Max. I think it *is* our employer."

"Then you would be the folks with the plants, right?" A man stepped around the back corner of the theater. He leveled a submachine gun at them, as did the two men who joined him a heartbeat later.

Sindje searched for the inner spark of mana that would fuel a stun bolt, but there was nothing there. More men came up behind them, and she could hear the distinct sound of safeties being clicked off. She looked at Max, both of them clinging to each other, too tired to resist.

"Frag, frag, frag."

"I agree, Max. I agree completely."

Khase crouched inside the auditorium doors, waiting for the first sec man. He almost argued with Hood about taking the fight in here, but once inside had realized this was a much more defensible place with all the rows of seats and the darkness. The smell of blood was strong, and he knew he was standing in a pool of it, possibly the troll's. It mingled with the scents of popcorn and various candies, and he spat to clear the taste filling his mouth. The unconscious forms of half a dozen sec men were sprawled nearby. Near the screen, another struggled to get up.

Hood backed into the auditorium, trying to use an earbud cell phone. For a moment it sounded like the troll was trying to contact one of the sec goons, and asked for someone by name. But then he growled and gave up, and Khase remembered what Pan had said about tech being blocked by a sophisticated system.

"Wouldn't want the movie interrupted; no, we certainly couldn't have that, now could we?" Khase mused as the first sec man passed the threshold. The elf's leg shot out, knocking the Predator IV away. Then he grabbed the man's sleeve and pulled him in and down, where Pan popped up from between banks of seats and delivered a hand chop where the man's helmet met the collar of his body armor. He went down with a groan.

The pair was able to pull off their snatch and grab a second time, then the sec team wised up. Someone in the lobby fired a sustained burst into the auditorium, chewing through the frame of the open double doors and punching holes in the plaster. Khase dove for the floor and Pan dropped between the rows of seats again. Hood started down the center aisle, making himself a target.

"I do not need protection, Hood-san! Save yourself!"

The troll ignored the old man. He tried to raise his bow to fire one of his last two arrows, but his arm was dead-weight again. This time he couldn't even move his fingers. Bullets ripped into the carpet at the troll's feet, more than one cutting through his shoes and stabbing into his toes.

Hood howled in pain and grabbed a seat back with his good arm.

"Stop, troll! Don't move!" This came from a barrel-chested man who stood a few meters back from the doorway. In the diffused lobby light his body armor held the hue of thick blood. "We want the plants, that's all. It's your choice if we have to kill you for them."

Hood swayed and leaned against the seat to keep from falling. "You can have the plants! Have all the fragging plants!" His eyes burned black with anger, but his shoulders were slumped in defeat. Softer: "Pan, Khase . . . stay put." He hobbled up the aisle. "I'll take you to the plants, then you'll take your sorry selves out of my theater!"

He managed to make it all the way to the back row when he stumbled. Khase darted out to help him and danced as more bullets chewed into the carpet. One ricocheted off a seat panel and buried itself in Khase's right hip, spinning the adept into a row of seats. Khase fought to block out the new pain that had blasted through his layers of concentration, competing with the ache in his arm from the bullet still lodged there from this afternoon.

"Watch it, elf!" the sec man warned.

Khase gritted his teeth, clamped one hand over his new wound, and held the other hand out as he limped toward Hood, keeping an eye on Pan. The old man peeked above a chair, gaze flitting from Hood to the sec men to Khase, lips working uttering silent Cantonese curses.

"You have no idea what you're doing." Hood glared at the lead sec man. He steadied himself and stepped into the middle of the aisle, swaying a bit. "This is the biggest mistake of your life and . . ."

Another shower of bullets into the aisle carpet cut Hood off.

"Listen, trog, your hoop is mine. So shut up and pay attention."

Hood growled softly, but gave the man a nod.

"You're going to take us to the plants, then we're going to take them out of here. If you play nice, you and the elf keep breathing. Understand?"

"We understand." This came from Khase. Under the watchful eye of the lead sec man, he moved to Hood's shoulder, then slipped under the troll's useless arm. "Let's do this and get them out of here. You can lean on me. I'm strong enough yet."

"Not that strong."

"Just wait." The elf breathed in and out, his eyelids fluttering as he forced himself deeper into a pain blocking trance. He straightened up, and any trace of the effects from his injuries seemed to be gone. "Try me, *tad*."

Though a full meter taller, Hood used Khase as a crutch, and the pair shambled up the last few meters to the waiting Keashee security men. Pan walked slowly behind them. A moment more and they were all in the lobby. A dozen security men had Predator IVs, FN HARs and Uzi IV subguns trained on the troll and the elf. Three more had weapons held to the heads of Sindje and Max, far up the winding marble staircase.

"Sindje!" The moment of panic cost Khase, as the mental wall he'd built against his pain tumbled down. He fell under the troll's weight, and he pushed Hood off him and blocked out the pain again as he forced himself to his feet. *"Chwaer!"*

"Don't take another step, pointy! You, get up!" The lead sec man kicked Hood in the side and then backed up beyond the reach of the troll's arms. "Get up now!" He pointed to the troll with the tip of his rifle, and then pointed up the stairs. "The plants have to be up there. Show us!"

It was evident the Keashee security force had already checked the lobby. The candy counter and antique popcorn machine had been thoroughly dismantled, and two storage closets had been ripped open, the broken contents strewn in heaps. Thumps and crashes from overhead showed that sec men were ransacking the projection room.

Khase helped Hood up, his eyes never leaving Sindje.

"I said we'd take you to the plants. Let them go." Hood gestured with his good arm at Max and Sindje.

"Insurance," said the man with the Predator IV pointed at Sindje's head. "Now show us. We're gonna take a little walk upstairs. You follow us, nice and easy. No tricks, or your sweetheart gets a bullet in the brain."

Hood and Khase lurched up the winding staircase, as the sec men prodded Sindje and Max to stay ahead. Despite Khase's adroitness, he fell once, slipping in blood that pulsed from the troll's injured arm and foot.

"You're in rough shape." Khase spoke so softly only the troll could hear him.

"No worse than you."

"This is gonna go real bad, real quick."

"Compared to what's happened already? Just remember, no geeking."

The elf opened his mouth to argue, but the squeal of a vehicle breaking just outside sliced through the air. It was followed by the slams of car doors and angry shouts.

"Now who else wants the fragging plants?" Hood growled.

36

Simon whistled as he watched the coordinated police ballet unfold before him. "Frag, one thing I can say about
the Ninety-Fifth, these Fast Response Teams are loaded
for bear. Must be the neighborhood."

Three Ares Mobmasters squealed to a stop in the street;
one blocking either end, and the third angling in front of
the Keashee vehicle, men spilling from its rear and side
doors to cover the driver, who raised his hands in surrender. A pair of Lone Star officers covered in heavy riot
armor popped the door and dragged the man out, throwing
him to the ground and covering him with their modified
HK 227X subguns.

"That is definitely our cue. Let's go." Jhones grabbed the
Remington modified combat shotgun he had removed from
the trunk earlier, slid out of his seat and—followed by
Simon—ran over to a man who looked like he was coordi-
nating the operation. "Officers Redrock and Chays, we
called this in. Thanks for the overwhelming reply."

"Tactical Sergeant Coneff, FR Team One. Look, unless
you got new intel, the best thing to do would be to stay
out of our way. We're about to go in." The officer turned
back to the building, issuing orders into his comm. "Longshot One, Longshot Two, assume your positions and check
in. Doorknocker, we're on in twenty, as soon as cover from

Mobile Command One is in place. Shots have been fired. Repeat, shots have been fired. Approach with caution."

Jhones tapped the guy on the arm, making sure he had the man's attention. "Look, I don't want to get in a pissing match here. This is your hood, you know best. But there are shadowrunners in there we need alive, a troll, an ork and two elves. Disable the sec team all you want, but we need those four to come out of this in one piece. I'd rather not pull rank on you, but I will if I have to."

Sergeant Coneff frowned down at him. "By the time you get command jurisdiction here, this op will be over. All right, I tell you what. Since you're so fraggin' interested, you can follow up with Bravo Squad. Michaels, get these two helmets and gills! This is not SOP, so both of you are responsible for your own hoops." He leaned down to Jhones. "Speak into the camera, boyo."

"Sergeant Jhones Redrock and Officer Simon Chays are entering target building on their own recognizance, and agree not to hold Precinct Ninety-Five's FR team responsible for any injuries they might sustain in said action. Good enough for you?"

Another FRT team member appeared holding riot helmets and breathers that he tossed to the two street cops. Coneff nodded. "You're golden. Bravo Squad, hold up a sec, you're getting two rubberneckers. Get those on, they're going in right after the door is cleared. And try not to get yourselves killed on my watch, okay?"

"No problem." Jhones and Simon ran around the Mob-master and found a tight cluster of Lone Star men near the side of the building motioning to them. A swarthy, freckled ork who looked too young to be in command of his own team shook his head. "You the locos hitting the lobby with us?"

Jhones grinned.

"Okay, it's your hoop—hold on—this is Bravo Squad, we are in position. Ready for execute." The freckled ork nodded toward the door. "All I want is for you to come in behind us and stay out of our way."

Jhones gave a thumb's up in reply and racked the Remington. Two men from what must have been Alpha Squad walked hunched over to the double doors. They opened them and another Lone Star officer brought up an Arm-Tech MGL-12 grenade launcher and put six rounds of CS gas inside. A white cloud immediately billowed out of the theater.

The Bravo Squad leader barked: "I'd put those filters on if I were you. It's gonna be hot in there. Stay low."

"We're ready when you are." This came from Simon.

A new voice was heard over everyone's commlinks. "Bravo Squad, this is Alpha. We are go on entry. Repeat, we are go on entry."

"Copy that, Alpha, Bravo is ready to rock and roll."

Six heavily armed and armored men ran to the door, lining up three to a side. One gave a hand signal, and they entered one by one, each covered by the next one. When the last one disappeared inside the cloud, the Bravo leader held up his hand and pointed toward the door. As one, the entire eight-man squad headed toward the entrance, with Jhones and Simon trailing.

The inside of the building had once been a plush theater lobby, now shredded. Popcorn crunched underneath Jhones's boots as he advanced into the building, Simon a bit behind and flanking him. Instead of the pitched gun battle they had been expecting, only eerie silence greeted them, with the rest of the FRT members fanning out as they looked for hostiles. Four peeled off and headed toward two double doors below a sign that said THEATER ONE.

"Where is everybody?" Simon subvocalized. *"Just a few minutes ago it sounded like World War Three in here. We should get those runners first before they meet the FR team and get shot."*

Jhones looked around, noting the rest of the squad was occupied clearing the rest of the floor. "Come on. We're not needed down here. Let's go up."

With Jhones leading, the two cops went up to the second floor, down the main hallway, to a narrow stairway in the back. Simon stopped at a glistening, dark patch on the wall. "Jhones." He pointed to the smear of fresh blood on the wall. "Someone wounded came through here."

Jhones rubbed his chin. "Still going up. We gotta be close to the roof now."

As they crept up the stairs, their commlinks crackled with the reports of the FRT squads. *"This is Alpha One, the*

*main theater is clear. Lots of firefight evidence and blood
here. Something big went down, but I think we may have
missed it."*

"This is Bravo Three, I have located an unconscious suspect behind the concession stand. Am arresting him now."

"Alpha Three and Alpha Four reporting, the rear bath-
rooms are clear. This finishes the sweep of the main floor."

"Alpha Squad, regroup to main lobby and execute sweep
of stairway and second level. Do we have any drones online
here yet?"

"They're providing extra security at Sea-Tac for the gover-
nor's visit, so no, we don't."

"Fraggin' great."

"This is Bravo One. Where are those two street officers
who came in with us?"

At the top of the stairway, Jhones switched channels to
a private line with Simon. "Well, they know we're missing
now. Let's go."

Simon nodded, fingers tight around the butt of his
Thunderbolt.

Jhones put his palm against the door, testing its strength.
"On three . . . One . . . Two . . . THREE!"

He kicked the door in and leveled the Remington, cybereyes scanning not just four thermal signatures, but a dozen
ranged around the room in between potted plants of various shapes and sizes that had been pushed against the wall.
Oh, frag.

"Lone Star law enforcement—" was as far as Simon got
before all hell rained down on them as multiple submachine
guns and shotguns opened fire.

37

As soon as the two cops kicked in the door and got their hoops shot off, Khase was in motion.

When they had hit the improvised greenhouse room a few minutes ago, the Keashee team leader had cordoned Hood, Khase, Max and Sindje off to the side, leaving four guards to watch them. He had separated six plants from the rest and detailed two guards to stay near them. The rest of his men had been assigned positions around the room to maximize their fields of fire when the reinforcements they knew were coming hit the room. The captain had been trying to raise their rotorcraft to set up an evac, but had been stymied by a strange communication breakdown. The adept had exchanged a grim smile with Hood as both of them realized that the Everett was still doing its job, keeping the outside world out a little longer.

Khase got the attention of one of their guards. "Hey, buddy, the elf and her friend aren't going anywhere. Why don't you let them lie down? You got us dead to rights."

The guard's eyes flicked to his leader, who was about to climb a ladder to the roof. He nodded, and the sec man motioned for Sindje and Max to lie down, which they did, Hood easing Max down, and Khase helping his sister.

"You be sure to stay here, all right? I'm sure Lone Star will be here any second."

Her lips rose in an infinitesimal smile. "You . . . say that like it's . . . an improvement over . . . our current situation."

"Don't worry, we're getting out of here. I've got an ace in the hole."

"Don't get killed, *brawd*."

"Not today, *chwaer*."

"No talking!" the guard nearest Khase swung his knee into the elf's wounded shoulder, knocking him off balance and reopening the clotted wound. Khase looked up at the sec man with eyes that should have burned with pure hatred, but instead were cold and calm. The guard covered the elf with his FN HAR assault rifle. "Just twitch once, and it'll be all over for you, leaf-eater, and your pointy-eared friend, too."

"Hey, knock it off, I've got movement!" a guard at the door hissed.

The rest of the guards readied their weapons while the leader and two others continued bringing the other six plants up to the rooftop. The head man pointed to a group by the door. "Take care of them. You two keep offloading these."

Just then the door burst open, and the room exploded in a firestorm of bullets and noise. Every guard's head turned to pinpoint the threat that might be coming through that door, leaving Hood and Khase free to act for vital seconds.

The adept's leg pistoned out, shattering the kneecap of the guard that had just hit him. He fell to the ground, and as he did, Khase snatched the subgun out of his hand and threw it at a second guard. The molded plastic stock slammed into his jaw, and the man toppled backward like a felled tree. Out of the corner of his eye, he saw Hood reach out with his good arm and hoist another Keashee guard into the air, then send him flying into the knot of men at the door. The airborne sec man collided with the shooters, sending them flying. The low roar of a shotgun pierced eardrums in the enclosed space, and Khase and Hood both hit the ground as slugs split the air above them, impacting two more guards and knocking them on their hoops.

Khase spotted the leader grabbing the last plant from one of his underlings, and ran for the ladder. The head man spotted him coming and barked, "Stop him!"

The other man who had been handing the plants up

swung his Uzi over, but Khase was already inside his threat range, levering the subgun out of the way to point at the second man as he leapt up, his knees slamming into the corp man's jaw three times before he landed. The man's eyes crossed, and he sank to his knees, then pitched forward on his face.

As he fell, Khase wrenched the Uzi out of his limp fingers and pointed it at the lone guard by the ladder, who raised his hands. The elf pressed the end of the barrel right between the man's eyes, like he was about to shoot him, and was rewarded with the pungent smell of urine as his terrified target wet himself.

"Gotcha." He brought the stock up and over, clubbing the man across the face and spinning him to the floor. "Hood, I'm on the leader." Khase held on to the gun and climbed up the ladder, checking one last time to make sure his sister and Max were safe. At the ruined remains of the door, he saw a dwarf with a Lone Star badge on his belt covering three disarmed guards, while another human lay nearby, his chest a pulped mass. In the dim light, he couldn't be sure, but Khase thought he saw tears on the dwarf's face.

Must have been the gas, he thought. Ignoring the troll's call for him to wait, he hit the door only to find it locked. Fortunately the hatch was old, and made of stamped sheet metal instead of anything really modern. Khase used the butt of the Uzi to hammer on it a few times, bending the lip around the lock, then slipped the end of the butt through and levered the hatch open. He ducked down immediately afterward, figuring the head guy would be shooting anything that came out—and he was right. Bullets spanged off the metal around him, and a long curl of steel sliced into his forearm, but Khase hung on. He poked the barrel of the Uzi out and fired off the entire magazine, the recoil jamming into his injured arm. Muffling a curse, he threw the gun out one way and hoisted himself out the other, praying that he had chosen the right way to roll.

The elf heard gunfire, but no bullets came close to him. *He went for the gun,* the adept thought. *But now where is he?*

The roar of an approaching rotorcraft blotted out every other sound on the roof. Khase looked up to see a maroon

Hughes WK-2 Stallion drop from the sky, its converted cargo bay doors yawning open, ready to take on the plants the sec leader was protecting as he motioned the rotorcraft closer.

Khase judged the distance to be about twenty meters. On a good day, he could make that distance in about two seconds. Now, with his arm and leg both injured, it would take three times as long, plenty of time for the sec man to see him and blow him away. *Unless. . . .*

He leaned against the battered hatch opening and focused every ounce of his will, gathering all of the aches and pains of his injuries and forcing them into a tight white ball in his mind. As he did this, the hurt in his physical body receded, becoming a dull ache, then vanishing altogether. He took that bright, white ball of pain and moved it to the middle of his abdomen, holding it there with all of his remaining strength, until it was vibrating with pent-up energy. Then he released it again, letting white-hot fire flow through his limbs, overwhelming his pain receptors and shutting them off.

For the adept, it was like he had just mainlined a jolt of pure adrenalin. Everything around him sharpened into focus, and he felt disassociated from his body, as if he were watching himself get up and move. There was no pain whatsoever in his arm and leg as he ran toward the guard, who was still trying to get the Hughes to land on the roof. Some instinctive combat sense made him turn just in time to see the adept a few steps away, one hand outstretched to grab his weapon, the other cocked to drive through his face.

The guy smoothly turned, obviously packing some impressive wired reflexes, and brought up his gun while trying to grasp Khase's leading arm to jerk it out of the way so he could shoot him. Khase evaded the grab and locked on to the man's Uzi, twisting it up at the descending rotorcraft while his other hand found the man's finger on the trigger and pressed down hard.

Thirty rounds punched through the thin skin of the Hughes, causing sparks to fly both inside and out of the helicopter. The steady beat of the engines changed as something was damaged inside, and smoke began pouring from the cowling as the Stallion lurched sideways, then corrected, but slowly lost altitude, whirling around as the pilot fought

for control. The rotorcraft started to sink below the level
of the rooftop, but Khase had one more thing to send after
it. He yanked the empty Uzi toward him, bringing the surprised guard's head with it. Khase butted him in the bridge
of the nose with his forehead, breaking his nose and causing
blood to spurt from his nostrils. He did that twice more,
then shoved the man toward the edge of the roof as hard
as he could.

"Khase, no!" Hood's shout from the hatch came too late.
Stunned and off balance, the Keashee sec man tumbled off
the edge of the roof, straight into the Stallion's main rotor.
There was a noise like a side of beef dropping into a
grinder, and a spray of red splattered at the elf's feet. Metal
screeched and crumpled as the Stallion's sudden descent
was stopped by something equally large, the rotors grinding
to a halt in the street below.

"What have you done? What have you done?" Khase
heard the roar as the troll lumbered toward him. When the
thick hand landed on his shoulder with the force of a pile
driver, Khase acted on instinct. He collapsed with the
blow, sinking to the ground and rolling back and off to
the side. As he came up, his hand grabbed Hood's thick
arm and kept swinging it with him, forcing it around the
troll's back, then up between his shoulder blades. A stomp
kick to the back of Hood's leg, and the troll was suddenly
down on one knee, his arm contorted and his face near
the gravel roof.

"What have I done? All my sister and I have ever done
is play by your rules. And all it's gotten us on this run is
almost killed—plus a big, fat pile of nothing. No easy run,
and certainly no cred."

The elf applied a little more pressure, making Hood gasp
as his arm was bent in a way it wasn't supposed to go.

"You've been holding out on us from the start, Hood,
playing coy all through this run. Neither my sister nor I like
being played for fools, yet we thought you would somehow
manage to turn this drekpile around. Ain't happened yet,
chummer, and from the party down below, it ain't gonna
happen, either."

Keeping Hood's arm up, he leaned down to whisper in
the troll's ear. "But here's what you're gonna do, Mr. Boe-

ing." The troll sucked in a noisy breath as Khase continued. "You're going to spin whatever story necessary to make sure that Max, Sindje and I come out of this with no charges, and paid. Otherwise, I'll just have to start talking to Lone Star about exactly who lured me into this run, and I'll bet your family wouldn't find that appealing at all."

"You're blackmailing me?" The troll tried to rise off the roof, but another twist sent his cheek against the small rocks.

"One more move like that, and I start breaking fingers." Khase was calm and collected now, but he still kept a vice grip on Hood's arm. "Let's call it our own little business arrangement, just between you and I. Face it, Hood, you owe us—Max, Sindje, and me. What I know now will just insure that you're going to pay us off, fair and square."

"And I'm supposed to trust your word on this?"

"Of course you are, *tad*. You see, unlike you, I've never withheld information that jeopardized a mission. With your connections, you could have made this run smooth as glass, instead of getting your kicks slumming with us."

"That was never the point. I think this thing might be larger than we can imagine." Hood looked at the spray of blood in front of him and winced. "I've been trying to work it through."

"We're out of time. Lone Star's gonna be pounding up here any second, so what's it gonna be, *tad*?" In one fluid step Khase both released Hood's arm and stepped away from the troll. Hood brought his aching arm around to his side and pushed himself back on his knees, pinning the elf with his glare. Khase wasn't worried, however, because he knew the troll was going to give in. *That's right,* omae, *mull it over, and then your strange sense of honor will kick in right about—now.*

"Agreed." The troll forced the one word out.

Khase held out his hand, and Hood took it, holding the elf's fingers in an undeniable grip that could pulp the adept's limb before he could escape. "But if I ever find out that this has leaked out into the street, you know who I'm coming after first."

"Well then, we'd better make sure that never happens, shouldn't we?" Khase pulled, and Hood pushed, and between the two of them, they managed to get the troll standing, just in time to see the first Lone Star officer surge out of the hatch and cover them with his HK.

"Stay right where you are!"

With twin weary sighs, Khase and Hood raised their arms, wincing with every inch.

38

Roland kept his hands clasped behind his back as he watched the plants being off-loaded from the back of the stock Ares Roadmaster. On the outside, he was the picture of tranquility, but his mind seethed with every pot that was brought in, checked against the missing manifest and rushed into the lab for evaluation.

And I'm looking at a couple of the fraggin' drekheads who stole them. Sure as the sun came up this morning, they're standing right in front of me.

Two elves stood near the Ares, both dressed in casual clothing. The male was in a black, raw silk shirt and loose coffee-colored linen slacks, but his arm was in a sling, and he gripped a cane in his free hand. Next to him, the female looked pale, but composed, dressed in a beautiful flower-print silk dress with an Asian cut, slit up both sides. The pair watched the security men unloading the plants. On Khase's other flank was Jhones, standing there much like Roland was, his hands clasped behind his back. Six other Plantech security men along with K-Tog watched the two elves, both of whom pointedly ignored them.

"Why all the fuss over these particular plants?" The troll gestured with a bandaged, hamlike fist toward the trays the guards were wheeling into the agricorp.

The security chief cleared his throat. "K, remember me telling you about the Shiawase deal?" He stepped close to the troll. Both of them had synthskin covering injuries they'd received at the house in Ballard. "The Shiawase execs—"

"Yeah . . . they bought plants, and they're coming by in a few hours to pick them up." The troll looked menacingly at Khase, clearly remembering him from yesterday's break-in."

Roland shook his head. "Most of these plants that were appropriated yesterday—"

"Stolen," K-Tog corrected loudly. If the elves heard, they gave no sign.

"Have valuable medicinal properties that Shiawase scientists will cultivate and turn into vaccines and pills and—"

"I remember from your talk before." K-Tog's fingers rested on the grip of an overlarge pistol at his hip, and one of his Roomsweepers was sheathed in a cross draw holster over his right shoulder. It was clear he was itching to draw either or both weapons, but a glance from Roland stayed him.

"Stand down, K." Much softer: "Our pensions, old friend."

K-Tog shifted his attention between Khase and Sindje, the tone in his voice making it evident that he didn't care who heard him. "I remember her, too. That skinny, ugly elf. Her and maybe that other elf were the ones who stole these plants. They were in Ballard, too. I know it was them. I paid good nuyen for these eyes."

"Maybe." Roland kept his voice low. "Maybe it was them." *Frag, I know it was them.*

"There was a third and a fourth one."

"K—"

"A troll and a stinking ork." K-Tog's fingers tapped his pistol. "They should go to jail. All of them, and for a long time."

Roland shook his head. "Maybe they stole the plants, and maybe it was folks who looked like them."

K-Tog's eyes narrowed and he softly growled.

"The big boss doesn't want any publicity. Bad for business. You know that."

K-Tog growled a little louder, but crossed his arms in front of his considerable chest. "So they get away with it."

"We got the plants back."

"That's something." K-Tog paused and gingerly rubbed his jaw. "But not much of something."

Considering no one on our side went to jail after that little Alki run, I'd say it was more than enough, Roland thought, but didn't bring that up in front of the elves and Jhones. "We got the plants back. And so we keep our jobs."

"And our pensions, like you said." Still, K-Tog continued to growl. "But giving the thieves a reward for returning the plants? Now that's two truckloads of drek."

When all the returned plants were safe inside, getting prepped for Shiawase to retrieve, Roland walked toward the two elves, a credstick held in his fingers. Sindje reached for it, but at the last second, Roland pulled his hand back.

"Is there a problem?" The male elf was all smooth manners and silky smiles.

"I just wanted to hear your incredible story one more time." The pause was slight, so slight that neither elf gave any visible sign of hearing it.

The female shifted, just enough for Roland to catch it out of the corner of his eye. *Uncomfortable, sweetheart? I'm just getting started.*

"Surely that's unnecessary, I mean, we did give our report to the officer—" she began.

"But to put yourselves in harm's way, all for a bunch of plants—I mean, even for elves, that is amazing." Roland's tone had verged on condescending with his compliments, and now it turned cold as ice. "Call it my need to know."

The elves' almond-shaped eyes flicked toward each other, then the male began. "Well, as I told the Lone Star officer, we were just watching the double feature at the Historic Everett Theatre, when these thugs burst in and started shooting up the place. Naturally, our concern was for the rest of the patrons, so we tried to make sure they escaped. And when the men turned on us, we defended ourselves as best we could."

The female elf chimed in. "Yes, but when we saw those men go to the second floor, we followed them, to try and make sure they didn't hurt anyone in the balcony."

The male took up the story again. "I'm not sure how it happened, but we found ourselves on the third floor, where one of the men was fleeing to the roof. I gave chase while my sister helped the poor Chinese family that had been taken hostage."

"And the guy who took a header off the roof into that Stallion's helicopter blades?"

The male's eyes regarded Roland, unblinking. "He slipped. By then Lone Star was there, and the rest of those thugs had been rounded up."

Roland looked at the elves for a long moment. His gaze even went to Jhones, standing there like the good public servant that he was. "By the way, what movies did you see?"

"What?" This from the female elf.

"It's a simple question. You claim you were watching a double feature. So, what were you watching?"

The male elf sighed. "Unfortunately, several of my brethren debasing themselves in remakes of old movie musicals. The double bill was *Grease 2040* and *Stayin' Alive: The Next Generation*. If you'd like, I can certainly howl a few bars for you."

"No, that won't be necessary." Their story checked out with other witness reports, including the family that ran the Everett. The movie question had been his last card, even if it was only for his own edification.

The sec chief lowered his hand, holding out the credstick. "It's not a large reward, though it's probably more than you deserve." Roland's voice was calm and even. "But it's by order of our company president, who is pleased that our deal can go through and that much-needed medicines will be manufactured."

The male elf looked at the amount and shrugged. "It will do, I suppose." He showed the stick to the female, who let out her breath in what Roland could only call relief.

"Thank you for your cooperation. You are both free to leave." Roland gestured to the main lobby doors as he stepped close. K-Tog shuffled over, fingers toying with his holstered pistol again. "And just so we're perfectly clear; I don't want to see either of you, or your two friends, the ork and troll, around here ever again. In fact, if you set foot in Snohomish just once more, I'll be on you like rain on Seattle."

He had to give them credit, their faces betrayed nothing. "Why, sir, I haven't the faintest clue what you are referring to. Come, my dear, let's go." The male elf put his cane down and, leaning on the female, the pair made their way to the door, the male elf still muttering something like, "No good deed goes unpunished."

K-Tog lumbered after them, and for a moment Roland was afraid he'd have to dress the troll down, but all he did was open the door for them. "Never return," the troll commanded. "Understand?"

The elves, noses almost in the air, strolled out to the waiting Ares. Roland walked over to Jhones, who was still standing in the atrium, smelling the air.

"Well, that ended about as well as could be expected." The sec chief's eyes never left the elves as they climbed into the Roadmaster. "I'm off duty after the delivery is made to Shiawase—want to head down to the Anything and grab a bite? I hear the special is liver and onions."

The dwarf didn't crack wise, just looked up at Roland with sad eyes. "Maybe another time, my friend. I've got some things to take care of."

"Sure, I understand. That reminds me, I'd better check in." Roland dialed the number for home, but a noise from outside distracted him.

A honk from the Ares made all three of them look up. The boxy truck had stopped in the circular driveway, and the male elf had rolled down his window, and was speaking to K-Tog.

Whatever he said made K-Tog furious, and the troll stomped toward the doors, drawing his pistol and his Roomsweeper as he did so. The elf laughed as the Ares took off in a swirl of gravel.

"K-Tog! Stand down right now!" Roland ordered.

"It was them, I know it!" The troll slammed his fist into the window of the main lobby, the impact making the entire wall shake.

Roland ran up to him, watching the Ares disappear at the end of the driveway. "Look, I told you that it might not have been them—"

"No sir! I *know* it was them!" K-Tog looked out down the driveway, panting as he tried to gain control of his anger. "It was what he said as they left."

"Which was?"

The huge troll looked at his boss. "He asked, 'How's your jaw?' "

39

Hood took a deep breath, holding the mingled scents of the various plants surrounding him in his lungs. *Should have done this a long time ago,* he thought.

He had decided with his second deep breath that he would hire some of Plantech's people to build a similar greenhouse for him—perhaps on top of one of the buildings he owned on Mercer Island. He would make the entire floor dirt, though, no walkways designed to keep visitors' shoes and feet clean. He ran through his mental list of which plants he'd like to include—definitely the small acacia with elephant ears, a miniature weeping cedar, perhaps a separate section for some orchids, which he'd always wanted to try growing, but never had the nerve. But after the last day or so, he figured it was now or never. Too bad he'd come home to find his cuttings gone. They would have made a nice addition to his collection. *Oh, well, easy come . . .*

After the debacle at the Historic Everett Theatre, he had been DocWagoned to a hospital, where he had spent sixteen hours in the Intensive Care Unit, healing his shot-up self. He had made them release him early—they had wanted to keep him there for another day. But he had insisted, and gotten in a stretch limousine that had been waiting for him. Inside, he had made a few calls to hold up his end of the bargain that he had made with Khase.

The troll sat in the high-backed massaging chair, feet up

on his coffee table, fingers of his left hand wrapped around a large, nearly empty mug of chilled lemonade. The remnants of two packages of oatmeal cookies were in his lap. He was still hungry, but he was too comfortable and too tired to go to the kitchen to get more.

His earplant beeped, and Hood picked it up, the distinctive chime indicating that he had a message. He inserted the device and played it, smiling in satisfaction. *The plants have been delivered safely, and Khase and Sindje left hours ago.* He took the phone out of his ear and tossed it on the table, then leaned his head back and turned it slightly, so he could see the tank with the large veiltails in it.

This condo was one of his favorites in the building, all of which—along with the rest of the block—he owned. Many of the other condos were rented out, but several were always kept empty so he and his associates could use them from time to time. It was convenient to bring runners to the building, and more convenient to take each group to a different condo, and sometimes to a different building he owned close to the International District. Hood thought he could help keep his real self hidden that way.

He dozed on and off, finding the fish more relaxing than a sleeping tablet. But after a few hours he roused himself and used his crutch to hobble into the kitchen for more cookies and lemonade. On the island was the collection of seed pods he'd culled from the bioware plants. Next to them was a prototype chip reader he had obtained from one of his family's labs. He gathered up the chips and reader, stuffing them under his aching left arm and managing to hold on to the refilled mug of lemonade with the hand. Then he lumbered back into the living room and set everything on the table.

This time he sat on the couch, not wanting the massage chair to lull him back to sleep. Hood drained half the lemonade in one swallow, then picked up the first chip and inserted it into the reader. There was a port and wire, so someone could jack into the affair and see and hear everything inside their head rather than just listening the old-fashioned way. Hood dug his fingernail into the port, ruining it, tore loose the wire, gingerly touched the PLAY button and turned up the volume.

It wasn't particularly interesting—a conversation between

a Plantech minor executive and someone from a downtown corp. Hood didn't bother sitting all the way through it. He slotted another, found nothing intriguing, and went on to a third and then a fourth. It wasn't until the sixth chip that something caught his attention.

It was a woman talking to a man. He recognized her voice: Belver Serra. And after listening for several minutes, he figured out her companion was the Plantech biologist who'd created the bioware plants.

"The dead biologist," Hood mused. "Plantech's Dr. Nansct."

The chip continued to play the conversation between Nansct and Belver. He told her about the six special plants, how to use them, and suggested that if she paid him enough nuyen not only would he sell her the recordings she wanted, but he'd sell her the plants, too.

"Greedy man. Greedy always gets you in trouble."

Another chip also had Belver's voice. She was talking to two men who never gave their names, though Hood was certain they were Shiawase officials. She was offering them miniaturized computer interfaces and tech-blocking prototypes from the Keashee Corporation in exchange for some serious nuyen.

"Greedy woman, too."

The deal was secured, and Hood guessed she handed over the prototypes. Then she made arrangements to sell them a variety of programs Keashee had in development.

Hood growled. "So, Ms. Serra, I figure Dr. Nansct blackmailed you about these recordings, hence your offer to buy them and the plants. Couldn't let your boss at Keashee discover you were a turncoat. Couldn't risk a leak. So that's why you hired runners."

Hood used the crutch to stand, pocketed the Belver chips, and lumbered to the entry closet. He selected a butter-soft, black Europa leather duster, and got into it with a little effort. "You know . . ." Hood continued to talk to himself, "I took the contract from your Johnson, Ms. Serra, 'cause I just couldn't figure out through the Keashee grapevine just what you were up to. Was curious why you wanted runners, and so I took the bait myself. Then I was curious why you wanted the plants. A lot of work and pain, it was, settling my curiosity. Almost got some associates of mine killed. You covered your tracks pretty well, Ms. Serra. A shrewd businesswoman. But not shrewd enough."

He opened the door and went out into the hallway, locking the condo behind him. He passed by the elevator and struggled up the stairs to the roof. "Now I got me one last piece of business to take care of."

It was raining. He tipped his warty visage up and let the drops patter against his rough hide. Then he ambled to a waiting helicopter.

40

Belver Serra finished up the last of her current workload by four o'clock, leaving her with two hours to pace the carpet and worry about what had gone wrong—a loyal corporate executive rarely left with the regular work shift.

Her hair was brushed back and lightly lacquered in place with a light hold, iridescent Tres Chic spray. An injection of ShadeAway had cleared up the dark circles under her eyes after a night of restless tossing and turning. When the sun had risen, and she had not been contacted by her Johnson or the Lone Star cop, Belver had started to seriously worry.

Even so, she had gotten up, dressed, and headed to the office like it had been any other workday. In fact, she had arrived two hours early. The thought of calling in had never crossed her mind, as that would have looked suspicious in and of itself. She, like any good corp *sarariman,* knew the first rule of playing in the big leagues: *Never admit anything you don't have to.*

But in my case, there's nothing to admit to. Anyone would have to know what the plants are about to understand what they could do. Otherwise, they're just decorative plants. And with my pet out of the picture, terminally, he cannot tie me back to this, and neither can those three local yokels. So I should be all right. At the office, she stuck to business as usual, the gnawing ball of worry in her stomach gradually dissipating as the day progressed.

Unfortunately, her secretary didn't seem to possess the same fortitude as Belver, and had called in sick, so the executive was also serving as her own doorkeeper. When the message came up from the lobby, she nearly choked on the peach tea she had been sipping in an attempt to stave off a headache.

"Ms. Serra, there is a Sergeant Jhones Redrock from Lone Star here to see you."

She dabbed at the droplets of steaming tea on the otherwise spotless desktop with one hand as she stabbed at the intercom pad with the other. "What does he want?" she asked, even though she already suspected the answer—he's here to deliver bad news about the plants. *Keep playing the part, they've got nothing on you.*

"He says he is here on a private matter that he will discuss only with you in person." In the background she heard a gruff voice say, *"Tell the big macher I'm coming up."*

"Very well, send him to my office. Tell him my secretary is out and he should just let himself in."

Belver took a moment to make sure everything was in place in her office, then sat in her leather chair, awaiting her visitor. She fumed inwardly, but was careful to not let any trace of her fury show. *How dare this insolent dreg come to see me at my corp! By the time I'm done with him, the sanitation crews won't hire him! They'll have to pick him up with the rest of the garbage!*

There was no knock at the door, it just swung open. The dwarf walked in, dressed in a well-cut double-breasted Victory suit. He crossed the main area of the office to stand in front of her desk.

"Officer, I'm very busy, so I would ask you to please state your business here quickly."

The dwarf hopped up into a chair, his eyes never leaving her face. "You can cut the corp bullspeak, Ms. Serra, there's really no reason for it. After all, we're old friends, you and I."

What the frag? The cop wasn't acting at all like she had expected him to. By now he should have practically been groveling at her feet, begging to atone for his complete and utter failure to deliver her those plants. "Officer—Redrock, was it? I'm afraid that I have no idea what you are talking about. If you do not have anything to discuss—"

"Oh, we have a great deal to discuss, but most of that can wait until later. What I wanted to come by to tell you personally was that I'm square with you. You and I are settled up."

That was too much for Belver. "Now you listen you runty little worm! You're not finished until *I* say you're finished! I know that those plants are out there, and you can still get them for me, and you will—"

"Really, Ms. Serra, unsuppressed rage does not become you." The dwarf leaned back in his chair, further fueling Belver's anger.

He's actually making himself comfortable! She was about to tear into him again when he started speaking.

"The plants were delivered to Plantech in time for them to complete their deal with Shiawase. They're gone, Ms. Serra, and whatever machinations you had in mind are gone with them."

Now it was Belver's turn to lean back in her chair. *Good, then the idiot never knew what was special about the plants. That's something, at least.* "I see. Well then, you leave me with no choice but let your—people—know that you didn't come through."

"Yeah, I figured you'd say that. Do what you like, but I'm clean." He slid off the seat and began heading toward the door. "Have a nice day."

Belver wanted to let this odious little man scuttle away back to the rock he'd crawled out from under, but she couldn't help herself. "Who was it?" she asked. "Who paid off your marker?"

Jhones smiled. "No one. But it doesn't matter to me anymore. I'm not going back to that world."

Suddenly, a figure appeared in the doorway: her boss. Not only her boss, but also the reclusive owner of Keashee, a man she had seen only once, when he had hired her six years ago.

"Mr. Boeing, please come in." She stepped around her desk, unnerved by his sudden appearance. Alarms jangled wildly through her mind, but she maintained her poise. "If I had known you were coming, I would have been prepared—"

The impeccably dressed troll held up his hand as he entered the room, leaning heavily on a polished, dark mahogany cane that was as thick as Belver's toned arm. Jhones stepped to the side to allow him entrance. "No, don't worry about it, this won't take long. Belver Serra, it has come to my attention that you have recently committed internal fraud by using company assets when you dispatched a Keashee security team to an address in Everett. While the gentleman whose name had been signed to that internal order is now deceased, recent evidence has come to light that implicates you in this affair."

Belver's stomach contracted violently, and she grabbed the corner of her desk for support. *He knows; I don't know how, but he knows.* And then her internal question was answered as the troll brought up a chip player and activated it. Belver's face turned pale as she heard her own voice discussing the details of her treason against Keashee.

Still, she rallied against the immutable evidence. "Sir, I find it hard to believe that you're giving any of this any credence. Voiceprints can be faked, and I can't believe you're going to take this—gentleman's—word over my own."

Hood limped across the room to her, looming over her as he leaned down next to her ear. "Ms. Serra, I saw your treachery with my own eyes at the Everett." He straightened again, and turned away from her. "Based on this evidence, I have no choice but to terminate your employment contract with us. You will immediately be escorted from the building by security. I'll have your personal effects sent to your home."

The dwarf chimed in at this point. "But I wouldn't think about starting your search for another corp anytime soon. There are two Lone Star officers waiting to speak to you on a whole battery of charges, including conspiracy to commit corporate larceny, unlawful use of corporate resources, conspiracy to commit murder, coercion of a Lone Star officer and I'll bet if we dig a little deeper, we'll find a link to that poor *zhlub* who died in his car early this morning. Belver Serra, you are under arrest on suspicion of committing the aforementioned crimes." He looked toward the door, where a Keashee security officer and a Lone Star officer both waited.

Belver was incredulous, watching her world collapse in a few short minutes. Even worse than the threat of possible jail time was the soon to be unalterable stain on her resume—that she had been fired with cause. It meant she would never be able to work in any reputable part of the corporate sector again. Her career was finished.

In desperation, she lashed out at the dwarf. "You're going to try to stick me on a coercion charge? But that means you're admitting your complicity in all this."

Jhones nodded. "I've already given my statement to my superiors, and I have accepted my punishment—which, I might add, pales in comparison to what's going to happen to you." He waved at the two men to take her away. "Sayonara, Ms. Belver."

Once the pale and shaken Belver had been escorted from the office down to a waiting Lone Star patrol car, Jhones turned to the huge troll and stuck out his hand. "*Domo arigato* for your invaluable assistance in this matter, Mr. Boeing."

The troll bent down to shake it, a wince of pain flitting across his features. "It was my pleasure. I cannot stand someone using my corporation for their own personal gain. Come, let me walk you out."

As they exited the office and headed for the elevators, Jhones kept glancing at the CEO. "Pardon me for asking, sir, but are you all right? I mean, your leg and all."

The troll smiled as they waited for the elevator to arrive. "Thank you for your concern, but it's nothing. I play competitive jai alai, and took a ball on the thigh in my most recent match. At one hundred-sixty kilometers an hour, they pack quite a wallop, even to me."

"Ah, of course. Well, I hope you're feeling better soon."

The elevator chimed, and they walked inside. Jhones' eyebrows raised when he saw Mr. Boeing wince again when he pushed the button for the lobby. *A jai alai hit shouldn't have bothered his leg at all. His arm is hurt as well.* He took a closer look at the troll, noting the swept-back horns, similar to the seriously wounded troll the DocWagon had hauled out of the Historic Everett Theatre. *Could this guy be—nah. Still, I've got the strangest feeling that I've seen him before.*

"Something on your mind?" Jhones looked up to realize Mr. Boeing was looking down at him.

"No, nothing at all. Once again, thanks for your help." The dwarf bowed, and had the satisfaction of seeing his bow returned just as deeply. *Could that have been him? Ah, frag it, who knows. After all, it's not like I have any hard evidence linking him to the run. He could have been catching a flick at the theater as well, as improbable as it sounds. Besides,* he thought wryly as he crossed the polished marble floor of the lobby toward the doors, *all those trolls look alike to me.*

41

From the main building of the Keashee Corp, Jhones took the light rail to Capitol Hill, getting off at a high-rise in the middle class neighborhood. He flashed his badge to the doorman, and walked inside to the elevators, where he pushed the button for the fourteenth floor. The lobby was quiet at this time of day, and a car arrived for him immediately. On the way up, he examined his hands, looking for any tremors, any trace of nervousness. *Just say your piece and get going,* he thought.

On the way up, he tried not to think about what had happened to Simon in the theater—how he had seen the storm of muzzle flashes, and had tried to pull his partner down with him to the floor as he had ducked out of the way. But it had been too late. By the time Alpha Squad had arrived to secure the area, the human was already dead, having taken a bullet in the throat and across his shoulders, shattering his neck and clavicle. If it hadn't been for Jhones' vest and helmet, he might have joined his partner, but the sec men had been aiming high, as usual, and most of the slugs had passed right over his head. The nightmares, however, would be a long time fading.

At the fourteenth floor, he got out and walked a route he had taken many times before, to a corner apartment door. He lifted his hand and rapped on the door.

"Who is it?" a speaker next to the door asked.

"It's Jhones." He waited for the maglocks to be turned off, trying not to fidget in the meantime. The door opened, and a pretty dwarf woman a few years younger than him looked out.

"Jhones, what a surprise, I wasn't expecting to see you until you came for Brenna this weekend." Suspicion flitted across her features. "Now, you've been doing a good job of keeping up with the payments, so don't tell me you're in trouble—"

Jhones held up both hands. "No, no, it's nothing like that. In fact, it's good news." He looked at her for a long moment before continuing. "I'm out, Mara, I'm done with the gambling." He sighed. "I know I've said it before, but this time, there's no falling off the wagon, I'm through with it forever. I have no choice this time."

She stared deep into his eyes, then smiled. "You know what? This time, I believe you. I'm not going to ask how or what happened, but I believe you." She stood back from the doorway, letting him see the hallway leading to the living room. "Do you want to come in for a bit?"

"I'd like to, but I have a wake to attend. My partner was killed in the line of duty, and the service starts at eight. Um—maybe, that is if you didn't mind, I could come by tomorrow, when Brenna is home from school?"

"Sure, she'd like that. And I'd like that, too. I'm proud of you, Jhones, I always have been, and I'm even more proud of you now."

The dwarf flushed and fidgeted in his shoes. "Thanks, Mara, and—I'm sorry for everything I put both of you through in the past few years. I just—couldn't help myself. But I've got my head on straight now."

She took another long look at him and nodded slightly. "Look, you'd better get going. Give us a call before you come by, I'll make gefilte fish, kishke and kreplach."

"Well, that is among the things I've missed about you—your cooking." Jhones grinned. "I'll call about six tomorrow night, all right?"

"Sounds good." Mara stepped close to him and kissed him on the cheek. "We'll see you then."

"Until tomorrow." Jhones waved to her one last time as the door closed, then walked back down the hall with a new spring in his step. *I don't know how I could have ever given them up. And to think it took a human, and a goy, no less, to show me the right way back to them.*

He reached the elevator door and pushed the lobby button. *Thank you, Simon, wherever your spirit is,* he thought as the door closed.

The streets of Ballard were quiet again after all of the excitement of two days ago, and the neighborhood had returned to its normal rhythms of life in downtown Seattle.

A shadow detached from the darkness and crept through a grocery store parking lot, checking to make sure no one was around, but also intent on finding something else as well.

The figure walked down an alley, turned a corner, and headed down a side street, its eyes sweeping back and forth. At length, it paused near a thick cluster of trees as it spotted its goal.

In the copse was a gray van, mostly hidden from the street. The figure walked to the door, fingers twitching as it reached for the handle. The door was locked, but some quick fiddling with a tool pulled from a pouch popped it, and the dark form slipped inside.

A low chuckle emanated from the driver's seat as the engine coughed once and turned over. The dashboard lights glowed, revealing Max's face in the neon radiance. "Well, it ain't no Nightsky, but a ride is a ride, all the same."

And with that she eased the van out of its hiding place, and took off down the street in a squeal of rubber.

Epilogue

Hood settled back into the cushy seat of the Rolls Royce Phaeton Deluxe. He straightened the tapered lapels of his perfectly tailored Wellington Brothers suit and reached for his commlink. It took only a few minutes to arrange for a completely new team of security for the Keashee Corporation. He fired all the sec men who followed Belver's orders and stormed the Historic Everett Theatre. Another call and he made provisions for the dead sec team members' families to be taken care of for the rest of their lives.

Afterward, he briefly contemplated taking legal action against Khase for killing the man, but then thought better of it. If he himself had a sister in jeopardy, maybe he would have done the same thing.

"Blood is important in some families," he mused. "And, as unfortunate as it seems, sometimes death is the high cost of doing business." But he didn't want it to happen again, so he would think twice about employing the two elves in the future. *Assuming I can even find them.*

One last call, this time to Pan Geng, to make sure repairs were scheduled to start in the morning. Then he watched the raindrops striking the windows and he listened to the gentle tat-a-tat-tat against the roof—and the scraping and snuffling sound coming from a box on the seat next to him.

Minutes later he stood on the tarmac in front of his private hangar at Sea-Tac, listening now to a staccato tat-a-tat of a harsher rain against his duster and the ground— it cut the noise of the planes coming and going.

As he had a few days ago, the troll stared into puddles

tinted neon by the reflected lights of the terminal and taxiway—seeing something far beyond the airport and Seattle. Rivulets of green, pink and electric yellow held his gaze for several moments.

"Sir?" The liveried driver hovered near him at the open rear door of the limo.

"I need you to deliver a package on your way home."

"Very good, sir. What package?"

Hood reached into the car and retrieved the box. The scratching intensified. He turned toward the light spilling from the hangar door and opened the box lid just enough so the driver could see inside.

"Is that what I think it is, sir?"

"A pug puppy," came Hood's gravelly reply. "A designer dog."

The creature's face was as black as the tarmac, eyes wide and corkscrew tail wriggling.

Hood replaced the lid and thrust the box at the driver. He reached into his pocket and pulled out a card with an address.

"Take it to the ork who lives here. And don't mention my name."

"Very good, sir."

Hood watched the Phaeton roll away, then took a long moment to enjoy the night air. Finally, he limped to one of his private jets. It was several minutes more before it roared down the runway, and only then did he start to relax.

Hood still thought the terminal looked like a giant arachnid from above. The concourses were its legs sprawled across a massive rain-slick slab that stretched toward the edge of the city proper, where myriad lights resembled a starry sky. The terminal where he was headed wasn't nearly so interesting, but the city was bigger . . . and so was the problem there that he would tend to next.

Aftershock Glossary

Foreign words and their meanings

Welsh

Brawd: brother
Cachu: drek
Chwaer: sister
Hurtyn: stupid
Plentyn: child, kid, faerie
Tad: dad, father

Japanese

Baka-gaijin: damn foreigner
Baka yaro: bastard, idiot
Chikushome: damn
Domo arigato: thank you very much
Hai: yes
Henjin: weird, eccentric
Kakkoii: awesome, cool
Kichigaijimata: insane
Kochi koi-yo: Come here!
Kónban wa: good evening
Kusatta: rotten
Kutabare: Frag you! Go to hell!
Omae: you, impolite form
Onara: fart
Oni: demon
Roba: donkey

Sarariman: corporate employee
Sayonara: good-bye
Shaikujin: honest citizen
Shakuhachi: end-blown flute
Sumimasen: excuse me, please forgive me

Ork slang (from *State of the Art: 2064*)

Buunda: expletive, similar to drek or frag
Cerri: sibling; brother or sister
Norgoz: weapon
Tharon: corporate
Ujnort: non-ork
Zakhan: enemy

Spanish

Cojones: genitals, testicles
Loco: crazy
Muchachos: men, comrades
Rapido: quick, fast

Cantonese

Mei sei goah?: You want to die?
Seung sei ah: You want to die?
Yat-zeu!: Go to hell!
Sei chun: stupid

Yiddish

B'emet: really?
Boychik: boys/men, affectionate
Chamalyeh: punch, hard hit
Chaver: close friend
Chazerai: disgusting stuff, trash
Chutzpah: audacity, nerve
Ganef, Ganefs: thieves, clever schemers
Gefilte fish: chopped, cooked fish
Goy: non-Jewish person
Kreplach; perogies
Macher: big shot
Meshuggener: crazy
Momzer: bastard

Nosh: snack, eats
Oy: Oh! Ouch!
Oy *vey:* Woe is me! Oh no!
Pisher: a nobody, a little squirt
Schlimazel: unlucky person
Sha: Shh, quiet
Tsuris: troubles
Verklempt: clenched; slang, uptight
Zhlub: a crude, unrefined person; a slob

About the Authors

Jean Rabe is the author of eighteen novels and more than three dozen short stories. When she isn't writing (which isn't often), she participates in fantasy football leagues; attempts to garden; constantly dabbles in all manner of war, board, and role-playing games; and tugs fiercely on old knotted socks with her two dogs. She lives in Kenosha, Wisconsin, with her husband, Bruce, who is also an avid gamer. In various Shadowrun campaigns, she favors playing trolls . . . just because. Visit her Web site at www.jeanrabe.com.

John Helfers is an author and editor currently living in Green Bay, Wisconsin. He has published more than thirty-five short stories in anthologies such as *The Sorcerer's Academy, Faerie Tales, Alien Pets,* and *Apprentice Fantastic.* He has written both fiction and nonfiction books, including a comprehensive history of the United States Navy. His novels include *Tom Clancy's Net Force Explorers: Cloak and Dagger, Twilight Zone: Deep in the Dark,* and *Siege of Night and Fire.* Future books include *Thunder Riders* and *Nightmare Expeditions,* a young adult novel illustrated by legendary comic book artist Bernie Wrightson.

STEPHEN KENSON
THE SHADOWRUN TRILOGY

Book I: BORN TO RUN   0-451-46058-8

Earth, 2063. Long-dormant magical forces have reawakened,
and the creatures of mankind's legends and nightmares have
come out of hiding. Megacorporations act as the new world
superpowers, and the dregs of society fight for their own
power. Sliding through the cracks in between are shadowrunners—underworld professionals who will do anything for a
profit, and anything it takes to get the job done. Kellan Colt
has come to Seattle to make a name for herself. But her first
run proves that in her line of work, there's no such thing as
a sure thing, and that in her world, there is only one law—
survival.

Book II: POISON AGENDAS   0-451-46063-4

Earth, 2063. Shadowrunner Kellan Colt thinks she's ready to
strike out on her own when she discovers the location of a
secret cache of military weaponry—right in the heart of the
supernatural creature-infested Awakened wilderness.

Book III: FALLEN ANGELS   0-451-46076-6

Kellan Colt has come far in her magical training. But she still
doesn't know the truth about her shadowrunner mother or the
secrets of the amulet she possessed. Troubled by disturbing
dreams, Kellan is drawn into the paranoid elven homeland of
Tir Tairngire where she must unravel the most difficult riddle
of all: who can she really trust in the shadows?

**Available wherever books are sold or at
penguin.com**

SHADOWRUN #4

Drops of Corruption

by Jason M. Hardy

Bannickburn is a burnt-out Scottish mage with
little power and even less going for him when he
falls into fast company with a crew of casino-run-
ning criminals. Soon he's back living the high life
he's used to. But just when Bannickburn thinks
he's hit the jackpot, he learns that in every game,
winners can turn into losers with the squeeze of
a trigger.

0-451-46063-4

**Available wherever books are sold or at
penguin.com**

THE ULTIMATE IN
SCIENCE FICTION AND FANTASY!

From magical tales of distant worlds to stories of
technological advances beyond the grasp of man, Penguin has
everything you need to stretch your imagination to its limits.

penguin.com

ACE
Get the latest information on favorites like
William Gibson, T.A. Barron, Brian Jacques,
Ursula Le Guin, Sharon Shinn, and Charlaine Harris,
as well as updates on the best new authors.

ROC
Escape with Harry Turtledove, Anne Bishop,
S.M. Stirling, Simon Green, Chris Bunch, Jim Butcher, E.E.
Knight, and many others—plus news on the
latest and hottest in science fiction and fantasy.

DAW
Mercedes Lackey, Kristen Britain, Tanya Huff,
Tad Williams, C.J. Cherryh, and many more—
DAW has something to satisfy the cravings of any
science fiction and fantasy lover.
Also visit dawbooks.com.

*Get the best of science fiction and fantasy
at your fingertips!*

Penguin Group (USA) Online

What will you be reading tomorrow?

Tom Clancy, Patricia Cornwell, W.E.B. Griffin,
Nora Roberts, William Gibson, Robin Cook,
Brian Jacques, Catherine Coulter, Stephen King,
Dean Koontz, Ken Follett, Clive Cussler,
Eric Jerome Dickey, John Sandford,
Terry McMillan, Sue Monk Kidd, Amy Tan,
John Berendt…

You'll find them all at
penguin.com

*Read excerpts and newsletters,
find tour schedules and reading group guides,
and enter contests.*

Subscribe to Penguin Group (USA) newsletters
and get an exclusive inside look
at exciting new titles and the authors you love
long before everyone else does.

PENGUIN GROUP (USA)
us.penguingroup.com